Catherine Ryan Hyde is the author of several highly acclaimed novels including the award-winning *Pay It Forward* (which was made into a feature film starring Kevin Spacey and Helen Hunt), *Love in the Present Tense* (a Richard & Judy Book Club bestseller), *Chasing Windmills*, *When I Found You*, *Second Hand Heart*, *Don't Let Me Go*, *When You Were Older*, *Walk Me Home* and *Where We Belong*.

PRAISE FOR CATHERINE RYAN HYDE

'This gritty love story is compelling reading'.
Sun

'Surprisingly wonderful'
Mirror

'A remarkable story of the magic of love'
Daily Express

'This novel has a steely core of gritty reality
beneath its optimism'
Amazon.com

'A quick read, told with lean sentences and an edge'
Los Angeles Times

'A sweet and honest look at the pains and pleasures of love'
JANE GREEN

'A work of art . . . enchanting'
San Francisco Chronicle

*Also by Catherine Ryan Hyde
and published by Black Swan*

DON'T LET ME GO
THE HARDEST PART OF LOVE
(previously published as *Electric God*)
SECOND HAND HEART
WHEN I FOUND YOU
CHASING WINDMILLS
PAY IT FORWARD
LOVE IN THE PRESENT TENSE
WHEN YOU WERE OLDER
WALK ME HOME
WHERE WE BELONG

Other books by Catherine Ryan Hyde

JUMPSTART THE WORLD
DIARY OF A WITNESS
THE DAY I KILLED JAMES
THE YEAR OF MY MIRACULOUS REAPPEARANCE
BECOMING CHLOE
WALTER'S PURPLE HEART
EARTHQUAKE WEATHER
FUNERALS FOR HORSES

TAKE ME WITH YOU

Catherine Ryan Hyde

BLACK SWAN

TRANSWORLD PUBLISHERS
61–63 Uxbridge Road, London W5 5SA
www.transworldbooks.co.uk

Transworld is part of the Penguin Random House group of companies
whose addresses can be found at global.penguinrandomhouse.com

First published in Great Britain in 2015 by Black Swan
an imprint of Transworld Publishers

A CIP catalogue record for this book
is available from the British Library.

ISBN
9780552778022 (B format)
9780857520609 (tpb)

Typeset in 11/14½pt Giovanni Book by Kestrel Data, Exeter, Devon
Printed and bound by CPI (UK) Ltd, Croydon, CR0 4YY

Penguin Random House is committed to a sustainable
future for our business, our readers and our planet. This book is
made from Forest Stewardship Council® certified paper.

MIX
Paper from
responsible sources
FSC® C018179

1 3 5 7 9 10 8 6 4 2

TAKE ME WITH YOU

Part One

Early June

1
August, Standing Still

August Schroeder stood at the rear door of his broken-down motorhome, looking out through the small, square window. Had he looked out any other window – the windshield, the side windows, the little window over the kitchen sink – he'd have seen the inside of a mechanic's garage. He wanted to see sky. He'd come out here to see sky. Not toolboxes and racks of new tires and hydraulic lifts.

He stepped out the door, down the two metal steps, turned and walked into the mechanic's garage.

He stepped in front of the open hood, where the mechanic could see him.

The man straightened up, stretching his lower back against one hand. He wiped his hands on a red shop rag. Wiped his forehead on one dirty sleeve.

He was unusually tall, the mechanic. Maybe six foot six or taller. His limbs appeared stretched, thin and lanky. His blond hair was long in the back, curling and tumbling and disappearing under the collar of his blue work shirt.

Wes. His name was Wes. August had been careful to learn this, because so much of his fate rested in the mechanic's hands. It seemed wise to remove as much of the distance between them as possible.

'How's it going?' August asked.

'I'm on schedule. If that's what you mean.'

August sighed. Took a seat on a stack of three unmounted tires, lowering himself with his hands. 'I don't even know what I mean. Just making conversation, I guess.'

Wes pulled a pack of cigarettes out of his breast pocket and shook one out, receiving it with his lips. 'What've you been doing to keep busy all day?'

'Not much. Just absorbing the fact that Yellowstone isn't going to happen.'

Wes lit the cigarette. Squinted at August through the smoke. 'You told me you're out all summer. Seems to me you'd still have plenty of time.'

'Time, yeah. I've got time. That's not the issue. Money is the issue. I budget just so much for gas every summer. Yellowstone is four states away.'

'You go out all summer every summer?'

'I do.'

'You a teacher?'

'Yes.'

'What do you teach?'

'High-school science.'

'Science,' Wes said. Like he was describing a shiny new car hardly anyone could afford. 'I used to be good at science. So . . . maybe Yellowstone *next* summer.'

'Yeah,' August said. 'I guess.' But when he thought again about giving up the part of the trip Phillip would have loved, should have shared, the pain came back, slicing him into two parts. The old and the new. It was so familiar now, that pain. He almost welcomed it. He'd almost missed it.

'But it was the whole point of the trip this year. It was really . . . kind of a big deal. But, anyway, you don't need to know all that, and it's kind of personal. I just won't be able to afford it, and that's just the way it is.'

He looked up into Wes's face, and saw something, but he didn't know what it was. Something that the mechanic was holding in. Something he could say, or not say. A weighing of options.

'I swear I'm not gouging you on this repair,' he said, but that wasn't the thing.

'I know you're not,' August said.

'I appreciate the trust.'

'It isn't exactly trust. I don't know you at all. I've known you for less than a full day. The reason I know your prices are fair is because my father owned a garage. I used to work summers there. I'm not exactly a mechanic but I know quite a bit about it. I know the things that tend to go wrong, and I know how many hours' labor it takes to fix them. If you were gouging me, I'd know it.'

*

About an hour later, August stood looking out his back door again, watching two boys play. One was maybe eleven or twelve, tall and lanky. He reminded August of a young horse – long-legged, and somehow managing to combine clumsiness with an odd grace. His hair was light brown and shaggy. The little one was quite little in comparison, maybe seven. His every move looked tentative. His very being had a tentative quality that drew August's eyes.

They were kicking a ball around in an enormous lot of dirt and weeds, close enough to the garage that August assumed they belonged to the mechanic into whose hands he had fallen. He guessed they were brothers, because boys of such disparate ages didn't tend to band together in play. Besides, they looked like brothers. They looked like two examples of the same theme.

As he stood watching, the long, familiar blade of pain sliced down from the pit of his throat, burned its way between his lungs. It was right there in his body, he now knew. It had never been in his head. It had always been real, but he had lived all those years without knowing it. Those years felt pointless and wasted now.

Woody wiggled by his left shin, whining. There was a low window, too, in the rear door. Woody could see the boys play, and he wanted out. His little docked tail quivered more than it wagged. The sound he made reminded August of the whine of his garden hose when the water was restrained by a closed nozzle.

He reached down and scratched between Woody's small shoulder blades, his fingertips disappearing in the wiry white fur. The dog let out a yip, almost as though accidentally. As though he'd been straining to hold it in, but then it got the better of him.

'OK,' August said. 'Why not?'

He opened the back door.

They were a good long way from the road. Even farther from the highway. Now, with the door open, August could hear it in the distance, the highway. Well, not the highway itself, but the cars on it. The distant drone of their travel. That sound sliced down through his chest, too. Because he was not on that highway with them. He should have been on that highway. He should have been gone. He should not have been here. Then again, the word 'should' repaired nothing. It definitely did not do engine repairs.

He stepped out of the air conditioning. Into the June heat.

He watched Woody blast over to the two boys, bounding up and down to chart his trajectory over the weeds. As he ran farther away from August, his image became distorted by wavy bands of rising heat.

The bigger boy's head came up, and his face brightened when he saw the dog. Woody was the perfect dog for a kid that age. A small-to-medium terrier mix, full of excitement, always up for play, happy to do tricks.

The littler boy turned to see what his brother had seen. He jumped, missed kicking the ball, and ran behind the tall boy to hide.

'He's friendly,' August called out. 'He just wants to play. He's been cooped up inside the motorhome too long.'

The little one emerged. Tentatively, as he seemed to do everything. Full of wonder and fear, warring with each other. August knew the wonder would win. He wished he could communicate what he knew to this frightened boy. But that never did any good anyway. People learned by what they experienced. It mattered little what anyone said to anyone.

The small guy held a nervous hand out to Woody, but the dog jumped away again, running in a wide circle and then doubling back for another invitation. He didn't want to be petted. He could get that much inside. He wanted to play.

August walked closer.

The older boy stood straight-backed and tall as August approached. He took charge, that boy. It seemed to be his nature. There was something unusually mature about his stance.

It made August's slicing pain ease and withdraw slightly. Because the boy in front of him was not Phillip. The boy in front of him was only who he was. He was only himself.

The younger boy retreated behind his brother again as August drew near.

'That's your rig, huh?' the tall boy asked, pointing with his chin to the rear one-third of the motorhome protruding from the garage. 'That's a real nice rig.'

'Thank you.'

'Nice dog, too. Is he a Jack Russell terrier?'

'Maybe part. I'm not sure. He's from the pound.'

'What's his name?'

'Woody,' August said, and Woody's ears twitched.

'He do any tricks?'

'Lots of them. But right now he's feeling cooped up. He wants to let off steam. Tell you what. I'll make you an offer. If you can catch him, I'll give you five bucks.'

'He won't come when you call him?'

'Oh, no,' August said. 'That's not it at all. He'll do whatever I tell him to do. But that's his favorite game. When kids try to catch him.'

The tall boy's eyes grew lighter.

'Hey, Henry,' he said. 'Five bucks. What do you think?'

They took off in pursuit of the dog, zero to full kid speed in seconds. Woody ran a wide, delighted arc, looking over his shoulder as if laughing.

They would never catch Woody. So it wasn't really fair. If they ran him until he was happy and worn down, August would offer them the five dollars anyway. Otherwise it was just a mean trick.

He wandered back into the mechanic's garage, because it hurt to watch children play. Despite the fact that he'd been doing so on purpose for some time.

About ten minutes after August took a seat on the stack of tires, the mechanic pulled his head out from under the hood. He looked at August as if he had something to say. But, if so, he never said it.

Instead he lit a cigarette, took a deep drag, then blew the smoke out again, watching it as if transfixed. As if he'd never seen such a thing before. 'How bad d'you want to make it to Yellowstone?' he asked.

'Bad,' August said. But it felt dicey. A little dangerous. There was an offer hovering somewhere. Everything was a mystery except the weight of it, which he could feel. 'If you have thoughts, I'd like to hear them.'

'Never mind,' Wes said, cutting his eyes down to the concrete floor. 'Forget I mentioned it.'

'You've got something to say, go ahead and say it.'

Just at that moment, the older boy stepped into the garage, carrying Woody in his arms. Woody's tongue lolled out, longer than seemed physically possible, and, as the dog panted, he flipped little drops of sweat on to the boy's bare arm. The effect was that of a wide grin on the dog's face. And that might have been exactly what it was. August looked up to the face of the boy. It was red and dripping from the heat and exertion.

'Seth,' the mechanic said. 'What're you doing with the man's dog?'

'It was his idea,' Seth said.

'It was my idea,' August said. 'He's doing exactly what I asked him to do.' Then, to the boy, 'I can't believe you caught him. Nobody ever caught him before. You must be one fast guy.'

'That's not how I did it. I didn't do it with my legs. I did it with my brain.'

Seth poured the dog into August's arms, and August set Woody on his paws on the concrete floor and went after his wallet. Pulled out a five-dollar bill and handed it to Seth.

'Pleasure doing business with you,' Seth said, with something almost like a small salute.

It seemed an odd expression for a child his age, until August considered that the boy lived in – or at least behind – a business. He must have heard it all the time.

August watched him walk back out into the shimmering heat.

'Nice boys,' August said.

No reply. Wes just crushed the cigarette into an ashtray on the workbench and stuck his head back under the hood.

August gathered Woody back on to his lap and watched for a few moments, to pass the time. But it was really no more interesting than staring at the sky. Right around the time he was ready to go back inside his rig, the upper part of Wes emerged again.

'When I finish up for the day,' he said, 'maybe you and me have a drink?'

'Oh. Um. I don't drink.'

'At all?'

'No. Not at all.'

'Oh. Well. The drink isn't the real deal of it. Coffee, then.'

August felt a rush of discomfort. This tall, odd man wanted something from him. And he couldn't imagine what it might be. He couldn't imagine what he had that the mechanic would need, or even want. He briefly tried on the idea that the man was hitting on him. But it didn't feel quite like that. But it felt equally personal, scary, and emotionally important.

'I have coffee inside,' August said. 'Come knock when you're done.'

'I'll prob'ly work late. Eight or nine at least. All the better to get you back on the road.'

'I'll be up,' August said. 'Just knock.'

Then he spent the rest of the day wondering how big a mistake he had actually made.

At the end of the day, the mechanic put away his tools, shut off the lights, and let himself out of the shop through a side door. He didn't knock.

August drank the coffee himself, and, predictably, couldn't sleep.

2
This Will Sound Crazy

In the morning, as he was making a fresh pot of coffee, August heard a shy, tentative knock on the motorhome's rear door. Woody barked.

And barked. And barked.

'You're late,' he said, out loud, but to himself. Quietly. Too quietly to be heard through the door.

He'd already pushed the side window blinds up, but had not yet opened the curtains on the back door. That was a more involved task, as they were blocked by the screen door. He had to open the back door to get to them. So that always happened last.

'Shhh,' he said to the dog, but to no effect.

He finished plugging in the coffee pot, and turned it on to brew.

Then he unlocked and opened the back door.

In the dirt at the bottom of his two metal steps stood Seth, a baseball cap held politely in front of him, his little brother Henry directly behind.

'Good morning, Seth,' August said.

'How'd you know my name was Seth?'

'I heard your father call you by it yesterday.'

'Oh. That's right. And this's—'

'Henry,' August said. 'I heard you call him by it yesterday.'

'Oh. Did I?'

'What can I do for you boys?'

'Sorry to bother you. Sir. Hope it's no trouble. If it is, just say, and we'll go right away. We wouldn't've knocked if we thought you were sleeping. We saw your shades go up. So we knew you were awake. Hope it's not a bother. It's just that . . . Henry . . . my brother . . . and me, we're just wondering . . . maybe could we play with that dog? No charge. We're not asking it for any five bucks. We just liked that dog. And we think he liked us back.'

'I know for a fact he liked you back,' August said. 'Look at him.'

He opened the door wider so the boys could see Woody standing on his hind legs – paws reaching up and raking the air – and jumping up and down. Yes. Jumping up and down on his hind legs only. Woody was half circus-dog. Woody could do that.

Henry let out a light shriek that August recognized only after the fact as excited laughter.

'He's good at that,' Seth said. 'How's he balance on his hind legs so good?'

'He's just built for it, I guess. He can walk all the way across a room on his hind legs.'

'We'd sure like to see him do his tricks sometime.'

'Sure. Maybe when you bring him back.'

Seth's face lightened, and only then did August realize the boy had been waiting for a yes or a no, and straining under the weight of the uncertainty.

'So we can take him out in the lot to play?'

'Sure.'

August opened the door wide for Woody and gave him the simple 'Go on' permission. The dog scrambled out the door and jumped all around the boys, and jumped up and put his paws on them, and licked at Henry's face, which he could reach by leaping.

'I like the way just that one ear on him is brown and the rest white,' Seth said.

'Yeah,' August said. 'I like that about him, too.'

'How long can we keep him out?'

'Well . . . I'll tell you what. Stay where I can see you, and if I want him back for some reason, I'll let you know.'

'OK, thanks,' Seth said, barely able to contain his grin.

'One condition, though,' August said.

The boy's face fell, and he stepped back as if he'd been slapped.

'Nothing bad,' August said. 'I just want you to tell me how you caught him.'

'Oh, that,' Seth said, and relaxed. And began to look a bit proud. 'I used my brain.'

'So you said. But you really didn't tell me how.'

'Well. See. I noticed how every time you go for him,

he runs. Even if you take a step at him. Even if you just move. But if I held still, or looked the other way, he'd come closer. So I got smart and sat on the ground and turned my back on him and pretended I didn't want nothing to do with him at all. And he just walked right up and climbed in my lap. But don't worry, 'cause we ran him real good before I thought of it. I don't want you to worry you didn't get your five dollars' worth.'

'I wasn't worried,' August said. 'You three have fun.'

August sat on the top metal step for half an hour or so, his feet on the bottom step, his elbows planted on his thighs, drinking coffee and watching them play. And waiting to feel the pain. But it didn't come. He felt for it. Poked at it. Questioned where it was hiding. Maybe it was because he knew the boys now, and they were so different from his own son. Maybe it was because he almost wanted the pain back, and it was determined to do exactly the opposite of what he wanted.

The weather was a thing of beauty, lightly cool, with no breeze at all. Over a distant mountain the sky still glowed faintly red from the tail end of dawn.

He heard a scuffing in the dirt, and turned his head to see Wes approach, head slightly tilted down.

'Morning,' August said. 'Not too late if you still want that cup of coffee.'

'Oh. Thanks, but I had mine with breakfast. Sorry I stood you up last night.'

'Up to you. You're the one who wanted to talk.'

'I decided . . .' And then he tailed off, and stood still

for the longest time, staring off into the distance like the answer was just on the line of the horizon. 'It was a stupid idea,' he said, finally. 'You would've thought I was crazy.'

August considered this for a moment, then decided he had no idea how to respond. He was curious now, but it seemed unwise to force someone's hand on an idea that was crazy even to the mind that created it.

Neither man spoke for a time.

August stared at Seth, off playing in the field. 'There's something . . . very . . .' Then he got stuck for a second or two, so he pushed the words harder. '. . . decent. There's something very decent about that boy.'

'Who, Seth?'

'Yeah. I'm not saying the little one isn't decent. Just that he hasn't said a word to me, so I don't know. But Seth . . .'

'Decent . . . meaning?'

'I don't know. There's something upstanding about him.'

Wes snorted laughter. 'Yeah, that's Seth, all right. He'll drive you crazy with how upstanding he is. And how upstanding he thinks you ought to be. You got any kids?'

'I had a son.'

'Had?'

August did not reply.

'Never mind. None of my business. Sorry.'

Then Wes got his feet unstuck and made his way into the shop.

August drained the last of his coffee and followed Wes inside.

The mechanic was going through drawers in a free-standing red metal tool chest as tall as his breast-bone. He picked and chose, gathered what he seemed to think he would need, then laid those tools out on the workbench before going on to the next drawer. He knew August was there, that much was obvious. But he didn't speak, or even turn his head.

'This . . . *thing*,' August said. 'The one you keep acting like you're going to say but then you don't say it. The one I'd think was crazy. Yesterday you made it sound like there was some tie-in between that and whether I could still afford to make it to Yellowstone. Was I right about that?'

'It was a possibility in that direction,' Wes said, without pausing in his tool selection or looking up.

'Do me a favor, then. Getting to Yellowstone was very important to me this year. More than you know. More than anybody can probably understand. So if you've got an idea, sometime between now and the time I get back on the road again, could you go ahead and spit it out? Let me decide for myself if it's crazy? I'll be driving away shortly after, and you'll never see me again, so I really don't see what you have to lose.'

'I expect to get 'er done tomorrow. But prob'ly late in the day. Seven, eight in the evening. Maybe later. If that was the case, would you drive out of here tomorrow night, or sleep another night and leave Monday morning?'

'Anything after seven I'd probably stay put for the night.'

'OK, then.'

'OK, what exactly?'

'OK, sometime between now and Monday morning I'll let you know what I was thinking so you can laugh in my face and call me a fool and drive away shaking your head.'

August held out his right hand. It took the mechanic a long time to notice. But then, when he finally did, they shook on that deal.

August didn't go out to the lot to ask for Woody back, because there was no reason why he should. And the boys didn't bring the dog back until a quarter to noon.

August opened the back door and Woody jumped in, circled twice, and flopped on to his side on the cool kitchen linoleum, his tongue hanging off on to the floor, his ribs heaving.

'You broke my dog,' August said. But when he saw the panic in Seth's eyes, he jumped to repair the damage. 'That was just a joke. It's nice to see him so tired. Maybe we give him a little break before we ask him to do tricks.'

'We have to go eat lunch,' Seth said. 'My dad takes off work every day around noon. We got to go in and eat with him. Henry and me. Then we'll come back and see tricks. If you're sure it's OK.'

'I'm sure it's OK,' August said.

*

When August looked at the clock again, it was after 2.30. And the boys had not come back. He looked out the window to see what he could see.

Seth was outside with an ancient wooden tennis racket, slamming a ball over and over against the side of the shop. As if he had a grudge to burn off, the ball was the cause of it, and the racket was righteous anger. Henry was nowhere to be seen.

August tried to go back to his reading, but he couldn't make his attention stick on the pages.

He let himself out the back door of the rig, Woody following behind at an uncharacteristically sedate pace.

Seth looked over once when he saw August coming. Then he looked away again. And smacked that tennis ball. And smacked it. And smacked it. The mood of the place had changed. Something had changed. There was no explanation in August's mind, but also no doubt.

'Where's Henry?' August asked.

'Inside.'

Seth missed the tennis ball in the process of answering. August expected him to run after it, but he didn't. He just dropped the old racket, turned, and flopped into a sit with his back up against the shop. Woody wiggled up to him, put his paws up on Seth's shoulder. Sniffed at the boy's face as though he'd lost something there. Seth wrapped his arms around the dog and drew him in, hugging Woody close to his chest.

August sat down next to them. Leaned back. It was a spot in the full midday sun, and August knew he wouldn't be able to stay there long. Seth lived out here in the hot valley. He must have been used to it.

They sat in silence for a time. How long a time, August found himself unable to judge.

'You never came by for dog tricks,' he said at last.

Seth said, 'Maybe some other time.'

Then more silence. August didn't want to ask straight out what was wrong, because he didn't feel it was his place to do so. And because he had rarely, if ever, met a young boy who wanted to talk about his heartaches and disappointments with a near stranger.

Seth startled him by speaking.

'Where're you going on your trip?'

'All kinds of places. National parks, mostly. Zion and Bryce Canyon on the way up. Salt Lake City. The big destination was Yellowstone, but I won't make it, what with the unexpected cost of breaking down and all. Then on the way back I want to swing east and see Arches and Canyonlands. Maybe Escalante and Capitol Reef. Maybe Canyon de Chelly. Depends on my timing. I like to leave things loose. It's the only time of year I get to.'

'That's a great trip.'

'I hope so. Didn't get off to much of a start. I'm hoping it'll pick up from here.'

'You got kids?'

August sighed. As quietly as possible. 'I used to have a boy.'

For the first time, Seth's head turned, and he looked right at the side of August's face. 'How do you *used* to have a boy? Isn't your boy your boy forever? Or do you just mean he grew up into a whole man?'

'He was killed in an accident,' August said. He waited for the pain to begin its path of travel. Nothing happened.

'Oh,' Seth said. 'I'm sorry. Was he my age?'

'No. He was older. He was nineteen.'

'I'm sorry that had to go and happen.'

'Me, too.'

A long silence fell. Seth was the one to break it.

'Do you miss having kids along when you go traveling?'

That was when the pain came back. Radiated down, almost more a burn than a slice, an irritating, humming burn. *So there you are again*, August told it, silently. *I wondered.*

It partially distracted him from the nagging sense that something was wrong in Seth's question. August had said he'd had one kid. One boy. Not kids, plural. More than that, though, was a sense of too much importance riding on what Seth seemed to be trying to camouflage as small talk.

'I miss him no matter what I'm doing,' August said. 'It never stops.'

Then neither said anything for a time, and August had just about reached his limit for sitting in the hot sun. He levered to his feet and walked to the open entrance of the shop, looking back over his shoulder once before ducking into the shade. Woody chose to stay with Seth for the time being.

He found Wes working under his hood with much the same energy Seth had used to smack the tennis ball.

'Whatever's wrong,' August said, 'please don't take it out on my engine.'

The mechanic's head appeared, and he straightened up to his full height and looked August in the eye, but only briefly. 'What's that mean?' He pulled a pack of cigarettes from his pocket and shook one out.

'Just that everything seemed so sunny and bright this morning, figuratively speaking, and now it's like a big dark storm cloud set its head down on this place while we were all eating lunch.'

Wes didn't answer for a long time. Instead he pulled out a bright-blue disposable lighter and torched the end of his cigarette, drawing hard. A cloud of smoke hung around his head. It was hot, and the air didn't move. Not even a little bit.

'Can't always tell kids what they want to hear,' Wes said at last. 'Sometimes you got to break bad news.'

'That's true, I suppose.' August took his usual seat on the low stack of tires. 'Talk to me about this idea.'

The hand that held Wes's cigarette came up to his face. But, rather than finding his mouth, it landed over his eyes and stayed there for a long time.

'You'll think I'm crazy,' Wes said.

'So you mentioned. But go ahead and let me think what I want. I believe it's time to get this out in the open. Whatever it is.'

Wes sighed. Squatted down on to his heels, which

put him somewhere in the neighborhood of August's level.

'Here's what I'm thinking,' Wes said. 'I can get you to Yellowstone by giving you this repair one hundred per cent free of charge. I'd even pick up the cost of the parts. I'll even take the cash out of my pocket you gave me for the tow and hand it back to you. Then you'll be right back where you were when this trip started. All you've lost is three days. And, like you said, you got plenty of time. Then you can go and do what you said was so important to you.'

August waited briefly, to see if Wes would continue on his own. He didn't.

'Yeah. That would get me there all right. But it leaves an obvious question. Why would you do that for me? Wait. Let me phrase it more directly. If you were to do all that for me, what would you want me to do for you in return?'

Wes took another drag of smoke and blew it out in a series of perfect rings that bent and collapsed as they floated over a hydraulic jack. He didn't seem inclined to answer.

'You're going to do this sooner or later, Wes. Please, let's just get it over with already.'

'Take my boys with you.'

In the silence that followed, August thought, *Yeah. You're right. I think you're crazy.*

But he only said, 'All summer?'

'Yeah. You're coming back through before school starts, right? You can drop 'em back to me then. Meanwhile they get to see the world. Some national parks. Geysers. They can go to Yellowstone and see geysers. You know what those boys've seen their whole lives? Nothing. Just what's within fifty or so miles of here. And let's face it. That's nothing.'

August breathed deeply two or three times.

'They don't want to see those places with a stranger. They want to go with you.'

'I'm not going. You are.'

'Even so. They'll wait for you. They want to be here at home with their dad all summer. They'll wait for a time when you can travel with them. They want to be with you.'

'Well, here's the thing about that. For the next ninety days or so, they don't get to be. This's the part where you find out I'm not crazy by nature. More like desperate. You know. Fresh out of options. I'm on my way to jail for ninety days.'

'I don't get it.'

'What's there not to get? I got sentenced to ninety days.'

'Then how can you be here? I thought when they sentenced you they put handcuffs on you and dragged you right out of court.' Part of him wanted badly to go on to ask, 'Sentenced to ninety days for what, exactly?' But he didn't. It was really none of his business, and besides, another part of him didn't want to know.

'Well. They can if they want. Judge can do pretty much what he wants to do. Thing is, I got these two kids. So I told the judge I needed a few days to get 'em settled in. You know. Make arrangements for some-body to take care of 'em. Kind of stupid, because I don't have much family, and what I have, I knew they were gonna say no. They said no last time. Why this time would be any better, I don't know. I guess I just figured if I had some time, maybe I could pull something out of my hat. So he gave me till Monday morning. Monday morning I have to surrender myself at the jail or they'll come get me and escort me there.'

'Where do the boys go if you can't pull something out of your hat?'

'County takes 'em.'

'Where did they go last time?'

'County took 'em.'

'Oh. Well. That's not bad, right? That's not the end of the world.'

Wes snorted, and smoke puffed through his nose. 'Not for *you*. But I'm sensing it's not such a great deal for them. Henry hasn't said a damn word since I got 'em back. I think he talks to his brother. But I can't prove that. It's just a suspicion.'

A long pause fell. August put it to good use by mentally rehearsing the kindest ways to say no.

'I'd send you with some extra cash for their food,' Wes said. 'They're good boys. You can see that with your own eyes. You said so yourself. Henry won't say a damn word. Seth is a talker but he'll stop if you ask him to. He'll do anything you ask him to. He can look after his brother, too. He's old enough. It's not like they're babies. You wouldn't have to watch 'em every second.'

'Wes—'

'No. Don't answer. Please. Don't answer yet. Just sleep on it. You got two nights to sleep on it. Tonight and tomorrow. Unless I get ahead of schedule. Sleep on it two nights and don't answer off the top of your head. They won't be much bother to you. They're good boys.'

On the last sentence, August distinctly saw the mechanic's lower lip quiver.

'OK. I'll sleep on it.' *And then I'll say no*, August added in his own head.

''Preciate that.'

A long, strained silence fell. August didn't like it much. So he worked harder to make it go away.

'Do they know you're on your way to jail?' But before the mechanic could even answer, August knew. 'No. Never mind. You don't even have to tell me. They didn't know before lunch. Now they do.'

Wes smoked in silence.

'Do they know you were going to ask me to take them?' But, again, he knew. He remembered Seth asking where August was planning to go. If he missed having kids along. 'Never mind. I think I know the answer to that one, too. How do they feel about that? Going away for three months with a stranger?'

'Thing of it is,' Wes said, 'there's strangers at that other place, too.'

'Right,' August said. And then fell back into the flurry of his own thoughts. 'Look,' he said, after a time.

'I know you're being the best father to them you know how to be. But you don't even know me. You don't even know for a fact that I can be trusted with a child.'

'I don't know everybody at the county can be trusted with a child, either.'

August didn't answer. Because he'd run out of arguments. The answer still felt like no. But he was out of logical reasons why it had to be. He wasn't going to do it because he didn't want to do it. Because it felt weird. Because it disturbed the familiar patterns he needed to cling to. Too late to dress it up as anything more noble than that.

When he looked up, Wes was staring straight into his eyes. As if taking some kind of measurements. '*Can* you be trusted with a child?'

'Yes,' August said quietly.

'Yeah,' Wes said. 'I thought so.'

Then he got up, smashed out his cigarette, and got himself back to work.

3

New Deal

Around the time the sun was going down, August wandered into the shop area again. Wes was on his back on a rolling cart, half underneath the engine. He couldn't put the rig up on a lift, because it was too tall and too heavy, and the shop ceiling wasn't high enough.

Wes did not pull his head out.

'Haven't seen your kids around all afternoon,' August said.

First nothing. As though he hadn't spoken at all.

Then Wes said, 'I told 'em stay away from you.'

'Now why would you do that?'

'Didn't want you to think I was playing dirty, like telling 'em to follow you around and look up at you with those big brown eyes. I said, "Give the man time to think."' Still Wes did not slide out from under the rig. The sound just filtered up. 'Also . . . if you're gonna say no, I don't want 'em to see it in your face.'

'Got it,' August said.

As he walked back to the door of the rig, he thought, *Yeah. Keep them far away if you don't want them to smell a 'no' coming.*

At twenty minutes to midnight, a knock blasted August out of sleep. Woody went nuts, letting off a stream of noise, more one long shriek than individual barks.

August stumbled to the door, rubbing his eyes. Woody followed behind him, close enough to bump the back of August's shin with his nose, a rumbly, rolling growl escaping his throat.

'Who's there?' he called out.

'It's Wes.'

August sighed and opened the door, and Woody sat close by, leaning against his leg and wagging faintly.

'Sorry,' Wes said. 'Sorry I woke you up. Maybe I'm wrong to. But I told you to sleep on it. But then I re-thought things and came up with a whole different sort of a deal. So now you're sleeping on the wrong thing. So, can I tell you the new thing, and then you go sleep on that?'

August looked at the mechanic's face in the half-dark. His hair was comically disarranged. Wes had obviously been in bed himself when the new deal had arrived in his brain. August looked over Wes's head, saw the moon hanging nearly full over the flat, mostly uninhabited landscape, and thought, *He's right. This is nothing. Those boys have seen nothing because there's nothing out here to see.*

'Well. I'm awake now. So I guess you might as well.'

'I'm giving you the repair. Either way. It's yours, no strings attached. I just decided. Know why I'm doing it? Because you need it. I'm seeing the need in you, one man to another, and we're both human, so I'm gonna reach out and help your situation. Because I can. If that makes you so happy you want to turn around and help *my* situation, that would be much appreciated. But whether you do or not, you're free to drive out of here when I'm done. No charge. So, congratulations. You're going to Yellowstone.'

August blinked a few times, too aware of his own blinking. He heard crickets. He hadn't heard crickets since he was a boy. At least, not that he could remember. Then it hit him that they must have been there all along, and he just hadn't registered hearing them. It seemed strange that he could be so unaware of it then and so aware of it now.

'I'm not sure what to say.'

'Don't say anything. Sleep on it.'

And, with that, Wes walked away, around the corner of the shop to whatever living quarters lay hidden back there. In the bright light of the full moon, August could see the little puffs of dry dust kicked up by the mechanic's shoes.

He closed the door and looked down at his dog.

'That was curious,' he said, and Woody gave him a puzzled look, like he should be helping August figure it out. 'I wonder what I'm to make of that.'

Woody tilted his head slightly, but left August to sort things.

'You know that just makes it even harder to say no.'

He sat down on the edge of the bed, set his forehead in one hand, and tried to figure out if the added sense of pressure had been purposely applied to him, or if the offer was a pure act of altruism and the guilt just a side effect.

He couldn't make even the slightest headway in telling the two apart, so he went back to sleep.

Eventually.

August slept much later than he meant to. When he woke, he dressed quickly and began the process of raising the window shades. He started with the driver's side, the window over the dinette table. The mechanic's face appeared just inches from the window screen, startling him. August jumped back and let out a small noise, immediately embarrassed that he had. Woody barked once, sharply.

'Sorry,' Wes said. 'Didn't mean to scare you. But I could tell you were up, because the rig moves a little when you walk around in it. You slept late. Did you know it's after ten?'

'Oh. Not exactly, but I knew it was weirdly late. I don't usually sleep in like that, but I was awake a long time in the night.'

'Right. Sorry. My fault, I know. Anyway . . . I just had some news, so I been waiting to tell you. I'm ahead of schedule. Looks like I'll be done early this afternoon. Well. Not early early. But maybe more like three instead of six. Thought you'd want to know.'

August leaned forward and pressed his hands down on the dinette table, because it felt too weird and awkward to stand, hands at his sides, and carry on a conversation through the window.

'Now how did you manage to pick up three hours just this morning?'

'Well,' Wes said, and scratched his head. As if it was a mystery to him as well. 'I didn't exactly. It's more that I always add a cushion of time. Because it seems like something always goes wrong. A bolt strips while I'm taking something apart. Or shears right off. And I got to drill it out or something. Or I get things apart and there's more going on in there than I thought. But now I'm putting it all back together. And nothing's gone wrong. And nothing much left *to* go wrong. So I thought I'd let you know. Because I figured . . . if I get you done by three, you'll be wanting to get on the road today.' Long pause. 'Right?'

'Probably so,' August said, identifying the subtext without addressing it.

'And you'll want to . . . you know. Get ready and all. And . . . like that.'

'Right,' August said. 'Like that.'

'Take her out for a test drive,' Wes said, a little after two thirty.

August climbed into the driver's seat for the first time in three days. Woody leapt into his position on the dog bed, on the floor between the driver and passenger seats. As he always did. He seemed to feel as though staying anywhere behind the cab of the rig while August drove away might amount to being left behind.

August started up the engine, a trifle apprehensive, but it started well and ran smoothly and quietly.

He looked up at Wes through the windshield. The mechanic gave him a thumbs up, the fear and need on his face nearly breaking August's heart. August looked away again and shifted into reverse. Put his foot on the gas. Just as the cab of the rig pulled level with the front of the garage, August glanced over and saw the boys.

They were leaning with their backs against the garage, in the hot sun. Their hair was freshly combed. Almost too neat and perfect to be real. Their clean white shirts were tucked into their shorts all the way around. *Two firsts*, August thought. *The first time their shirts were clean, and the first time they stayed tucked in.* Then again, for your shirt to untuck, you have to move. The boys weren't moving.

Beside each boy sat a small, ancient, hard-side suit-case. One was dark green, the other a battered tan with one dark maroon vertical stripe.

August looked away quickly, because it was too sad.

When he pulled back up in front of the garage, the boys had not moved. Wes had not moved. It was as though August had thrown them all into a state of suspended animation by failing to make – or at least announce – a clear decision.

August shifted out of gear and stepped on the park-ing brake.

Wes dropped to the ground and looked underneath the rig for a long time. Checking for leaks, August assumed.

August braved another look at the boys. They reminded him of children alone on a train platform during the war, waiting for possible strangers to possibly transport them to safety. Hoping for rescue, despite their parents being left behind. Not that he had ever witnessed such a scene with his own eyes. But still.

Henry turned his head to look off into the distance, and, in doing so, he caused one lock of his otherwise perfectly combed hair to fall out of place. It trailed on to his forehead, the tiniest possible rebellion. As August watched, Seth pulled a black plastic comb from his shorts pocket, leaned over closer to his brother, and combed the errant lock back into position.

August's heart broke. Cleanly, and decisively.

And now he had to go break theirs.

A strong push-back rose in his chest. It made him angry. It felt unfair, that he had been put in this position. Then he remembered what he'd been given in return. He told himself that breaking bad news to them was the whole price he had to pay for Yellowstone, and three days' worth of expensive repair work. Thing is, it wasn't a small price to pay. Maybe it should have been, but it wasn't. Or at least it didn't feel small.

He opened the door and stepped down, leaving the engine running. He walked around the back – the long way – to avoid Wes.

Predictably, the boys turned their eyes up to him.

Just the way their father had told them not to do in the interim. Because it wasn't fair.

It just so wasn't fair.

'You boys look like you're sure you're going somewhere,' he said. Hoping to ease into the thing.

'Our dad told us to be all ready,' Seth said. 'Just in case. He said that way if you said yes, we wouldn't keep you waiting. But he said he didn't think you were gonna say yes.'

Henry shifted his eyes down to the dirt, and the lock of hair fell on to his forehead again. Seth twitched but did not ultimately move, as if he'd been about to reach for it, then changed his mind. August could see the stress it caused him. He watched Seth unable to take his eyes off his brother's forehead, unable to focus off an imperfection he apparently felt was his responsibility.

August heard a slight whimper, and turned to see Woody in the passenger seat, front paws up on the window, longing to get to the boys.

'Here's the thing,' August said.

Then he stopped talking for a time. He would later go over the moment again and again in his head, examining what he knew and when. The boys both looked up into his face with those eyes. Those unfair brown eyes.

They didn't say a word. They waited.

'There are drawers in the rig,' August said at last, 'and there are cupboards. The cupboards are high, but it's OK for Henry to stand on the couch to reach them if he takes his dirty shoes off first. I'll clear out a drawer to share and a cupboard for each of you. And then when you get your stuff in them, I want you to leave the suitcases behind. Because they'll only get in the way. It'll be small in there for three people and a dog. Even though the dog is small. Anyway. We'll have to do our best to work around each other.'

Then he stopped talking, and the silence resonated, and seemed to last a long time.

Seth broke it.

'Dad!' he screamed. Loud enough to hurt August's Seth-side ear. 'Dad! Guess what? He said yes!'

And August thought, *Oh, holy crap. Did I? Did I say yes? And why exactly did I do that? And how could I have done a thing like that without at least talking to myself about it first?*

Then he realized that none of that nonsense mattered anyway. It was too late to take it back. It was done.

'I'm writing down my cell-phone number,' August said.

He and Wes were standing in the tiny office. The place where you meet with the garage owner at the end of the repair, usually so you can settle up your bill. Usually not so you can exchange information for the purpose of returning his children at the end of the summer.

August glanced over his shoulder, through the wide-open office door. Seth was belted into the passenger seat of the rig, and Henry was standing up between the seats, one hand stretched out to each. They both stared at the adults through the windshield. Their elation seemed to have worn off quickly, revealing the miscellaneous uncertainties beneath.

'Thanks,' Wes said. 'And I looked up the number of the county jail and wrote it down. I gave it to Seth. And I gave him some money so they can call from a payphone. I can get calls up to three times a week. Monday, Wednesday and Friday. Just inside certain hours. I wrote down the hours.'

'You can receive calls? I didn't think inmates could receive calls.'

Wes seemed to wince at the word 'inmates'. 'Rule is, only in an emergency or by special permission. I got permission on account of I'm the sole provider for these two kids, and I knew they'd be in no position to come visit. Either way.'

'Oh,' August said. 'OK. Seth can call from my cell phone. I've got minutes coming out of my ears.'

'Good. Thanks.'

August watched the mechanic carefully. Watched his eyes, his mood, his reactions. Because he wanted to see how a man felt as he sent his kids off to spend the summer with a relative stranger. But Wes either felt very little emotion, or, more likely, didn't like to give his feelings away.

'It's no problem. It costs me nothing. We'll call three times a week.'

'Yeah. That would be good. That would help a lot. Help them and me, both. Hey, hope you don't mind, I wrote down your license number, and I thought you could put your full name and address on this paper.

It's just that . . . if the authorities ask me where I put my kids . . . you know . . . sounds kind of bad if I don't specifically know. I mean, what do I say? "Well, they drove off with some guy but he seemed OK and he said he'd bring 'em back later." I mean, I can't just tell people I gave my kids to this guy I don't even know.'

The mechanic's own words twisted his face into a wry smile, and he ended on a snort that was almost laughter. Sardonic laughter. Then his face changed suddenly. His eyes went wide, and he lowered himself into his desk chair. He brought one of his hands to his chest as though he was having trouble breathing.

'Hey,' August said. 'Wes. You all right?'

At first Wes just looked up at him, eyes still showing whites all around. Looking, but clearly not seeing. Then he said, 'Is that what I'm doing? My God. That's what I'm doing, isn't it? I'm giving my kids to this guy I don't even know.'

August leaned over the desk and grabbed Wes hard by both shoulders. 'Look at me,' he said. It didn't take at first, so he tried again. 'Wes. Look at me.' This time Wes's panicked eyes met his own. 'I'm going to take good care of those boys. And we're going to call you three times a week. They're going to see some amazing things. Places they never knew existed. And I'll bring them back in September. And if you ever want to know how they are, I'm on the other end of my cell phone.'

'I'd have to call collect.'

'Go ahead if you need to. If it feels important.'

'Let me give you some money for their food.'

Wes pulled out his wallet and removed every bill it contained. August accepted it without looking or counting, and without comment.

'Thanks. Seriously. Thanks, August. I mean it. I knew you were OK. I knew I didn't make a mistake with you. I don't know why I lost track of that for a minute. I just . . .'

'Love those boys?'

Wes began to cry. Not openly, like sobbing. It was silent, and he obviously tried to resist it. But August clearly saw the tears well up and spill over.

'They're my whole life,' he said, swiping hard at his eyes with the back of one hand. 'My whole world. You know?'

'I know,' August said.

'Mind if I go in the rig alone and say goodbye?'

'Go ahead.'

In fact, August didn't even watch them through the windshield. He considered the moment entirely theirs, and let them have it.

'Was my dad OK?' Seth asked as they pulled out on to the road that would take them back to the highway.

'Pretty OK.'

'He looked like he was having a heart attack or something.'

'No. Nothing like that. I think he just got scared, because he was sending you away with me.'

'But you're OK. Aren't you?'

'I am. Which I reminded him. And then he felt better. He just loves you guys a lot.'

Seth smiled, but it was a sad, lost little smile.

August looked in the rear-view mirror at Henry. He was sitting on the couch. Wearing his lap belt, as instructed. Woody was sitting with his front end draped over Henry's lap, his back end on the couch. Henry was stroking the dog with one hand. And crying. And wiping his nose on the sleeve of his clean white shirt.

'I don't remember your name,' Seth said. 'I remember the dog's name, but not yours.'

'August.'

'Like the month?'

'Yes. Like the month.'

'Mr August?'

'No. Just August. It's my first name.'

'Oh. I never knew anybody named after a month before.'

'Ever known a girl named April? Or May? Or June?'

'Um. Let me think. No. Not really *known*. But I guess I've heard of such a thing. But I never heard of a man named after a month. So what do I call you?'

'August.'

'You sure that's not disrespectful? My dad said to be real respectful.'

'It might be disrespectful to call a grown-up by their first name if they haven't asked you to, and if you're not sure how they feel about that. But if a grown-up says, "Call me August," then that's what you do.'

'And then it's not disrespectful.'

'Right.'

'I'm talking too much. Aren't I?'

'Well. I don't know about that. Too much for who?'

'My dad said I shouldn't talk too much.'

'But how do you know what's too much?'

'I asked him that exact same thing. He said if I talk the way I usually do, that would be too much.'

August laughed, and it surprised Seth, who didn't seem to understand what part of that was funny.

'Tell you what,' August said. 'If I think it's too much, I'll say something. Something like, "How about some quiet for a while?" If I don't say that, it's not too much.'

'Sure, OK,' Seth said.

Then he was dead silent through the rest of California.

4
Meetings

'Nevada state line,' August said. 'Two miles.'

Seth's head snapped up. 'Henry! You hear that?' He craned his neck around to check on his little brother.

August glanced in the rear-view mirror. Henry was struggling to wake up. Woody was still hanging half over his lap.

'Henry! Listen! A whole new state! Nevada. We never been to Nevada before. You gotta wake up. You gotta see this.'

'Really never been to Nevada?' August asked.

'Never.'

'Not so very far from where you live.'

'Really? Seems far. Anyway, we never went.'

'What other states have you been in besides California?'

'None of 'em. Can we stop?'

'Stop? I'm not sure what you mean. Stop where?'

'In Nevada.'

'Well . . . Seth . . . we'll be going through Nevada for a while. We'll be making lots of stops.'

'But I mean when we first get there. I want to see if it's different.'

'It's not very different. One mile this side of the state line is a lot like one mile across it.'

'Oh,' Seth said. 'OK.' His disappointment was heart-breakingly obvious. 'It's up to you where you stop or where you don't. That's fine. And you're probably right. I just kind of wanted to feel it for myself.'

'It feels different to me,' Seth said. 'I can't even really say how. It just does.'

He stood on the curb at a highway rest stop. They were close enough to the state-line sign to read it. August held Woody's leash, partially standing his ground as the dog pulled him over toward more interesting smells. Better places to lift his leg.

'I'll accept that,' August said.

He looked down at Henry, who huddled close to his brother's side. 'What do you think, Henry? Is Nevada different?'

Henry quickly turned his face away.

'Do you have a camera?' Seth asked. 'Would you get mad if I asked you to take a picture of that sign? The one that says we're in Nevada?'

'Seth, I won't get mad no matter what you ask me. I might say yes or I might say no, but I won't get mad at you for asking. I'll take a picture of the sign. Only thing is, we're on the wrong side of it now.'

'No, we're on the perfect side of it, August.'

'But you want to see the sign that says, "Welcome to Nevada". Or however it says it. From this direction you'll get "Welcome to California". And "Nevada says Drive Carefully, Come Back Soon".'

'No, this is right. This way. Because if the sign says we're just getting into Nevada, then we didn't yet. But if it's Nevada saying drive careful, then that's where we are.'

'That's actually reasonable logic,' August said. 'Here. Hold Woody's leash.'

He walked the few paces back to the motorhome, unlocked and opened the driver's side, and pulled his camera out of the door's inside map pocket.

Then he lined up a good view of the sign, zoomed in close, and snapped off a shot. Even though he had been to Nevada many times.

'Thanks,' Seth said. 'I want to remember this.'

'No problem. You guys hungry?'

'I am,' Seth said. He leaned over and whispered in his brother's ear. Although August could see or hear no response, Seth quickly added, 'Yeah. We are. Thank you for asking.'

'How do you feel about ham and cheese sandwiches?'

'We like ham and cheese sandwiches. Don't we, Henry?'

Henry didn't answer.

*

They ate at a rest-stop picnic table, under a stand of shade trees, to give everybody more time outside. Woody sat rapt on the grass between Henry and Seth, head shifting back and forth like he was watching a tennis match, clearly hoping for a dropped – or contributed – bite.

'This's a good sandwich,' Seth said. 'Thank you, August. Henry, isn't this a good sandwich?'

A barely perceptible nod from Henry.

'See, that's Henry's way of saying thank you.'

'Look. Seth. You're a very polite guy. And I appreciate that about you. But, really . . . it's kind of a given that I'm going to feed you. I wouldn't have you along if I didn't plan to take decent care of you.'

Seth nodded, seeming a trifle chastened.

They ate in silence for a time.

Then Seth asked, 'Do you hate this?'

August looked up suddenly, but the boy wouldn't meet his eyes.

'Do I . . . what? Do I hate what?'

'This. You know. Having to take us. I know you didn't really want to.'

'I don't hate it. No.'

'Who would want somebody else's kids along all summer? Nobody I know.'

'I wouldn't have said yes if I hated the idea.'

'Really?'

'Yes. Really.'

'But you don't exactly like it, I guess.'

'Maybe a little quiet for a while,' August said.

And Seth gave him that.

*

About sixty miles down the road, August stopped and filled up the gas tank. It was hot outside, so, even though they were driving with the air conditioning on, and even though he was paying for the gas with a credit card at the pump, August ducked into the convenience store to buy three sodas.

As he stood in line at the cash register, he noticed disposable cameras for sale in a rack on the counter. So he took down two, checking to be sure he was getting thirty-six exposures each, and slid them across the counter with the cold drinks.

A bored-looking teenaged boy rang it up and put it all in a paper sack for him.

August carried it back out into the heat, opened the driver's-side door and set the bag on the seat. Then he cleaned the windshield, stepping up on the front bumper to be able to reach it all. He replaced the gas nozzle, snagged his receipt from the pump, and climbed back into the driver's seat, moving the bag so he could sit down.

He pulled out one cold soda, then handed the bag to Seth.

'This is for you and your brother,' he said.

Seth looked inside, but apprehensively. As though August might have brought him a bag of snakes.

'Just the sodas, though. Right?'

'No. Everything in there is for you and Henry.'

'You bought us cameras?'

'Just the cheap disposable kind.'

'I never had a camera before. Not any kind.'

'I thought it might be nice if you could decide for yourself what you want to remember. Put your seat belt back on. We're going to drive again.'

'OK,' Seth said, and he did.

August looked over his shoulder at Henry, but could see that Henry had never taken his off.

'How many pictures is it?' Seth asked.

'Thirty-six each. But you can have copies of all my pictures when we get back. Just that, if it's something I wouldn't think to take a picture of, like the Nevada sign, but it feels important to you for some reason, you can have some pictures of your own.'

Silence.

August pulled away from the pump and merged back into traffic, headed for the freeway ramp. As he was pulling on to the ramp, Seth spoke.

'I can say thank you for that. Right?'

'You can say thank you for anything you want. But I know what you mean. The cameras are a little more above-and-beyond than food. So . . . you're welcome.'

Out of the corner of his eye, August watched Seth open the little box around the camera and tear open the foil pouch that contained it. Seth peered closely at the printed directions on the cardboard sleeve for a minute.

'Here, Henry,' Seth said. 'I'm going to give you this one for yours. And you do it like this. You wind it this way till it stops. Then you press this button to take the picture. Then you wind it till it stops again, so you're ready for the next picture.'

He reached the camera as far as he could behind his seat, and Henry leaned forward and stretched his hands out to receive it. It caused him to lean part of his torso on to Woody's head, but Woody didn't move, or appear to mind. In fact, he didn't wake up.

August watched in the rear-view mirror as Henry carefully wound the camera and aimed it straight down at the sleeping dog on his lap. August heard the click of the shutter button. Then Henry wound to the next stop and slid the camera into his shirt pocket, turned his head, and stared back out the window again.

'Seth,' August said, and shook him lightly by the shoulder. 'Hey. Buddy.'

It was three minutes before 8 p.m. Probably earlier than the boys were used to falling asleep. But there was something about a moving vehicle. And all those hypnotizing miles.

August looked up again at the windows of the building, glowing with light. He'd found a double parking space on the street right beside it, a stroke of luck. He was only ninety per cent sure it was the building he was looking for. But the handful of parked cars indicated just enough activity to feel right.

Seth stirred, stretched. Looked around and rubbed his eyes.

'Where are we, August?'

'No place special. This is not where we'll spend the

night or anything. We're just in a little town in Nevada, and I wanted you to know I'm going to be gone for an hour and a half.'

'Where're you going?' Seth asked, sounding a bit alarmed.

'Just into this building right here,' he said, and pointed. 'Henry's fast asleep. You can look after him, right?'

'Sure, I look after Henry all the time, but . . .'

'I just have to go to a meeting.'

'A meeting? But you're on vacation.'

'Different kind of meeting. Not a business meeting.'

'But you don't know anybody in this town, do you?'

'It's kind of a long story, buddy. And the meeting's about to start. How about if I tell you what it's about, but later?'

'OK.'

'I'll lock up. So nobody can get in. And Woody'll guard the place, anyway. But if you have any problems, or get scared, or anything feels like it's wrong, just honk the horn.'

'Does the ignition have to be turned on?'

'No. The horn works without the ignition on.'

''Cause with some horns, the ignition has to be on.'

'Not this one. It's wired to the battery. Comes in handy in bear country. Sometimes you have to make a lot of noise to chase them out of your campsite in the middle of the night.'

'Are we going where there are bears?' Seth asked. Trying to sound casual. Not quite succeeding.

'We're going where there are *grizzly* bears.'

Seth's eyes widened slightly, but he didn't answer.

'But we'll be careful. Gotta go, buddy.'

August patted Woody on the head and walked through the rig to the back door. Just as his hand touched the door handle, Seth spoke up again.

'August? Am I really your buddy?'

'Sure. Why wouldn't you be?'

'I don't know. I just didn't know that.'

'Well . . . I figure we'll all be buddies soon enough. So I jumped ahead a little.'

August walked into the warm, softly lit room just as the secretary of the meeting asked if there were any newcomers. If there had been, that might've taken up time, but as there weren't, the secretary moved right on to visitors.

August found a seat and sat down with his hand raised. 'My name is August, and I'm an alcoholic from San Diego. And I'm sorry I'm late.'

There were eight other people at the long table. Six men and two women. They said, nearly in unison, 'Hi, August. Welcome.'

Because that's the way they did things at a meeting. Didn't matter where you were from, or even where you were now. It didn't matter if they knew you. At some very basic level it didn't even matter if you'd been drinking, though fortunately August hadn't needed to test that theory. You just showed up, and you were welcome.

*

When the basket had been passed, and secretary announcements and reports handled, it was suggested that August might want to lead. Share his story first. If he was willing. Not terribly unusual for a visitor, in his experience. Still, he'd expected the reading of the steps and traditions to buy him some time. But apparently he had missed them by being late.

Immediately he felt a push-back against sharing. These other people were at home. He was not. They'd had time to adjust to the energy of the room and the people, which were familiar to begin with. He had not.

He pushed the feeling away again and did it anyway.

'My name is August and I'm an alcoholic,' he said again.

Then he paused while they greeted him a second time.

It's how things were done.

'I'll just go ahead and say what I say at every meeting, every time I share. The only difference is the count of days. I have nineteen months and three days sober as of today. My sobriety date is a year ago last November third. The day my nineteen-year-old son died. I haven't had a drink since that day.

'I'm going to be really honest and say I never exactly thought of myself as a falling-down drunk. I drank a lot, probably too much. I never got in trouble for it, but maybe I would have, if nothing had stopped me. I always figured I could stop if I wanted, but I can't prove that for a fact, because I never wanted.'

A light ripple of reaction. What might have been laughter if he hadn't started his story on such a serious note. August briefly waited it out.

'Nobody told me to stop, probably because my wife drank just about the way I did, and my son had too much respect for me to give advice. Maybe he thought my drinking was still within some kind of acceptable range. I don't know what he thought. I wish he were here. I'd ask him.

'A year ago November third he was riding in the car with my wife, and she started up at a green light . . . pulled into the intersection. But somebody was in the process of running the red. Easy enough to put it off on a red-light runner, and I think we both tried. But usually before you start up at a green, you take some little glance to make sure the way is clear. You know. There's that situational awareness born out of survival instinct. Anyway, the guy T-boned our car on the passenger side and my son was killed instantly. My wife walked away. Well, my wife at the time. My ex-wife now. Not as lucky for her as it may sound, walking away. At least, that's my view of the situation. We kept waiting for toxicology reports. It was probably a day before we heard, but it felt like a month. I kept asking her to tell me, but she said she'd been fine. But I figured she'd been drunk. But the reports came back, and she hadn't been drunk. And she wasn't charged with any crime. But she had alcohol in her system. She always had alcohol in her system. Just not over the legal limit. Close to the limit, but not over it.'

August braved a glance at the faces of the three men right across the table. They leaned forward in absolute silent and undivided attention. He looked away again.

'I swear to God I think it would've been kinder for her if they'd thrown her in jail. At least then she'd get out after a while. But when nobody punishes you, you have to do it yourself, and there's no release date on that. We're always harder on ourselves than any governing body could ever get away with being.

'To this day I can't say for a fact that things would've gone differently if her blood alcohol had been zero. But I feel like it would have been different, and I guess I'll always feel that way. Her reflexes would've been a little bit sharper. Our splitting up wasn't because I needed to punish her. It wasn't like that. I don't know what I needed. I don't even know what I need now. She still hasn't stopped drinking. I don't want to judge her for that. Maybe I wouldn't have been able to stop, either, if I'd been driving that car that day. I don't *want* to judge her, but maybe at some level I judge her every day whether I want to or not. Whether I mean to or not. It's one thing to know the right path and another thing to take it. But I never set out to throw her away. I never set out to throw anything away. It just all fell apart. I'd look at her every day and try to fathom how I'd feel if I were her, and I couldn't imagine, but I knew I didn't want to find out. I knew that if a couple of drinks could turn into that kind of life-or-death situation, at any moment, without any warning, then I wasn't going to have even one. Not even a sip.

'It's funny. Well . . . maybe not really funny, under the circumstances, but . . . The principal of my school – where I teach – lost her husband. A few months ago. I was sitting with her one day at lunch, and she knew I'd lost my son, so we were talking. So finally I asked her what had happened to her husband. You know. If she didn't mind saying. I was kind of shocked, but what she said was, "He drank too much." She never said what actually killed him. If it was his liver, or . . . I don't know, and I didn't want to press for details. But she made it clear that the direct answer to the question of how he died was that he drank too much. And she didn't seem ashamed of the fact, either. She sounded very . . . understanding. Very tolerant. She said he had a lot of stress in his job, in his life, and this is what he did to handle it.

'So of course by this time I had a little over a year in the program, and I said, "Not to pry, and you don't have to answer if you don't want, but did he ever try AA?"

'She looked at me with the most astonished look on her face. I swear, this is going to sound like a joke, but this is what she said. Word for word. She said, "Oh, my goodness. No. He wasn't *that* bad."'

August paused to allow a burst of reaction. It could have been a big laugh. AA was known for big bursts of spontaneous laughter over confessions that outsiders might consider too somber to evoke cheer. But August's son had died. So the burst took the shape of puffs of breath and the shaking of heads.

'Anyway,' he continued, 'I couldn't get it out of my head. Because my wife didn't think she was bad enough for AA, either. At least, she never thought so when we were together. And it's not for me to say. But it's funny how you can take something that turns out to be fatal and classify it as not worth fixing. So I haven't had one drink since I got the phone call about the accident. Not one sip. I don't know if I'm what you might call a true alcoholic or not, I just know I came in with the desire to stop drinking and that's all I need to claim my seat. And, whatever I was, it's bad enough because I decided it's bad enough, and that's my call to make. And I hope you respect that and accept that I qualify for this program, but I figure you will, because I've told a version of that same story to a lot of people at a lot of AA groups, and not one person has failed to respect me yet.

'And . . . I don't know . . . now I'm just suddenly running out of steam. I think there was something else I was going to say, but now it flew away completely. But I guess that's enough out of me anyway. I know that's not really much of a proper lead. I didn't do the whole "what it used to be like, what happened, what it's like now" thing. I'm not sure how much you adhere to that here. I just feel done. Thanks for asking me to lead. Thanks for being here with a meeting when I needed one.'

August sat back against the hard wood of the chair. Pulled in a long breath. The group applauded, which made him jump. His home group didn't applaud speakers. He knew some groups did, and he had even been to some groups that did. But it caught him by surprise all the same.

'Want to call on somebody, August?' the group secretary asked.

So August pointed to one of the men across the table from him, because the man had been listening with the look that made August feel most understood.

The man said, 'I'm Tom, I'm an alcoholic.'

And the group said, 'Hi, Tom.'

'Really glad you found your way in here tonight, August. Partly because you've got a hell of a story. Partly because this is a damn small town and we've been sick to death of each other's stories for a very long time.'

And with that, the mood lightened, and the hard part was over. And August just listened. And breathed.

After the meeting, a woman approached August, as he was doing his best to make it to the door.

'What do you teach?' she asked. 'I'm a teacher myself. That's the only reason I'm asking.'

She was ten or fifteen years older than August, with a kindly face, and eyes that still had some spark left. She didn't look the least bit burned out or worn down.

'How long?' he asked, thinking maybe it was a second career for her.

'How long have I been a teacher? Almost thirty years.'

'Wow,' he said. But then he chose not to elaborate.

'So what do you teach? What grade level?'

'Science,' he said. 'High school.'

'That must be hard since your son died.'

'No,' he said. Then, noting the odd look on her face, he added, 'Well. Everything's hard since Phillip died.'

'All those kids around his age. It must make you feel . . .'

After she trailed off, it took a minute for August to realize she was waiting for him to finish the thought. And the fact that he didn't see that right away let him know that he was disconnecting. The way he did during the school year.

'Nothing,' he said. 'I feel nothing.' Silence. August thought about just heading out the door. But he hit the thought head-on instead. 'I teach like I'm walking in a dream. The kids in front of me, I teach them, and I talk to them, but they don't even look three-dimensional to me. They don't even look full color. And I feel nothing. I keep waiting for somebody to say they notice the difference. Or even let on without saying it straight out. The kids, the other teachers. Nobody ever does.'

'It must be one of those things that you're more aware of from the inside.'

'I guess,' he said.

'I don't suppose that numbness will last for ever,' she said.

'No,' August said. 'Unfortunately, I think you're right about that.'

5
The Glove Compartment

When August opened his eyes, it was light. He was asleep on the fold-out couch bed in the motorhome. The boys were sleeping on the thick cushions of the folded-down dinette area on the other side. Except Seth wasn't sleeping. He was half sitting up. He had the window shade partly raised, and was peering out.

Woody had chosen their side. Their bed.

August sat up and stretched, and Woody leapt on to his bed to wag good morning. He rubbed against August's side like a cat.

Seth said, 'What is this place, August? It doesn't look like a campground at all.'

'It's not. It's just some guy's driveway.'

'What guy?'

'Just a guy I met at my meeting last night. By the time the meeting was over I was too tired to go much farther, so I asked a couple of people at the meeting if there was a campground close by. But there was nothing really as close as I wanted. But one of the guys invited me to park in his driveway for the night.'

'Oh,' Seth said. He didn't say more, but the 'oh' was loaded with questions he seemed to know he shouldn't ask.

'Come on,' August said. 'Let's get up and get dressed and get Woody outside to pee. And I'll make us some breakfast. And then I'll tell you what the meetings are all about.'

'These pancakes are good,' Seth said.

'Glad you like them. Woody. Get down.'

Woody, who had briefly been standing with his paws on Henry's lap, slunk into the corner by the back door.

'Ever heard of AA?' August asked Seth.

'That's not the one you call for a tow when you break down on the road, is it? 'Cause my dad always calls it Triple A.'

'No. This is Alcoholics Anonymous.'

'Yeah,' Seth said after a time. 'I've heard of it. It's for people who can't stop drinking, right?'

'I guess that's as good a way to say it as any. It's for people who want to stop drinking and haven't had much luck stopping on their own. It seems to work a lot better than when people just sit home and try to use willpower. It's not an issue that willpower has much effect on. Not if you're really an alcoholic.'

Seth looked up into August's face. 'Are you an alcoholic, August?'

'I think so. The main thing is, I decided I wanted to stop drinking.'

'So that's why you go to meetings.'

'Right.'

'Even when you're out on the road.'

'Yes. I try to be regular about meetings.'

'If you skipped 'em in the summer, would you go back and drink?'

'Probably not. I probably won't get in an accident this summer, either. I may never get in an accident in my whole life, but I still put on my seat belt every time I drive. Besides, I feel better when I go to meetings.'

'How can you not know for sure if you're an alcoholic?'

'Well . . .' August began. He glanced at Henry, who wasn't looking at either of them. But August had to assume he was taking it all in. Hard not to wonder what a little guy like that makes of the world. When he won't ever say. 'I didn't drink the way some of the people in the meetings did. But I drank enough that I wanted to stop.'

'So, how do you know? How do you know if somebody's an alcoholic?'

'In the program, we more or less leave it that you're an alcoholic if you say you are.'

'But you don't even know if you are.'

'I say I am, and I've chosen to stop drinking. So I am.'

'Oh.'

A long silence. Henry finished shoveling in his

pancakes. Seth took a few more bites, but also pushed a few bites of pancake around, leaving little patterns in the syrup on his plate.

'Can I go to one of the meetings, August?'

August thought a minute before answering. It seemed like a complicated question. He had no immediate answer to toss off the top of his head.

'Not sure you'd want to, buddy. You'd probably think they were hopelessly boring.'

'No. I wouldn't. I really want to go.'

'Why?'

Seth looked down at his plate. Then he stuffed two bites of pancake into his mouth at once. He never answered.

'You don't drink, do you?'

Seth burst out laughing. Almost spit out some of the mouthful he was chewing. 'August,' he said with his mouth still full. 'I'm twelve.'

'You wouldn't be the first twelve-year-old alcoholic ever.'

'I don't drink.'

'Then why do you want to go to a meeting?'

Seth finished his chewing slowly. Thoughtfully. He swallowed hard. Woody wiggled back and sat at Henry's feet. But he stayed down, so August said nothing.

'If I tell you,' Seth said, 'is it just 'cause you want to know? Or if I tell you will you really maybe take me to one?'

'It depends on the meeting. Some are open meetings, and that means everyone is welcome. A lot of meetings are closed, so they're for alcoholics only. I'd have to find an open meeting. I have lists of meetings all along our route, but I didn't write down if they were open or closed, because I didn't think I'd need to know.'

'I still don't know if that means yes or no.'

'I can ask. Next time I go to a meeting, I can ask if it's open. And if it is, you can come in, too. What about Henry?'

'I guess he'd have to come in with us. He won't mind. He'll go wherever I go. But I still have to tell you why before you'll take me. Don't I?'

'It's something of an unusual request for a kid to make. So . . . let's just say I'd appreciate knowing.'

'I just want to know why people drink.'

'Hard question to answer. It's probably different for everyone.'

'And why they don't stop. You know. Even when it's making problems.'

'OK.'

'You'll take me?'

'Sure. Why not? First open meeting I can find.'

'We've got another state line coming up,' August said.

'Yeah? Really? What's the state?'

'Arizona. But we won't be in it too long. Although we'll hit more of it on the way home. But we're just going through the very corner of it today. You'll see what I mean if you look at the map. Then we'll hit another state line and we'll be in Utah.'

'Two more states, and all just today?'

And, on that thought, Seth reached forward to open the glove compartment.

August stamped on the brake, almost without thinking. The driver behind him honked long and loud, then pulled around and passed him on the left.

'What are you doing?' August asked Seth.

Seth froze, his eyes wide.

'I was just gonna get my camera.'

'What the hell is your camera doing in my glove compartment?'

'I don't know. I mean, I put it there last night. I just wanted to put it where it would be safe.'

'That's why I cleared you out drawers and cupboards. So you'd have a safe place to put your stuff and you could stay the hell out of mine.'

'Why are you yelling at me?' Seth shouted, obviously working to hold back tears.

August hadn't realized he'd been yelling. But, having had it pointed out, it was clear that Seth was right.

An exit came up, and August took it. At the end of the ramp, he found a wide patch of dirt alongside a roughly paved road in the middle of absolutely nothing and nowhere. He pulled on to it and shut off the engine.

He looked in the rear-view mirror to see Henry crying, and Woody nudging and licking the tears. He looked over at Seth, who was looking away. Out the window. As if there were something out there to see.

'Is this about that soda bottle?' Seth asked, his voice heavy and resentful.

August shut his eyes tightly. Careful not to yell. 'You have no right to ask me about that.'

When he opened his eyes, August was surprised to see Seth staring at him not with fear, but with something fierce in his eyes. Something that looked almost like . . . contempt.

'Seth, I'm sorry I yelled before. Some things are just private.'

Seth continued to stare, his nostrils flaring slightly.

August leaned over, opened the glove compartment, and pulled out Seth's disposable camera. It was lying right on top of the plastic iced-tea bottle. Seth couldn't possibly have missed seeing it. He closed the compartment door and held the camera out to Seth, who was still staring fiercely.

'Here's your camera.'

Seth did not reach out and take it.

'You said I could ask you *anything*. You said I could ask any question I wanted, and you'd either say yes or you'd say no, but you wouldn't get mad at me for asking. And you just got mad at me for asking. I don't see what can be so private about it. It's just an old soda bottle. I just wondered what that was. In it.'

'It's not soda. It's an old iced-tea bottle. And you're right. I said you could ask anything. I'm sorry. This was my fault, not yours. I apologize. Here, take your camera.'

Seth took the camera and stuck it in his shirt pocket without comment. He turned his head and stared out the window again.

They sat that way for a time, silent except for the sounds of Henry's sobs.

'You'd better go comfort your brother. Tell him I'm sorry I yelled.'

A little after six that night, August pulled into an RV park just north of St George, Utah. He paid up at the office, then – rather than drive straight to his assigned site – he made a stop at the dump station.

He turned off the engine, and glanced over once at Seth. Seth was awake, staring out the window. He hadn't said another word to August all day.

August sighed, and walked back through the rig to pick up a pair of disposable plastic gloves from the utility drawer. Henry stared at him as he did. Woody wagged and wiggled and let out one long whine.

August sighed again. 'Can it wait, buddy?'

'I'll take him out,' Seth said.

'Thank you,' August said, without trying to define whether that qualified as Seth speaking to him or not.

'What are you doing?' Seth asked, appearing suddenly at his right shoulder.

It made August jump. He was in a squatting position, and almost fell over.

'I'm dumping the tanks.'

'The tanks? Like . . .'

'Yeah. Like when we use the sink or the toilet or the shower. It goes into a holding tank. And every few days I have to dump it.'

'Ick.'

'Now you know why I use plastic gloves. So, you're speaking to me again.'

Seth squatted down next to August. They watched foamy, soapy graywater from the kitchen sink flow from the end of the hose and down the sewer drain.

'I'm sorry,' Seth said. 'For not talking to you all day.'

'I thought that was my fault, not yours.'

'You said you were sorry for yelling. That should have been the end of it.'

August nodded thoughtfully a few times. He'd been thinking the same thing himself at various points during the day, but was surprised to hear it come out of Seth's mouth.

'I put Woody back inside with Henry,' Seth said.

'Thank you.'

'He did both things. Peed, and . . . you know. I picked it up. I brought one of those bags. I put it in the dumpster at the end of the road. I didn't think you'd want it in the inside trash.'

'Thank you.'

'Maybe you could teach me to do this.'

'What? The tanks?'

'Yeah.'

'Why would you want to do the tanks?'

'Just to be helpful.'

'You know you don't have to be perfect, don't you, Seth?'

'What?'

'You know you can't be all things to all people. Right?'

'I don't know what you mean.'

'No. I guess you wouldn't.'

They stared at the flow in silence for a minute more.

'I've just been in a bad mood all day,' Seth said. 'That's why I was sorry.'

'That'll happen,' August said.

'I sort of know why. But I don't want to say. You'll think it's stupid.'

August shut off the final dribble of flow from the sink and disconnected the motorhome's sewer hose. Before he stood up to rinse it with the provided non-potable water nozzle, he looked Seth dead in the eye.

'Don't take this the wrong way, buddy, but it seems like you *do* want to say.'

'No. I don't.'

'Then why even bring it up again?'

'You'll think it's stupid.'

August sighed. It had been that kind of day. Full of sighs. He stood and began rinsing out his sewer hose.

'Seth,' he said. 'The longer you live, the more you'll see that the inside of everybody is a lot like the inside of everybody else. If you're feeling something, more likely than not it's just what anyone would feel.'

'So you think I should say.'

'I do, actually.'

'I'm already homesick.'

'I don't think that's stupid.'

'Really?'

'Not at all.'

'Don't get mad when I say this. I don't mean to be

ungrateful. But I sort of thought we'd be seeing so much great interesting stuff that I wouldn't have time to get homesick. Not that we haven't seen places. I think this town is nice. You know. With the mountains and all. Seems like the mountains are all different colors. But it wasn't enough to keep me from getting homesick.'

'Give it a little time. We're just stuck in one of the in-between bits. We haven't gotten anywhere yet.'

He looked up to see Henry watching them from inside, both hands against the glass of the window. Woody panted beside him, leaving nose prints on the glass.

'When do we get somewhere?'

'Tomorrow. Tomorrow we'll be at Zion National Park. There'll be a lot more to do. I think you'll like it.'

'What's it like? Tell me about it.'

'Seth. We'll be there tomorrow morning. Can't I just show it to you?'

Seth's shoulders fell. He seemed to deflate on a huge exhale. He turned on his heel to go back inside.

There it was, August thought. *There it goes again.*

'Seth. Wait.'

Seth stopped and turned. Waited to see what August would say. And, in many respects, so did August.

'The old plastic iced-tea bottle in the glove compartment has a little of my son Phillip's ashes in it.'

An awkward silence.

'His? What do you mean, his? He had, like, an ashes collection?'

'No. Not ashes that used to belong to him. Ashes of him.'

'Oh,' Seth said.

'I know. It's weird. That's why I didn't want to talk about it.'

'Shouldn't it be in, like . . . a fancy . . . what do you call those things?'

'Urn?'

'Yeah. That.'

'The rest of them are. This is just a little part of his ashes.'

'Oh. But still. Why an old iced-tea bottle?'

'Maybe that's another story for another day,' August said.

August sat in his camp chair, eating a hot dog grilled on the grate over their open campfire. And vaguely wishing he had brought three camp chairs. He had three, left over from the days when his family traveled together. But he'd left two in the garage, never imagining he would need them.

It was late dusk. Nearly dark.

'This is more how I thought it would be,' Seth said. 'Like camping.'

The boys sat side by side on a folded blanket, staring into the fire. The wind changed, and blew smoke into their eyes and faces. They scrambled away. Seth started to drag the blanket around to the other side of the fire.

August said, 'I wouldn't bother if I were you. The wind'll just shift again. Wherever you sit it'll hit you in the face part of the time. We'll mostly be camping. But when you're driving long distances, you have to be prepared for some in-between days.'

'It's OK. We don't mind. Especially now that we know. This hot dog is really good. I never had a hot dog this good. I think it's cooking them on the fire. Our dad always just boils them in a pot.'

And, at the mention of their father, things went silent for a long time. Until they were done eating.

Then Seth asked, 'Can I have another? Please? I know three is a lot . . .'

'It's fine, Seth. You can have all you want. But you'll have to throw another one on to cook.'

'I don't mind that. But is it really OK? I'm not being selfish?'

'It's fine. It's not a problem.'

'I feel like it might cost you too much to have us along.'

'Your dad gave me some food money for you.'

'Oh. I didn't know that. I feel better now.'

Seth unwrapped the package of hot dogs, pulled out one, carefully rewrapped what was left, and threw his third hot dog on the fire. He didn't sit down again. Just stood and watched it cook.

'My dad drinks,' he said. 'Not so much that he should go to AA. Well . . . maybe. I don't know. That's the thing. I don't know how bad is bad enough.'

'Nobody really does,' August said, 'from the outside.'

He looked down at Henry, who was eating his hot

dog with ketchup only, and staring at it with a slight frown.

'Thing is, it gets him in trouble. So I wonder why he doesn't just not do it, then. That's not how he got in trouble this time. This time it was checks. Not bad checks, exactly. He wasn't trying to steal or anything. Just checks that weren't good fast enough. You know how sometimes you write a check, and you don't really have that much in the bank, but you think you will. You know. That you can get the money and put it in the bank in time. Before the check comes in. But the first three times. The first three times he was drunk driving. And he still drives home from the bar. Even though they haven't caught him at it again.'

Then he stopped suddenly, and looked confused and a little bit ashamed. As if he had no idea who'd said all that, or why.

August said, 'I thought this was only the second time he had to go to jail.'

'No. Fourth.'

'He told me it was the second.'

'Oh. Well. Maybe he forgot those other times.'

But August couldn't imagine how anybody could forget going to jail. He didn't say so, though. He just said, 'So that's why you want to go to a meeting with me.'

'Sort of. Yeah.'

'There's a whole other program for that. When it's about somebody else's drinking. It's called Al-Anon. They even have Alateen. For kids.'

'That would be OK. If we find one. But I figure you're going to these anyway. We don't need to talk about this. I don't really even know why I—'

And just at that moment, Woody, who was sitting close by Henry and his hot dog, sat up and begged. It was something he'd been taught not to do while people were eating. So, on the one hand, August was surprised. Then there was another part of him that wondered why the dog hadn't used it on the boys meals ages ago.

Henry laughed and gave him a piece of bun.

'Oh, dear,' August said. 'Now there'll be no living with him.'

'Henry,' Seth said. 'Don't feed him like that, or he won't be polite any more. Hey. We never saw Woody do his tricks.'

So August cut up a hot dog and ran Woody through his paces.

He held a piece behind his back, made his other hand into a gun shape, and pointed straight at Woody's heart. 'Stick 'em up,' he said to the dog.

Woody stood straight up on his hind legs with his front paws reaching for the sky. Henry shrieked laughter.

Then August had Woody twirl like a ballerina, and walk all the way around the fire ring on his hind legs. He held Woody, then told him to play dead. Woody drooped in his hands, head and paws hanging limply down. Both boys laughed.

For a finale, he had Woody stand up and give him both a high five and a high ten.

'That's the best dog,' Seth said. 'You got any marsh-mallows, August?'

'We have, in fact, three bags,' August said.

He didn't bring up the fact that the boys were feeling better, because sometimes such things were better left unexamined.

6
There

'So you can't drive into this valley at all?' Seth asked. 'You have to ride the bus?'

They had just found themselves seats on the shuttle. It was mid-morning, maybe an hour after arriving at the park.

It was finally time to be 'there'. Somewhere. Any of the many 'theres' of the summer. They had spent too much time only *headed* for there. Even August, with his adult patience, could feel the insistence of that need.

'In the off season you can drive. In the summer you have to use the shuttle. It's not exactly a valley. It's a canyon. Zion Canyon.'

'Is it nice?'

'You're about to find out.'

The shuttle started up, easing along the narrow but perfectly paved road. Henry perched on the edge of Seth's seat so they could all sit on the same side as each other. August had given them the window seat, because he'd seen Zion before.

'That was a stupid question,' Seth said. 'I'm sorry. Because I already know it's nice, because it's even nice from our camp place. I like the way you can see the great big mountains of rock, but you see them with the nice green trees in front of them. And that stuff from the trees that flies around. That makes it even nicer. What did you say the trees were again?'

'Cottonwoods.'

'So does that make it cotton, what's flying around?'

'It's just a common name. Somebody thought it looked like cotton. Real cotton doesn't grow on a tree.'

'Am I talking too much?'

'I don't know. Maybe not. It's OK to be excited. But you might want to listen to the driver, because he'll announce the different things we're seeing.'

They traveled along the road for several minutes in silence before the driver announced the Court of the Patriarchs.

'The what?' Seth asked, leaning toward the window to see.

'The Court of the Patriarchs.'

'Those three big . . . sort of . . . mountains? Why do they call them that?'

'I'm not sure I remember. Tell you what. We'll stop in the visitor's center on the way back and pick up some brochures. And if they don't answer all your questions, there are people there you can ask.'

'They're really pretty,' Seth said.

They were more than pretty, August thought. *They were majestic. They made you miss one breath, no matter how many times you'd seen them.* He didn't speak.

'I like how they're red, but then sort of white at the top. I never saw mountains that were red and white both. And sort of green at the bottom. Will the stuff at the visitor's center tell me why the rock is red, white and green?'

'If it doesn't, I will. But the rock isn't green. The Patriarchs have some trees growing out of them. Near the bottom.'

'How can trees grow out of solid rock?'

'Nature's funny that way.'

'Seriously, though, August. Will you explain it to me?'

'I will. But right now we have to decide if we want to get off by the lodge. We could go up the Emerald Pools Trail. But it's steep. Can Henry do steep?'

'I'm not sure. Are there other trails that aren't steep?'

'Sure. We can ride all the way to the end and take the River Trail. Along the Virgin River.'

'But we can see that river out the back door of your rig at our camp place.'

'It's different in the canyon. Believe me.'

As they neared the stop for Angels Landing, the driver slowed and pointed out a group of climbers going straight up the sheer side of the reddish cliff. They looked like ants, hanging at a thousand feet or more, three-quarters of the way up the wall.

August heard all the breath go out of Seth in slow

motion. But Seth didn't comment, and neither did August.

But when they got to the Angels Landing stop, the one called The Grotto, Seth said, 'Can we get off here and see it?'

'Sure, I guess.'

'But then we can't walk by the river?'

'We can do both. We can catch another shuttle bus when we're done.'

They stepped out into bright sun. Stood under a startlingly blue sky. The heat of the day was already quite evident, though not in full gear. August guessed it was already close to ninety.

Seth pulled his disposable camera from his shirt pocket and aimed it at the climbers on the rock face.

'You'd do better with my camera for that,' August said. 'You're not going to see much without a strong zoom.'

August pulled out his camera, turned it on. Took off the lens cap. Handed it to Seth, who seemed afraid to hold it.

'Here, put the strap around your neck. Then you can't possibly drop it.'

'OK.'

'Now point it at the climbers.'

'OK.'

'Now move this lever to the right.'

August placed Seth's finger on the zoom.

'OK.'

'Still got the climbers in your view?'

'Yeah, but they're all blurry.'

'Then put your finger on the shutter,' August said, pointing out the shutter. 'And press it down halfway. Not hard. Just press lightly.'

'Whoa!' Seth shouted. Loud enough to make Henry jump. 'Wow! I can see them. I can see them so good, August. Like they were right in front of me. I can see what color shirts they're wearing. Now what do I do?'

'Press the shutter down the rest of the way.'

August heard the click.

'Now let's see what you got.'

He took the camera back from Seth, lifting the strap from around his neck. He pulled up a display of the picture. It looked great. A perfect close-up of three climbers and their ropes on the rock wall.

He showed it to Seth.

'See? You got a good shot.'

'It *is* good. Isn't it? Thanks for letting me use your camera.'

'You're welcome.'

'I totally want to do that,' Seth said, pointing again at the climbers.

August snorted laughter. 'No way in hell,' he said.

'I didn't mean *now*. I'm not stupid, August. I know that's too hard to do *now*. I mean I want to *learn* to do that. When I get older. When I'm big enough that it's up to me what I do, and nobody can stop me.'

'Oh. That's different. But be careful. It's a dangerous sport.'

'But maybe not if you're good at it and you do it right. You think I shouldn't *ever* do it?'

'It's not up to me to tell you what you should or shouldn't ever do. I think you should be careful. But in general I think you should do what you want to do, if you really want to do it.'

'I really want to do it,' Seth said.

They got off the shuttle again at Weeping Rock. They walked the short uphill trail to the rock face, and ducked under the steady drops of falling water to stand under the rock overhang and look out.

Henry stared straight up at the drops as they came off the ledge, purposely leaning out, his face turned up and wet, his hair increasingly drenched. There was a low rock wall, built as a ledge, to hold him in. So he could lean out without falling.

'I hope Woody's OK,' Seth said.

'Why wouldn't he be OK? You took him for a walk before we left. He got to go to the bathroom and all. He's fine in the motorhome by himself.'

'But doesn't it make him sad?'

'He knows there are some places dogs can go and other places they can't.'

'But doesn't it make him sad?'

August sighed. And, unfortunately, considered the idea. 'Maybe. I don't know. I just know it's the way it has to be.'

They watched the raining moisture in silence for a time. Henry's head and shoulders were soaked, but he didn't pull back under the rock overhang.

'They should call this Raining Rock,' Seth said.

'Well. I guess they could have. But they chose Weeping Rock instead.'

'But that's too sad,' Seth said.

'August! Look! You can walk up to Angels Landing on a trail!'

They stood back outside the visitor's center, a quarter-mile walk from their campground, in front of a detailed map of Zion Canyon.

'Yeah. I know. But it's a tough trail. I've done it. It's steep.'

'Let's do it. Let's go.'

'I'm not sure Henry could get up there. I'm not even sure you could get up there, if you're not used to steep hikes.'

'I can do it. I can even carry Henry on my back if I have to.'

'I'm not as sure as you are that you can do all that.'

'But can't we try? Can't we even try, August? I want to get up there really bad.'

'Not today, no. It's already too hot. And too crowded. But if you really want to try, we'll get up while it's still dark tomorrow. And we'll catch the very first shuttle. And I'll pack some water and some snacks. And we'll see how high we can get.'

'All the way. I want to get all the way up to the top.'

'We'll see how high we can get,' August said. 'What about calling your father, though? Tomorrow morning will be the first day you can call your father. Don't you want to do that tomorrow morning?'

Seth bit his upper lip for a minute.

It hit August that he'd had just about all the hot sun he could take. Thank God the River Trail had been in shade. But they hadn't walked much of it. Just enough to get the feel of the cool walls of the canyon, and marvel at the way the river had carved them.

'Couldn't we call him when we get back down?'

'Up to you,' August said.

Then he thought, without saying, *That's a lot of want for a kid. He wants to get to the top of Angels Landing more than I thought.*

'Can we get cell-phone reception up on top?' Seth asked, straining with hope.

'I'm not sure.'

'Bring your cell phone and let's find out. We could call him from the top. From way up there on the very top of the world. And I could tell him what it looks like up there. What I see. It'll be like he's on top of the world with us. Instead of being, you know . . .'

Then he trailed off and didn't finish the thought.

'If we even get that high. It's a tough trail.'

'I can get to the top,' Seth said. Without the slightest hint of doubt.

'We'll see how high we can get,' August said.

'I think I'm too excited to sleep,' Seth said.

August propped up on one elbow. Looked over at the boys, tucked into their bed on the dinette side, but wide awake. Henry was staring at the ceiling, one hand stroking the back of Woody's neck. Even Woody was wide awake.

'I know it's early,' August said. 'But we have to get up before four.'

'I don't think I ever got up *that* early before. We're all ready, though. You have your pack all ready with water and stuff.'

'But we have to get Woody out for a walk before we go.'

'Oh. That's right.'

Seth reached out and petted the back end of the dog. The part Henry didn't already have covered in the petting department.

'What was your favorite thing you saw today?' August asked. Then, just as Seth opened his mouth to speak, he added, 'Other than the climbers.'

'Oh. Other than the climbers. Then I think it was that wild turkey we saw near the Temple of . . . what was it the Temple of again, August?'

'Sinawava.'

'Right. I still don't understand how they got those names. That court and all, and the temple. When we looked at the brochures, it just said stuff like somebody thought it looked like that thing. But that didn't really explain it.'

'But you understand now about the mineral difference in the rocks.'

'Yeah, you explained that real good. Better than the brochures.'

Silence for a time. Still nobody was sleeping. And sleep would be required for the following morning's climb. It would be hard enough for the well-rested.

'Will you talk to me about something, August?'

'What do you mean? About what?'

'Anything. It'll help me sleep.'

'Just talk to you about anything?'

'Yeah.'

'Hmm,' August said. He lay back again, his hands clasped behind his neck. 'Let me see. I could tell you about Bryce Canyon, but it's hard to describe. I can't tell you about Yellowstone, because I haven't seen it yet myself.'

'But you saw the trail up Angels Landing. Tell me about that.'

'Won't that just make you more excited? And make it even harder to sleep?'

'Oh. Yeah. Right. Well. Tell me anything, then. Doesn't have to be about things we're gonna see. Tell me anything. Tell me something about you. Because me and Henry, we don't even know you very well.'

August took a deep breath, and tried to think of something. He thought he'd tell them about his job teaching high-school science, but it struck him as too boring. Then he remembered that boring might be good. He could potentially literally bore them to sleep. Then he realized it was he himself who would be too bored by it. He had to do it all school year long, but he didn't have to think or talk about it during the summer.

'I'm thinking,' August said.

More time passed. During it, August wondered about the number of times Wes had been in jail. And why the impression he'd been given had turned out to be a lie. It felt like a harsh word, lie. But it didn't seem reasonable to believe it could have been a mistake.

He had two brief flashes of fear. The first was that he was responsible for these boys, and he was taking them up to the top of a narrow rock formation fifteen hundred feet over the canyon floor. And there were no guard rails. This wasn't Disneyland. It really was possible to tumble right off the edge.

The second fear was that the summer might bring more surprises about the boys' life at home. More bits of information withheld. It briefly flashed through August's mind that by the time it was September, and his job was to return the boys, he might no longer be sure returning them was the right thing to do.

He pushed the thought away again. Hard. But it left a pinching feeling in his gut, a sense that he had taken on too much. That he had started down a long trail of taking responsibility for the boys, with no idea where it might lead.

'I really am thinking,' he said.

'OK,' Seth said.

And a silence fell again.

'My son's name was Phillip,' August said after a time. 'I won't tell you all about him, because I want you to get to sleep faster than that. But I'll tell you about him and the iced tea. He used to love this bottled iced tea. Drank maybe five bottles a day. He bought it out of his own money, because it had sugar in it. I thought he shouldn't drink so much sugar, so I wouldn't buy it for him after a while. So he bought it for himself. He was like that. He had a very strongly developed sense of fairness. He'd play by my rules, but he was the first to call me on it if my rules overreached. We used to call him The Enforcer.'

'We?'

'My wife and I. I mean, my ex-wife and I. Anyway. There was only one time I can ever remember him not finishing a bottle. We were sitting at the dining-room table, and he was drinking this iced tea, and we were talking about whether I was going to let him go on a camping trip with his friends over the Christmas break. That boy loved camping more than just about anything. But before we finished talking about it, and before he finished the bottle, his mom came in and asked him to go to the store with her. She had a big shopping to do, and she wanted help carrying everything. He never said no to helping out his mom. Never. I guess he figured he wouldn't be gone too long. So he just left the half bottle of iced tea sitting there on the table. Because he knew he'd be right back. But he wasn't right back.'

'When was he back, August?'

'He never came back. That's when he and his mother got in that accident.'

'Oh.'

'So for the next couple of weeks, that bottle just sat there on the dining-room table. I'd go in and look at it. But I couldn't bring myself to throw it away. I still didn't get it on an emotional level that he was gone. I don't know how to explain that part. It's like I knew, but I didn't know. My head knew, but there was this part of me that couldn't make sense out of it. I felt like the bottle was proof of something. Like it made it so real that he was just about to come back and finish it. It made it almost seem possible. But then time went by, and the bottle started getting moldy. And I couldn't bear to see it get moldy, so I washed it out and put it away. But I still couldn't bring myself to throw it out.'

'So that's why you put the ashes in an old plastic bottle instead of a fancy urn.'

'Right.'

'Do you take 'em with you everywhere you go?'

'No. I don't. I'm taking them with me to Yellowstone because I'm going to leave them there.'

'Leave 'em there?'

'Right.'

'Just leave that bottle somewhere? What if somebody throws it away?'

'No, not leave it there like that. I mean just leave the ashes. Not the bottle.'

'Oh. You mean like sprinkle 'em. I've heard of that.'

'Thing is, I don't think it's . . . strictly speaking . . . it's probably not technically legal. But he was supposed to come on this trip with me. And this is the closest I can get to taking him along. But it's probably best if you don't say anything about that plan to anyone.'

A brief silence fell.

Then Seth said, 'That's a really sad story, August.'

'I know. You're right. I'm sorry. I don't know what I was thinking with that.'

'It's OK. I said it could be anything. Besides, now we know a little bit more about you.'

True, August thought. *Only, now they knew more about his sadness and not much else. Then again*, he thought, *maybe that's all there really was to know about him. At least for the time being.*

He thought for a while about something else he could tell them. A happier note on which to go to sleep. He made up his mind to tell them the story of how he found Woody at a humane society that he hadn't even known existed. A place he stumbled upon while in the process of being lost.

He lifted up his head to look at the boys, and found they had already gone to sleep. Or, at least, close enough to look asleep to an outsider.

Unfortunately, for August, sleep did not come so easily.

7

The Very Top

They got off the nearly empty shuttle at the stop called The Grotto. No one else did.

They stood in the morning twilight, August un-twisting the straps of his pack as he slipped them on to his shoulders. In the near-darkness, he could see Seth bouncing on his toes, hardly able to contain his enthusiasm.

'Save your energy,' August said. 'You'll need every ounce of it.'

He looked at Henry, who stood quietly, arms at his sides, revealing nothing at all. No excitement, no dread. No anything. He was just along.

'I'm really surprised we're the only ones going up from the first shuttle. This is the most popular hike in the park. Granted, most people like to sleep later than four. But there are usually half a dozen or a dozen on the first shuttle out. Looking to beat the crowds.'

'So today it's just us beating the crowds?' Seth asked.

'Looks that way.'

'So let's hurry up and beat them.'

'I thought this trail would be dirt,' Seth said.

'It's not,' August said. 'It's mostly paved.'

'What's this we're walking on? Looks like pink concrete. Well. Not pink. You know. Like the color of the rocks.'

'Not sure,' August said. 'It might be.'

'You said this was steep. But it's not steep at all. It's easy.'

August stopped. Henry noticed and stopped with him. August waited for Seth to notice, but after ten long Seth strides, he gave up on that system.

'Seth,' he called.

Seth came back.

'Why'd we stop?'

'I want you to use your head. Which, no offense, you're not doing. You saw Angels Landing yesterday and you saw it across the river when we started this trip. You can see how tall it is. And the hike is only about five miles round trip. Less up to Scout Lookout, which is the farthest we're going. Which means at some point the trail has to go more or less straight up.'

'Why aren't we going all the way?'

'You haven't seen the last bit of climb, or you wouldn't ask.'

'I want to do it all.'

'Seth. Focus. My point is that the trail goes through this canyon—'

'Yeah! We are in a canyon, aren't we? That's why it's still kind of dark. And cool.'

'Seth. I'm trying to tell you something important.'

'I don't know what it is, though.'

'I'm trying to tell you not to underestimate this hike. It's pretty mellow through this canyon, and then it gets steep. And there are drop-offs. Like, more than a thousand feet up. And there are no railings, or anything like that. I want you to pay good attention and not underestimate this trail. And when we get up high, and we're exposed to drop-offs, I want Henry in the middle. And I might even ask that we hold hands, just for extra safety.'

'I sure don't see that we'll need all that.'

'You will,' August said. 'Keep your head in the game.'

They stopped just below the dreaded series of almost comically tight switchbacks. August knew they had a name, but he didn't tell the boys what they were called. Because Walter's Wiggles made them sound too cute and friendly.

A light wind made the aspen leaves shiver.

'Doesn't even look like a trail,' Seth said. 'Looks like a brick wall.'

The trail was built with brick retaining walls under each switchback, and the section of trail was so steep that from this angle one could see only the retaining bricks. Not the trail they helped retain.

'This is where it gets a little harder,' August said.

'Well, let's do it already,' Seth replied without pause.

August moved forward. Seth moved forward. Henry stayed put.

Seth made his way back to his little brother while August waited.

'You tired?' he heard Seth ask.

Then August watched as Seth boosted Henry on to his back, the younger boy's hands clutching at the shoulders of Seth's light-blue shirt.

They started up the tight switchbacks.

They still hadn't seen another soul. A second shuttle might well have offloaded passenger hikers by then, but, if so, they had not caught up. Their pace had been good.

August sensed that was about to change.

Seth stopped on the trail, sagging down to the point where his brother's feet touched the ground. Henry planted his feet and stood on his own power while Seth fell into a crouch, panting.

'This is hard,' Seth said. 'But only because I'm carrying him. If it was just me, I'd be doing fine.'

'You remember what I said. I said we'd see how high we could get. Maybe this is it.'

'No! I'll take him. I can carry him. We can't even see the view down into the canyon from where we are. Please, August. I can do it.'

August sighed.

He slipped off his pack, and pulled out two bottles of water, handing one to each of the boys. They drank gratefully. August savored the silence. The only sound was the wind, and Seth's labored breathing.

'I could go on ahead by myself,' Seth said. 'And you could wait for me here.'

'No. No way. It's dangerous up there. It's no place for a lone inexperienced kid hiker.'

'Please, August. I want to get to the top so bad. I'll never get back here again. When else will I have a chance? I'll take Henry. I just will. Will you walk more with me if I can take Henry?'

August sighed again. 'Here, you carry my pack,' he said. 'If Henry isn't too afraid of me to get on my back, I'll carry him up.'

No reaction from Henry. Even the look on his face remained unchanged.

'Please, Henry,' Seth said. 'For me?'

Henry walked the three steps over to August and reached up his arms. August crouched down and turned his back to the boy, and Henry climbed on. August felt the grip of small but determined hands on the shoulders of his shirt. He heard and felt Henry's slow, calm breathing against his right ear.

He slid one arm under each of the boy's bare knees and clasped his hands to lock them into place.

'You need to hold on tight, Henry. This is going to be no place to take a fall.'

Henry let go of August's shirt and wrapped his arms around August's neck instead, gripping just low enough not to cut off his breathing.

Seth shouldered the pack and they trudged on. With many stops for August to catch his breath.

*

'This is Scout Lookout,' August said. 'This is where the trail ends.'

He eased Henry down on to the uneven red stone and pale dirt. Then he straightened, and felt so bizarrely light that he could imagine his body levitating. Floating away.

The sun, which had long been up by any reasonable measure, was just glaring over the cliffs to their left. Across the canyon. Ahead, chains were bolted into the rock for hikers to grab on to as they made their way along the edge of a narrow rock spine rising to the cap of Angels Landing. Directly ahead, the way was more or less horizontal. Then, farther up, it seemed nearly vertical. He'd taken that last piece of climb once before. He didn't want to take it again. Not with two young boys, one of whom was overtired. Not even if he'd been alone.

The first rays of sun glinted off the Virgin River, which wound like a gold snake nearly fifteen hundred feet below.

They stood on the wide, flat dirt expanse of the lookout. The last wide anything this hike had to offer.

'But that's the very top, up there,' Seth said, predictably pointing up the near-vertical spine to the cap of the rock formation.

'Seth. Go up to that sign and then come back and tell me what it says.'

On the sign was a photo of the same vertical climb that rose before them. In the corner was a graphic of a person – depicted in about the same detail as the guy on a men's room sign – falling. They stood too far away to read the information on the sign, but August had been up here before. He knew approximately what it said.

Seth walked straight-backed to read the sign, then rejoined them again with a noticeable sag to his posture.

'So, how many people does it say fell to their death from that route?'

'Six,' Seth said.

'I believe it also says something about parents watching their children. And I'm not going up there. I'm not sending you up there with nobody watching you.'

Seth flopped on to his butt in the tan dirt, obviously holding back tears.

'The view is really good from here,' August said. 'Let's just enjoy it.'

'When will I ever get another chance? I wanted to go to the very top. You said this was the most popular hike in the park. So, like, hundreds of people have gone up there.'

'More like tens of thousands.'

'So almost everybody who went up there didn't die.'

'Listen. Seth.' August eased his tired legs into a squat in front of the boy, angled in such a way that he could still keep a close eye on Henry. Henry didn't move a muscle. 'I want you to see this situation from my point of view. You're not my kid. You're somebody else's kid. And I'm responsible for you. That's even harder than being responsible for your own kid. How can I let you do something dangerous? What would I tell your father if something went wrong?'

A tear slipped loose and rolled down Seth's cheek. He wiped it away furiously with the back of one dusty hand.

'My father would let me go.'

August sat in the dirt and sighed. He briefly wondered if he had always sighed so often. He pulled his cell phone from his shirt pocket and checked for reception. Two bars.

'Did you bring his number?' he asked Seth.

'Yeah. I did. 'Cause we said we might call him from up here.'

'Did he say how early you could call?'

'Seven. Seven to three. Is it after seven?'

'It is.'

'Is it the same time here as there?'

'No. It's an hour later in Utah. But it's still after seven there.'

'So I should just call him from here? And tell him I'm almost on top of the world and that's as high as August says I get to go?'

'No. You should ask his permission to go up to the top. If he says you can, you can. But I want to talk to him. Make sure this thing is properly explained.'

It took a good five minutes of waiting just to get Wes on the line. August wondered if that meant his cell minutes wouldn't last as long as he'd thought.

Then he heard, 'Hey, Dad.' And watched Seth's face brighten to match the moment. 'Yeah . . . How is it?' Long silence. 'Yeah, you always say that. Every time. I get it. The food is bad . . . Yeah, I am . . . Yeah, it's good . . . He is . . . Listen, you won't believe where I am. I have to tell you where I am. I'm on top of this huge rock thing in Zion National Park called Angels Landing . . . Oh, you've heard of it? I'd never heard of it . . . Well, I carried him part of the way, and August carried him part of the way. Anyway, we're not at the very top because August thinks the last part is too dangerous . . . Yeah, that's what *I* said. Thousands of people do it and they don't fall. I think so, too . . .'

A long pause, and then Seth extended the phone at the end of one long arm.

'He wants to talk to Henry and then to you.'

Henry grabbed the phone and held it to his ear, but said nothing. August watched closely for some emotional tell. A change in Henry's eyes, or expression. But Henry's face remained cool and blank, as if he were only listening to the recording of the lady giving the correct time over and over again.

August closed his eyes, then opened them and watched the sun glaring over the cliff on the eastern wall of the canyon. It was warm already. Very warm. Thank God all their hiking from this point on would be down. He watched the ant-sized long box of a shuttle bus snake its way along the narrow, brick-colored road below.

He thought briefly of the dog, alone in the

104   CATHERINE RYAN HYDE

motorhome back in camp. August wondered if it made Woody sad.

Then the phone was thrust in his direction, and he took it.

'Wes,' he said, turning his back to the boys and taking a few steps away.

'August. How you doin', my friend?'

August turned back to the boys, covered the phone, and said, 'Don't move. Not one muscle. No exploring. No walking closer to the edge.' Then, to Wes, 'I'm OK, except it turns out it's a crushing weight being responsible for the life or death of somebody else's kid.'

'Let him go. He'll be careful. He's light, and he's pretty athletic. I did that hike once. Years and years ago. There're chains to hold on to, right?'

'Yeah. There are chains. But not like chain railings. Just something to grab on to. If your hand slips off the chain, you'll still fall.'

'Let him go. It means a lot to him.'

'Listen. Wes. Not to get too personal here, but what number jail run is this?'

'What number?'

'Yeah. What number. I was sure you said this was the second time.'

'Second. Yeah. That sounds about right.'

'Seth says it's your fourth. He wasn't trying to rat you out or anything. He didn't know what you'd told me. It just came up in conversation.'

A long, long silence.

Then Wes said, 'I guess I was hoping you'd be having conversations about redrock and how to get Henry up steep trails.'

'And I guess I was hoping I could count on everything you told me to be the truth.'

Silence.

Then, 'I wasn't thinking clear when you left with 'em, OK? So I guess I made a mistake. Anybody can make a mistake. Right?'

August looked around to check on the boys. They hadn't moved a muscle. Seth smiled weakly at him. Dying to know.

'OK. Look, he'll be happy. I'll go tell him the good news. We'll call again.'

'Roger, my friend. Ciao.'

August clicked the phone closed.

'You can go,' he said to Seth, who leapt straight into the air from a sit and landed on his feet. 'One condition, though. We have to wait until—'

A movement caught August's eye, and he turned to see two hikers arrive on the flat lookout. Two young men in their twenties.

'Hey,' he called to them. 'Can I ask you guys a favor?'

They moved closer, panting lightly.

'Problem?' one of them said.

'Not really. Just that this boy wants to go up. But I don't want to go, and his little brother here doesn't want to go. And I don't feel so good sending him off as a solo hiker. So I was wondering if he could go up with you.'

'No worries,' one said.

And the other one flipped his head in the direction of the chained route and said, 'Let's go, dude. Let's get 'er done.'

After what seemed like fifteen or twenty minutes of sitting in the dirt with Henry, who looked out over the huge and variegated canyon and never at August, they heard a scream at a great distance.

August's heart jumped, thinking he was hearing a cry of disaster. But as the scream wound on, it became more obvious that it was a shout of triumph. A sort of high-pitched 'Yee hah!' And the more he listened, the more sure he became that he was listening to Seth.

Henry smiled. Not a big, open smile like the ones he reserved for Woody's tricks. A wry little half-secret smile that curled his mouth on one side only.

'I do believe he made it to the very top,' August said.

Henry nodded once.

They trudged about a third of the hot way down before Henry stopped dead in the trail.

'Hmm,' Seth said. 'I thought down would be OK for him.'

Seth put his head together with his little brother for a moment. If words were spoken, August didn't hear them.

Then Seth's head came up and he told August, calmly, 'His feet hurt.'

So August sat him down on the trail in the full sun

and unlaced and pulled off Henry's running shoes. The socks he wore underneath were black and thin, like dress socks. They had holes in the toes.

'Geez. I should have looked at the socks you guys were wearing. We need to get you something thicker. More like hiking socks.'

A full busload of hikers were now making their way up the trail in the growing heat. The trail was just barely wide enough for passing, and August felt legs brushing his shoulder as they scraped by.

'Sorry,' he said, to no one in particular.

He pulled off Henry's socks. The boy had blisters on both heels, and on the ball of one foot.

August took out his pack and extracted a first-aid kit, and a ziplock bag full of moleskin.

'I can put moleskin on these to cushion the blisters,' he told the solemn little boy, 'but it's still going to hurt to walk on them. Because they're big and puffed up. That's what makes them hurt. Or I could lance them and drain them and then put a little spot bandage on and moleskin over that. And then they'll be flat and it won't hurt so much to walk. But you have to be willing to let me stick a big needle into your blisters. I don't know. What do you think?'

'He'll hold still for it,' Seth said. 'He's good.'

'I'd rather hear it from him.'

'You know you're not going to hear nothing from him.'

'He can nod.'

'Henry,' Seth said. Sharply. As if Henry were hard

of hearing. Or, more likely, for August's benefit. 'Can August use a needle on your blisters?'

Henry nodded.

So August opened a little packet with a sterile needle-sized lance and lanced and drained Henry's blisters, and dressed them. Henry never winced. Never pulled away. Never made a sound.

Then the boy put his own shoes back on, double-tied the laces, and they began to walk downhill again, bucking the crowd headed up. Like floating downstream while the rest of the world swam upriver.

They made their way down the trail for another few hundred yards before Henry stopped dead again.

Seth went to him for another head-to-head.

'His blisters still hurt?' August asked.

'Only a little. Mostly he's just tired.'

August sighed and slipped off his pack, handing it to Seth. Then he crouched on the trail and Henry climbed on to his back. More soft puffing of breath against August's right ear.

They plodded downhill again.

'That was the best thing I've ever done in my whole life so far,' Seth said.

August only smiled. He felt the sweat growing on his back, which had a child pressed against it, and no air circulation. He didn't answer. He knew what Seth said was true, and the statement didn't feel as though anybody or anything needed to add much to it.

'You're a nice man, August,' Seth said, surprising him.

'Why do you say that?'

'Because you carried Henry. So I could get up there. You told me yesterday I couldn't get all the way up there and carry Henry, too. And you were right. Most grown-ups, when it turns out they're right, they say, "I told you so." You didn't say, "I told you so." You just carried Henry.'

'It meant a lot to you,' August said.

'It did,' Seth agreed. 'I took a picture from the very top. On my camera. Because my camera was just about as good as yours for this, 'cause there was nothing to zoom in at.'

'True.'

'I can't believe it's the first I took a picture on my own camera. But it's really two pictures, because I handed it to one of those guys and they took a picture of me standing on the very top. You know. Just in case nobody believes I really did it. Should I have taken more pictures by now, August?'

'Good idea to pace yourself. We've got a lot left to see. Our summer's barely even started.'

8
What He Told Me

The following evening not long before sunset, they made their way along the paved Pa'rus Trail, the three of them and Woody. It was the only trail in the park that allowed you to take your dog.

They walked slowly, nursing stiff quads and tight Achilles tendons.

'You know,' Seth said, 'I thought this trail would be nothing much, on account of how it starts right in the campground and you can take bikes and dogs and all. But it's the prettiest to look at that we've seen yet. The sky is so blue and the rocks are so red and white and you can see the cliffs and the courts and the temples like you're seeing the whole thing almost all at one time.'

'This is actually my favorite trail in the whole park.'

'And Woody gets to go.'

'That's part of why.'

'And I love how it keeps going back and forth over the river. I like the bridges.'

As they approached another bridge, Seth stopped in his tracks, and pulled his disposable camera out of his pocket.

'What do you see?' August asked.

'I just like the way that rock mountain lines up behind the bridge like that. Looks nice. Real scenic, you know?'

August looked at it over Seth's shoulder.

'You have a good eye.'

'Think so?'

'I do. But I think you should use my camera. It's digital, so we'll never run out of shots.'

'What if the card fills up?'

'Not likely. It's sixteen gigs. But even if we did fill it up, I have my laptop along. I can download them and erase the card.'

August slipped the strap of his camera off from around his neck and handed it to Seth.

'I can really take as many pictures as I want?'

'Knock yourself out.'

They walked in silence for about ten photos.

Then Seth asked, 'How long is this hike?'

'Two miles.'

'Both ways?'

'Just one way.'

'Oh. That's long. I mean, it's not really, but . . . after yesterday . . .'

'I thought we'd walk down to the end of the trail, and up to the road. It lets off up at the Canyon Junction, which is a shuttle stop. You and Henry can jump the shuttle and Woody and I'll walk back. I'll meet you back at the visitor's center.'

'Oh. That's a really good idea, August.'

'That tired?'

'My feet hurt. I think I sort of have blisters, too.'

'How do you *sort of* have blisters?'

'Oh. Well. You don't, I guess. I guess I just have 'em.

'Why didn't you tell me?'

'I figured Henry having blisters was trouble enough.'

The minute the boys stepped on the shuttle, August fished out his cell phone and checked for reception. Surprisingly, it looked good.

He started back down the trail to the visitor's center, and, as he walked, he pressed the speed-dial number for Harvey, his AA sponsor in San Diego.

Harvey picked up on the fourth ring.

'So. Are you having fun yet?'

Harvey had never been one to say hello.

'Yes and no. It's not going exactly the way I pictured it.'

'One of those effing growth opportunities?'

'Maybe not that bad.'

Woody took off after a movement in the brush, maybe a rabbit or a squirrel, and hit the end of the leash hard. August reeled him in again.

August filled Harvey in on the short version of his mechanical breakdown, and the sudden addition of the boys. As he talked, he watched the late sun turn the western-facing rocks a deeper and deeper gold.

'So, basically, I just have a question for you,' August said.

Harvey said nothing. Harvey didn't say things like, 'What's the question?' He waited. He didn't call the men he sponsored, either, to ask how they were doing. He figured August had his number and knew how to use it.

'Do you think it's even vaguely possible to forget how many times you've been in jail?'

'Potentially. Maybe if you get up around a few dozen. You might get to the point where you're like, "Was that twenty-nine or was that thirty?"'

'But if you've been in jail four times, you wouldn't honestly think it was twice.'

'No. Not honestly. I mean, outside of a dementia situation. Who are we talking about here?'

'The boys' father.'

'Alcohol-related offenses?'

'Mostly.'

'Aren't I a good guesser?'

'You're amazing, Harv.'

He tramped across a bridge. It rang with a metallic clanging sound under his footsteps, and Woody found it unnerving. August walked down the bank on the other side to let the dog drink from the river.

'So, now that I know he lied to me, I'm starting to wonder what else I'm about to find out.'

'Me, too. Hope you're prepared to be in this for the long haul.'

'It's just till the end of the summer.'

'You hope.'

'He only has to do ninety days.'

'How do you know?'

'He told me.'

'He also told you it was his second time.'

August stopped and stood still in the fading light. Wondered at the beauty outside him, and the contrast between that and his inner landscape.

'Why would he do that? Why ask me to take them for three months if he really needs someone to take them longer?'

'Maybe he figured by then you'd be attached to them. Which I'm guessing you already are.'

'You think I should call the jail and find out?'

'I don't know if they'll tell you. But I think you should do as much independent verification as possible. Why'd you take 'em, anyway?'

'You know how bad I wanted to get to Yellowstone. And why.'

'You could've gone next year. Phillip wouldn't have minded.'

'They're such good boys, though.'

'Ah,' Harvey said. 'Now I think we're getting closer. Fills a hole in your life having kids around again?'

'It's not that. It's nothing like that. They're so not Phillip. Phillip was nineteen. They're like twelve and seven.'

'Right. Got it. I see your point. That's so completely unlike Phillip. Because we all know Phillip never used to be twelve and seven. Anyway, what does any of this matter now? You're in it. You're not about to dump them now. Time will tell what you've gotten your . . .'

Harvey may have said much more, but the cell reception faded and the call dropped. August checked a dozen times, hoping to be able to call Harvey back. But he never got another single bar of reception on the canyon floor for the rest of the week they were there. He could have called Harvey back from the payphone, but he never did.

'This is so different,' Seth said. They stood on the hard-packed dirt trail that formed the rim of Bryce Canyon. In a light, misting rain. 'I've never seen anything like it.'

'I'm not sure there's anything like Bryce Canyon to see.'

'I love those . . . what do you call them again?'

'Hoodoos.'

'That's a funny word.'

'It is.'

'Why do they call them that, again?'

'I don't know. We'll look at the brochure when we get back inside the rig.'

'Geez, August. I think I read it ten times while we were in there waiting for the rain to stop. I'm glad we just went ahead and came out here in the rain anyway. I mean, so we get wet. Who cares?'

August set one hand down on Henry's shoulder. Henry let him.

'What about you, Henry?' August asked.

Henry responded by ducking his head and sliding under August's slicker. Then he unsnapped one snap and stuck his face out, holding the plastic material tightly to the sides of his head.

'I think Henry's not too thrilled about being wet,' August said.

'Well, I don't mind.'

'I'm sorry I don't have rain gear for you guys.'

'That's not your fault, August. We were supposed to bring whatever we needed. It was nice enough that you bought us socks. Besides, who knew it was going to rain? Didn't you say it never rains this late in the year?'

'I don't know the statistics, exactly. But I think it's pretty unusual.'

'You know what they look like to me? The hoodoos? They look like pictures I've seen of caves. When they have those long . . . what do you call them?'

'Stalactites and stalagmites.'

'Right. That. Except these all go up from the ground. This may sound weird. But we were at Zion so long . . . what was it, eight or nine days? I got used to it there. Like I lived there or something. Like the whole world just looked like Zion. And now it's so weird that it looks like Bryce. I never knew all this was out here. I mean, I saw pictures in books. Like, the Grand Canyon and the Rocky Mountains. But I never saw pictures of hoodoos at Bryce. I want to take pictures of them, but I don't want the camera to get wet.'

'There's no hurry on that. We'll get plenty of pictures. We'll be here a while.'

'How long, August?'

August shrugged. 'As long as we want. Until we've seen enough hoodoos to last us. Until we're tired of them and ready to move on.'

'I don't think I could ever get tired of them.'

'How about until you know them so well you can see them in your head when you close your eyes?'

'That'll do,' Seth said.

August left the boys in the motorhome and walked to the only payphone at the campground. The rain was just barely tapering off, and cell-phone reception was close to non-existent.

August used his calling card – instead of quarters – to call the county jail that held Wes, because he was sure he'd spend a long time on hold.

He was wrong.

The woman who answered the phone and heard his question asked if he was family, or Wes's attorney.

When he said he was neither, that was more or less the end of that.

'But I'm taking care of his children,' August said. 'That's why it's so important I know his exact release date.'

'I'm sorry, sir,' she said. 'The prisoner would have to authorize us to give you that information.'

'OK, got it,' he said. 'Thanks.'

He hung up and walked back to the rig, thinking the news had not exactly come as a surprise. Still, it felt depressing in ways he couldn't quite pin down.

The rain had let up, and as he stepped level with the next camp site, Seth came running at him, babbling and excited.

'You missed it, August! You missed it and it was amazing. Well, not missed it missed it. It's still there, but it's fading out. You should've seen it before. It was so amazing. I took your camera to take a picture of it. Boy, I sure hope that's OK, but I just couldn't miss it. I did it mostly for you, August. I wanted you to see it while it was still good, so I took a picture of it. I didn't want to take it with my camera because then you wouldn't see it, because you won't even still be around when we get home and get our film developed. I wanted you to see it now, today.'

'Whoa,' August said. 'Whoa. Slow down, Seth. Took a picture of what? What was so amazing?'

'The two rainbows!'

He pointed along the steep-use trail that led up to the canyon rim. Henry stood transfixed, faced away from them. Beyond him, a double rainbow arched across the canyon. It was hard for August to imagine that he was seeing the faded version.

'Where's the camera now?' August asked.

'Right here in my pocket. Where it'll stay dry. But it'd stopped raining before I took it outside. But I just want you to know, if it had started to rain again, I'd have kept it dry.'

'Hand it to me, would you?'

'OK.'

Seth pulled the camera from his pocket and gave it

to August, who lined up a shot.

'I got great pictures of it, though, August. And it was brighter.'

'But did you get Henry in there staring at it?'

'Oh. No. He was standing beside me. So no.'

'I just thought it looked nice with him in the picture.'

August snapped off a shot, then brought up all the photos to view. Seth's were amazing, with both arcs of the rainbow visible, and a perfect framing of the red rock canyon and hoodoos beneath.

'That was quite a rainbow,' August said. 'You're a good photographer, you know that?'

'No, I didn't know that. How could I know? I never took a picture in my whole life until we came on this trip. How can I be good at something if I just now started?'

'I think you just have a natural feel for it. Glad you captured this.'

'I think it might be a good sign. You know what I mean?'

'I'm not sure. You mean like an omen?'

'Maybe. Just, when I saw it . . . I sort of felt like maybe now everything is going to be OK.'

August offered no opinion. He wanted to go with Seth's idea. It was appealing, and it drew him. But he still had a lot of questions and misgivings in his head and in his gut.

When August woke the next morning it was light, and something hard was pressed against his back, between his shoulder blades. Something too round and heavy to be Woody.

He raised his head and rolled partly over, which involved pushing the something out of the way. But it mostly shifted away on its own.

August sat up.

The something was Henry. In August's bed on the couch side. He'd been sleeping – or maybe just lying still – with his forehead up against August's back.

August looked around for Seth and the dog. Woody might have been up front in the driver's seat, watching out the window for squirrels. With the privacy curtain up, it was hard to tell. August listened for a minute, expecting to hear Seth in the bathroom. But all was still except for the rumbling of coffee percolating. Apparently Seth had put on a pot of coffee for August to enjoy when he woke up.

'Where's Seth and Woody?' he asked, making eye contact with Henry, who quickly looked away. Of course, August had intended it as a rhetorical question.

'Out for a walk,' Henry said.

He had a small voice, like the sound one might imagine coming from a shy animated mouse.

August felt his eyebrows rise. He watched Henry for a moment, in case there was more. Henry made a point of avoiding his eyes.

'So you can talk,' August said.

Henry nodded faintly.

'You just choose not to?'

Henry nodded again.

'What made you change your mind?'

Henry shrugged.

August lay back down, and Henry moved up closer and pressed his forehead between August's shoulder blades again.

When Seth and Woody got back, August was sitting at the dinette table, drinking coffee. Henry was seated across from him, buttering toast.

'Thanks for the pot of coffee.'

'You're welcome. I hope you didn't worry about where we were.'

'Not at all,' August said. 'Henry told me.'

Seth laughed a little snort of a laugh, but didn't answer.

'No, seriously. Henry told me.'

Seth's eyes widened. 'In words?'

'Yes. In words.'

'Well, I'll be damned. Whoops. Sorry.'

'For what?'

'For cussing.'

'That's not very strong cussing.'

'But maybe you don't want me to cuss at all. Like, ever.'

'Seth. Sit down.'

Seth took off Woody's leash and sat next to Henry, still holding the leash nervously in his hands, his eyes cast down toward the table. 'What?'

'You worry too much. You think you have to do too much. Like you think you're always just about to make some terrible mistake. There's nothing wrong with wanting to learn to dump the tanks. There's nothing wrong with making coffee for me or walking the dog. It's nice. But I get a feeling you're doing it because you always feel like you need to do more. To be more. Like if you don't make yourself useful you're not entitled to the air you breathe. Why not just relax and be a kid on vacation?'

Seth's eyes came up to his, then darted down again.

'I could try.'

'For your own sake. Yeah.'

'It's just . . . I've been like this for so long.'

August pulled in a deep breath. Sighed it out again. 'Yeah, I imagine you have. But I'd still appreciate it if you'd let go of the idea that you constantly need to impress me.'

'I'll try.' But he didn't sound too sure about his chances of succeeding.

'Toast? Henry will share, I think, and then we can make more.'

'OK,' Seth said. Then he looked down at his brother. 'Henry. You said something to August?'

Henry nodded. A bit more decisively this time.

'What made you go and decide to do a thing like that?'

Henry shrugged.

'Have you ever seen a hoodoo?' Seth asked. Then he fell silent while he listened to his father's reply.

They stood in the baking sun, at the payphone. Henry hunkered down into a squat in August's shade.

'Well, I'd never even heard of them. I wish you could see them, but at least I got pictures. I'm getting pictures of everything. Mostly I'm taking them on August's camera, but he says he'll give me a copy of all of them when we get home in September. Yesterday we walked all the way down to the bottom of the canyon and around this loop trail. And then we were right in with the hoodoos, right near the bottom of some of them. They're like these . . . like spires. But rough, you know? And all these colors like red and orange and gold and white. I mean, rock colors, but more color than I ever saw in rocks before. Colors like in pictures of the Grand Canyon, only even more colorful. I wish I could describe them better. They're hard to describe. I wanted to call you from down there on the trail at the bottom of the canyon, 'cause I kind of wanted to describe a hoodoo while I was looking right at one. But I'm not sure even that would've helped. Besides, we didn't get any reception down there. But it was a great hike. And Henry's getting in pretty good shape. August didn't have to carry him until we were most of the way back up to the rim again. He has better socks now. We both do. August bought us socks for hiking, so we don't get blisters. That helps.'

A pause.

'Yeah, he is . . . Yeah, we are . . . Yeah, OK.'

Seth held the receiver out to Henry. 'He wants to talk to you.'

Henry took the phone and squatted down again, but in the sun this time. He closed his eyes.

A minute later he held the phone out to August.

When August put it to his ear, Wes was still talking.

'So, I know you're being a good boy because you always—'

'Wes?'

'Oh. What happened to Henry?'

'I don't know. He just handed the phone to me. I thought you wanted to talk to me.'

'Oh. Well. Not really. But—'

'I need to talk to *you*, though. Actually.' August looked at the boys, who were watching him carefully. 'Boys, could you give me a second alone here?'

Seth's face closed up slightly. Tightened. But he took hold of his brother's sleeve and they moved away.

'So, what's up?' Wes asked. 'What's the deal? Is there a problem?'

'No. No problem. I just wanted to know your exact release date. You know. So I can make my plans.'

'Hmm,' Wes said.

'Not sure why that would be hard.'

'Well. It's ninety days. Like I said.'

'So you should know the exact date.'

'I'd have to be looking at a calendar.'

'I find it really hard to imagine that you're not counting the days. What about all those prison films where guys mark off the number of days on the wall?'

'That's mostly just in the movies,' Wes said.

'No, I don't think it is. I think it's human nature to count the days until something you hate is over. Anyway, this is getting us nowhere. So here's what I'd like you to do. I'd like you to authorize me to get information straight from the people at the jail.'

A stony silence. August's mind raced, wondering how much to read into it.

'I can just find out the date and tell you.'

'I'd still like to hear it from them.'

'You think I'd lie to you?'

'Honest answer? I'm not sure. You told me you'd been in jail twice and it turns out it's four times.'

'This's not about how many times I've been in,' Wes said, his voice hardening some. 'That's really none of your business. It's just your business when I'm here to take the kids back.'

'OK, I accept that. It's none of my business. But you volunteered the information that it's your second time in jail. Then you said you forgot the other two times. I don't know if you forgot or you lied about it. That's not even so much the issue. The issue is that I'm not sure I can trust the information I get from you. I'd like to hear it from the jail as well.'

Another silence.

Then, 'Fine.'

'So you'll authorize me with them?'

'Yeah.'

'Like, today?'

'Before the next time you call, yeah.'

'But I can call them on any day. It's you who can only get incoming calls three days a week. So how about today, while you're thinking about it?'

'Yeah, whatever, August.'

August squeezed his eyes shut. Opened them again and watched Seth and Henry petting a woman's golden retriever.

'I've taught high school just about all my life, Wes. I've lived long enough to know that "whatever" basically means "kiss my ass".'

'What do you want from me, man?'

'I want you to tell the prison officials that August Schroeder, the guy who's taking care of your children, is authorized to receive information, same as blood family.'

'Fine. OK.'

August opened his mouth to add something about timing, but was interrupted in that thought. Not by Wes. By a dial tone.

August locked up the rig, and the three of them and Woody crossed the parking lot and stood at the wood-post and stone-pillar railing of the lookout into Bryce Canyon. Just to break things up, they had stowed all the moveable items in the rig and set off on a morning's drive down the long road that paralleled the canyon, stopping at every lookout.

It was higher in elevation here than at camp. Over nine thousand feet. August could feel the slight difference in his breathing.

The tiny cones of bristlecone pines littered the area, and Henry began to gather them up and place them in an impromptu sack made by holding up the bottom of his tee-shirt. August wondered whether to tell him it was against park rules to gather anything. He weighed its importance, then let it go. When they got back to the motorhome, maybe August would encourage him to choose his favorite and only keep that one.

A raven almost the size of a hawk sat on one of the stone pillars, eyeing them and cawing.

Seth stared off into the canyon, transfixed.

August pulled his cell phone from his pocket, and was surprised to see bars of reception.

'Hey,' he said to the boys. 'I can get cell reception here. I'm going to go off a ways and make a phone call, and then when I get back maybe we can call your dad.'

'OK,' Seth said. As though barely paying attention.

'Will you take Woody for me?'

'Sure,' Seth said, and reached out a hand for the leash. Without ever taking his eyes off the canyon.

'Harvey,' August said. 'Good. You're there.'

'Thought you were mad at me.'

'No, you didn't. You knew I just lost reception.'

'Pretty much. Maybe a little of both. Any updates?'

'Yes and no. I talked to the jail. And they wouldn't give me any information. So then next time I talked to Wes, I asked him to authorize me. Right then. That day. While he was thinking about it. He didn't seem very happy about it. In fact, he hung up on me. But he said he'd do it. But then I called the jail again, and he still hasn't. Or at least he hadn't as of yesterday.'

'Surprised?'

August looked up to see that the raven had followed him. Either that or a different one had landed nearby. The bird stared at August with one shiny black eye. August watched the odd shape of the top of his enormous beak as he opened and closed it, letting out his strange call.

'Not really. I'm just not sure if I should allow for some possibility that he might have forgotten. Or if I should just assume he blew me off.'

'Like there's a difference.'

'Well. There's some difference.'

'There's no difference, August. People remember what they want to remember and forget what they want to forget. If you told him something was important to you, and he forgot to do it, he blew you off.'

'Yeah,' August said. 'I guess I see your point about that.'

'I need to talk to him,' August told Seth as Seth waited on the line for his father.

'OK.'

About a minute passed before more words burst out of Seth.

'Dad! Great. You're there. So, look. I'm standing at the railing looking right into Bryce Canyon. I'm going to try to describe it to you. But . . . you know what? It's still hard. The hoodoos have stripes. Sideways stripes. That's the best way I can say it. Like the rock is really red like a brick, but even redder, but then it'll have this wide white stripe through it. And even the part that's red looks like it has stripes. And some of the hoodoos are all together, like one big wall of hoodoos all attached. And some of 'em are just standing all by themselves. Shoot. That doesn't help at all, does it? I bet you still can't picture it. So, listen. August needs to talk to you . . . No, he specifically said he needed to talk to you.'

August reached out for the phone and Seth handed it over. Quickly. But not quickly enough. By the time August got it to his ear and said hello, there was no Wes on the line. There was no open line. The call had ended.

'Hmm,' Seth said. 'Must've lost reception.'

August looked at the readout for reception. Four bars, same as when the call had started.

'Yeah, maybe so,' August said.

Henry fell asleep on the drive back to camp. Seth stared out the window for the first two-thirds of the way.

Then he said, 'How long have we been at Bryce, August?'

'Five days, I think.'

'Oh.'

'Why? Does it feel like enough?'

'Well. It's not up to me, August. It's up to you how long we stay in a place. It's your rig and your gas money and your trip.'

'But how does it feel to you? I'm asking. Does it feel like time to move on?'

'Maybe. Maybe, yeah. I think as long as I live I'll be able to close my eyes and see hoodoos. Even if I never *can* figure out how to describe 'em. It'd be kind of nice to go where there are meetings.'

'Meetings.'

'Yeah. You know. If you can find ones that're open. That aren't for alcoholics only. Which way do we go next? What's the next stop? Are there meetings in between here and where we're going next?'

'There are meetings just about everywhere,' August said. 'When we leave here we drive quite a ways before we get to any more good national parks where we plan to stop and stay for a while. We go through Salt Lake City next, and some other parts of Utah where there are fewer rocks and more people. So, yeah, I'd say there are meetings ahead of us.'

'Well, then I'm ready to go on when you are,' Seth said.

'Look, I want to say this while Henry is still asleep,' August said.

They were back in their campsite, and August was standing at the kitchen counter making tuna sandwiches for lunch. Henry was still asleep sitting up in his seat belt, Woody draped over his lap. The dog's paws were twitching, as though running in his dreams.

'Sure, OK, August. What?'

'I'm going to need you to ask your dad exactly when he gets out of jail.'

'Don't you know?'

'I thought I did. Now I'm not sure.'

'Can't you just count from the date he went in? That Monday the day after we left?'

'Yeah. I could do that. But when I ask him about it,

I'm not getting a clear answer. And once he even hung up on me.'

'I don't think he'd do that on purpose, August. I think your phone just lost reception.'

'I was talking about that time on the payphone.'

'Oh.'

'So I just thought maybe it might be good if you asked. Maybe he'd be more inclined to talk to you.'

'OK.'

Silence.

August finished the sandwiches – three of them – and placed them on paper plates on the dinette table.

Seth sat down in front of one.

'What if he's getting out later than you thought? What happens to us then?'

'We don't know that's the case,' August said. 'So let's cross that bridge when we come to it.'

'OK,' Seth said. And took a big bite of sandwich.

August looked up to see Henry's eyes come open. Not so much as though he'd just wakened up. More as though he'd just decided to open them.

'Henry is fast asleep for the night,' August said. 'What do you think we should do?'

'I think it's OK to leave him.'

'Do you?'

'We'll be locking up. Right? And Woody would bark like crazy if anybody tried to get in. We can put down those curtains so nobody can even see there's a kid in here. I think he'll be fine, August.'

'And I've got an alarm system anyway.'

'And we'd hear it, right? We'll be right in *there*, right?' Seth pointed through the window of the rig at the open doorway of the meeting place. Light spilled out on to the street, looking inviting. Warm. 'It'll be fine, August.'

'What if he wakes up and gets scared because he's alone?'

'He's not alone. Woody's here.'

'Think that counts?'

'To Henry? Are you kidding? Nobody counts more than Woody.'

'Oh, look,' August said. 'There are cookies. And coffee, but don't drink any.'

'I don't drink coffee, August.'

'Good.'

'But I can go take some cookies?'

'Why not?'

But Seth didn't move.

They were standing just inside the entryway of the small meeting hall. It was a good ten minutes before the meeting started, so only about three people puttered around. Four folding tables had been pushed together into one big table, and a huge, broad-shouldered man was placing stacking chairs around it.

'My dad doesn't like it when I eat sugar. He says I talk too much as it is.'

'I'm sure it will have worn off by the time you see him again.'

Seth smiled a crooked smile, and set off in the direction of the cookies.

The man, about the size of a linebacker in a football game, approached August.

'I'm Ray,' he said. 'Welcome.'

'August.'

'Newcomer?'

'Visitor. This meeting is open, right? They told me on the phone at central office that you're men's stag, but otherwise open.'

'We are,' he said. 'But I think your son would be happier in the next room. A few of our regulars bring kids, because they can't afford a sitter. There's a TV in there and some comic books and stuff.'

'Thanks,' August said, 'but you don't know Seth. He begged me to take him to a meeting.'

'It won't bore him to death?'

'Like I said, you don't know Seth.'

August looked up to see that Seth had never made it to the cookie table. He'd been waylaid by a table full of AA literature, clearly marked as free. He was choosing brochures, and stuffing them into his pockets until they bulged.

The leader of that night's sharing was the guy with the least time sober. Only five days.

August glanced at Seth's face occasionally as the young meeting leader shared his experience of throwing away seven months of sobriety.

'Everybody asks me what I was thinking,' the guy

– whose name was Greg – said. 'And it's absolutely impossible to explain. Because I wasn't. I wasn't thinking. There was no thought process. None. It just happened. I'm not saying it did itself, because I know I'm responsible. I just don't know where I was when it happened.

'Nothing bad was going on. I wasn't celebrating anything. I was hungry, and in kind of a scratchy mood, and I went into this place to get fish and chips. I figured it would settle me down to have a full stomach, you know? My nerves just felt a little raw. Not even really much more so than usual. And then . . . I don't even want to say I got an idea to. It didn't even feel like an idea. I just ordered a beer because it seemed like it couldn't do me any harm on a full stomach. All of a sudden two beers and a plate of fish and chips looked like a good plan. Just totally reasonable. I keep looking back at it, but I don't know how I would've stopped it, because it's almost like I didn't even see what I was doing until it was done.

'Oh, I've talked to my sponsor a lot, and I know in a broader sense how I could've prevented it. If I'd stayed closer to the program and called him every day like I'm supposed to and worked the steps and gone to more meetings I probably wouldn't have been set up for a slip. But once I was in that place, it's like I didn't even see it happening. I knew I ordered that first beer. And I knew I was drinking it. I just had this idea that it was OK. And then it was later that night, and I needed to go out and get more, and then it was so obvious that it wasn't OK. And I just couldn't imagine how I'd sat there in that fish and chips place not knowing it. I'll just never get over how this disease works.'

As he wound down his sharing, Seth folded his arms on the table in front of him and set his head down in that cradle. August figured he was just tired. Though it was only a little after eight.

Ray shared next, and said, 'Welcome back, Greg. The main thing is, you're here now. You're back. I'll tell you exactly what happened. There's a name for that crazy thing where you drink and you can't even say why. It's called alcoholism. The only disease that tries to convince you that you don't have a disease. Sneakiest damn thing on the planet.'

August leaned over and whispered in Seth's ear. 'You OK, buddy?'

Seth turned his head and looked into August's face. He looked a little queasy.

'I'm fine,' he said.

'You sure? You look sick.'

'I'm fine.'

Ray was in the middle of sharing about a drinking dream he'd had a few days prior. 'And then I sort of come to – in the dream, I mean; I don't mean I woke up yet – and I'm sitting at the bar with a half-drunk whiskey in my hand. And it was that same feeling. Like, how the hell did that happen? I mean, I know it's a dream and all. But I was in and out of this program eleven or twelve times before it stuck. And believe me, this was realistic. That's just how it was in real life. No real reason why I fell back except I'm an alcoholic. I think it's because I came in for my wife. You know. Not for me. I hadn't hit my bottom yet. I'd hit what she thought was my bottom. But I wasn't done and that's just how it is.'

Ray said more, but August was watching Seth again. Wondering if he should offer him the chance to go back to the motorhome. August lifted up in his chair and leaned to his right, looking through the window to see if all was still and quiet inside the rig. If there was any movement, any indication that Henry was awake. But nothing seemed to move.

'What about our visitor?' Ray said in closing. 'And his young friend. Care to share tonight?'

Seth's head came up and he shot August a panicky look. 'Do I have to share, August?' he asked in a loud, tense whisper.

'No. You don't. It's up to you.'

A long breath came out of Seth, audibly, and his shoulders dropped.

'My name is August, and I'm an alcoholic from San Diego, California.'

Of course, the group said, 'Hi, August.' As groups do.

'I related a lot to the part about the drinking dreams. I still have them. Maybe two or three times a month. They scare the crap out of me, but it's almost worth it for that sense of relief when I wake up and realize I didn't really do it. I didn't really throw my time away.

'They're a little different from what Ray was describing, but that denial factor is the same. That sneakiness of the disease. Like in the dream I've been having a couple of drinks a couple of times a week, but it doesn't matter. It's OK. I haven't told my sponsor or the group, I haven't changed my sobriety date. Because it doesn't matter. But then in the dream it suddenly hits me that it totally matters and I totally have to come clean. But I don't want to. But by then there's no other choice.

'In my home group there's this one guy who tries to tell you there's something wrong with your program if you're having drinking dreams. And I've already told him he better never say that to me again. Because I completely disagree. I know exactly why I have those dreams. It's not because I want to drink, it's because I'm scared of that denial Greg was talking about. I'm scared it's going to get me when I'm not paying attention. And that fear comes out in my sleep. If I wanted to drink, I would have by now. For whatever reason, I've been here since I got here. Probably because I was ready. I didn't come here for anybody but me. Nobody told me it was time. *I* decided.'

Normally he would have shared more, but he looked over at Seth. Seth was sitting upright again, looking even more distressed.

'You want to share, Seth? You don't have to.'

Seth shook his head in fast, panicky motions.

'You feel OK? You want to go back to the rig and lie down?'

Seth nodded, white-faced and silent.

So August dug the keys out of his pocket and handed them to Seth, who scrambled out.

He listened to two more people share, then left the meeting early, to check on Seth and make sure he was OK.

He found Seth sitting up on the couch, next to the sleeping Henry, poring through the literature.

'You OK, Seth?'

Seth sighed. But he didn't speak.

Woody wove around August's feet in greeting, and August reached down and scratched between the dog's shoulder blades, gently.

'You looked like you were physically ill. Did you have a headache or a stomachache or something?'

Seth shook his head no.

August perched on the edge of the couch and draped an arm around the boy's shoulders.

'Want to talk about it?'

Seth began to cry. He wiped at the tears with the back of his sleeve, but they just kept coming. 'Shit,' he said. 'I hate it when I cry. Oh, great. And now I cussed, too. Sorry, August.'

'Don't really care,' August said. 'What's going on?'

'I'm so stupid.'

'Why are you stupid? I don't think you're stupid at all. Why do you think you're stupid?'

'I thought if I went to a meeting I could sort of pick up something there that I could bring home to my dad. Like I could find this thing that works for people to stop drinking . . . and . . . you know . . . give it to him. But it totally doesn't work like that. Does it, August?'

'No. It doesn't.'

'You have to want it for yourself, and even then it doesn't always work.'

'True.'

'You have to be really ready. And you can't even help somebody else get ready. They have to get themselves ready. So what do I do, August?'

August sighed deeply. Pulled Seth closer in to his side.

'I have no idea, Seth. I'm sorry.'

'Do you think my father's an alcoholic? I know what you always say. Like how you can't tell from the outside, and you are if you say you are and stuff like that. But now that feels like you're just ducking the question. I know you can't say for sure, but I'm asking what you think. And I really want to know, August. I want to know what you think.'

'OK, then,' August said. 'I'll tell you. Here's what I think. I think the vast majority of people with three drunk-driving convictions are alcoholics. Because most people who are not, who are just heavy drinkers . . . if they get two DUIs, they're going to do one of two things. Either stop drinking or stop driving when they drink. The only people I know who are crazy enough to set themselves up for a third are alcoholics. So, I don't really know your father well enough to judge him. But based on knowing that, if I had to guess, I'd guess yes, he is. And there's another reason I think he is. Because if he wasn't, I don't think you'd be as upset as you are right now.'

Seth turned his wet face up to August, no longer trying to hide the tears.

'And there's not a damn thing I can do about it?'

'If there was anything you could do, it wouldn't be bringing him something from an AA meeting. If there was any way you could make a difference, I would think it would be by telling him something very honest from your own experience. Like sitting him down and telling him from your heart how his drinking affects you.'

'Think it might help?'

'I don't know, Seth. It might or it might not. All I really know is that you have a right to do it. And that nothing short of that is likely to do much good.'

'Thanks for telling me what you really think, August.'

'Wish I could do more.'

'It's not *your* problem.'

But I wish it was, August thought. *So I could do more to fix it.* He didn't say so out loud.

He made a mental note to call Harvey in the morning and get a second opinion on the wisdom of planning an intervention for a guy you only know because he towed you to his repair shop and got you back on the road at no charge. Oh, yeah. And because you have his kids.

When August woke up, both Henry and Woody were looking out the window on the opposite side of the rig, their hands and paws against the glass. Seth was nowhere to be seen.

August rose and leaned over to the other side of his motorhome, bracing one hand against the back of the couch. He looked out to see what they saw.

Seeing nothing but their empty campsite, he looked down at Henry.

'Good morning, Henry. What are we watching with such fascination?'

Henry looked up into August's face and frowned. Then he pointed out the window.

Seth had paced back into their field of vision, audibly talking on August's cell phone. His face looked pinched and clouded. The volume of his voice betrayed anger, but August couldn't make out individual words.

Seth looked up briefly and saw the three of them

staring at him. He turned his back and paced directly away from the rig.

August pulled on his sheepskin boots and let himself out the back door, pulling a light coat over his pajamas.

By the time he got outside, Seth had ended the call and apparently set the phone down, or slipped it into his pocket. He was picking up small rocks, one after the other, and hurling them fiercely at the trunk of the campsite's biggest fir tree. August could hear the thwack, thwack, thwack sounds of the rocks striking their target. On one hit, he saw a piece of bark burst free and land a foot from the base of the tree.

Seth looked over his shoulder at August. Cast him one miserable glance, as if every part of life was wrong and August was the worst of it. Then he picked up another rock and landed it with an even louder thwack.

'Seth,' August said.

No reaction.

He walked closer to the boy's back. Seth's shoulders looked high and tight around the back of his neck.

'Seth, how about we give that poor tree a break? Maybe tell me what's going on. Bet you anything it's not the tree's fault.'

Seth shot him another dark look over his shoulder, then picked up a new rock. August stepped in and took a firm hold on the boy's right hand. Seth dropped the rock and let out a strangled sound of objection. He fought wildly to get free. For lack of a better plan, August threw his arms around the boy and wrapped him up tightly. It was something like trying to restrain a medium-sized wildcat, but August held on.

'Let me go!' Seth shot out.

'Tell me what's going on.'

'Not with you holding me prisoner.'

'I'm not holding you prisoner. I'm trying to hold you. I'm trying to put my arms around you and give you a hug, but you're fighting so hard you can't tell.'

Seth stopped moving. All the fight silently drained out of him. August could feel it go. Then Seth began to cry quietly.

August walked him over to their picnic table and sat them both down on one of its benches, still wrapping Seth in his arms. He glanced up to see Woody and Henry still watching them out the window. He wondered which of them looked more concerned. He finally decided it was a tie.

'Was that your dad you were talking to?'

Seth answered with a sniffle. Then a nod against August's shoulder.

'Want to tell me what the bad news is?'

At first, Seth didn't. Then, a minute later, August could feel him gear up to begin. A straightening of his shoulders. A big deep breath.

'I'm OK now, August,' he said.

It was clearly a lie. But August released him.

Seth looked around as though a tissue would magically appear. Then he wiped his nose on his sleeve.

'He says they're trying to pin another charge on him. He could be in for another ninety days. So when you go back through at the end of the summer, maybe his jail sentence'll only be half over.'

August sat a minute, consciously breathing. The news settled in as a long fall. Like something falling into a long well of a space, so deep as to be nearly bottomless. But it did have a bottom. And when the news reached it, August realized that part of him had known this all along. This or something quite like it.

'When will we find out?'

'I don't know,' Seth said, 'but one thing I can tell you for sure. We don't have to ask *him* any more. Because he lies. I always try to think maybe he just made a mistake, but I really think he lies, August. So, anyway, I made him tell the guard right while we were on the phone that he wanted to talk to somebody and give permission for the jail to tell things straight to you.'

'Oh,' August said. A bit surprised at Seth's careful thinking. 'That was good. Think he'll do it?'

'He better. Anyway, once he told the guard I think probably he'll have to. Don't tell Henry,' he added on a sharp outrush of breath. 'It'll kill him.'

August indicated with a flip of his head where Henry knelt on the couch inside the rig, overlooking the scene.

'I think you better tell him something,' August said. 'I think what he's imagining might be even worse.'

'What do we *do*, August? What are we supposed to do if he has to stay in jail until *December*?' Seth spat out the word December as if giving a date decades into the future, when he and his brother Henry would be old and gray.

'Um. I don't know, buddy. I need to think. Let me call the jail and see what's what before we do anything else.'

Seth sat without comment for a moment, then sniffled once and rose to his feet.

'And when you're done talking to Henry, start putting everything away so we can go. I want to get on the road early today. Because we'll be at Yellowstone by nightfall.'

The woman August talked to had a high, thin voice. A voice like a little girl. August briefly wondered if her office was literally on site at the prison. She sounded so defenseless. But that was not a useful observation, he realized, and it was probably way off base.

He pushed such thoughts away again.

'I don't know what you mean about this "extra" charge you keep referring to,' she said. 'There's no extra charge. The inmate in question was charged and convicted on one count. Driving while under the influence.'

'Oh,' August said, his head swimming with confusion. 'So you're not in the process of charging him with anything else.'

'We're not,' she said. 'No.'

August looked up at the window of the rig to see if the boys were staring at him. Woody was sitting in the passenger seat of the cab, but he was apparently watching for squirrels. The boys crossed back and forth by the window, scurrying to get everything cleaned up and put away.

It struck August as strange that Wes would present the worst possible news if it wasn't true. It just didn't add up right.

'Hey, wait,' he said suddenly. 'Driving under the influence? I thought this time he was charged with kiting checks.'

'No, sir. Driving under the influence.'

'Oh. Well. I guess that doesn't matter. At least, not right now. The main thing is that I get his release date straight.'

'The second of December,' she said.

News of the date sent a ringing numbness through August's body. He held still and felt it echo around, touching one part of his insides at a time.

'You said there were no additional charges.'

'Correct.'

'But he was supposed to get out in September.'

'No.'

'No?'

'No, sir. He was never scheduled for release in September.'

'So he was originally sentenced to . . .'

'Six months.'

Another ringing silence. Though it was a thought out of place, it struck August that the woman must be having trouble understanding his inability to grasp simple information. And that she must have been looking forward to the call being over.

'Right from the beginning he was sentenced to six months?'

'Correct.'

'For DUI?'

'It was his fourth offense.'

'Understood.'

Another long silence.

Then the woman said, 'Is there anything else I can do for you?'

August noticed that her voice had deepened just slightly, and become a trace more adult-sounding. As if she needed to be big and strong to push August off the phone.

'Um, I don't think so. So, that's . . . I mean, that's non-negotiable, right? That's definite? December second? That's not going to change? No time off for good behavior or anything?'

'On his fourth offense, I think you can trust that he'll serve every day of that sentence.'

'OK,' August said. It wasn't OK at all, but there was nothing this woman could do about that. 'Thanks.'

He clicked the phone closed and walked to the back door of the rig. Woody met him with wags, and, as August opened the door, he was careful to keep looking at Woody. In his peripheral vision, he could see that all bustling had stopped. The boys were holding still.

Waiting.

When he finally looked up at their faces, August didn't have to say that the news was bad. They already knew. Apparently it was right there in his eyes. Just sitting right there for them to gather for themselves.

'Just . . .' August said, then stalled, unsure where he was headed. 'Just . . . I don't know. Give me time to think. I just need to think about this.'

'Whoa, look at those mountains,' Seth cried, startling Woody. 'I never saw anything like that in my life! They look like the Alps! Is this Yellowstone?'

It broke the stunned silence that had haunted them all day.

'Not quite,' August said. 'We came up from the south end so we could go through Grand Teton National Park. I wanted to see it, and I thought you guys would, too.'

'So those are the Grand Teton mountains?'

'They are.'

'I never even heard of them.'

'Never studied them in school, or saw a picture?'

'I don't think so. They're so . . .'

He was never able to finish the thought. But August thought he knew. They were so sheer in their height, great narrow caps that pointed straight up, or even seemed to bend over a bit. They were genuine mountain peaks. The kind it would be hard to imagine trying to climb. They harbored veins of old snow, even in the summer. They did look a bit the way August pictured the Alps.

'Let's stop and have lunch, and we can really take them in,' he said.

*

August made tuna sandwiches, parked in a turnout near the shore of a lake. Seth stood outside, staring at those mountains. August had to call him to come in and get his sandwich.

'Can I take it back outside to eat it, August?'

'Sure,' August said.

And he and Henry settled on opposite sides of the dinette table. August watched the Grand Tetons out the window. Henry stared as well, but August couldn't tell if he was watching the mountains, or watching his brother watch the mountains. Or both.

A few minutes later, his mouth still full of tuna fish, Henry said, 'He's thinking about climbing.'

It surprised August, to hear so many words from the boy.

'How do you know?' August asked.

Henry only shrugged.

'No, really,' August said. 'I'm curious. How can you tell?'

Henry shrugged again. 'Just know,' he said.

August finished the last of his sandwich, then stepped out the back door, leaving Woody inside with Henry. So he could continue to stare while the boy finished eating.

August stood next to Seth, nearly shoulder to shoulder. Seth's sandwich drooped in his hand, barely touched. He showed no special sign that he knew August had joined him.

'Thinking of climbing?' August asked.

A brief silence.

Then Seth said, 'Oh, yeah.'

They looked on in silence for a few minutes more.

'Don't let your lunch go to waste,' August said.

'I've been trying to think of words to tell you how all this makes me feel.'

'The Tetons?'

'Yeah, but not just them. All of this. All this . . . you know. These places. Nature. It makes me feel different. But I just can't figure out what words to use.'

'Most people say it makes them feel smaller. Like the world is so big, it makes them feel insignificant.'

'No,' Seth said. But then he didn't immediately elaborate. 'Bigger,' he said after a time.

'Really?'

'Just on the inside, though,' Seth said. 'Like in my chest. Like I breathe air into my chest, and there's more space in my lungs than before. But not my lungs, really. I just feel like there's more room inside me than there used to be.'

August briefly tried that on for size. Wondered if he longed for summer because summer made it so much easier to breathe.

'Is that how it feels to you, August?'

'I'm not sure,' August said. 'But I guess that's as good a way to describe the feeling as any.'

'We're in Yellowstone,' Seth said weakly as they pulled into their campsite. It was the first thing he'd said in many hours.

It was a thing everybody already knew. But nobody

had said it. Because nobody had said anything since passing through the park entrance.

'Yes we are,' August replied.

Then he turned off the engine of the rig, and the headlights. And the campground was thrown into darkness. The trees disappeared, and the tents and motorhomes that surrounded them. Then, as they sat a minute, it all came back into soft focus, aided by lights on in the windows of other rigs, and an occasional campfire.

'You wanted to get here real bad, didn't you, August?'

'Yes,' August said, disliking where this was headed, but unsure why.

'So . . . that's good. Right? I mean . . . you're here. That's good.'

They sat still, August in the driver's seat, Seth in the passenger seat beside him. Henry and Woody on the couch in the back. For some reason, none of them had even taken off his seat belt. As if the inertia was something contagious.

'I'm not sure what you're asking, Seth.'

'I think I mean . . . do you feel better now?'

August pulled in a big breath. Forced it out again.

'No. And I really thought I would.'

'Can I ask you a question, August?'

August squeezed his eyes tightly shut. Gripped the steering wheel more tightly. 'I still need more time to think about that, Seth.'

'No, it wasn't about that. It was about the iced-tea bottle. I just wondered . . . I mean . . . we're here. So is that all we have to be? Here? Are you going to leave those ashes anywhere just so long as it's Yellowstone? Or do they have to go someplace really special in Yellowstone?'

'I'm not sure. I think it might be a lot of different places. But I didn't really think it out all that well. Yet.'

Much the same way I didn't think out why just arriving here was supposed to solve anything, he thought. He did not say it.

'Do you want to think of places all on your own, August, or do you want us to help you?'

They all three sat cross-legged on a blanket in front of their campfire, the glow of the flames illuminating the boys' faces. And his own, August realized as an afterthought, but he didn't care to think about that. He wanted to feel invisible.

August got the distinct impression that Seth desperately wanted to talk about what they would do during the second half of his father's sentence. And, since August couldn't, his only option was to desperately talk. In general.

'You can make suggestions if you want. I figured when I saw a good place, I'd just know it. It would feel right, you know?'

'But you haven't seen anything yet? Oh, never mind. I'm sorry. That's a stupid question. We just drove in. And it was dark. How could you have seen anything yet? I'm sorry, August. I know I'm talking too much but I can't make myself stop.'

'It's OK,' August said. 'We're all a little off balance.'

'Thanks, August. Can I go inside and get the marsh-mallows?'

'You can if you want, but this fire will have to burn way down before we can toast them properly. All it's going to do now is set them on fire.'

'I could sharpen some sticks while we're waiting.'

'Fine,' August said.

Seth sprang to his feet and disappeared. Woody ran after him. Just in case there was trouble. Or fun.

August looked over – and down – at Henry. Henry looked up to August, completely unguarded, the boy's face like a door thrown open to invite visitors into his house. He smiled a tiny smile that August could only characterize as excruciating. The look in his eyes reminded August of the last day the boys spent at home. The way their father instructed them to steer clear of him. So they wouldn't unfairly burden him with looks like this one.

August smiled, against odds, and quickly looked away again.

Seth squatted beside Henry at the edge of the fire, sharpening the end of a long stick with August's Swiss army knife. Cutting away from himself and his own hand, just the way August had taught him.

August could hear a light rustling of wind in the trees, and some kind of insect noise. And distant voices of their fellow campers.

'The fire!' August said suddenly.

He surprised even himself by saying it. Seth was so startled that he fell forward and had to brace himself with one hand to keep from tumbling into the fire pit.

'Sorry,' August said.

'It's OK. You just surprised me.'

'You cut yourself?'

'No. I'm fine. What about the fire?'

'That's where I should put the first little bit of Phillip's ashes. In our campfire.'

Seth said nothing for a time, and August could see and feel his stare in the fire glow.

'In the *fire*?' he asked after a time. Sounding opposed.

'Yes. Why not? If he were here with us, he'd be sitting here enjoying this campfire. It's our first night here, and he'd be thrilled to be here. But it's too late and too dark to go exploring. So he'd just be sitting here enjoying the campfire. Enjoying the fact that we're here. So the first place we should put some of his ashes is in the fire.'

'But . . . August . . .'

'What?'

'He wouldn't be *in* the fire. If he was here. He'd be sitting beside it.'

'Well . . . That's true. But I don't want to just dump his ashes on the ground next to the fire pit. Because then we'll be scuffing through them for the next week or two. Getting them on the bottom of our shoes. That's not good enough. This way he'll actually *be* the fire. He'll be part of it.'

'But . . . August . . .'

'What, Seth?'

'It's a *fire*. Nobody wants to be in a *fire*.'

'Seth, he's already been cremated.'

'Oh. Well, that's true. But still . . .'

August looked down at Henry again, who returned his gaze immediately.

'What do you think, Henry? Should we sprinkle a little of Phillip's ashes on the fire?'

Henry nodded once. Immediately and decisively.

'We should?' Seth asked. 'Why?'

Henry shrugged. 'I dunno,' he said in his little cartoon-mouse voice. 'Just seems good.'

August squatted on the balls of his feet, one knee braced against a stone of the fire pit, and held his two hands out, together, palms up.

'How much?' Seth asked.

His role in the proceedings clearly made Seth nervous.

'Go slow. I'll say when.'

The ashes felt gritty hitting August's palms. Like the tiniest pebbles imaginable. Sharp, even. When a mound of about a quarter of a cup had been poured into his hands, he said, 'That's good. That's enough.'

Then he just remained there, squatting, uncomfortable, watching Seth put the cap back on the bottle. Henry extended his neck comically and stared at the ashes in August's hands as if expecting some kind of sudden movement from them.

'Should we say something?' Seth asked.

'I don't know. I didn't really think about that.'

'If we say something, it should be you. You were his father. I didn't even know him.'

'You would have liked him.'

'I bet I would've. I wish he was here.'

'Yeah,' August said. 'Me, too.'

'So . . . you gonna say something?'

'I don't know. Maybe not. I don't know what to say.'

He'd been feeling around inside himself ever since the bottle came out of the glove compartment. He'd found nothing at all so far.

'Can I say something, then?'

'Sure.'

'Phillip, his name was?'

'Yes. Phillip.'

'Phillip, we wish you were here for this trip. I know you don't know me, but I know I would've liked you, because I like your dad so much. And this would be a much nicer trip with you here, because then he wouldn't be so sad. But I hope when we put a little bit of you in the fire, he'll feel better. I'm still not so sure about that fire thing, but . . . well . . . never mind.'

August waited briefly to see if he was done.

'We'll have a really nice trip for you,' Seth added. 'I know that's not as good as you having it for yourself. But it's all we can do, and we'll do a really good job. Won't we, Henry?'

Henry nodded once, hard.

'OK, I'm done, August. You can do it now.'

August leaned forward until the fire made his hands uncomfortably hot. Just for a moment, he didn't want to open his hands. But the fire was beginning to burn them. And he didn't want to pull them away with the job left undone. He didn't want to fail at this.

So he opened his hands with a slight tossing motion. The fire bent lightly from the wind of his motions.

Then . . . nothing.

August had no idea how long he stared at the fire, wondering what he expected it to do and why it wasn't doing it. In truth, he didn't know what he'd expected. Anything except nothing. He hadn't expected everything to remain perfectly unchanged.

He looked down at his hands, which were still coated with ash.

Suddenly he found it nearly impossible to breathe. His chest felt constricted, as though something was holding him too tightly.

He rose to his feet, feeling slightly dizzy.

'I have to go wash my hands,' he said. It came out as a half-coherent mumble.

He vaulted up the back steps and into the rig, where he closed himself into the tiny bathroom. He purposely avoided his own eyes in the mirror as he scrubbed his hands with antibacterial soap. He looked down at them as he washed, and saw that they were shaking. He washed harder, hoping the pressure would keep them steady. The feeling in his chest, that constriction, was not easing. If anything, breathing was more of a struggle. When his hands were entirely clean, he splashed cold water on his face, somehow thinking that would help. It didn't.

Still avoiding the mirror, he dried his face and hands and came out of the bathroom, needing to sit.

He perched on the edge of the couch, his head in his hands. Then, feeling even sicker, he tried putting his head down between his knees.

A few seconds later he heard the back screen door swing open. Woody appeared under his face, and licked his nose. He straightened up as best he could.

'August!' he heard Seth say. But the word sounded far away, as if making its way to him down a long tunnel. 'What's wrong? Are you sick?'

'No, I'm OK,' he said.

'You don't look OK.'

'I am.'

'Are you lying to me, August?'

Seth sat on the couch close to him, one thin arm draped over August's back.

'Yes. I guess I am.'

'What's wrong? Do you feel sick?'

'No, it's not that.'

'What is it?'

August worked hard to pull in a deep breath.

'I just . . . I don't know, buddy. I don't know how to say it. I wanted to get here. You know. For him. But now I'm here. And I don't know what I expected it to fix. It didn't fix anything. Nothing changed.'

'Henry!' Seth screamed. 'You have to get in here! August's sad! We have to help him!'

Then Seth wrapped himself around August, rising to his feet to get a better hold. August could feel the boy's hair pressed against his face. He worked hard at holding in tears. So as not to alarm the boys. No, that was a pathetic excuse, he realized. He always worked hard at holding in tears. He would have to stop doing that.

Someday. Not now.

After a moment, August felt Henry's arms wrap around his chest, and the little guy's face pressed up hard on his shoulder.

'Don't be sad, August,' the little mouse voice said.

August's tears let go. And stayed for a long time. As long as they damn well pleased. Until they were fully cried out.

The boys stayed as well.

Henry held on tight with one arm, and with his other hand he stroked the back of August's hair. Almost exactly the way he petted Woody.

And he didn't stop.

In time, August straightened slightly.

'I think I'm going to be all right now,' he said.

'You sure?' Seth asked.

'At least as all right as I was before.'

'OK,' Seth said, letting go. 'I guess that'll do.'

'You guys go back out by the fire. I bet it's just right for marshmallows by now.'

'OK, we'll start one for you, August. I know just how you like 'em.'

And that was true. He did.

August stepped back into the bathroom and washed his face well in the sink. For longer than necessary. Then he looked up at his own face in the mirror. It jolted him. His eyes were swollen and red, and he looked so completely . . . ruined. He quickly looked away again. The image in the mirror made him seem so vulnerable. *Well*, he thought, *the mirror didn't play any part in that*. He was vulnerable. He just didn't feel quite ready to view the full extent of it.

He dried his face and joined the boys by the fire.

He could still feel his hands shaking. The pressure around his chest was gone, but had been replaced by a scraped-out, scoured feeling in his chest and gut. He tried to decide if it was just as bad. Or worse.

He sat cross-legged on the blanket, and Seth handed him a perfectly toasted marshmallow on the end of a stick. He bit it tentatively, but it was still too hot to eat.

'Here's what we're going to do,' August said.

Seth leapt to his feet, dropping one of the sticks.

'Now?'

It almost made August laugh. Or cry again. It was hard to know which one fit. It was just so perfectly Seth. Always tripping over his own feet, trying to do what you wanted of him, before you even had time to say what that was.

'No, not now, Seth. At the end of the summer.'

A silence fell.

Seth sat back down.

'I can't stay with you boys at your place. I have to get back to work. So the only thing we can do is take you guys back home to San Diego with me. It's going to be hard, because you'll have to be in a new school, but just for a few months. Just until Christmas vacation. And that's another thing. I can't drive you home until Christmas break. I just have too much to do on the weekends. And that's more than two weeks later than your dad gets out of jail. If he wants to come get you sooner, that's fine. But that's the soonest I can get away to take you home.'

Silence. As if the boys thought there might be more.

'That OK with you guys?'

'OK? August, that's great!'

'It's going to be hard. Change to a new school and then change right back again. And you'll have to take the bus to school. Either that or I'll have to drop you there almost an hour early.'

'That's not hard, August, that's great.'

'You sure?'

'Are you kidding?'

August heard a light sniffle, and looked over at Henry just in time to see him wipe his nose on his sleeve.

'If it's so great, why is Henry crying?'

'He does that sometimes when he's happy. Well, not happy exactly. When he thought he was in trouble and then it turns out he's safe. When he feels . . . what's the word?'

'Relieved?'

'Yeah,' Seth said. 'That.'

August ate his marshmallow, and they sat in silence

for a time, staring at the embers of the slowly dying fire.

In time, Henry's sniffles subsided.

'Know what's nice?' Seth asked.

August didn't know. But he assumed it had something to do with avoiding a county facility for children.

'No, what?'

'Now it's like a little bit of Phillip is in the smoke. I'm watching this smoke, and it's going up to the stars, and part of it is him. I just thought that was nice.'

'That *is* nice,' August said.

'So something did change. At least a little bit, anyway.'

'I think you're right about that,' August said.

In A Barrel

August woke them early the next morning. Barely dawn. So they could see a few of the sights before the bulk of the crowds massed in.

As they drove the empty road between Madison Campground and Old Faithful, they had just enough light to see geothermal steam, rising in the distance, on both sides of the road. A spooky moon hung over a low stand of mountains, half obscured in the mist.

'Whoa!' Seth cried, and Henry craned his neck to see. 'Why does it do that, August?'

'You knew there were geothermal features at Yellowstone.'

'Huh?'

'You knew there were geysers, at least.'

'Are geysers geothermal?'

'Yes. They are.'

They pulled into a parking lot next to a network of boardwalks that wove through boiling mudpots, hot springs, fumaroles, and beside a small geyser. They were the third vehicle to park, but the owners of the other two vehicles were nowhere to be seen.

'Can Woody come?' Seth asked.

'No. Sorry. No dogs on any of the boardwalks or trails in the park. It's not a very dog-friendly place.'

'Sorry, Woody,' Henry said, and August watched in the rear-view mirror as Woody laid his ears down.

They stepped out into the barely light morning. The very ground under the boardwalks steamed, running with hot liquid from under the surface of the ground. The decimated bare trees looked as though they'd just survived a volcano.

'Whoa,' Seth said again, and Henry grabbed at August's hand. 'It's kind of cool. But not exactly pretty. It sort of looks like one of those movies about the end of the world. Like we're the only ones who survived.'

'I guess so,' August said. 'I've seen a lot of pictures of Yellowstone. There's definitely beauty here. But these dense geothermal areas are a little spooky.'

They stopped near a paintpot and stared. Its middle was a deep pool of clear emerald blue, stained iron red at the eroded road-map edges. The rising steam nearly obscured their view, so they stared longer, waiting for the occasional breeze to bend the steam and help them see. Henry gripped August's hand tighter.

'I should've paid better attention in science class,' Seth breathed, his voice weighted with wonder.

Everybody should pay better attention in science class,

August thought. He was so tired of teaching something that nobody seemed to care much about.

'You knew there was heat inside the Earth,' August said.

'I did?'

'I assume you did. You know about volcanoes, right?'

'Oh. Yeah. But this is not lava.'

'No, but it's all part of that same super-heated system.'

'I had no idea all this was going on under the Earth. I'll never look at the ground the same way again. It's like the planet is alive.'

'The planet *is* alive. No "like" about it.'

'I always thought living stuff grew out of it, but . . . Will you tell us why it does all this, August?'

August felt the deep sigh rise up in his chest, then heard it exit through his nostrils again.

'I'm sure it explains all about it in the brochure,' he said.

Seth shot him a wounded look, but said nothing.

They walked on, around a bend in the boardwalk where a small geyser was spitting water a few feet into the air, almost hard to distinguish from the rolls and coils of steam in the barely-dawn. Two couples with a camera on a tripod were cheering the geyser on.

Without discussion, August and the boys walked on, wanting to be where there were no other people again. It would be their last chance for the day. The crowds would wake up soon.

'But you're a *science teacher*,' Seth breathed, heavy

with complaint. 'And every time I ask you about science, you tell me to look at the brochure.'

August sighed again.

'I know,' he said. 'I'm sorry. It's just that I do this all year. I get kind of burned out.' *Well*, he thought. *I don't get burned out. I got burned out years ago, and still haven't come back from it.*

'But you don't even seem like you *like* science.'

'I used to,' he said.

'But now you don't.'

'I guess I'm just kind of tired of what I do.'

They rounded the boardwalk back toward the parking lot. Dark birds perched in the decimated and completely bare tree skeletons, then flew away again.

'Do you like teaching kids?'

'Well, they're not exactly kids. It's high school. They're more like jaded teenagers.'

'But do you like them?'

August walked a few more steps, wondering if he should lie.

'I used to.'

'Well, what do you like now?' Seth asked, sounding exasperated.

August thought for a long moment, hoping for a more noble answer. Then he told the truth.

'Summer,' he said.

They sat on a stretch of bare, backless bench, watching the rising steam of Old Faithful. Waiting for the geyser to blow. A few dozen people waited with them, but there was a lot of bench, so no sense of being packed too tightly.

'I wish we had something to do while we were waiting,' Seth said.

August filled his lungs in preparation for a sigh, then decided he did that sighing thing far too much.

'Quick science lesson?' he asked.

'Yeah!' both boys shouted at once.

They looked up at him with eager faces. August wondered if his job would be different if kids looked up at him with eager faces. And if even these two kids would have been the slightest bit eager for a science lesson if they had been in school.

Maybe the school was the problem, August thought. *Maybe everybody wants a science lesson if they're sitting in the middle of one of the greatest geothermal wonders of the world. Maybe we've removed all the relevance from the information we teach kids, so they have no idea why they should care. Maybe it's not the kids' fault. Maybe we made the first mistake.*

'I'll start with geysers,' he said. 'They're a lot like the hot springs we saw before, but less open. They have very narrow openings. So the heat can't rise and escape very well. It gets bottled up. And there's pressure created by the rock and water sitting on top of all this heat. So these bubbles form, and stay trapped, until they're so big and powerful that they actually lift the water above them. Kind of a splash thing. And that lets pressure off the system, so you get this violent boiling. And the extra steam it creates forces the water up and out of this narrow opening.'

Then he went on to explain the terraces, and mud-pots, and paintpots, half aware that the people on either side of him had gone silent and were leaning in a bit to listen. Right before he wrapped up the lesson, he felt a faint memory of what he had once liked about science. And, in the faces of the boys, what he had liked about teaching kids.

But the thought was interrupted by Old Faithful, as had been destined. Everyone shouted and cheered, and then August was just another person glad to see the eruption, glad it did what it consistently did. In that moment, it didn't matter that he knew more about the geological process than those around him. Everybody likes a good geyser.

As both the crowd and the geyser were winding down, Seth asked, 'If Phillip were here, would he have wanted a lesson in science?'

'He wouldn't have needed one,' August said. 'He knew almost as much about it as I did. He was a science whiz. Almost a science nerd, though I don't mean that in a bad way.'

They all three stood, and began the long walk across the network of big parking lots to the motorhome.

'He liked it because you liked it,' Seth said. It didn't sound like a question.

'Maybe. Or maybe it runs in the family.'

Henry glanced up at August, almost as though he had an opinion. If so, he never shared it.

'No, I think you're right,' August said. 'I think he liked it because he looked up to me. And because it was something we could be interested in together. Something we could share.'

'Huh,' Seth said. 'So I bet you liked science a lot better before he died.'

August never answered.

'August! Buffaloes!'

August instinctively pressed his foot on the brake, glancing in the rear-view mirror to see how closely the car behind them was following. He swerved on to a pullout, and so did most of the cars on that stretch of park road. As many as could fit. The rest just came to an illegal stop in the roadway.

'Bison, actually,' August said, stepping on the parking brake.

'What's the difference?'

'You're not the first to confuse the two. But there's a difference.'

August stared out Seth's open passenger window. The animals grazed in a vast green field, a stand of mountains a sharp contrast behind. The sky was perfectly cloudless, a color almost navy blue at the edges. A narrow river snaked through the field. The animals looked a bit silly from this close vantage point, their shoulders and necks massive, shedding the last scraps of ragged winter coat, their hips tiny, as if the two ends of the animals had been put together in an accidental mismatch. August briefly wondered how it felt for a female bison to give birth.

He glanced over his shoulder at Henry, who had taken off his seat belt and was kneeling on the couch, looking out the window. Woody stood just to his right, paws up on the back of the couch, growling at the bison low in his throat.

When August looked back, Seth had picked up August's camera and was clicking off shots, the zoom fully extended.

'I can see them real good through your camera, August.' Then, about twelve clicks later, 'Can I get out and go closer to 'em?'

'No! No way, Seth. They can be dangerous. They're huge animals. You don't want to approach them.'

'Oh. Too bad. I guess I just have to settle for the zoom.'

He clicked off about ten more shots, then set the camera in his lap and just stared for a time.

August watched the side of the boy's face. It looked placid. Ecstatic, almost. But strangely calm. For Seth.

'I'm glad you boys got to see bison,' August said.

'I hope it's OK that I took, like, thirty shots with your camera.'

'It's fine, Seth. Digital pictures don't cost anything.'

'I can't wait to show the kids at my school. Oh. Wait. I forgot. I won't see 'em till after Christmas. Well. It doesn't matter, I guess. I'll just show 'em the pictures next year. They'll still know I got to see all this. Just not so soon.'

They sat quietly for a moment. Then that long, dividing ache sliced through August's chest again.

At almost that exact same moment, Seth said, 'Phillip should've seen the bisons.'

'That would have been nice,' August said.

'We should put some of his ashes here. Right here where we sat and watched them.'

August looked around. Out the windshield, his side window. The rear-view mirror. There were a lot of cars holding still. A lot of tourists watching the bison.

'I don't know, Seth. I like the idea in principle. But there are too many people around.'

'I could scatter a little handful right out the window and nobody would ever know. You could just put a little bit of 'em in my right hand. And I'll just hang my hand out the window. And just as you start to drive, I'll open up my hand. Nobody'll even notice. And if they do, it'll just look like a little puff of smoke or something.'

August let the idea settle briefly. Then he opened the glove compartment, took out the iced-tea bottle. Slowly unscrewed the cap. He filled the cap with ashes, then poured them into Seth's waiting hand.

Then he sealed the bottle again and tucked it into the map pocket in the door. Close to his left knee.

He had a sense he might be reaching for it often on this drive.

'Seen enough?'

'Let's just look a little more, August, please? It's so pretty here.'

They sat in silence for two or three minutes, Seth's right hand in his lap, balled tightly around his big responsibility.

Then Seth sighed. 'OK. I guess we can go see more great stuff now.'

'Henry. Seat belt on.'

But when August looked over his shoulder to check, Henry was already back in his seat with his seat belt on.

Seth hung his right hand out the window as August pulled back on to the road. A moment later, the hand was back inside again. August never saw the ashes go. He felt cheated somehow. He wished he had seen them go.

'Wet wipes in the glove compartment,' he told Seth.

'Thought I wasn't allowed in the glove compartment.'

'Seth . . .' But before August could finish the thought, he looked over to see Seth grinning widely, pleased with his own . . . not joke exactly, but . . . August couldn't find the word.

'Funny guy, Seth,' he said. 'You are a funny guy.'

But it struck August as odd. Because Seth wasn't a funny guy. At least, he never had been before.

The following morning they drove the park road alongside Yellowstone Lake. Headed toward the canyon, and its waterfalls. The sky was just beginning to lighten. They'd left camp early in the hope of being the first up to the viewing spot at the brink of the upper falls. But August felt sure that was a battle already lost.

'That's a big lake,' Seth said. He whistled low between his teeth. 'Man. That's the biggest lake I ever saw.'

The road ran close to the edge of the water, and nearly at the same level.

'What other lakes have you seen?'

August glanced over to see Seth redden slightly.

'I've never seen a lake before,' he said. 'Any lake. So I guess I didn't say that right.'

'Really? Never seen any lake at all?'

'Kind of like desert where we live.'

'Definitely like desert where you live.'

'I've seen lakes in books. You know. And movies. And on TV . . .'

Before he could go on, Henry surprised them both by piping up.

'Stop!' he squeaked.

'What, Henry? What's wrong?'

'Nothing. I just want you to stop here.'

August found a safe place to pull over.

'You need to go to the bathroom?'

'No.'

'What do you need, then?'

'The bottle.'

August exchanged a glance with Seth, who shrugged.

'What bottle, buddy?'

'The Phillip bottle.'

August blinked a few times, then pulled the plastic iced-tea bottle out from its place in the map pocket. He undid his seat belt and held the bottle out to Henry, who was by then unbelted and standing.

Henry held both hands out, together. Palms up.

'Just put a little,' Henry said.

August opened the bottle and poured a mound of ashes into the small waiting hands. Henry closed both hands tightly around them.

'Wait, let me open the door for you.'

August held the back door wide and Henry made his way carefully down the back steps. August followed him out into the surprisingly chilly morning twilight. Henry stepped out on to a narrow bank by the water's edge. Took off his sneakers by stepping on each heel with the other foot.

'Let me help you with your socks,' August said.

Henry patiently lifted one foot at a time for August to pull his socks off. Then August rolled the hems of Henry's jeans up as high as possible around his skinny legs.

Henry walked into the lake, deep enough to get his rolled pant legs soaking wet. If the water was cold, which it surely must have been, he didn't let on.

August heard a small sound and looked behind him to see that Seth had come outside to watch. He had Woody on a leash. Woody also seemed intent on watching Henry's movements.

Henry spun around three times, his arms straight out in front of him, hands still tightly balled around the ashes. As if he planned on shot-putting them into the lake. Then he stopped, and held his hands up high, as if someone might reach down and take the ashes from his waiting hands. August expected him to open his hands and let them go, in which case the ashes would have rained down on Henry instead of the lake.

Instead, Henry suddenly plunged his hands down into the water. When they came out again, they were open, and separate. Henry stared at them for a moment, as if to gauge what remained. August could see a dull film of ash rise to the surface of the water between Henry's wet pant legs.

Then the boy waded ashore.

'OK,' he said as he walked past them.

August picked up the boy's shoes and socks and followed him inside, Seth and Woody trailing after.

'You want to change into dry pants before we go?' August asked him.

'No. It's OK.'

'Want to wash your hands?'

'No.'

Henry settled into his usual spot on the couch and put on his lap belt. Woody, freshly relieved of the leash, bounded into his lap.

August shrugged inwardly and settled back into the driver's seat, where he waited for Seth to belt himself in. He glanced back over his shoulder at Henry, who was holding out his hands and staring at the open palms.

August opened the glove compartment and retrieved the canister of wet wipes he kept on hand for Woody's muddy paws. He reached it back to Henry.

'Here,' he said. 'For your hands.'

Henry shook his head. 'No,' he said in that little mouse voice. 'It's OK. He can stay.'

August thought that over for a moment before

pulling his hand back and dropping the wipes into the glove compartment again.

He fired up the engine and they drove on, alongside the vast mountain lake, the sky just beginning to take on color.

'This is Wednesday,' August said as they drove. 'You'll want to call your dad today.'

Nothing. Absolute silence.

August glanced over at Seth, who stared out the window as if he hadn't heard.

'You *do* want to talk to your dad. Don't you?'

First no answer.

Then, after a time, Seth said, 'Not really. No.' Quietly. As if he'd suddenly run out of that seemingly endless Seth energy.

August glanced at Henry in the rear-view mirror. Their eyes met as Henry instinctively returned August's glance.

'What about you, Henry? You want to talk to your dad today?'

Henry shook his head.

'Oh, no,' Seth said when they pulled into the parking lot for the short trail to the brink of Upper Yosemite falls. 'There are already people here.'

Their rig was the sixth vehicle parked.

'I thought there might be.'

'But we're gonna go see it anyway, right?'

'Yeah. Hell, yeah. We're here. Let's go see it.'

They stepped out into the cool early morning.

'Wow,' Seth said. 'That must be some waterfall. I can already hear it!'

August took Henry's hand for the walk to the falls, though he wasn't sure why. It was impossible to lose him until they reached the platform at the brink of the falls. And the platform was railed. They had seen that from earlier overlooks. So it would be damned hard to lose him even then. Yet August instinctively reached down, and was a bit surprised when Henry reached up to meet him halfway.

As they walked hand in hand, August thought of the ashes on Henry's hands. And it made him comfortable. Not afraid, as he'd thought it would.

For the first time, August understood why Henry had declined to wash them away.

They stood on the platform together, as apart as possible from the other tourists, the roar of the falls making communication nearly impossible. Henry leaned forward, pressing his belly and chest against the rocks that formed the edge of the platform, his head underneath the rail. Even though the rocks were wet from mist. August stood over him and held the waistband of his jeans, for no real reason except to make himself feel more secure.

As the water pitched over the very brink of the falls, August felt he could see through it. See the greenish depth, the sheer bulk of it, alone in the air with nothing to support it.

Seth gripped the rail tightly and stared over it for a few minutes.

He took out his own disposable camera and snapped off a shot.

Then he tugged at August's jacket.

August leaned down to hear him better.

'Let's go now,' Seth shouted into his ear.

August had to give Henry's jeans a good pull to get his attention, but then they walked together up the short, steep path back to the parking lot.

'That was a let-down,' Seth said.

'Really? I thought it was a great waterfall.'

'That's not what I mean. I wanted us to be able to put some of the ashes in. So they'd go over the falls. But there were all those people.'

'We could go even earlier tomorrow. We could get up at four. Get here while it's still dark.'

'But maybe we'll do all that and somebody else will've done the same thing.'

'Maybe. But what other options do we have?'

'We should go further up the river. Is there a place to get down to the river further up?'

'Farther,' August said, without thinking. Then he wished he hadn't corrected the boy. 'I don't like that plan. There's nothing much more dangerous than a fast-moving river above a waterfall. A lot of people die that way in national parks. They fall into the river and the current takes them right over the falls.'

'There has to be a place where we can go and still be careful.'

'I don't know, Seth. I think the best way to be careful is not to do it at all.'

They walked the rest of the way back to the rig in silence. Woody sat in the driver's seat, watching them from the window as they approached, his whole body wagging.

When they were belted in and ready to drive, August looked over at Seth. The boy looked sulky, his face shut down.

'What's up, Seth?'

'I know you think I'm not careful enough, August. But sometimes I think you're *too* careful.'

'Don't say that like it's a bad thing.'

'It can be.'

'It keeps people safe.'

'Not always, it doesn't. Everybody goes around missing all the best stuff because they don't want anything bad to happen. But then when something bad wants to happen it just does. Anyway. No matter how careful you're being.'

'That's not entirely true,' August said, still not starting the engine. 'There are bad things you can prevent by being careful and others you can't. Lots of people get into lots of trouble when they could have avoided it by being more careful.'

'But not by being *too* careful,' Seth said, clearly exasperated. 'By being just careful enough. I think we should go further . . . farther . . . up the river. And be just careful enough.'

August sat with his inner resistance for a moment, then sighed.

'You might be right,' he said. 'Maybe we should go upriver and just be careful. Maybe I was being overly cautious.'

'Sure were,' Seth said. Then he glanced quickly over at August. 'I mean . . . thank you. That's what I meant. Thank you.'

'I figured that's what you meant,' August said.

'Oh, this is a great place!' Seth shouted as the river came into view between the trees.

But August didn't like the look of it at all. Because there was no guard rail. Just a racing river.

'I could climb up on that big rock,' Seth continued.

He pointed to a rock about the length of a school bus and three times as wide, at the edge of the rapids, the river curving and roiling around one edge of its base.

'But there are places with no rocks. You can just stand at the edge of the river. Wouldn't that be safer?'

'I don't know, August. I think if I stood in a safe place and threw the ashes they'd just land in the dirt by the side of the river. And I sure don't want to lean over. Look at the top of that huge rock. It's almost flat. And it's higher on the river end. So if I slipped climbing up it, I could only fall back away from the water.'

'I don't like it,' August said.

Yet they were walking in the rock's direction.

'Tell you what, August. I'll get down on my belly and

inch my way up that rock. Till I can get just my arms over the edge. My whole body'll be lying on the rock. I couldn't fall. It's not even possible.'

'On one condition,' August said. 'That I go up there with you and hang on to the waistband of your jeans.'

'August, it's impossible to fall off that rock.'

'Humor me.'

'I don't really know what that means,' Seth said. 'Except I think it means you're going to be hanging on to the waistband of my jeans.'

August lifted Henry by his waist and set him on top of the rock, which was much lower on its non-river end.

'Promise me you'll stay here and not move a muscle.'

'I promise, August,' Henry said.

'Because this is a dangerous place for you to be walking around alone.'

Henry crossed his heart with one hand, solemnly. 'Double, triple promise,' he said.

'Good boy. OK, Seth. Let's go.'

They inched their way along the rock, Seth in the lead. And it felt safe enough. Until they got out closer to the end, and August could look off and see river below them. But the rock was so wide, he couldn't even look straight down. It really was safe. His brain told him so. And yet his heart began to pound.

'OK, hand me the bottle, August.'

It surprised him to hear Seth say it, because it meant the boy had reached the edge. August instinctively reached up and grabbed the waistband of Seth's jeans, hooking his thumb through a belt loop. He looked back at Henry, who hadn't moved. With his free hand, he took the plastic bottle out of his jacket pocket and handed it up to Seth.

Then he looked at the rushing river again and got a bad feeling. The feeling said this was a mistake. That he was right in the very act of doing something he should have known better than to do.

At that exact moment, Seth let out a gasp, followed by, 'Oh, *shit!*'

August yanked hard on the jeans and the boy came tumbling back toward him, and they rolled a few feet back away from the river and then came to a stop, partly tangled. August's heart pounded like it might break loose, and he grabbed Seth's shirt as if to assure himself that he had the boy, and Seth could not get away.

'What just happened, Seth?'

Seth stared at his own hands and said nothing at all.

August looked down at the hands. They were empty.

'I dropped it, August.'

August breathed deeply for the first time in a long time.

'Oh, hell, Seth. Is that all? You scared the crap out of me.'

'August. I dropped it. Phillip's bottle. It's gone.'

'So? The plan was to put it into the river. And you did.'

'But not the whole bottle. You wanted to put him other places, too.'

'Well, now he's on his way down the river. So he's going all kinds of places, isn't he? Places we never could have thought of. He's on a big tour of Yellowstone, right now.'

'You're just saying that to make me feel better.'

'I'm not, actually. Come on. Let's get off this rock. Let's go get your brother.'

Seth stared forlornly out the window for most of the drive back to camp.

Finally he spoke up.

'You were right, August. I'm sorry.'

'What was I right about?'

'You said we shouldn't do it. It was too dangerous. You said something bad might happen. And you were right. And it's all my fault.'

'Seth, nothing bad happened. We're all fine. It was a plastic bottle. With about half a cup of the ashes of my son, the rest of which are safe at home. When I heard you scream, I thought you were falling. It was a *bottle*, Seth. You're a living, breathing kid. When I said something bad could happen, I meant to *you*. Not to the bottle. You're safe, so nothing went wrong.'

'I know you're just saying that to make me feel better.'

'Seth, you have to let it go.'

Seth turned his face to August and fixed him with a scorching stare.

'People say that to me all the time. And I have no idea what they're talking about at all.'

'I know,' August said. 'I'm sorry.'

*

Later that night they lay in their respective beds, August staring at the ceiling. In time he could hear Henry's sleep breathing, something like a light shadow of a snore. But so far as he could tell, Seth was still awake.

'August?' Seth said after a time.

And August was not surprised.

'What is it, Seth?'

'If you don't want to take us back to San Diego with you now, I understand.'

'Oh, Seth. I wish you wouldn't say things like that.'

'Why not?'

'Because . . . of course I'm going to still take you with me. I would never change my mind about you because you accidentally dropped something.'

'But you told me it wasn't safe.'

August sighed deeply. There was a wall inside Seth, and he had hit it again. He could never seem to get over, under, or around it. And it hardly seemed ready to crack. No matter how many times he told that boy to take it easy on himself, it was something like talking to the wind.

'Let me tell you a little story about Phillip,' he said.

'OK.'

'He was a first class thrill-seeker. I remember one time we saw this documentary about people who've gone over Niagara Falls in a barrel. At first, it was like a suicide mission. In the early days of barrels. But lately they've been making them tougher. Anyway, a lot of people still die. It's just about one of the most dangerous things in the world a person can do.'

'Don't tell me he wanted to do it.'

'Yes and no. I think he knew better than to actually try. But he was just so fascinated by it. I know he would have done it in a heartbeat if he could somehow have been sure he'd survive.'

'I'm not sure why you're telling me.'

'Think about it. What could be a more fitting tribute? You put some of his ashes in the equivalent of a barrel and sent them over two very high waterfalls. It's perfect. It's more perfect than anything I could ever have thought of.'

'You're not just saying that to make me feel better?'

'I think it was perfect.'

'Thanks, August. I do feel a little better now.'

August lay awake for a few more minutes, pondering his tall tale. Phillip had never been a thrill-seeker. They had never watched a documentary about Niagara Falls and barrels. Nor had the idea ever been discussed.

But it had been worth it to say so. Because in just a matter of minutes, Seth was snoring peacefully.

And August slept well, too.

Part Two

Late August

1
Sad Good News

They stepped out into the warm sun at a parking lot in Arches National Park. Walked down a flat path to an area from which they could view the famous Delicate Arch at a distance.

'How much more time left to our vacation, August?' Seth asked as they walked.

He asked once or twice a week, and never seemed to remember from one asking to the next. Or maybe he just liked to hear it spoken out loud.

'About two weeks. Thirteen days until we head back. A couple more until we get there. There it is. See it up there?'

August pointed up to a cliff-like slope of sandy-colored Utah red rock. There it stood in the distance, a perfect free-standing, flat-topped arch. Just about everybody August knew had at least seen a picture of Delicate Arch. Except Seth and Henry.

'Oooh, nice,' Seth said, and zoomed in for a shot

with August's camera. 'Too bad we can't get closer up.'

'We can. We're about to hike up there. I told you that. You don't remember?'

'Hmm,' Seth said. 'Maybe I was thinking about something else.'

'*I* remember,' Henry said. Since the beginning of summer his voice had gradually morphed into that of a fairly confident cartoon mouse.

'Great,' Seth said. 'He finally gets to talking again and he mostly uses it to make me look bad.'

'This is kind of steep,' Henry said.

They were making their way up a slickrock slope, following the stacked rock cairns marking the trail. There's really no other way to mark a trail over slickrock. Except blue paint blazes. Which August was glad the park service hadn't chosen.

'You want a ride?' August asked.

'No. I'm OK. I just want you guys to slow down a little.'

They all stopped, and Henry leaned on his own knees and breathed for a minute. Then he straightened up again.

'OK. That's good. Let's walk some more.'

They started uphill again.

'What did you say they called those stacks of rocks again, August?' Seth asked.

'*Cairns*,' Henry said. Before August even could.

'Right,' August said.

'There he goes again,' Seth said. 'I wonder why they call them that.'

'No idea,' August said. 'Some people call them ducks.'

'Even weirder. But maybe that was because they looked like ducks to somebody.'

'Maybe.'

'They don't look very much like ducks to me,' Henry said.

They all three stopped to lean and breathe again, but even more briefly this time.

'Will you take a picture of Henry and me in front of the arch, August?'

'Sure I will.'

'Good. I want my friends from school to see we were there. After Christmas, that is.'

'You know, Henry,' August said when they began to climb again, 'you've gotten to be a darn good little hiker.'

'I know,' Henry said. 'I think so, too.'

They pulled into an RV park in Moab around lunchtime.

Seth dumped the tanks while August fed Woody and hooked up the water and electricity. Then he checked his cell-phone messages.

'Another message from your dad,' he told Henry, who frowned at the news.

'Seth!' Henry called through the window. 'Dad called again!'

'So what?' Seth called back in. 'I didn't care the first ten times, either.'

'Did he really call eleven times?' Henry asked August, more quietly.

'No. Five or six, maybe. Seven, tops.'

After lunch they took a walk on a high dirt berm, almost a levee, that ran along a canal that let off into the Colorado River on the other end of the campground.

Seth had Woody's leash, and August decided he should probably listen to the phone message. In case Wes was getting desperate. In case he was about to put out an all-points bulletin. Report August for stealing his children.

He dropped a few paces behind the boys and called his voicemail.

'August,' the message began. 'Seth. Henry. OK, part of me gets it. You don't want to talk to me. But I have some news, and you'll like it. It's good news and nobody'll call me. Do you have any idea how hard it is to talk my way into the office to make a non-collect call? How many times do you think I can do this? And it's good news. Did I say that already? And I worked damn hard on it and this is getting frustrating, so no matter how much you hate me right now, could somebody *please call me back and hear my good news?*' Wes's voice rose to almost shouting by the end of the sentence.

Then a click.

No goodbye.

The message had been left earlier that morning. Which meant that, even though August wasn't entirely sure what day of the week it was, it was definitely one of the days he could call Wes back.

'Your dad says he has good news,' he called to the boys.

Henry kept walking. Seth stopped and spun almost defensively. It had definitely caught him off guard. Then he talked over his caring again.

'So what? Who cares? How good could it be? I bet he's just saying that to get us to call. I bet he's lying. Maybe he's always lying.'

August caught up with the boys, and Henry slipped a hand into August's hand.

'I think we should at least hear what it is.'

'Will *you* call him, August?'

'Yeah. OK.'

They reached the corner where the canal met the Colorado River. To their left, a highway bridge spanned the river, with an impressive wall of red rock behind it. They sat in the dirt on the berm.

'Look,' Seth said, pointing up at the rock face. 'That's going to be an arch, isn't it, August?'

August looked up to see what looked like an arched doorway protruding from the rock. Yes, that's how they began, all right.

'Someday,' he said. 'But those things take a lot of time.'

He punched number five for the jail, which was now on speed dial. He read the person who answered both Wes's name and inmate number It didn't take Wes long to come on the line. It surprised August, who pictured him running down a prison hallway to grab up the phone.

'Seth?'

'No, Wes. It's me. August.'

'Oh.' If Wes was trying to hide his disappointment, he wasn't doing well. 'Look. I know Seth has a very well-developed sense of right and wrong. But . . . he has to talk to me sometime.'

August covered the mouthpiece of the phone with the heel of one hand. 'He says you have to talk to him sometime,' he told Seth.

Seth snorted derisively.

'No comment on that at the moment,' August said into the phone. 'But in the long run I tend to agree with you. I'm sure you can understand why we're not your biggest fans right now. I mean . . . what did you think you were doing, Wes?'

A long silence. Knowing what he knew about Wes, August was half prepared to find that Wes had hung up the phone and gone.

'I didn't think you'd take 'em if you knew it only solved half the problem.'

'You got that right.'

'Look. You want to hear the good news or don't you?'

'I do. Actually.'

'I'll be there when you come back through. I'll be home September third.'

August held still, watching the river flow and absorbing the news. He'd been primed for something good.

But it didn't feel good. It hit his gut hard. A distinct loss. He'd completely adjusted to the idea that the boys were with him nearly until Christmas.

At his left side, he could feel them straining to listen to the other side of the conversation, which they could not possibly hear from where they sat.

'You're not saying anything,' Wes said.

'How did you manage that?'

'It wasn't easy. But I got 'em to let me do the second half of my time at home. You know. With one of those ankle-monitor things. The first two times I put in for it they turned me down. But I just kept at it. You know. Letting 'em know it was for the kids. Not for me. That I had nobody to watch 'em after the first week of September.'

'I don't suppose you told them you knew exactly how much child care you did and did not have going in.'

'Well, no. Couldn't very well tell 'em that. I told 'em you had something come up that you had to bring the kids back early.'

'So you lied to them, too.'

'Listen. August. You really gonna bust my . . . chops? When I finally got this thing worked out?'

'No, I guess not. I'll tell them.'

'That's it? I don't even get to talk to my boys?'

August put his hand over the mouthpiece again. 'You guys want to talk to him?'

They both shook their heads vehemently.

'When they're ready,' August told Wes. 'Right now they say they're not.'

'Shit,' Wes said. And hung up on him. It was a conversation-ender to which August had almost become accustomed.

He looked over at the boys.

'*Was* it good news?' Seth asked.

'Um. Yeah. It was.' But August noticed that he didn't sound all that convincing. 'He's going to be home when he first said he would. At the end of the summer. He's going to be on house arrest. You know. With an ankle monitor. He won't be able to leave the house. But he'll be there anytime after the third of next month.'

They all stared at the pull of the river in silence for a moment or two.

Then Seth said, 'In thirteen days?'

'More or less.'

'In thirteen days we won't ever see you again?'

'Oh, sure you will. We'll see each other again.'

'But we don't get to go back to San Diego with you at all?'

'Guess not.' He looked at Henry, who refused to meet his eyes. For the first time in a long time. 'What about you, Henry? What do you think of all this?'

Henry only shrugged.

It jolted August in a place in his gut. Because Henry had been talking to him for quite a while now. Long enough that August was used to it, and not expecting it to go away again.

'Hey. Henry. You in there? Talk to me.'

Henry continued to look away.

'We haven't lost you again, have we, buddy?'

Henry only shrugged.

August took a few deep breaths, trying to breathe around an uncomfortable obstruction in his gut. As if he'd swallowed something whole that remained undigested.

'You guys take Woody back to the motorhome, OK? I need to make one more phone call.'

The boys got up, brushed off the seats of their shorts, and scuffed away without comment.

August dialed his sponsor, Harvey.

'You must be having a good time out there,' Harvey said, skipping 'hello' as usual. 'Because when you're having a bad time, you call.'

'Well, I'm busted then, Harv. Because we were having a good time until just now.'

'The story of my life,' Harvey said.

August filled him in on the sudden news. 'I don't know what to do,' he said. As a sort of wrap-up.

'What do you mean you don't know what to do?'

'I thought it was self-explanatory.'

'There's only one thing you *can* do. Give the kids back and go home. Get on with your life.'

'But I'm not sure they want to be there,' August said, in what skirted embarrassingly close to a whiny tone. 'I'm not even sure if they're safe there.'

'Doesn't matter, August. He's their father.'

'He's also a practicing alcoholic.'

'Indeed. Imagine if that was all it took to get kids away from their parents. Where would we have been in our drinking days, eh? Lots of parents drink. Some of them way too much. But they mostly get to keep the kids.'

'Every word out of his mouth is a lie, Harvey.'

'Which also does not relieve him of custody.'

'Shit, Harv.'

'Yeah. You're right. I agree with you, August. It's shitty. It's one of those things in life you wish would be some other way. But it's not some other way. Is it? You're a smart guy, so I suspect you know what I'm going to say next. What am I going to say next?'

August squeezed his eyes closed.

'I expect you're going to say that those boys have their own higher power looking out for them. And that I'm not it.'

'I'm relieved to know you occasionally pay attention,' Harvey said.

'What would you think about an intervention? You know. The boys and me. Before I leave them alone there.'

'Sure,' Harvey said. 'Good idea. Knock yourself out. That and two-fifty will buy Wes his next bottle of beer.'

At sunset they stood at the railing at Dead Horse Point, in a state park of the same name adjacent to Canyon-lands, just across the highway from Arches, and an easy drive from the campground.

The Colorado River snaked hundreds of feet below, flowing straight toward the spot where they stood, then bending away again in a horseshoe turn. The river had carved itself a red-rock canyon, leaving a teardrop-shaped mesa of colorful, striated rock above the horseshoe. The late sun hit the water at a slant, making it glow a flat gold.

Henry hadn't said a word all day. Seth had said maybe ten.

'This is one of the prettiest things we've seen on the whole trip,' Seth said, lining up a photo. 'And that's saying a lot. Because we've seen some amazing stuff. I don't like the name, though. Why do they call it Dead Horse Point?'

'You're better off not knowing. It's not a happy story.'

'But you know it?'

'It's on that sign over there. But I don't recommend it. There are actual dead horses involved. It's depressing.'

They stared in silence for a moment or two, the sun blinking off the water. In a minute it would disappear behind the red mesas.

'I hate things that are sad, August.'

'I know you do, buddy.'

'It's sad that you live so far away from us.'

'I figured that was what you meant. But you can call me. I'll leave you with my number. You can call me collect. Anytime. If you need help. Or even if you just want to talk.'

'And if our dad has to go to jail again, can we come stay with you?'

'Of course you can.'

As they headed back to the motorhome, Seth said, 'Remember when you told me that if anything would stop my dad drinking it might be me telling him the truth about how it hurts us when he does?'

'Yeah. I do remember. And I'm way ahead of you on that, buddy. I've already talked to my sponsor about doing an intervention.'

'Oh. Yeah. I know about those. I saw them on TV. What's a sponsor?'

'A person in the program who has more time sober. Who helps you with the one-on-one stuff.'

'Maybe you could be my dad's sponsor.'

'Not a good idea, Seth. First of all, your sponsor is supposed to be completely on your side. And I'm really not on your dad's side. I'm on your and Henry's side. And he knows it.'

They walked in silence for a minute more.

'What's the other thing?' Seth asked.

'Other thing?'

'The thing that's not first of all.'

'You have to be sober to have a sponsor. Sponsorship is a relationship between two sober people. You can't sponsor someone who's drinking. It just doesn't work. Sponsorship is help staying sober. And your dad's not sober. And even though I'm totally willing to do this thing with you and support you, I need you to understand that it usually doesn't work.'

'I know,' Seth said.

'Just be prepared for that.'

'I am,' Seth said.

Henry said nothing at all.

2
Stay Found

The meeting place consisted of a long silver travel trailer, maybe thirty feet, parked on a dirt lot. There were only four cars parked. Well. Two cars and two pickup trucks.

August and Seth crossed the lot together in the light dusk, the toes of their shoes scuffing in the reddish dirt. A thin buff-colored dog wiggled out to greet them, his friendliness tentative and nearly excruciating. His tail beat a rhythm between his hind legs. Seth bent down to pet him, and the dog gazed up into the boy's face as if he had never been so in love.

August looked over his shoulder to see Woody wagging and rearing at the back door of the motor-home. Clearly jealous. August didn't mention it, because he didn't want Seth to feel guilty.

But a moment later Woody began to whine and scratch at the door.

'We should go in,' August said, placing one hand on Seth's shoulder. 'Before Henry wakes up.'

'Why would Henry wake up?'

'Never mind. Let's just go in.'

They walked two steps together, then Seth planted his feet in a dead halt.

'I'm worried, August,' he said.

'About what?'

'You said this is the Navajo Nation.'

'Yeah . . .'

'I just . . .' But he never said just what.

'Look. Seth. It's normal to be afraid of what you don't know, but—'

'No, it's not that, August. I'll like 'em fine, I know I will. It's more whether they'll like me. It's just that . . . this is their country. Sort of. This reservation. It's their land. What if they don't want us here?'

'It's an AA meeting, Seth. That crosses all kinds of boundaries. Tell you what. Let's go meet them and see if we're welcome. I'd be willing to bet money we will be.'

'OK,' Seth said.

And they walked again.

Seth hung back slightly as August held the trailer door wide. Inside were two Native American men, one in his fifties, the other quite old, a Caucasian man, and an older Native woman.

'Evening,' he said, when they all turned to look.

'Well, I'll be damned,' the younger Native man said. 'Visitors.'

'Is that OK?' August asked, infected with a tiny bit of Seth's issue, the worry over not being welcome.

'OK? It's great. Only happens every once or twice a year. Rest of the time it's just us. C'mon in. Who's your friend here?'

'I'm August,' he said, stepping in. He reached back and took Seth gently by the shoulder, pulling him inside. 'This is my friend Seth.'

'I'm Emory,' the fifty-something Native man said. 'This is Jack and Dora. And this is my father, Kenneth. You both here for an AA meeting?'

'Seth's not an alcoholic,' August said. 'But he's interested in meetings, because his father drinks. I couldn't see online if this was an open meeting or not, and nobody at the AA info line could tell me.'

The old man, Kenneth, pulled at his wrinkled chin. 'Now, let's see. Never had to decide that, because we all are, and so it never came up. What say we take a real fast group conscience? All in favor of Seth at our meeting?'

All four members raised one hand without hesitation.

'Done.'

August looked down at Seth, who seemed relieved.

'See? Told you we'd be welcome.'

'Did he think we'd keep him out because he's not an alcoholic?' Dora asked.

August was about to answer when Seth beat him to it.

'No, ma'am,' he said. 'I just thought . . . I mean, this

is your country. August told me this is a sovereign nation. So I thought maybe we had no right to come here. Well. I guess we can drive down the road. But I wasn't sure if you'd want us to stop for a visit.'

'The US is a sovereign nation,' the white man, Jack, said. 'Right?'

'Guess so,' Seth said. 'Yeah.'

'You mind when people from other countries come for a visit?'

'Oh,' Seth said. 'Yeah. I get your point. OK, good. Because August said he really needs a meeting. And I got some stuff to get off my chest, too.'

'Most of the time he's a pretty good dad,' Seth said. August noticed Seth's hands were shaking. 'And even when he drinks. He's not mean. He doesn't hit us. Once he swatted Henry on his . . . you know . . . behind. But that's the worst he ever hit us. And during the day he talks to us, and he makes sure we eat. But then when he gets off working at seven or eight, he just disappears. Sometimes he comes in real late, drunk. Never makes any trouble for us or anything. Just goes to bed. But lots of times he doesn't come home at all. Now it's not so bad. Because I'm twelve. You know. Big enough to babysit. But when I was seven and Henry was two, it was scary. You know. When he didn't come home at all.'

Seth's words dried up briefly. He looked around at the faces. Licked his lips. The group waited in rapt attention. Trusted him to continue.

'Before that it was OK because our mom was there. That's when she left. When I was seven and Henry was two. I still don't know why. My dad would never tell us. I don't know if she had some other guy or if there was something she wanted real bad to do with her life. I just know there was something, and it was more important than us. So . . .'

He froze again for a long time. August could see something moving and changing in Seth's face, and in his eyes.

'That's what I should tell him! I just figured out what I should tell him when we do our intervention. That when your mom leaves because you're not important enough to stay for, you need your dad to stick around. And I know he'll say he did. That he stays with us every day and takes care of us. But every night he leaves us alone, because the drinking is more important. Yeah. So it's not my imagination. Your kids are supposed to be the most important thing. But we had to go to a child services group home thing because he put drinking first, which . . . I guess I can see he didn't know that would happen. But then . . . even then, he didn't stop. He didn't stop drinking and he didn't stop driving after he drinks. So it's just like what mom did. He was supposed to put us first but he didn't. And it makes us feel terrible. And I think that's what I should tell him when we have our intervention.'

Seth looked around again at the faces. Every head nodded. August could feel himself nod. Even though you were supposed to just listen when someone was sharing. But it was impossible not to nod.

'I'm scared about that,' Seth said. 'Not even that he won't stop drinking. I mean, that's no worse than what we've already got. It's . . . wait. I don't know what it is. Or do I? I feel like I'm about to say what it is even though I don't even know, and then it'll be like I'll hear it from myself for the first time. Or maybe I do know. Yeah. I'm scared because if he doesn't quit drinking it'll be my fault. Because the only thing that could help is if I tell him how his drinking makes me feel, and I'm really good, and the words are just right. And maybe I won't be good, and then it'll be my fault it doesn't work.'

Seth stalled again. August could hear the boy's breathing from a couple of feet away. As though this had been a hard physical slog. Not just a hard emotional one.

'I wish we could just stay with August,' Seth said. It seemed to burst out of him all at once. Then he glanced around as if trying to identify where the words had come from. 'Did I just say that out loud? Why did I say that? I never should have. I'm sorry. He's my dad. I love him. It's not that I don't love him. I really do. And I know I need to stick with him and try to help him. And I'd miss him. I know I would. I'd miss him and I'd miss home. I don't even really know why I said that. Well . . . yeah, I sort of do. It's just different with August. Not like he's perfect. But like you know what's going to happen next, and it makes sense. And even when it doesn't work like that, I can just say so to him . . .

and then we talk about it and then things make sense again. I talk to my dad all the time but nothing ever changes. It's like everything I say just sort of bounces off him. But when August and I talk, stuff actually gets worked out. And it's such a relief.'

Seth paused again. August stole a glance at his watch. It was 9.32. Seth was talking over the end of the meeting. No one seemed about to stop him.

'But I know I have to go back,' Seth said. 'I'm sorry for everything I said. Maybe I shouldn't have shared at all. I'm done now.'

'I'm Emory and I'm an alcoholic,' Emory said.

The group said, 'Hi, Emory.' Including Seth.

'I'm going to bend a rule and tell you something straight, son. We're not supposed to crosstalk. And that's not just interrupting someone. It's speaking right to their situation. We're supposed to stick to our own story in meetings, but I'm going to push that rule some. Son, don't you ever be sorry for saying what's really true, especially not in a room like this, that's just made for that. The way you feel is the way you feel, and no matter how much you think you should feel some other way, you can't change that. There's some things in this life you can change and some you can't. I'm sure August tells you the same thing. Here's what you do when the time comes to talk to your dad. Here's what I do. I say to my creator, "I'm about to open my mouth here. And, historically, that's been a dicey thing, as we both know. So some help is in order. So let me know what you want me to say to this person in this situation. Say it through me." So that's my advice to you where your dad is concerned. Whatever you believe in, whatever you can pray to in this big world, say to it, "What would you have me say to my father?" If you do that, the words'll be right. And if the words are right, you did what you could. If he doesn't shape up after that, it's none of your doing. That's out of your control, and don't take it on yourself.'

He paused for a big breath, and as he did, Dora spoke up.

'Emory. We're over time.'

'I know it,' Emory said. 'I know we are. But that felt important.'

Chair legs squeaked over tired old linoleum as each member pushed his or her chair back away from the table and stood. They formed a tight circle around the table and took each other's hands. August held the hand of Seth and Dora, Seth held hands with August and Emory.

They recited the serenity prayer together.

August was surprised to hear that Seth knew it by heart. After all, it was only his second meeting.

Then they broke the circle for the night.

'Glad you came,' Emory said, clapping August on the shoulder. 'Come visit us again if you're ever driving through.'

'That could happen,' August said.

'I like that boy,' Emory said, pointing with his chin to Seth, who was outside the open trailer door petting the sweet buff-colored dog.

'I like him, too,' August said. 'He deserves better.'

'It's his path.'

'You sound just like my sponsor.'

'How long has your sponsor been sober?'

'Twenty-two years.'

'I been sober thirty-six. Thirty-six years. I'm not saying I know it all. In one way, we've all just got the time since we got up this morning. But I've seen a lot of people walk a lot of roads. Some not so happy. And it makes them what they are. So if you run around putting a pillow under people to cushion their fall . . . well, I'm just not sure it's quite the favor we think it is.'

They stood quietly a moment, looking out the door at Seth and the dog. Then August's eyes landed on the rig, parked in the distance. The dome light was on inside the cab. It took August's tired brain a minute to figure out what that could mean. Only one thing, really. It meant one of the cab doors was standing open.

'Excuse me,' he said. 'I have to go check on Henry.'

He crossed the parking lot at a dead run. Seth called some question to him as he streaked by, but he couldn't make it out, and didn't stop to clarify.

All looked normal on the driver's side, which was all he could see from that angle. He ran around the back of the rig. The passenger door was standing wide open. His mind cold and blank, August thrust his upper body into the rig.

'Henry? Woody?'

No Henry. No Woody.

Henry and Woody were gone.

*

Three white SUVs parked in the dirt surrounding the rig, each marked with the Navajo Nation Police insignia, their light bars spinning. August wished the lights would stop. The state of emergency it raised in his head and gut was making it hard to stay inside his own skin.

One brown-uniformed officer examined August's passenger door by flashlight for a long time. Too long. A ridiculous length of time. Or maybe it was only a few seconds and the ability to gauge time had completely abandoned August.

'I'm not seeing any forced entry,' the officer said at last.

'So you think he opened the door.'

'You have an alarm system in this rig?'

'I do, yes.'

'Was it on?'

'Yeah, anytime I lock up with the key it's on.'

'Then yeah, I think he opened the door. Was he upset? Any reason he would want to run away?'

August exchanged a panicky glance with Seth, who he'd almost forgotten was standing near his right side. Seth returned the glance but said nothing.

'Potentially. Yes. But I really can't see him just walking off into that dark night by himself. No lights, no buildings, no place to hide. I can't see him making a decision to bring that on himself. He's kind of a jumpy little guy.'

Seth tugged at his sleeve. Lightly. As if trying to get

August's attention while not existing at all. Both at the same time.

'In a minute, Seth. So here's another scenario we haven't considered. Maybe he was taken by somebody who tricked him into opening the door.'

The officer scratched his head. 'Don't really want to rule out anything at this point. But you were right in that trailer where they have the meetings, right?'

'Yeah . . .'

'Wouldn't the dog have barked if a stranger came up to the rig?'

'Oh. Yeah. Definitely. Well, that's good, then. That's good if nobody took him. I think. I guess. Except it means he's out there by himself . . .'

August fell silent for a moment, and in that slight pause, a chorus of coyote howls split the air. Split August. Right down the same line in his chest where the pain always split him. It seemed unfair. The world was always conspiring to take advantage of that deep flaw in him.

'You have coyotes out here?'

'Oh, yeah,' the officer said. As if it should have gone without saying. Which was possible.

'How much of a danger are they to the boy?'

The officer sighed deeply. 'I'd worry more about the dog,' he said.

August's head swam, and he straightened his knees against the sense that they were melting.

'I have a flashlight in the motorhome,' August said. 'Just tell me which way to go. Tell me which direction doesn't already have police searching on it.'

'Sir. I really think it's best if you and your other boy just sit inside and wait.'

The panic surged inside August at the idea that he would be stripped of all distractions that might help him outrun the panic.

'Why shouldn't we look? Isn't more people looking better?'

'Sir. No offense against you personally, but . . . if you don't know this land . . . and you don't . . . we got enough to do looking for your boy. We don't want to have to call a search for the two of you as well. You just stay found for now, and let us see what we can do about the little one.'

'August,' Seth hissed, the minute they got inside the motorhome.

'What, Seth?'

'Henry ran away from the county place. A bunch of times.'

'Oh, geez, Seth. Why didn't you tell me that before?'

'I tried! I really did. But you told me to wait. And I wanted to whisper it to you. I didn't want to just yell it out. I wasn't sure what I should say in front of the cop. I didn't know what to do, August. Don't get mad at me. Please. When I'm scared and people get mad at me I feel like I'm gonna explode or something. Fall apart.'

August calmed his own panic with a deep sigh. Then

he pulled Seth in for a hug. The boy remained tightly wound in his arms.

'I didn't mean to seem mad, Seth. I'm sorry. Nothing that happened tonight was your fault. This is all my fault.'

'Isn't it Henry's fault?' Seth mumbled against August's chest. 'He's the one who took off.'

August tried the idea on, but it slid away again.

'No. It's my fault. Henry is seven. I'm in charge of taking care of him. I have to take responsibility for this. Let me just go tell the officer what you told me.'

Seth pulled out of the hug. Awkwardly, it seemed. As though he wasn't sure he knew how.

August paused at the back door to be sure Woody wouldn't push through the door with him. Then he remembered, and his heart sank.

He tried to take back the numbness again. He was only partially successful. He climbed down, leaving the back door flapping wide open, because there was no reason to close it.

'Sir?' he called out, scuffing through the red dirt.

The officer stood at the open door of his white SUV, talking on a two-way radio.

'Yeah?'

'Turns out I didn't give you the best information. The boy has more of a history of running away than I knew.'

'OK.'

'I just thought I should tell you.'

'OK.'

'You know. So we know what we're dealing with.'

'Oh. Got it. To be frank, we been treating this as a runaway all along. So this doesn't change the thinking much. You go wait in the rig. We'll let you know what we find.'

3
One Real Good Dog

'You OK, August?' Seth asked suddenly, startling him.

He sat up on his unmade bed. Blinked into the light.

'Yeah. I guess.'

'It kind of freaks me out how you've just been lying still for like an hour with your hands over your face. Could you . . . I don't know . . . talk to me or something?'

August looked around the inside of the rig for reasons he couldn't pin down.

'Has it really been an hour?'

'Pretty much. I think he'll turn up, August. He always did before.'

'This is not exactly the same kind of landscape he was lost on before.'

'Oh.'

A long silence. August was trying hard to keep the inside of his head and gut still. He felt an overall sense of heavy, sickening dread, but it was surprisingly low-level. He knew if he jostled it he'd be in for an unpleasant surprise.

'Or *I* could talk,' Seth said. 'But I really need *somebody* to talk. What've you been thinking all this time, August?'

August sighed.

'I was thinking I was too hard on my ex-wife.'

August expected Seth to ask what he meant.

Instead Seth just asked, 'You mean about the accident?'

'Right. That.'

'But somebody got killed. That's big.'

'But what if somebody gets killed tonight, because I left Henry alone while we went to that meeting? Remember how we talked about it? The first time we did it? We said, "We'll just be right in there. We can see him and hear him from here. And Woody is here to bark. And there's an alarm." And all that time what we were saying is that we knew something *could* happen, but we figured the chances were pretty slim that it *would*. And how many times do we do that every day of our damn lives? We take all these little calculated risks. All the time. Nine hundred and ninety-nine times out of a thousand nothing goes wrong. And the one time it does, we blame the person who took the risk, tell them they should have known better than to ever do such a thing. Which I'm not saying is wrong, but we know *we* take risks, too. Maybe we even blame them more because we want to pretend it never could have happened to us. But of course it could have. We make life-and-death decisions every day. The odds are just really good on most of them. But if something goes wrong, we're still responsible. And we don't get to do it over, either.'

'But she drove while she was drinking, August. That's so big.'

'Under the legal limit. I'm not saying it was OK, Seth. I don't know what I'm saying. Yes, I do. I think. I drove when I'd been drinking, too. But I never got into an accident. And now who the hell am I to act like I'm better than her because she was sitting at a red light when someone ran it? And I wasn't? That's luck. That's not to my credit. We're responsible for everything. Everything we do. Not just when it backfires on us.'

A silence.

Then Seth said, 'This is making my brain hurt, August.'

'Sorry.'

'It's OK. I'm the one who said you should talk to me about anything. It's my fault too he took off.'

'No, it isn't.'

'But you said we're responsible for everything we do. And I was the one who said it would be OK to leave him alone in here.'

'I'm still the adult.'

'But I'm supposed to look after my brother. So how can it be your fault but not mine? What's the difference?'

'The difference . . . Seth . . . is that you already think everything is your fault. You try to hold the whole world on your shoulders. I need to step up a little. You need to dial it back.'

A knock on the door startled them both.

'It's just Emory,' the familiar voice said.

August bolted to the back door and swung it open so hard that Emory had to jump out of the way.

'Sorry,' August said.

'No worries. Look. I've been doing a little poking around with the police but I think I'm going to head on home now. Hope that's OK. I got work in the morning.'

'Oh. Yeah, of course. I didn't even know you were searching.'

'Well, I wanted to do what I could. But I really think the police have it covered.' He turned his head and looked off to the horizon in the moonlight. 'They're good at what they do. They got a grid thing worked out . . .' Then he tailed off again. Just as August was beginning to wonder what he was looking at, Emory said, 'Is your dog about so big?'

He held his two hands, one above the other, in an approximation of a dog about Woody's size.

'Yeah. Why?'

'That him right there?'

August stepped out into the moonlight, and looked where Emory pointed. About a hundred feet away he just barely made out Woody, at a dead run in their direction. Stretched out, running so hard and so flattened that he appeared closer to the ground than he ever had before. His hugely extended tongue flapped out of his mouth on one side.

'Woody! Seth, come see! Woody's back!'

As Seth stepped off the bottom step into the dirt, Woody hit August. Literally. Took off from the ground a few feet away and slammed against August's chest, landing in his arms. August could feel the little dog's labored breathing. And the pounding of his heart.

For a moment he worried that Woody's heart might explode.

'August, why did he leave Henry?'

'I have no idea,' August said.

But before he could even finish the reply, Woody was back in the dirt. Apparently the name Henry, spoken out loud, set him back into motion. He ran a few yards away, back into the open landscape. In the direction from which he'd just come. Then he stopped. Looked over his shoulder, his tongue still lolling ridiculously from one side of his mouth, flipping sweat. He ran back to August and whined desperately.

'I think you need to see where he's trying to take you,' Emory said.

August looked around. There were still police vehicles parked in the dirt. But no policemen. They were all out sorting a grid.

'I was thinking that, too. But the policeman told me I had to stay put. So they wouldn't end up having to send out a search party for *me*. Because I don't know the land.'

'I know the land,' Emory said.

'But you have work in the morning.'

'Guess I'll be tired, then.'

August resisted the urge to bear hug the man. He wasn't quite sure how that would be received.

'Seth, you wait here.'

'I want to go, August.'

'I know, son,' Emory said. 'I understand. But I think you should stay here, just on the off chance he comes wandering back.'

Seth's shoulders slumped.

'I guess,' he said. 'Yeah.'

Emory's flashlight provided just enough illumination to see the footing of each next step. To make sure they weren't about to trip over rocks, or low vegetation. Every now and then Emory had to raise the beam to see Woody, who was always ten or twenty feet ahead of them, tongue hanging out straight now, waiting impatiently.

It struck August how incredibly easy it would be to get his sense of direction completely turned around out here in the dark, without being able to look up and see landmarks of any kind. He wondered if even Emory had a good enough grasp of their direction of travel to get them back to the rig again.

Then he wondered how a seven-year-old was supposed to find his way, but he swallowed the lump in his throat – and whatever else was trying to push up behind it – and tried to shake the thought away again.

'This is a long way for a boy of seven to come,' Emory said after a couple of miles. 'You sure he could even get this far on his own steam?'

'Definitely. Henry's a great hiker. We've been train-
ing all summer.'

'Ah,' Emory said. 'Just our luck.'

They picked their way along in silence for another
half hour or so. Then Emory said, 'Aha.'

August looked around, but saw nothing in the darkness.

'Aha what?'

'Dog's taking us to a house. Walt and Velma Begay's
house, to be exact.'

'I don't even see a house.'

'There.'

He shone the light, but it didn't reach quite as far as
the house. But it served as a pointer, and August saw
the dark shape of a modest, blocky stone home. There
were no lights on. No sign that anybody was inside.

'What's that scratching noise?' August asked.

'I think the dog is scratching on the door.'

They walked up on to the porch in the weakening
flashlight beam. Woody was indeed scratching at the
wooden door. With both front paws, as if digging.

'Woody, stop,' August said, worried that he would
mar Walt and Velma Begay's front door. Woody responded by jumping into August's arms.

Emory knocked. There was no movement in the
house. No reply.

'Lemme go look in the carport,' Emory said, and
took the weak beam of light away.

August sank down into a sit on their front stoop,
holding Woody in his arms. A chorus of coyote yips

and barks split the night again, morphing into spooky howls, and August tightened his grip on the dog, who shivered once.

A few minutes later Emory came back and sat beside him on the stoop, turning off the flashlight. To save batteries, August assumed.

'They're not home,' Emory said.

'I can't imagine Woody would lead us here for no reason.'

'Especially with that scratching on the door and all. I looked through the windows as best I could, but it's all locked up and no sign anyone's in there. Maybe the boy was here but he's not here now.'

'Where would he be if that was the case?'

'Well, if we're having a lucky night, they might've run him down to the police station. See who he belongs to.'

'I hope we're having a lucky night.'

'You and me both, my friend.'

In that dark moment, it struck August as strangely right to be referred to as Emory's friend. That was really how he felt. All things being what they were.

Emory pulled out a cigarette and lit it with a paper match. August caught a whiff of the smell of its smoke as it wafted past him. It woke things up in him that he would have preferred to leave sleeping.

'I haven't smoked in sixteen years,' August said, 'but you have no idea how tempting that smells.'

'Want one?'

'Yes. But no. Don't give me one. I couldn't bear to

have to quit all over again. I quit smoking more times than anybody I know. Twenty times, maybe. Maybe twenty-five. I think the reason it finally stuck is because I just couldn't bear to do it all over again. Just, when you lit that, it hit me all at once how it would feel to smoke a cigarette and drink about three glasses of bourbon. That would take the edge off these feelings, all right.'

Emory smoked in silence for a few moments.

Then he said, 'Boy needs you to keep your head together.'

'I know. I wasn't really going to do it. It's just one of those things that goes through your head. No, not even your head, really. It bypasses your head and goes through your gut. I wasn't going to act on it, but . . . I don't know. I sure felt it. You think that's a bad sign?'

'I do,' Emory said.

'Really?'

'Very bad sign. I think it means you're an alcoholic.'

Both men laughed briefly, and then the silence came back to stay.

While it was sitting on them August thought, *Maybe I really was that bad. Maybe I am a real alcoholic. Maybe all that stuff about how I didn't drink quite the way the other people in the meeting did is just one of those things you tell yourself when you don't want to know.*

Emory spoke again, startling him.

'Think he ran away because he doesn't want to go home to his dad?'

'That's a possibility. Yeah.'

'I feel bad for those kids.'

'Me, too. I feel like I should be doing more for them.'

'Like what?'

'Like not making them go back.'

'Not sure you even have that option.'

'That's what my sponsor says.'

'Well, it's the second time your sponsor and I agree, so I'm thinking he's a very wise man and you should listen to him. Don't answer this question off the top of your head, August, and don't answer it out of your emotions. Think like a lawyer for a second. Has their father done enough bad that somebody should go to court and try to strip custody?'

August sat on the question for a moment.

Then he said, 'Probably not.'

'You have any kind of standing to fight him on custody? Are you blood to those kids?'

'No.'

'Then I don't see much point in considering something that's well out of your reach anyway.'

They sat quietly in the pale moonlight for a moment more. August was surprised by how much his eyes had adjusted. He wondered if he and Emory were going back anytime soon. He wondered what their next move was from here.

'It's not so much what's happened so far,' August said. 'It's more what *could* happen.'

'Never heard of somebody losing custody of their kids for what they might be about to do. Or, then again, might not. Look. August. I grew up with an alcoholic dad, too.'

'You did?'

Emory didn't answer. Just waited. As though August would get it on his own in time.

'Oh. Your father. Right. Duh. He was in the meeting.'

'There were some tough times. But, you know what? I grew up. Kids are pretty sturdy. Even when times are tough, mostly they grow up. So maybe something'll happen if they're with their dad. Then again, maybe it won't. I mean, they made it this far. And, not to make you feel bad, but . . . you're sober, and something bad happened tonight. Sometimes stuff just happens, you know? There's not always some simple thing to point to, like if you just don't do this, nothing can go wrong. Something can always go wrong. But we don't like to think that way, so we point a lot.'

They sat silent a moment more.

Then Emory said, 'My advice is give 'em back. Not like you have much choice. And try to trust they'll keep growing up. Just like they did before they met you.' He smashed out his cigarette under the heel of his big boot. 'We'd best be getting back. No point just sitting here.'

'Please tell me you know the way.'

'Sure I do. We're on the road now. Way led us right back to the road. All we got to do is walk right down it a few miles.'

They set off on foot without the help of the flashlight. With his eyes adjusted, August could just see the white stripe marking the center divider of the paved road, and they walked on it, right down the middle of that little highway.

They never saw a car.

August let Woody walk alongside them for a few minutes, but when the dog stopped to sniff by the side of the road, August thought about coyotes again, and scooped him up and carried him.

'If it turns out that boy was ever at Walt and Velma's,' Emory said, 'that's one real good dog you got there.'

When August saw the rig off in the distance, the lights were on inside. Not surprisingly, Seth was awake and waiting up.

There were no police cars.

'Where do you think all the police cars went?' he asked Emory.

'Hmm. Not sure. Could be good. Maybe they got a tip or something.'

A hard knot began to form in August's stomach. The pain and fear of not knowing had seemed so over-whelming. This was the first moment it dawned on him that the pain and fear of finding out could be far worse.

When they were no more than twenty or thirty steps from the motorhome, Woody jumped down and ran to the back door of the rig. And a police SUV appeared over the rise, headed in their direction, red lights silently spinning.

August stopped in the road, and Emory stopped to see why August stopped.

August clutched at the man's arm, because in a distant and numb way he felt like he might tumble.

'Oh, God. They know something.'

It surprised August when words came out of him, because he felt completely immobile. As if made of stone.

Emory put one hand on August's shoulder, clearly understanding how much support was needed.

'Maybe they know something good.'

'It's my fault, Emory. If something happened to that boy, I have to live with it for ever.'

'There's no real negligence here, August. Kids run away. Been doing it since the beginning of time.'

'But this one did it on my watch. How am I going to tell his father?'

'Hold yourself together. Don't write your own ending here before we know. Let's go see what's what.'

They began to put one foot in front of the other again just as a brown-uniformed policeman stepped out of his SUV and opened its back door. That broke through the cold stone and concrete of August, and struck him as a possible good sign.

The policeman turned around to face them in the thin moonlight, clearly holding the shape of a child on his hip.

'Well, well,' Emory said. 'Looks like we get our lucky night after all.'

August ran to them.

'This the young man you lost, sir?' the policeman asked.

Henry reached out for August, and August grabbed

him into his arms. Held him so tightly that it must have been hard for the boy to breathe fully. But he didn't loosen his grip and Henry didn't complain.

'I have no idea how to thank you enough,' August said to the policeman when he could finally breathe and speak.

'These things happen.'

'Where'd you find him?'

'We didn't. Actually. A couple of our local folks found the boy walking and took him home with them. Then they ran him down to the police station to see who might be looking for him. They said to tell you sorry about the dog. They tried to get the dog, but he was worried about them taking the boy, and he wouldn't come. They couldn't catch him.'

'Walt and Velma Begay?'

'Now how on earth did you know that?'

'He knows that,' said Emory, who was suddenly at August's shoulder, 'because he has a real good dog.'

'Thank you so much, officer,' August said. 'I'm so sorry I put you in this position.'

'These things happen,' the man said again.

4
Last Stop

'I'm thinking maybe I should just take you boys straight home,' August said.

It was first thing in the morning. The first words August had spoken. They were still in bed. Still parked on that patch of Navajo Nation dirt, because August had been too entirely exhausted and wrung out to drive again.

Seth sat up fast.

'What? Why?'

'I just don't like the idea that he could take off again. I can't be responsible for that.'

'But we were gonna see that canyon. You said we could take a ride in a four-wheel-drive thing and see cliff houses and cave paintings and stuff. And Spider Rock. Why can't we see Spider Rock? And you said maybe even the Grand Canyon as a last stop. I'll never be out here again, August.'

'I don't know. I think we're skipping Canyon de

Chelly and the Grand Canyon. I think I just lost my stomach for all this.'

August threw the covers back, disturbing Woody. He got up and walked to the tiny bathroom, closing himself inside.

He heard the voice of Seth filter in, and he moved his ear closer to the door to hear what he was saying to his brother. It wasn't hard to do that and pee at the same time. It was a very small space.

'This is all your fault, Henry. I can't believe you did that. What a bonehead move. You could've killed that dog, you know. He could've been eaten by coyotes and it would've been all your fault. Why do you always have to ruin everything? I wanted to see that Navajo canyon. That Canyon . . . whatever.'

August opened the door a crack and peered out, before even washing his hands. Just in time to see Seth punch his brother on the arm. It looked like a pretty solid punch, but Henry didn't let out so much as a peep.

'There will be no hitting,' August said, and Seth startled.

'Sorry, August,' he said quickly.

'No matter how anybody behaves. No matter what anybody thinks anybody else has done. No hitting.'

'Sorry,' Seth said again.

August washed and dried his hands and then stepped out of the bathroom and began making a pot of coffee.

'August?'

'Yes, Seth.'

'If we go back now we'll be a few days early. And our dad won't be home. Then what'll we do?'

'I won't just leave you there, if that's what you mean. We'll park the rig outside the shop till he gets back.'

Silence for a long time. Long enough that August could hear the coffee maker begin to sigh and spit.

Then Seth said, 'August? Couldn't he pretty much run away from there, too?'

'Oh,' August said. And sighed. 'I guess I hadn't thought of that.'

They rode down the middle of the flat, winding wash on the back of a strange and ancient vehicle. It was something like an old four-wheel-drive construction truck, but converted to a flatbed with six rows of seats, protected by railings.

Their Navajo guide, Benson, had already announced that this was informally called the Shake and Bake Tour. Benson had a canvas roof over his cab area. August and the boys, and the other sightseers, just had to sit out in the hot sun.

The truck lurched as their guide downshifted the gears, then wobbled wildly as it climbed the bank out of the wash again. Six horses made their way hock-deep through the wash of Canyon de Chelly, completely unaccompanied.

August looked over at the boys, neither of whom had said much all day. Well, Seth hadn't said much. Henry hadn't said anything at all since Moab.

Seth looked up and caught August watching.

'I liked the Native rock paintings best. Or carvings. Or whatever they were. Or . . . best so far, anyway.' He waited, a bit awkwardly, then added, 'The ones that looked like people on horses hunting a deer were my favorites.'

'You haven't seen White House yet.'

'Is that one of the old dwellings?' Before August could answer, Seth suddenly shouted, 'Emory!'

August could not imagine why, and was too surprised to answer.

'Look, August! It's Emory. Hi, Emory!'

August looked up just in time to see Emory driving a tour truck full of sightseers in the opposite direction, passing them in the wash. A Navajo man on a paint horse rode through the water behind.

Emory tipped his hat to them as he passed, with a broad smile. August raised his hand in greeting, then felt a pull at his heart as the deeply familiar man drove away again.

A woman sitting in front of Seth turned around and said, 'You know that other tour guide? Where do you know him from?'

August elbowed Seth in the ribs. He had no idea if Seth would know what the elbow stood for. He had no idea if he had properly educated the boy regarding the anonymity of the people he saw in meetings.

'He helped us when my brother got lost,' Seth told her.

She smiled thinly, nodded, then looked forward again, as if she hadn't cared all that much to begin with. August wondered why she had even asked.

'I wasn't going to forget,' Seth whispered in his ear.

They stood out in the sandy dirt by the White House ruins, a partially collapsed ancient dwelling, some parts built in front of the vertical canyon wall, some seemingly carved right out of it. They were taking a break from the shaking, but not the baking.

A big, tall Navajo man with a big, round belly was playing haunting tunes on hand-carved wooden flutes. More flutes were for sale on a table in front of him, as were CDs of his music.

Henry was staring up into the man's face, listening with rapt attention, something akin to pained bliss on his face.

'Now that I see it,' Seth said, 'I'm not sure why they call it White House. It's not really white.'

'Once again we'll have to refer to the brochure. Or you can ask Benson when the break is over. Is Henry mad at me?'

'No,' Seth said. Simply.

'Seems like he's mad at me.'

August watched Henry the whole time he talked. August watched Henry constantly. He was beginning to find it tiring.

'No. He thinks you're mad at *him*. He always tunes people out when he thinks they're mad at him.'

'I'm not mad at him.'

'Really? Seems like you are. I sure am. Oh! Look, August! A snake!'

August looked away from Henry for the first time in a long time. The snake twisted through the tan dirt near where they stood, maybe three feet long, an intricate series of black and tan diamond patterns. Then August looked up again, relieved to see Henry right where he had left him.

'He's pretty,' Seth said. 'Can I pick him up?'

'No! Don't, Seth!'

'I don't think he's poisonous.'

'Snakes can bite without being poisonous. Don't touch it.'

'OK. I'll just take his picture, then.'

He snapped off a few shots with August's camera. Seth always had August's camera now. He paid better attention to the scenery than August did, had a better eye, and his pictures turned out better anyway.

Then Seth said, 'Don't tell Henry. He's scared of snakes. You sure you're not mad at Henry? Kind of seems like you are.'

'Does it?'

August breathed the question in. Resisted the temptation to slough it off again. Let it sit inside him for a minute.

'I don't mean to be,' he said, because it was the most honest thing he had. 'I think he's mad at me because he thinks I shouldn't take you guys home. But I don't have any choice. I'm not your father. Legally there's nothing I can do.'

Seth looked away from the snake for the first time since he'd spotted it.

'August,' he said. 'I can't believe you thought that. Nobody's mad at you for that.'

'He seems mad.'

'He's mad that the summer's almost over. And that our dad's telling lies. But he doesn't blame it on you. How could he? Geez, August, you took us all summer. Nobody else would have done that. We knew you'd take us home when it was over. Who could get mad at you for that?'

Probably no one, August thought. *Other than me.*

'So, have you been there before?' Seth asked.

He was belted into the passenger seat, watching through the windshield as the Interstate 40 gained altitude.

'The Grand Canyon?'

'Right.'

'Several times. Phillip and I even hiked a big piece of it. Not all the way down to the river. Just a day hike. But it was quite an adventure all the same.' Silence. Then he wondered if there was more subtext to the question, if it was less just small talk. 'Why do you ask?'

The boy shrugged, and August thought he would add no more to the discussion. A good five miles later, Seth said, 'It just seems awfully nice. That you would take us to see it. You know. If it's really for us.'

'Summer's almost over,' August said. 'And I just think we should end it at the Grand Canyon.'

*

August parked the motorhome in a pullout on Desert View Drive, the east side of the Grand Canyon. Shut off the engine. This would be their first view. Well, the boys' first view.

'Whoa,' Seth said, stretching the word out long and low.

They stepped out through the back door, leaving Woody inside. August reached down for Henry's hand, and Henry instinctively reached back. It was the new rule.

They stood at the low stone wall together, absolutely silent. The often vibrant shapes and curves and colors of the rock canyon had a dusty look in the midday sun. August made a mental note to take the boys to the lookout tower at Desert View, so they could look down into the canyon from atop the tower and see the Colorado River snaking below.

'I've seen lots of pictures of it,' Seth said. 'But it's better.'

'Pictures don't do it justice.'

'But I can take some anyway?'

'Sure.'

Seth sighted through the lens of August's camera and said, 'The colors are not really that much better than Zion or Bryce Canyon. But I think what's so amazing about it is that it's so huge.'

'Grand,' August said.

'Oh,' Seth said. 'Right.'

'I'm sorry this has to be such a quick visit. It's too late for any first-come, first-served camping. And we can't wait outside the park till morning and snag one like we usually do, because we have to get you guys home.'

Seth let the camera down to the end of its strap again. His shoulders lost their usual straightness.

'I still think it was nice of you to bring us here, since you've already seen it. I can't believe this is it for our summer.'

'I know,' August said.

'You're gonna stay and help us talk to our dad, right?'

'I am.'

'Maybe we should practice what we're gonna say.'

'I don't think so,' August said.

'Really? Usually practice is good.'

'Remember what Emory told you at the meeting?'

'No. Oh! Yeah! I do! He said I should tell whatever I believe in that I'm going to open my mouth. And then ask what I should say to my dad.'

'Right. Straight from the heart without rehearsal is usually best. Otherwise it just comes out sounding rehearsed. Instead of heartfelt.'

'Too bad. I'm better with things I get to practice. But so long as you're there, August . . . I never did anything like this before, and I think if I was alone with just him and Henry like I always was before I might chicken out. How long will you stay?'

'As long as it takes, I guess. It shouldn't take more than an hour or two to talk to him, right?'

'Oh. I was hoping you'd stay longer.'

'Why? You need me there longer for something?'

'Not exactly,' Seth said. 'I just hate to see you go.'

Henry said nothing at all.

After quite a few more minutes staring into the vast, silent void Seth said, 'I wonder if all this stuff we saw, this really big, pretty world, will keep seeming real to me. Or if after a while I'll remember it, but kind of far away, like in a dream. Like I know it happened, but it doesn't feel like it *really* did. Know what I mean?'

'You'll have all the pictures.'

'That only helps a little,' Seth said. 'I mean, at first it helps a lot. But then you look at 'em every time you want it to feel real. And then after you do that a bunch of times it turns out you looked at 'em too much. So then after a while they're just more like pictures of a thing and not the actual thing. After a while you look at a picture and all it helps you remember is the picture. And then it gets kind of memorized and you hardly even see it. I have lots of pictures of my mom. But it only helped for a while. You know what I mean, August?'

'Unfortunately,' August said, 'yes. I do.'

5
Some Kind Of It

'His car is here,' Seth said.

'Did he drive himself to the jail?'

'I dunno. I was with you.'

August was surprised by how much his heart and gut sank as he drove into the familiar dirt lot of the mechanic's shop. It had that sickening familiarity of something you got stuck with for many interminable days against your will. Like driving all the way across the country with only one music CD. Especially if the CD was one you hadn't liked much to begin with.

They all piled out the back of the rig and into the most oppressive midday heat. Much worse than the weather when they'd left in June.

Woody ran around sniffing and lifting his leg on every interesting bush.

'The shop is closed,' August said.

'That doesn't mean he isn't home. That just means he doesn't have any cars to fix.'

August followed the boys around to the back of the shop, a place August had never seen. Purposely. It hadn't been his business, when the rig was in for repair, where these people actually lived.

It wasn't a house, exactly. It was a wing of the same sheet-metal, high-windowed building as the shop. But the door was wide open, and through it August could see that it had been decorated as a simple, functional home inside. At least, from what he could see of the living room.

Wes stood in the doorway, his shoulder leaned against the jamb, smoking. August expected him to greet the boys before anything else, but instead he looked directly into August's face and narrowed his eyes in a way that made August uneasy.

Henry pushed past his dad and trudged inside. Seth stopped and waited. For something.

'I don't even get a hello?' Wes shot over his shoulder as Henry disappeared from sight.

'Let him go, Dad,' Seth said.

Wes and Seth regarded each other for a long moment. Then Seth's eyes moved down to the level of his father's shoes. Wes was wearing baggy cargo pants. Much baggier than anything August had seen him wear before. There was a definite unnatural bulk around his left ankle.

'Is that it?' Seth asked.

'What else would it be?'

'Can I see it?'

'No. You can't see it. Why would you need to see it?

What would the point of that be? You know what it is. What it looks like has nothing to do with anything. It's what it does we got to worry about. You're gonna have to walk to the store for us all, you know. I know it's a long way, but maybe they'll let you borrow a cart if we promise to bring it back. You're responsible to bring back everything we all need.'

A brief silence. Seth was still looking down at his father's shoes. Or maybe at the brown dirt right in front of them.

'Fine,' he said. 'But I'm not buying you any liquor.'

Wes straightened up and rocked back a little, but said nothing at all.

Seth broke free from his statue pose and pushed past his dad into the house. 'August's coming in,' he said on the way by.

Wes's eyes came up to meet August's again. Woody sidled up to Wes and wagged his tail, but Wes ignored the dog, or failed to even notice.

'There's a lot I appreciate,' Wes said. 'A lot I have to thank you for. Putting ideas like that in my kid's head is not one of 'em.'

'We didn't talk about that. That was Seth's own idea.'

'Yeah. Interesting coincidence. Goes off on a trip with a man who never takes a single drink at all and comes back with ideas like that.'

'If it helps any to know,' August said, 'I drank more than my share in my life. I just don't any more.'

'Oh, an ex-drinker. The only thing that could be worse.'

'Do you honestly believe that before Seth met me he was happy with how things were going around here? You really think that dissatisfaction is coming from me? Like if I hadn't told him to mind, he wouldn't?'

'Why're you coming in, again?'

'Because I promised Seth I would.'

Wes took another draw on his cigarette, then stamped the butt out in the dirt just in front of the doorjamb. And left it there, with dozens of others.

'I have a feeling I'm not gonna like this much. But you gave your word to Seth, and I owe you a debt of gratitude. So I guess you best come in.'

August sat in the living room – or, anyway, the main area of the house – uncomfortably and silently perched on the edge of one of two sofas. Both were covered with blankets that hid some but not all of their age and defects. Wes sat across from him, also silent.

Woody had been returned to the motorhome, with the air conditioning running, because August wasn't sure whether he was welcome in the mechanic's home.

Seth was off in another part of the house trying to talk Henry into joining them.

Time was stretching out painfully, so August could only assume the fetching of Henry wasn't going well.

A crushing amount of time later – though it may have been less than five minutes – Seth came out again, literally towing Henry by one wrist. He towed the boy over to the couch next to August and physically sat him down.

'I know you're not going to talk,' Seth told his brother. 'So, fine. Don't talk. But we're all in this together, so sit there. While we do this. Like it or not. I don't like it, either, Henry, but that's not the thing and you know it.'

Then Seth sat on the other side of August. Which August knew would give Wes the distinct impression of three against one. But it was a mistake August didn't know how to correct.

Then he took it a step further in his mind and thought, *Just because Wes doesn't like it doesn't make it a mistake.* The three-against-one impression was an accurate one. *That's what an intervention is*, he thought. *That moment when everybody else is on one side and you're on the other. That's how you know it's time to change. Because you're fresh out of support.*

'Shit,' Wes hissed, not quite under his breath. 'I knew I wasn't gonna like this.'

'Dad,' Seth said. 'It would really be good if you could just listen.'

In the ringing silence that followed, it felt clear to August that this was a level of directness Seth had not used with his father in the past. He could see something rise up in Wes, that instinctive alpha-dog reaction. Then Wes glanced at August and August watched him tamp that instinct back down again.

Wes put his feet up on the coffee table, one ankle crossed over the other. Then he had to take them apart and cross them the other way when the ankle monitor interfered.

'Fine,' he said. 'I have a feeling I know where this is going, but . . . talk away.'

'When Mom left—' Seth began.

'Wait. Mom?' Wes interjected. 'Where does your mom fit into this?'

'Dad. You're not listening.'

'Sorry,' Wes said, his embarrassment appearing strangely genuine.

'When Mom left, we never talked about it. Ever. At all. That was five years ago and I still don't know where she went. Or why. I still don't know if she left because she had another . . . you know . . . guy . . . or if she had something she wanted to do with her life that she couldn't do at home.'

Seth paused.

After several seconds of silence, Wes asked, 'Am I supposed to talk here?'

Seth only nodded.

'She had both.'

'Oh. OK. Well, anyway. What I'm trying to say . . . Oh, wait. I forgot to do something.'

Seth went silent and closed his eyes. August glanced at Wes, who was watching his son's face with some confusion. August was not confused. He knew exactly what Seth was doing. He was asking for the right words.

'OK,' Seth said a few seconds later. 'What I'm trying to say is, all I knew is that we weren't the most important thing to her. I'm just a kid, and maybe I don't know as much as you, or maybe I don't know much at all, period. But I really think a person's kids should be the most important thing to them. But if you've got stuff you want to do and you just walk away and do it and never see them again, then they're not. I mean, we're not. We weren't important enough to her.'

'I don't see what—' Wes began.

'Dad.'

'Right. I know. Sorry. Listen.'

'And then you stayed with us. I know that. I know you'll say you stayed, and didn't go off after anything else. And I know it's true. But it's not all true. Because as soon as you were done with work, you'd go off to the bar and leave us home by ourselves. Sometimes for hours and sometimes for all night. I was seven. I wasn't old enough to look after a kid who was two, and I knew it. And you should've known it, too. I wouldn't have known what to do if the house was on fire, or somebody tried to break in, or Henry was choking or something.'

'None of which happened,' Wes interjected.

'But that was just luck. You didn't control that none of that happened. You just got lucky and it didn't. August says we're responsible for everything we do, even if we take a risk and nothing bad happens, because it could have. We don't get to feel good that it didn't. It's just by luck that it didn't.'

Wes's eyes came up to August's, and he sat back and crossed his arms in front of his chest defensively.

'I said that about an entirely different situation,' August said. 'I was talking about myself at the time.'

A pause, while everyone gauged whether Wes had

anything to say. When he remained silent, Seth took over again.

'And then you got put in jail and we had to go to Aunt Patty's, which was sort of OK, because at least we were OK there. But it still sucked, because it meant you left us. First Mom left us, for whatever. Then you left us because drinking was more important than us. And then you did it again. And then Patty said this was the last time, which I still think sucked, because she was mad at you, not us, because we were always good when we were there. It sucked that she took it out on us that you wouldn't stop, but she warned you she would. So Henry and me, we figured you wouldn't do it again, because we'd have no place to go if you did. But you did. And we had to go to this place where kids go when they're orphans, because you cared more about drinking. We weren't the most important thing to you.'

Seth stopped. Then sighed.

A long silence fell on the proceedings.

When it became too awkward, Wes said, 'Is that it?'

'I don't know,' Seth said. 'Maybe.'

Wes looked at Henry, who did not look back.

'What about you, Henry? You want to yell at me, too?'

Henry predictably declined to respond.

Wes looked to August, his eyes smoldering.

'What about you? You want to add anything?'

It might go better if he didn't, and August knew that. But he glanced down at Seth, who looked up at him with the most pathetically pleading eyes. He'd promised to support Seth. Which probably involved opening his mouth. Besides, the idea of a successful intervention – which August had never really expected this one to be – was to break down the offending family member's defenses. And that was clearly not yet accomplished.

'Sure,' August said. 'OK. Remember when you told me that Henry hadn't said a word to you since he came back from the county home? You said you thought he talked to his brother, but you couldn't prove it. I just want to add that Henry talked to me for most of this summer. I won't say he talked my ear off, exactly. But he talked. Which for him is a lot. Which means the only person he isn't speaking to is you. And if it were me, I'd take that seriously as a parent. I'd figure that meant there really is a problem. And since it'd been going on before the guy who doesn't drink any more came into the picture, I would figure the problem pre-dates him. And I wouldn't try to convince myself that this could all be put off on the outsider.'

Wes took his feet off the coffee table. Sat forward. Placed his head in his hands. For a long time. So long that Seth looked up at August for answers. August had none, so he just shrugged.

Finally the hands came down.

'Well, this is some kind of bullshit,' Wes said.

August felt Seth tense and coil at his side, and he placed a hand on the boy's shoulder to calm him.

'No,' August said. 'It's not. It's the damn truth. Your son's trying to tell you the damn truth.'

'No, it's some bullshit,' Wes said. 'And I'll tell you why. Because I'm stuck in the house with this damn ankle monitor, and my responsible son just threw me a curve ball, telling me he'd shop, but not for what I want. That came as quite a shock, you know? So first he fixes it so I literally can't possibly drink for the next three months, and then he sits me down and tells me I shouldn't. When I couldn't if I tried. Which is sort of adding insult to injury, don't you think?'

'How did you think Seth was going to buy alcohol for you? He's twelve.'

'I could've arranged it. Guy at the liquor store's a friend of mine. I could've sent Seth with my ID.'

'Which is totally illegal.'

'So's driving over the speed limit, but everybody does it.'

'So, you'd order your son to drive over the speed limit because of something you want from him?'

'I'm done here,' Wes said, and swung to his feet.

'Dad, wait!' Seth nearly shrieked it.

'What, Seth? What? Why is nothing I do ever good enough? What do you want from me now?'

'I want to know what happens at the end of the three months.'

Wes stood still for a few seconds, chewing on the inside of his lip.

Then he said, 'Tell you what. You got a point about the drinking and driving. God knows I've caused enough trouble with that, for you guys and me both. So when this damn thing comes off . . .' He kicked at the monitor with the toe of one boot. '. . . I'll go out and get a stock at the store and keep it here at the house and not go out at night. OK? Two or three good drinks a night won't hurt anybody if I'm not out on the road. Right? That's all I ever needed – just a couple to let off steam, you know? Calm me down. Now . . . are you ready to get off my case about this, Seth? Is that gonna be good enough for you?'

'How slow do you drink?' Seth asked.

August couldn't tell if it was a serious question or a sarcastic complaint.

'What're you talking about?' Wes asked.

'You were gone for four, five, six hours. All night. And you were only drinking two drinks?'

Wes sighed.

'All right, maybe sometimes I had more. But that doesn't mean I always have to. I'm saying I'll keep it to two or three. Now. I ask you again . . . is that good enough for you?'

'I don't know,' Seth said.

'Well, it's gonna have to be.' Wes broke his statue-like pose and headed for the door. 'I'm going out for a smoke.'

And he did.

Seth sat blinking for half a minute or so. Then Henry got up and stomped off into the back of the house again.

Seth looked up at August.

'That didn't exactly take an hour or two, did it?'

'No. That might have been a new record.'

'I don't know if it went OK or not.'

'Me, neither,' August said. 'Come on. Help me get all your stuff out of the rig.'

'And then you're going?'

August looked at Seth's face, and saw the visual version of what he felt in his gut. It seemed so cold and final to drive away. Like a lifeline being severed, too hastily, and without looking back.

'Want to have lunch in the rig with Woody and me before I go?'

Seth sighed a sigh that seemed to deflate him, but was clearly full of relief.

'Thanks, August,' he said. 'I'll go get Henry.'

When Seth showed up at the back door of the rig a few minutes later, he did not have his brother with him.

'Where's Henry?' August asked as Seth let himself in.

'Inside. I can't get him to do anything today. I told him it was his last chance to say goodbye. But it's like he's a robot and the switch got turned off. He just won't do anything.'

'Wow. That's too bad. He's going to come out and say goodbye to me, isn't he? I hate to leave without saying goodbye.'

'I don't know,' Seth said, sitting down at the little dinette table. 'With Henry you never can tell. Is that OK, what my dad promised? If he doesn't drive, and he keeps to two drinks a day, that'll be OK. Right?'

'I hope so,' August said, and took down a can of tuna fish for their lunch.

'So you don't think it will be.'

'I think it could be, and I hope it is.'

'You have to tell me the truth, August. You have to tell me what you really think.'

August paused before opening the can. Turned to look at Seth. Leaned back on the counter. In case this took a while.

'All right. Here's the truth of what I think. If your dad's an alcoholic, he'll make a lot of promises about cutting down. But he won't keep them. Because . . . well, that's more or less the textbook definition of an alcoholic. Someone who knows it's time to cut down, but can't. So I think it's going to be a few months before we know how that's going.'

'Hmm,' Seth said. 'I hate things like that.'

'Everybody does,' August said.

Then he made them a couple of sandwiches. And it felt strange to make two. Instead of three. It struck him that next time there was a meal to be made, he would only make one. But it felt uncomfortable and bad, so he put it out of his mind as best he could.

6
Goodbye

'I feel bad leaving you here,' August said.

He couldn't remember if he'd already said that twenty or thirty times before, or if the rest of the times had all been in his head.

'It's fine, August.'

They sat on the motorhome couch, a huge black trash bag between them, filled with both boys' clothes and belongings. There were more belongings than when the trip had begun. August would have to carry it in. It would be too much for Seth.

So August would have to see Wes one more time.

'It's not the best place in the world for a kid to be.'

'True,' Seth said. 'It's not the best place. But it's our place. It's where we live. We didn't expect you to fix that, August.'

'Right. I guess I have to stop doing that. You don't even know my last name, do you?'

'I think I heard you say it once, but now I forgot.'

'It's Schroeder.'

'I wouldn't have any idea how to spell that.'

'I'll write it down for you.'

August took his blank journal down from one of the cupboards. The one he'd intended to use to chronicle every moment of the summer. The one he hadn't written one word in.

He tore off the first blank page.

'I'm writing down my name and my address. And my phone numbers. Home and cell. And . . . do you have Internet?'

'I do! My dad just got me a nice new computer for my schoolwork. Well. New to me.'

'I'll write down my email then, too.'

'Do you Skype? I Skype with a friend from school. That would be cool if we could talk on video. And it doesn't cost like the phone. Put down your Skype handle.'

'I don't have one,' August said. 'But I'll get one when I get back. I'll start an account and email it to you.'

'Cool.'

August handed Seth the sheet of paper, and he studied it carefully, as if it were his job to memorize it on the spot.

August took out his wallet and sorted through the bills. He still had the fifty-dollar bill Wes had given him, because it was vaguely inconvenient to break a fifty.

He tried to hand it to Seth, who just stared at it.

'What's that for?'

'It's what women in the old days used to call mad money. Once upon a time when a woman went out on a date, the man was driving and the man was paying. So the woman would bring some mad money in case it didn't go well. If she had to walk away, she could call a cab or something. It's for safety. You could take Henry and walk to the nearest payphone and call me. You could even get on a bus to the next town and call from there. Where your dad would never think to look.'

'I'm not sure why we'd have to do all that.'

'Just in case,' August said.

Seth continued to stare at the bill.

'I really don't feel right taking your money, August.'

'It's not mine. It's part of the money your dad gave me for your food. We didn't quite spend it all. It's really yours. Just promise me you won't use it for anything else.'

'I promise.'

He slipped the bill out of August's hand and into his shorts pocket.

'You're forgetting something, August.'

'What am I forgetting?'

'You really don't know?'

'Oh! The pictures.'

'Right. I want to show my friends at school.'

'I'll put them on a DVD for you.'

Seth watched in silence as August booted up his laptop, downloaded the last shots from the photo card, and popped a blank DVD into the slot. He brought up the folder of all the trip photos, and the thumbnails stared back at him from the screen.

Seth got up and looked over his shoulder as he scrolled through them.

'Damn, you got some nice shots,' August said.

'They do look pretty good, don't they?'

A long silence as the DVD began to burn.

Then Seth said, 'It already doesn't seem totally real that we got to do all that.'

'You sit here while the DVD burns,' August said. 'I'll go carry all your stuff into the house.'

Wes stood smoking in the doorway, just like before.

August stopped and faced him, the trash bag slung over his shoulder.

'I know you think you're better than me,' Wes said. Without meeting August's eyes.

'No. I don't. You're right around in the same neighborhood I was in about two years ago.'

'Well, there,' Wes said, his eyes coming up to meet August's. 'Right there. You just said it. I'm where you were two years ago, and you're much better now.'

August cut his eyes away to indicate that he didn't care to fight.

'Wes, I know you think this was all my doing . . .'

'Not really,' Wes said. 'Let's face it. Seth was always voted most likely to stage an intervention on his own dad. It's just who he is. He wants the world to be a certain way. Everything in order. Tries to get all his ducks in a row, all the time. And of course it never works. Unfortunately he thinks I'm one of his ducks.

I don't know which is worse, the way he thinks he can run all our lives better than I ever did, or the times I worry he might be right.'

August relaxed a little. Felt one side of his mouth twitch into a half smile.

'Maybe you can pool your resources and work it out.'

'Sure,' Wes said. 'Maybe. Thanks for everything you did.'

'No worries. We had a pretty good summer. A few exceptions here and there. I was hoping to say goodbye to Henry.'

Wes dropped his cigarette in the dirt and ground it out with the toe of his boot. He exhaled smoke, turned and cupped both hands around his mouth.

'Henry! Come say bye to the man!'

Then they waited. And waited. And waited.

Henry never came out.

'You shouldn't be sad, August,' Seth said.

They stood in the dirt by the driver's-side door of the rig. It was becoming increasingly obvious that it was time for August to get in and drive.

'You're not sad?'

'Yeah. I am. But *you* shouldn't be.'

'Now why is that?'

'Because I don't want you to be sad.'

August heard a thin whimper and looked over his shoulder to see Woody in the driver's seat, paws up on the glass.

'Speaking of sad . . . he's going to miss you boys like crazy.'

'I don't want to think about that, August.'

'OK. Sorry.'

August gave Seth a fast hug and climbed into the driver's seat, pushing Woody out of the way.

'Take care of your brother.'

'I will. I always do.'

Then Seth turned and walked back toward the house, purposely kicking up dirt with the toes of his shoes. Woody jumped on to August's lap and watched him go in silence. Then he jumped down into his bed between the seats, ready for the trip.

August started the engine and drove slowly over the rutted dirt toward the road. Before he even reached the end of the lot, he heard his name called, faintly in the distance.

'August!'

It wasn't Seth's voice. And it wasn't Wes.

Woody ran to the back door, whining.

August braked, and looked in his side-view mirror. Henry was running after the rig. August stepped on the footbrake, threw the door wide. Jumped down into the dirt and the heat, the engine still running.

When Henry caught up, he leapt into August's arms much the way Woody often did. Except August had to be more careful to keep from being bowled over backwards.

'I'm sorry Woody could've got eaten by coyotes,

August,' Henry said in a great whispery rush into August's ear.

'That's in the past. Why didn't you come out and say goodbye?'

'I thought if I said goodbye you'd go.'

'You knew I had to go, Henry. I have to get back to work.'

'It was dumb. I'm sorry.'

Henry jumped down, kicking up dirt when he landed. He walked over to the open door of the rig. Reaching up on his tiptoes, he hugged Woody and kissed him on the ear.

August said, 'Maybe I'll come back and see you on my way out of town next summer. If it's OK with your dad.'

'It won't be,' Henry said. 'Bye, August.'

And he waved.

August stood frozen a moment, searching for choices. But he had only one. Wave back and drive away.

So that's what he did.

August should have been able to make it home in six or seven hours. But he didn't. Because he didn't even try. Fatigue overcame him, and he couldn't figure out if it was physical or emotional in origin. Or maybe he didn't have enough energy to care.

He pulled into a Walmart parking lot in one of those California desert towns that look just like all the other California desert towns.

It was only 4.30 in the afternoon, and the parking lot was busy, and noisy. So he parked at the very farthest, most remote corner. But it was still busy and noisy enough.

He pulled the curtains and almost immediately fell asleep on the couch, with all his clothes on.

When he woke up, it was dark. And fairly quiet. He squinted at his watch face, which faintly glowed. It was a little after nine. And now he felt wide awake.

He took Woody out to pee, then checked his cell phone for messages. He had none.

He hit number two on the speed dial of his phone, which was still his ex-wife, Maggie. After all this time.

She picked up on the second ring.

'Maggie,' he said, thinking he should have thought this call out much more carefully before making it.

'August? My God. What are you doing calling?'

'Shouldn't I?'

'Hell, I don't know. Should, shouldn't. I just know you never did before. You know. Not never, but . . .'

'Right. I wanted to ask you a question about Phillip.'

A long silence on the line. August wondered briefly if she had been drinking. At this hour of the evening, most likely yes. She sounded fine. But then, she always did. She always had.

'What makes you think I knew something about him you didn't?'

'I don't know. I think I'm just looking for a different perspective. Or maybe just perspective, period. Any perspective at all.'

'OK,' she said, her voice tight. 'Try me.'

'I know he never acted like much of a thrill-seeker. But did he have a sense of adventure that he just wasn't acting out?'

'I have no idea how to make heads or tails out of that question.'

'Would he have wanted to go over Niagara Falls in a barrel? I mean, in some mythical world where he would be absolutely assured of survival.'

'August . . . to borrow an expression from our late son . . . that is one weird-ass question.'

'Is it? I think I've lost the ability to even judge.'

'Have you been drinking?'

'No! No, I still haven't had a drink for . . . well, coming up on two years pretty soon here.'

An awkward silence.

Then she said, 'That's good, August. Good for you. I'm happy for you.'

'Thank you. I guess it's OK if you don't have an answer. Maybe there isn't one.'

August pulled up the shade slightly to investigate a roaring noise, like an airplane taxiing through the Walmart parking lot. Instead he saw an employee cleaning up trash with a leaf blower. He stuck a finger in his free ear.

'I'll give you an answer if you want, August, but it's only my answer. It may be accurate or it may not. I think everybody would like to go over Niagara Falls in a barrel if they could be magically assured they wouldn't die. The reason people don't do things like that is because they don't want to die. Not because it doesn't sound like fun. I think Phillip had a pretty good sense of adventure, but he'd seen us run into a few brick walls, so he was cautious. Take away that caution, I think he would have climbed into that barrel in a heartbeat. He had his moments. Remember the toboggan incident?'

'I don't.'

'You must. Before we moved west. His friend Frankie. And that hill that dumped right out on to the highway.'

'Oh, God. That. Yeah. But there were no toboggans involved with that.'

'Well, so they were using cardboard for toboggans. What's the difference? It was foolhardy. Although . . . I was never entirely convinced that he knew about the highway connection in advance.'

'If he hadn't known, wouldn't he have said he hadn't known? In his own defense?'

'You know he always misplaced his tongue when anybody was mad at him. Now, come on. Really, August. What's this all about?'

'I was just thinking about it since we put a few of his ashes in the Yellowstone River just above the water-falls.'

'We? You're seeing someone? Good for you.'

'No. It's not like that. I had somebody else's kids with me this summer. It's . . . kind of a long story.'

Silence for a time. It took August a minute to realize she was waiting for him to say something more.

'Is that really all you called to say?'

'No,' he said. And it was the first he had heard of it. Just as it came out of his mouth.

'Didn't think so.'

'I owe you an amends.'

'For . . .'

'I drove plenty of times with him in the car. With . . . you know . . . not huge amounts of alcohol in my system, but some. Enough.'

'But you weren't driving when something bad happened.'

'But I could have been.'

'But you weren't.'

'But it's not to my credit that I wasn't. That's what I'm trying to say. There's no real difference between your situation and mine. Luck, is all.'

'You never said anything to make me feel otherwise.'

'No.'

'Are you saying you felt it, though?'

'I'm saying I was careful not to. It was an effort. I don't know how to put it any better than that.'

'Listen. August,' she said, her voice hardening. 'It's very big of you to call and . . . No, you know what? I'm sorry. I'm being defensive out of force of habit. It really was nice of you to call and tell me it could just as easily have been you. I appreciate that. But it still wasn't.'

'I know.'

'And you have no idea how I feel.'

'I never claimed to.'

'But anyway, thanks.'

'Sure,' he said. 'Least I could do.'

Then they said goodbye.

August couldn't get back to sleep, no matter how hard he tried.

So he drove.

7
It Won't Be

It was close to ten at night, and August sat in a coffee shop post-meeting with Harvey. It was a place that served breakfast twenty-four hours a day if you wanted it. August was having a Denver omelet. Harvey was drinking cup after cup of coffee. How he managed to do that so late at night August could never fathom. Did he sleep? And if so, how?

August had school in the morning. His first day of the new school year. That fact sat in his stomach, feeling a little queasy and sour. He probably should have skipped the talking and gone for the sleep.

And yet he was talking.

'So the last thing he said to me . . .'

'Which one?'

'Henry. The little one. I'd just said, "Maybe I'll come visit you guys on my way out of town next year. If it's OK with your dad." And just really casually, he said, "It won't be."'

'I'm sure he's right,' Harvey said.

Harvey had jet-black hair slicked back with some product that made it look wet. He was older than August by a good fifteen or twenty years, and had recently had several skin cancers removed from his forehead and jaw, slightly marring a face that was otherwise aging-movie-star handsome, but in a distinctly old-fashioned way. Like the star of a silent movie. Except he was rarely silent.

'Why do you say that?'

'Because it's true. And even a seven-year-old can figure it out.'

'I would think he might respect the bonds we formed.'

'Right. Because he's such a deeply respectful person. Open your eyes a little here. Look at the thing this way: he's under no obligation to respect the relationship between you and his kids. And he doesn't want to. So he won't. You've seen him in a very bad light. And his kids have seen there's a better way. He feels inferior to you. So my guess is he'll try to wipe away the evidence that anybody named August ever existed in his life.'

'Seth will still keep in touch with me.'

'Hopefully.'

'You never tell me what I want to hear, Harvey.'

'Right. I don't. It's not my job to tell you what you want to hear. It's my job to point out what is. Maybe I'm wrong. I hope I'm wrong. But you might want to be open to the idea that the closeness you shared with those boys was more situational than anything else.

Seems big now, but people get on with their lives. They don't have much choice. This is a big deal to you, isn't it? Why is this such a big deal to you? Did you forget these were someone else's kids?'

'Not exactly.'

'Making you feel the loss of Phillip all over again?'

'Or for the first time.' Then August stopped cold, and listened to the silent but tangible echo of those words. Once again he had surprised himself by saying something he didn't know he knew. 'That sounds weird, huh?'

'Not really.'

'Really?'

'Really not really. You just said yourself I never tell you what you want to hear. It's been not quite two years. People think two years is long enough, but not for a big loss like that one. It tends to go through in phases. This is not just you, it's everybody. It's just human. The truth is not exactly that you're feeling it for the first time, even though I can understand how it might feel that way. The truth is that giving those kids back is making you feel the loss at a new level. In a new way. Here's my advice: don't cling to your bond with those boys. You'll only be hurting yourself. Make up your mind that it was a one-time thing. That they'll promise to keep in touch but they won't. Make your peace with that. Then, if you get to keep talking to them or seeing them, it'll be a happy surprise.'

*

August was working on his class notes at the dining-room table the first time his laptop rang. It sounded just like a phone, but not like *his* phone. He could tell it was coming from the computer, but it had never rung before, and he had no idea what to do about it.

It wasn't until the fourth ring that he noticed the Skype icon jumping up and down.

He clicked on it, and immediately saw Seth's face in a pop-up window, dimly lighted, and slightly distorted from Seth's leaning in so close to the screen.

He'd had Skype for over a week, and he'd wanted to call the boys, but Seth said it was better to wait and let him call. He didn't say why, but August had a pretty good idea.

'I can see you!' August said, a bit surprised by the level of joy in his own voice.

Seth frowned. 'I can't see you. Turn your camera on, August. You do have a camera, don't you?'

'I've never used it before, but I know I do. How do I get it to come on?'

'See that little icon that looks like an eye? Does it have a circle around it and a line through it?'

'It does, yeah.'

'Click on it.'

August clicked, and the icon changed.

'I see you now,' Seth said. 'Hey, Henry. I got August. Come say hi.'

Henry's tentative face appeared over his brother's shoulder, and he waved silently.

August felt Woody's front paws on his thigh, and he

looked down. The dog was curious about the familiar voices. Or just voices in the otherwise empty room. August wasn't sure if a dog could recognize a voice through electronics.

He reached down and lifted Woody into his lap.

'Woody!' both boys said almost in unison.

Woody cocked his head to one side, and the boys both laughed.

Then Seth said, 'Nothing. I'm doing my homework.'

The pop-up window froze, then disappeared. The call had ended.

August tried to go back to his class notes, but his mind was too active, too distracted. Instead he got up and made himself a sandwich, brought it back to the table, and checked email.

It was all junk except for an email from Maggie that he couldn't bring himself to open just yet.

The computer rang again and he jumped to answer the call.

Seth's face appeared on the screen again.

'Sorry, August. My dad came in the room.'

'So, he literally can't know I'm in touch with you at all?' August asked, thinking he sounded a bit too much like a resentful child.

Henry's face appeared over Seth's shoulder again. Again, a silent wave.

'Maybe just for a while,' Seth said. 'He's in the worst mood. Isn't that right, Henry?'

Henry answered by pinching his nose closed with his thumb and forefinger.

'Very stinky mood,' Seth said.

'But you're OK with him . . . right?'

'Well, he's not violent, if that's what you mean. He just yells a lot and he always seems aggravated. He tells us we're aggravating him about twenty times a day. Yesterday it was so bad I swear I almost thought about taking his ID and going and buying him some liquor. I didn't, of course. But it was tempting. Just today Henry said to me how much better it would have been if we could've just gone to stay with you in San Diego until December.'

Henry nodded silently. Solemnly.

'Turns out he's much nicer when he's drinking than when he's not. But I shouldn't talk about him, because I sure wouldn't want him to hear me. The pictures are so great, August. I took 'em to school, and my teacher let me show 'em like a slide show to the whole class, and I stood up and told what everything was and what we did there. I'm like a rock star now. Everybody is so jealous. Even the kids that get to go places. Like Randy Simmons. He got to go to the Grand Canyon last summer. Lots of the kids get to go one place on vacation. But nobody I know ever got to go all those places in the same summer. It's like a vacation to everywhere. Everyone is so jealous. But not really in a bad way. Well, not with most of 'em.'

A brief silence fell. And before it ended, August heard a knock on his front door. Which struck him as odd. Because he wasn't expecting anyone. And no one ever showed up at his house unannounced, because everyone knew he was not the sort to tolerate it.

'Someone's at my door,' he said.

'Oh, that's OK, August, we'll talk later.'

'I hate to cut this short. I've been wanting to talk to you boys.'

'It doesn't matter. We'll just call back soon.'

'Promise?'

'Absolutely. I promise. Go get the door.'

Then the image of Seth froze, and disappeared. And August felt as though a little piece of himself, a chunk of aliveness in his gut, disappeared with it. Like a small flame snuffed out.

He crossed the house to the door, already angry at whoever might be on the other side of it.

He threw the door open wide to find his ex-wife standing on the doorstep. She'd cut her hair. It had always been shoulder length, now it was decidedly short. She'd also stopped coloring it, leaving it shot through with gray. Which looked fine to August, and left him wondering why it hadn't always been.

Her sudden presence made it feel hard to swallow.

'I was on an important call,' he said, knowing it was too harsh but not entirely caring.

'I could come back some other time.'

August sighed. Leaned his forehead on the edge of the door.

'Well, I'm off it now, so you might as well come in.'

*

'You have anything to drink around here?' she asked, wandering through the dining room as though she planned to find it on her own.

It had been her house, too, for almost twenty years. She'd volunteered to walk out with nothing but her personal belongings. She'd asked for almost nothing in the divorce. A function of guilt, maybe.

August watched her look around and wondered how it felt to her. Comfortingly familiar? Painfully familiar? He wondered if she now knew she'd given away far too much.

'I have two kinds of soda . . . coffee and tea . . .'

'That wasn't exactly what I meant.'

'It should have been. You know I don't drink now.'

'What, you don't even keep a little in the house to serve to company?'

'Of course not. Why would I?'

'People like a drink when they come visit.'

'I never invite anybody to come visit. And if they show up unannounced, it's not much of my concern what they like. Anybody who wants a drink and comes to my house is barking up the wrong tree. You can have a drink before you get here and after you leave.'

August wondered if she had. If she would.

She looked directly into his face for a long time. Then she wandered back into the living room and sat on the couch.

'I guess I was mistaken,' she said.

August sat on his big stuffed easy chair beside the

couch. She made a point of refusing to meet his eyes again.

'About what?'

'I didn't think you would have called me that night unless you were trying to re-establish contact.'

'Oh,' he said.

He knew he should say more, but not what the more should be. The true answer was no. He had not been trying to get back in touch with her on any kind of permanent basis. But she knew that now, and it felt unnecessarily cruel to say it out loud.

'All that weird stuff about Phillip didn't seem to make much sense, so I thought it was a pretext.'

'I'm sorry if I gave you the wrong impression,' he said. 'It was exactly what I said it was.' Then he realized he was restating what she already knew, which he had decided not to do. But he was doing it, and he couldn't seem to stop. 'I really wanted to know the answer to that question about Phillip, and then once we were talking I wanted to make that amends. I'd already told one of the boys I was traveling with that I owed it to you, and yet somehow until I had you on the phone it never consciously occurred to me to say so directly to you.'

He stopped talking. Ran out of words. He felt for the part of himself that had loved her for so long, even though he knew it would hurt to touch it. He couldn't find anything. But he didn't necessarily think that proved it wasn't there.

There was a little three-dimensional wooden jigsaw

puzzle on the coffee table that Phillip had made in high-school woodshop, and August watched her finger it almost absent-mindedly. Her face gave away nothing. She'd always had a perfect poker face. Quite the opposite of August, whose face gave away everything at all times.

'What's the deal with the kids? Whose kids?'

'Oh. I met a couple of kids on my way up to Yellowstone whose father had to be in jail for the summer, so I took them with me.'

'For . . . ?'

'I don't know. They were nice boys. They needed it.'

'I meant what did he go to jail for?'

'Oh. DUI.'

August felt unsettled, and almost unable to talk. Unable to grasp the thoughts he would need to make the conversation work. His mind was a jumble, as if he had the flu, or had knocked his head. As if he just woke up. Meanwhile Maggie looked calm and sharp. But maybe that was a function of comparing the inside of his head with the outside of hers.

'Don't tell me you're doing missionary work.'

'I don't know what that means.'

'Is it part of the program to find and save alcoholics?'

'No. I didn't find these people. They found me. The motorhome broke down, so I called the Auto Club and that's who came out and towed me into his shop.'

'Coincidence,' she said.

August had no idea how she meant it. In fact, he

increasingly felt himself losing his grasp. Having less and less idea about anything.

'Is that a joke?'

'No, why would it be?'

'If I found someone else whose son died in a car accident about two years ago, that would be a coincidence worth noting. You can barely throw a rock into a crowd without hitting an alcoholic.'

She looked up into his face, and he flushed and averted his eyes. Again, he found her face impossible to read.

'I guess it depends on how you define an alcoholic,' she said.

A buzzy silence followed, during which August weighed the trouble they'd already hit. There was a scratchiness to the conversational topic off which they had just glanced. It reminded him of why things had gone wrong between them. Why it seemed they always would.

He wanted to express the feeling, but before he could even gather his thoughts, she spoke.

'We were good together,' she said. 'Whatever happened to that?'

It stunned August to hear her say it, just as he was absorbing how good they weren't. He didn't – couldn't – speak.

'Oh, I didn't really mean that,' she said. 'I know what happened to it. That's obvious. I guess what I mean is, are we sure that what happened to it is permanent?'

August opened his mouth to speak, and promptly

fell into even deeper waters. Because he suddenly tried on her idea. What if it was less of a dead end and more of the world's biggest speed bump, what had happened to their marriage?

Part of August raced forward with the idea, while another more subtle, more hidden part of himself tugged at his sleeve, warning him there was something he was forgetting. There was a reason. There *was* a dead end. And he knew it. But now he couldn't think what it was.

'Oh,' he said out loud when he'd reclaimed it.

He hadn't meant to say it out loud.

'Oh, what?'

'You drink and I don't,' he said.

'And that's a deal-breaker?'

'I believe it is.'

'There's no such thing as a couple where one drinks and the other doesn't?'

'There may be,' he said. 'But I don't think it's a workable plan at all. When you were on your way over here to tell me we should think about being together again . . . tell the truth now . . . did you think maybe you would stop drinking? Or did you think maybe I would start again? Or did you think the divide really didn't matter?'

'I didn't think about it at all,' she said. 'So let me get this straight. You'd never be with anyone again who lets even a drop of alcohol pass her lips?'

August straightened himself physically, and tried to clear his head. He felt a little too on the defensive, and resolved to take himself off it again before proceeding. He mostly succeeded.

'If I met a woman who had a glass of champagne at a celebration, or ordered a glass of wine during a dinner out . . . I wouldn't see that as being a big problem.'

'Interesting,' she said. 'Sounds like you've made yourself the judge, jury and executioner on how much is enough and how much is too much.'

'Not at all,' August said, feeling he was pulling himself on to more solid ground at last.

'So where's the dividing line? If it's not arbitrary and not your own judgement, where do you draw the line?'

'It's simple,' he said. 'One takes place in a restaurant. The other in my home. People can do whatever they want in restaurants. It's really none of my concern. I can't make the world alcohol-free, and I wouldn't try. Those are things I can't control. But I control my home. And when I walk into the dining room or the kitchen and find an open bottle of booze in my living space, that's over the line. It has nothing to do with judging anybody else. I just know how I want to live in my own home.'

He waited, but she said nothing. She'd picked up the little wooden puzzle and was holding it in her palm, shaking it lightly back and forth. Watching the smoothly sanded pieces shift in place.

If Phillip had been there, he'd have taken it off her palm and placed it back on the table. He hated any kind of nervous habits, unnecessary repetitive movements. He said they made it too hard to think, and that thinking was already hard enough.

It struck August that he might have found his footing and she might have lost hers.

She never answered.

'So, tell me,' August said, 'Could you live in a house with no booze?'

To his surprise, he felt something rise in his chest, a desperately flapping small bird of anticipation and hope. He hadn't known any hope was even still alive in there. He'd been so preoccupied by the loss of his son that all other losses had been forced into seating deep in the shadows. So deep he'd lost track of them entirely.

'Of course I could,' she said. 'I just don't see why I should have to.'

The bird closed its wings and retreated back into the shadows.

'I have class notes still to do,' August said. 'I'm not sure what possessed you to come by here without calling first.'

'Still always feel the need to control everything, don't you?'

But August didn't. In fact, he noted with some pleasant sense of surprise, he didn't even need to convince her that he didn't.

'I'll walk you to the door,' he said.

August sat at the dining-room table for another half an hour, willing his computer to ring. He desperately wanted his conversation with the boys back. Too desperately, in fact, and he knew it. As if he needed their call to save himself. Which he knew wasn't right. Yet he couldn't quite grasp how to repair it.

He couldn't work on his notes, because he couldn't make his brain hold still.

He glanced at his watch to see that he was already twenty minutes late for his regular meeting. He would be thirty minutes late by the time he arrived. But it was the only option that made any sense, so he threw on a jacket, grabbed his car keys and ran.

'I wanted to talk to the boys,' August told Harvey over coffee, 'because I wanted them to know I know exactly how they feel.'

Harvey narrowed his eyes suspiciously.

'Because their ex-wives are also trying to win them back?'

'Because I wasn't the most important thing to her. I asked her if she'd put me before drinking. And the answer was no.'

'She's your ex, August. There's no such thing as an ex-parent. They needed their parents to put them first. And it's a parent's job to put their kids first. How many people do you know whose exes put their welfare above all else?'

'I think you're missing the point,' August said. 'I was married to her for almost twenty years. We raised a son together. She came over to my house to try to tell me we could work through the things that had split us.

Do you honestly not think part of me jumped at that idea? Do you think there wasn't any part of me that still wants that?'

The waitress inconveniently arrived to refill Harvey's coffee cup. The two men fell silent until she was gone.

'OK, I see your point,' Harvey said. 'I didn't mean to be dismissive. But let me throw another idea out there for you to consider. You wanted to talk to the boys to tell them you knew how they felt. Fine. Maybe. We're all human beings and there are things we all feel. You know how they feel when they're lonely, too, but you don't necessarily feel compelled to call them up and tell them so. I think you needed to talk to them because you need an emotional lifeline right now. And because you've made them your emotional lifeline. And that's not fair to them. They're kids. Somebody else's. You were supposed to be bailing *them* out, not vice versa.'

August frowned and stabbed his fork into the left-over pancakes he no longer wanted. He knew Harvey was right, but he resisted letting that truth in, because it meant he had to cut the cord.

'Why do I even bother to come talk to you, Harv?'

'If you don't want to hear the truth you're always welcome to stay away until you do.'

August sighed.

'So what do I do?'

'Same thing you did before you met them. Go to work, go to meetings. Call your sponsor. Work the steps. Get on with your life and let those boys get on with theirs. It's really the only thing you *can* do.'

*

In his sleep that night, August had a dream about
Phillip. The first he'd ever had. Well, that's not entirely
true. The first one in which Phillip had actually
appeared. In the weeks after the accident, August had
nearly nightly entertained a dream in which he learned
by phone call that Phillip was in the hospital. As in,
injured but alive. And almost nightly he raced to the
hospital to tell his son that he'd been told he was dead.
That he'd truly believed he was dead. But he always
woke up before he could get there.

This dream felt entirely different.

August dreamed he sat at the dining-room table, rolling that long-lost plastic bottle of iced tea around in his
fingers. But it wasn't half-full of iced tea. It was half-full
of ashes, the way it had been on the motorhome trip.

When he finally looked up, Phillip had come to sit at
the table with him. And August did not feel surprised.
He felt gratified. In fact, he felt as though his heart was
stretching, growing a size or two at a time. But he did
not feel the least bit surprised.

He tried to speak but couldn't. Literally couldn't.

'I would *so* go over Niagara Falls in a barrel,' Phillip
said.

'Would you?' August said, suddenly finding his voice.
'I thought maybe you were the sort who wouldn't.'

'I was alive. And that might have killed me. So back
then, no. But now I would. In a heartbeat.'

August looked down at the bottle again, thinking of what difference Phillip's words might make to

any plans for scattering the rest of the ashes. When he looked up Phillip was gone.

August woke up sitting upright in bed. The clock said it was ten after four in the morning, and all he could think was how much he wished he could call Henry and Seth and tell them about his dream. It wasn't until later that he realized he couldn't, even if they called the very next day, because he'd told Seth that Phillip was a thrill-seeker in life. This would have to be his little secret.

But the urge to connect with them remained. Which is how he knew Harvey was right. He had made those boys his lifeline. And that wasn't fair to them. It had been his job to bail them out. Definitely not the other way around.

It took ten or eleven days to move it all the way down into his gut, but August accepted those words. It was good that he did, too. Because Seth didn't call again until Christmas.

When he did, he reported that his father was indeed staying true to his word and having only two or three drinks a night.

With a catch. The drinks kept getting bigger.

By the time Seth called, a drink – by their dad's standards – was a twelve-ounce water glass full of straight scotch or vodka. No water, no ice, no nothing.

But the boys were OK, Seth said, because he stayed home.

At the end of the conversation, Seth thanked August

for the open offer that the boys could stay with him in a pinch. And he did so in a way that made it clear to August that he was an important factor in that OK-ness. Nothing was guaranteed in that world, but Seth and Henry lived in a reasonable state of relaxation because they always had August as a Plan B.

August remembered Harvey's words, and when he said goodbye he silently let them go. Released them into their own lives. He wished for their father to stay out of trouble, even if it meant he'd never see the boys again. Because that's just what you do.

You let go.

Part Three

Late May, Eight Years On

1
Weakness

August made his way through the living room slowly, careful not to trip over Woody, and sat down at his computer. He closed his eyes and made a simple, silent wish.

Please let Seth be there.

He'd geared himself up to do this, and it hadn't been easy. If Seth was away from his dorm room, August would lose his nerve. He could feel it. And he had no idea how long it would take him to gear up again.

He booted up his laptop and opened Skype.

After eight years, he still had only one Skype contact. Seth.

He clicked on the icon to call him, relieved that Seth's status showed as online.

August could call Seth now without worry, now that Seth was away at the university. The previous year, his freshman year, they'd talked often. Eight or ten times, which was more than all the years before that put together. This year Harvey's prediction about life going on seemed to have been borne out again.

Either that or August had been trying to avoid the conversation he was about to have now.

'August,' Seth said, appearing in a window on his screen.

He was tall now, like his father. Awkwardly tall, as if life had stretched him. He wore small, round, wire-rimmed glasses, and his hair hung down long in the back, curling into – and over – his collar. Like his father.

He'd grown a beard, a small, neatly-trimmed goatee that August had never seen. Last time August called, Seth had been clean-shaven.

'Hey, Seth. This is new, huh?'

August pulled at his own chin so Seth would know what he meant.

'Oh. Yeah,' Seth said, seeming embarrassed. 'Grand experiment. I might keep it or I might not. Listen, August. I'm sorry it's been so many months. I've just been so busy with school. My class load is insane this semester. I have no idea what I was thinking signing up for all this.'

'It's not you,' August said. 'I could have called, too. But I've been having some stuff going on. Some health issues . . .'

'Yeah, you mentioned that last time we talked, but you didn't really go into detail about it. And you looked great. Still do, by the way. So . . . OK now?'

'No, there are some ongoing problems . . .'

Seth's face changed as he caught the fear.

I did this badly, August thought. *I should have come into it through a different door. Not worried him so.*

'Oh, please, August, spit it out fast. How bad is it?'

'It's not life-threatening,' he said quickly.

Seth sat back against his chair with a thump August could hear. 'Well, thank God for that,' he said. 'Talk to me. What's going on? You look great.'

'It's not the kind of thing you'd see when I'm sitting at the computer. It's not that kind of sick. It's just . . . the last few months . . . I've been having trouble with my legs.'

Seth's eyebrows scrunched down. Almost comically, if this hadn't been such a serious moment.

'Your legs?'

'Yeah. They're getting weaker. Really for a lot longer than a few months, but you know how you have a million explanations for things. And then after a while it kind of breaks through that it's something more than normal. I've been running after a diagnosis for a while. I think that's why I haven't called in months. I didn't want to tell you I had something like that hanging over my head but no diagnosis yet.'

'But you have one now?'

'I do. As of today. It's a type of muscular dystrophy.'

August paused. He wasn't sure why. Maybe in case Seth had thoughts he wanted to express. Maybe because it was hard to go on.

'You have no idea how much I wish I could talk to you and Google something at the same time,' Seth said.

'Well, don't scare yourself too much with the research. Because there are some very nasty forms that I don't have. Distal, they call this. It affects the extremities. Hands and arms, calves, feet. My hands are good now but they might not stay that way. But there are a lot of forms of the disease and this is not the worst of them. It'll keep progressing, but this one tends to go slowly. And it's not life-threatening. I'll probably live about as long as I was going to anyway.'

Seth blinked a few times, then took off his glasses and rubbed his eyes.

Seth's room-mate came bounding in behind him, noisily, with a string of words August couldn't quite make out.

'Pete, I'm right in the middle of something important,' Seth said. 'So either shut up or get out.'

'Geez,' Pete said, peering into the computer screen at August. 'Someone's in a mood.'

Then he disappeared again.

Seth took an audible deep breath and composed himself. 'This sounds scary,' he said.

And August, who was in no mood to play games, said, 'It is.'

'What's the upshot of all this? How does your life change?'

'Kind of hard to predict. Depends on how fast it progresses. But I'm already having some trouble walking. I've been using a cane for a month or two, but pretty soon it's going to be two canes. Maybe leg braces. Worst case, I suppose I could end up in a wheelchair, but it might not get as bad as all that. Just depends on how fast it progresses.'

'Can you still drive?'

August wondered if Seth had accidentally bumped into August's reason for calling, or if he knew exactly where August was headed next.

'I've been driving. Up until just recently. Right now my car is in being fitted with hand controls. But later, if I start to have trouble with my hands . . . I may not always drive. Which leads me to what I actually called to tell you. I mean, I called to tell you about my diagnosis, of course. But I had to make a decision. And, maybe I'm wrong. Maybe it won't mean a thing to you, but . . .'

'August, what?'

'The motorhome has to go. I have to sell it.'

Seth fell silent. August tried to read his face, but without success.

Maybe August had too much hopeful speculation wrapped up in whether or not the boys cared about that old rig. Maybe he was only telling himself this story about their unforgettable summer, and how the rig represented that time, making it historic and sentimental. Maybe it was just a big piece of metal to them. Maybe it should just be a big piece of metal to August.

'Couldn't you get hand controls in the rig?' Seth asked after a time.

'It's more than just that, though. It's going up and down those narrow back stairs. And dumping the tanks and hooking up the water and the electric. You have to stand up and have your hands free for that stuff. It's just a little too much for me now. Already. And it's not going to get any better.'

'Oh,' Seth said. And turned his eyes down, away from the screen.

'I didn't know if it would be a big deal to you or not. I know you have some memories tied up in it . . .'

'You can say that again,' Seth said.

It warmed a place in August's chest. He tried to answer but couldn't find words.

'How much're you asking for it?'

'I haven't figured that out yet. I'll have to do some research on what it's worth. It's old, and it has a lot of miles on it.'

'Let *me* buy it, August.'

It was something August hadn't expected Seth to say, and it took him a minute to regroup and pull his thoughts together.

'You sure you want it just for sentimental reasons?'

'No, not *just* for sentimental reasons. To take trips in. I can use it when I go climbing. I'd have to pay you a little every month, though. I mean . . . maybe a *really* little. Would that be OK?'

'Of course it would. But are you sure about this? Like I say, it's old, and it has a lot of miles on it.'

'August. I grew up in a mechanic's shop. I can fix seventy-five per cent of what goes wrong with it and the other twenty-five per cent my dad'll fix for free.'

'Well, that's a good point.'

'It's settled, then. As soon as school lets out for the summer I'll come down to San Diego and pick it up.'

It lifted something in August's chest to think of Seth coming for a visit. It was something he'd never considered when he'd made the call.

'OK, then. Settled. Listen. Will you tell Henry the news?'

'No.' Seth shook his head vehemently. 'No, I couldn't, August. It's big stuff. He needs to hear it from you. I'll tell you what. I'll have him call you. I'll have him call you on the phone next time my dad's out of the house. Shouldn't take long. He's gone all night again, most nights.'

'Oh, no. I thought your dad was keeping his word on that.'

'That was a long time ago, August. Since I've been away at school . . . well . . . I guess he thinks I was the policeman on that plan. And, you know . . . Henry's fifteen. Not exactly a kid.'

'You didn't tell me, though.'

'I didn't want you to worry.' A silence, during which Seth didn't meet August's eyes on the screen. 'So, anyway, Henry'll call you, and you can tell him yourself, OK?'

'OK,' August said. 'That's good.'

He dreaded the idea of having the conversation a second time. But Seth was right. Henry needed to hear it first-hand.

'Be nice to see you again,' Seth said, breaking into a shy smile. 'Gosh, it's only been eight years. Huh?

How'd we let so much time go by, August? When we swore we wouldn't?'

'No idea,' August said. 'I have no idea why time does what it does. Or why people do what we do. It's all a mystery to me.'

Henry called a little before ten that night, blasting August out of sleep. August was too freshly awakened to understand that it was not the middle of the night, and therefore assumed it was a sign of big trouble.

When he realized it was Henry, August was not so much perturbed that Henry would call so late. More humiliated to have gone to bed so early.

'I'm sorry, August,' Henry said. 'I know it's not polite to call this late but I just got off the phone with Seth and I have to know what's going on.'

'Henry?' August asked, knowing but still doubting.

'Yeah, it's me.'

'My God. Your voice has changed. You sound like a grown man.'

'Oh, come on. You've talked to us since my voice changed.'

'Maybe. But Seth did all the talking.'

August raised up on to one elbow, and Woody came and rubbed against him, as if asking what all the commotion was about.

'What's going on, August? Seth said you're selling the motorhome. And he told me we're buying it. Well, him. Well, sort of we. He said he'd take me with him when he goes climbing.'

'You climb too?'

'No! Me? Are you kidding? He's taking me to Yosemite and Joshua Tree with him, but not up the walls. He'd never get me up the walls, not even with a pitchfork or a bayonet. Not even with both. But why are you selling the rig? First I didn't think much of it because I figured you were just trading up on a newer one. You know. Must be pretty old by now. But he said no. No more going away all summer. But you love going away all summer. The national parks and the hiking and the driving. It's almost like you wouldn't be you without that. And he wouldn't tell me why. He said I had to call you and let you tell me. So now I'm nervous and there's no way I could've gotten any sleep. So tell me. Please?'

When he finally wound down, August almost felt a desire to ask one more time, 'Henry?' He had never heard Henry string so many words together at one time. Had he changed so much in that regard? Or was his worry bringing it out?

It took August a beat or two to begin. He was still reverberating from Henry's assessment. That he wouldn't be August without those summers. It had been playing at the edges of his mind since the diagnosis, but he hadn't phrased it quite so succinctly to himself. Now that Henry had, he felt a little stunned, and wondered who he would be from now on. He couldn't escape the feeling that it would be someone not nearly as good.

'I'm facing some health issues—' he began.

'Oh God. That's what I was afraid of. If you say you're

dying, August, I swear I'll die right along with you. Right here, right now.'

'I'm not dying.'

'Oh, thank God. Thank God you're not dying. I don't think I could've taken that. So what's so bad that you can't get out in that motorhome again?'

'Distal muscular dystrophy.'

A long silence.

'Hold on,' Henry said, in his still-surprising man voice. 'I'm looking that up.'

August waited. Gratefully. He was relieved not to have to run through the whole thing again.

'Oh,' Henry said after a time.

'Could be worse,' August said.

'Could be better,' Henry replied without pause.

Then another long silence fell. August didn't know whether Henry was reading, or just absorbing what he'd already read.

'This totally sucks,' Henry said after a time. 'The only thing that doesn't suck about it is that we get to see you soon. The tenth, Seth said.'

'We? I didn't know you were coming, too. That's great!'

'Shit,' Henry said. 'Oh. Sorry. Sorry I cussed, August. I just did something stupid. It was supposed to be a surprise. So don't tell Seth I told you. I said I'd come along to help him drive.'

'You drive?'

'I have my learner's permit.'

'And that's all you need?'

'I can't drive alone. But I can drive with an adult.'

'How old is an adult for these purposes? Eighteen? Or twenty-one? Because Seth isn't twenty-one.'

'Oh. I didn't think of that. I don't know. But . . . Well. Even if I can't drive, I can help keep him awake while *he* drives.'

'It's only six or seven hours, you know.'

Henry offered no reply. It was as though August's comment had just stopped him cold. And August had no idea why.

'But listen to me,' August said. 'What am I saying? Of course I want you to come, no matter what the reason. I miss you even more than I miss Seth, because I talk to him more now that he's away at college.'

A brief pause.

Then Henry asked, 'You miss us?'

'Of course I do.'

'I'm sorry I don't keep in touch the way Seth does. You know how it is. He's more of a rebel than I am. Always has been.'

'I don't understand. Why would you have to be a rebel to keep in touch with me?'

'Argh!' Henry said, a breathy exclamation. 'Stupid, stupid, stupid. I'm really messing this up, August. I shouldn't even be talking. I should go back to my mute routine, because I ruin everything. See you in fifteen days. Can't wait.'

And then he was gone.

*

August sat up for a long time, watching TV but not really hearing or seeing it. Wondering if he was right to think that something about that conversation had seemed strange.

Harvey pulled into the driveway and honked at about seven thirty the following evening. Just as August's lack of sleep was beginning to catch up with him. Woody leapt up on to the back of the couch and barked loudly enough to hurt August's ears.

'Hush,' he said to the dog, running a hand along the wiry fur on his back. 'It's just my ride. It's just Harvey.'

The use of Harvey's name brought silence, and caused Woody's tail to twitch.

August made his way to his feet and reached for his two canes, which were leaning against the coffee table. He was disappointed, but not entirely surprised, when Harvey beat him to the door.

'Yeah, I'm coming, Harv,' he said. 'Give me a second.'

Opening the door was a bit tricky, because it opened in. He didn't want to lean forward too far. He didn't want the door flying open and hitting him or his canes. So he sidled up close to the door, unlocked it, then carefully stepped back several feet.

'Come in,' he said.

Harvey stepped into his living room, got down on one knee, and greeted the bouncing dog.

'He never changes, does he? Still acts like a puppy. Ready to go?'

'As I'll ever be. Woody, stay and be a good dog. I just have to go to my meeting. I'll be home soon.'

Harvey held the door for him, then locked it behind them. While August carefully made his way along the walkway, Harvey trotted ahead to his car and opened the passenger door for August.

The way everybody did these days.

Doors flew open for him at school. Chairs magically pulled back, in the grip of people he hadn't even seen coming, and were held steady for him as he sat. Seemingly disembodied hands braced his elbows as he stood. Except at home, of course. Where he was on his own.

Part of him wanted to tell people to stop. That he had to adjust, to find his way. But each logistical movement through his day was so tiring. It was so much easier to take the easy way out each time.

Harvey took August's canes from him and placed them in the back seat, then reached for August's elbow.

'No, I'm good,' August said. 'I'll just get a good hold on this handle over the door.'

He seated himself with a sigh.

Woody sat in the window, wagging faintly and watching them go. A flash of a memory darted into August's brain. Standing under Weeping Rock with the boys, at Zion. Seth asking if it made Woody sad to have to stay behind. Which August had never considered before.

It must, though.

Still, every one of us has something that makes him

sad, August thought. *And no one can save us from all of it.*

Harvey plunked down in the driver's seat and started the engine.

'So. Two canes now. Does that means it's progressing faster than you thought?'

'No. It means I waited much too long to go to two canes. I took a couple of falls, and everything was harder than it should have been. Denial. Not that you'd know anything about that.'

'Hopefully this will do it for awhile.'

'Unless I develop any weakness in my hands. Then I'll have to go with those metal ones that go around my forearms.'

They pulled out of the driveway in silence.

A block or two later, Harvey said, 'And yet you look so blissfully happy. Why is that? If I didn't know you better, I'd think you were seeing someone new. That you'd fallen in love. But I'm your sponsor. So surely you'd have told me if that was the case.'

'I'm not seeing anyone new.'

'I suspected as much. It's the boys. Right? Coming for a visit.'

'I think so, yeah. I mean, I had no idea I looked blissfully happy. But if I do, that's why.'

'I think your life has gotten too small when a visit from a couple of kids makes you look like you're falling in love.'

'I don't think that's a very nice thing to say. You know how I feel about those guys.'

'I'm sorry,' Harvey said. 'I didn't mean to be dismissive. Love is love. I just wish you'd be more open to trying other kinds of relationships.'

'I know you do.'

He didn't say more because they'd been through it before.

'When do you get your car back?'

'They're being a little vague about it. But hopefully next week. I really want it back in time to go pick up the boys at the bus station.'

'Thought they were driving.'

'Change of plans. Not sure why. Maybe they want to drive home together. Or maybe they're going straight to some kind of trip.'

'You get to ask, you know.' August ignored that. 'Well, if they don't get your car done on time, you know I'll drive you.'

'Thanks.'

A few more blocks of silence.

Then August said, 'Did I tell you about the somewhat odd conversation I had with Henry the other night?'

'You told me you talked to both of them. You didn't say it was odd.'

'It might be my imagination.'

'I doubt it. If it felt odd, it was probably odd.'

'He just . . . he kept acting like there was stuff he was avoiding saying. Turns out I wasn't supposed to know he was coming. It was a surprise. But he blew that, so he told me not to tell Seth he had. And then later he got all flustered and acted like he was doing nothing but make mistakes. But I don't know what the other mistakes were.'

'Try to be optimistic about it. The one secret he let slip was a happy one. Maybe there are more happy surprises.'

'That would be nice,' August said. Then, because it was too heavy and obvious to leave unsaid, he added, 'For a change.'

Harvey frowned but said nothing. They'd been doing quite a bit of work lately on helping August walk a good line with the diagnosis. Not minimizing the seriousness of the issue, but also not falling to the other extreme. Self-pity.

August briefly wondered if that was the real reason behind why he always felt so tired lately. Seemed the figurative, internal straight line was harder to walk than the literal, physical one.

'And then he said something to me at the end of the conversation that I still don't understand. He was apologizing for the fact that Seth keeps in better touch than he does—'

'Helps when you're verbal,' Harvey interjected.

'Well, Henry was verbal when he called the other night. So he can be if he wants to be. Anyway, he said it was because Seth's more of a rebel. And I didn't get that.'

'Seems self-explanatory. Their dad told them not to.'

'But they've ignored that from the start and gone behind his back. That's a given. I don't know. Maybe I'm making it out to be a bigger thing than it is.'

'You know,' Harvey said, in that tone he usually adopted when about to say something that would make August want to slug him, 'if you don't know what somebody means by something, you can ask. It's called communication.'

'Funny. I did ask. That's when he got all flustered and acted like everything he said was a mistake. And then he hurried off the phone and that was that.'

'Well. They'll be here soon. And more will be revealed.'

And then they'll go to Yosemite, August thought. *And Joshua Tree. And they'll hike. And camp. And Seth will climb. And they'll have campfires in the evening. And spend all day on the trail, or the open road.*

And I won't.

And with that, August felt himself fall off the center line for the first time. Deeply into self-pity. He didn't even bother to try to break his own fall. He just sank all the way down. Let the current take him away.

2
Grown

August leaned his back up against the outside wall of the bus station, grateful to ease his weight off his tired arms. He waited for the bus to pull up out front, so he could meet the boys before they walked into the station. To minimize his own walking.

It was the end of the last day of school, and he was painfully tired.

Three buses pulled in, but all turned out to be disappointingly from somewhere else.

By the time he saw the bus that would prove to be the right one, August deeply regretted having no place to sit down.

He saw them in the window as the bus drew by – too far by. He would have to walk again. He watched their hands go up in a static wave, their faces changing with emotion and relief.

He did not feel what he had expected to feel.

In his imagination, it was a moment marked by a

swell of positive emotion. It resolved the eight years of semi-silence. And it was simple. It was all good. It was just good.

When will I ever learn, he thought. *Nothing is ever that simple. Nothing is ever all good.*

Instead he felt a ringing emptiness, a sense of profound loss. One of the people he'd just waved to was a man. A young man, but a man. The other was a teenager. A young adult. They were not the children he remembered. They were not children. They had grown into people he knew little about. And they had done so without his help or influence, or even – for the most part – his witness.

It made him feel as though something precious had been taken from him.

He shook himself free of the moment and began the long – by his new standards – walk to the spot where the bus had stopped.

He looked down to be sure he wasn't about to tangle his canes with the feet of other people headed for the bus. When he looked up, Seth was coming in his direction, fast. Apparently Seth planned to bowl him over with a hug. Unfortunately, Seth probably didn't realize how easily bowled over August could be these days. How literal that phrase could become.

'Careful!' he said, suddenly, and without much thought.

Seth froze, his face falling, and closing up fast. He was clean-shaven now. August was vaguely aware of people brushing past their shoulders.

'It's easier than you think to knock me down. Do give me a big hug. But when I lift my arms to hug you back, you're going to be the only thing holding me up. So don't let go without notice.'

Seth's face softened, but not into simple relief. More like a mixture of relief and a shot of pain, or even pity, over August's new condition.

Next thing August knew, he was wrapped in Seth's surprisingly strong arms. He was still thin, but the climbing had changed him. Again it struck August that Seth was a grown man.

He raised his arms, canes and all, and hugged Seth in return.

Over Seth's shoulder he saw Henry, looking shy as ever. August smiled, and Henry averted his eyes and then smiled back. But by then Henry was smiling at the concrete of the bus-station sidewalk.

August carefully braced on his canes again.

'OK, I'm good,' he said.

Seth let him go and stepped back. He held August briefly by the shoulders and smiled into his face in a way that looked worried and a little sad. Whether the shoulder hold was intended as physical or emotional support, August had no idea. Maybe both.

Henry stepped up for his turn.

'Careful how you hug him,' Seth told his brother. 'Don't knock him down. And let him know before you let go.'

'Yeah, yeah,' Henry said, 'I heard all that. I can do it just as carefully as you can.'

Henry's hug was different. Gentler, and with more of a sense that he was not only giving support to August, but taking support from him as well.

'We have to get our bags,' Henry said quietly into August's ear. 'We have lots of bags.'

August braced with his canes, and Henry carefully released him.

'Why so much stuff? Aren't you going straight home?'

August watched the boys exchange a cryptic look between them.

'No,' Seth said. 'We're going climbing.'

'Straight from here? I didn't know. Good thing I left so much in the rig. Flashlights and screwdrivers and pots and dishes and a million other things I would have taken out if I'd sold it to a stranger.'

Or if I were in any shape to haul a million things up and down those narrow back stairs, he thought. He didn't say it.

For a moment he was struck with a second great wave of loss. Seth and Henry were going to Yosemite and Joshua Tree. And August was not. And he probably never would again.

'Where's Woody?' Seth asked as they made their way through the parking lot at a painfully slow pace. 'We thought you'd bring him.'

'He's waiting in the car. It's hard for me to walk him on leash these days, because I need both hands to walk. I pay a neighbor's girl to take him out now.'

August could feel his tiredness translating into un-coordinated movements. And they just got slower. He could sense how hard it was for the boys to move at this pace. How they had to keep reminding themselves. They both had two massive olive-green duffle bags, one on each shoulder. August wondered if they would have offered to help him walk if they weren't so burdened. But he had to be able to walk on his own, even at the end of an extra-long day.

'Well, don't you worry,' Seth said. 'We'll take him for lots of walks.'

'Oh? I thought you were leaving in the morning.'

He tried to keep his tone flat and even. It hurt him a little – no, maybe more than a little – that they hadn't chosen to make a longer visit out of it. But of course he hadn't said so out loud.

He watched another look pass between the boys.

'Right,' Seth said. 'Well. We'll have to work fast, then.'

August almost said it then. Stay a little longer. What's your hurry? We haven't seen each other in eight years. Yosemite and Joshua Tree will still be there in a few days.

But he felt himself skating dangerously close to the line of self-pity. So he said nothing at all.

'He doesn't remember us,' Henry said, his voice betraying his surprise and disappointment.

Woody stood with his paws on the passenger-side window and barked at the boys. And barked and barked. And barked.

'You look a little different, you know,' August said. 'Wait till he gets a sniff of you. Then he might change his tune.'

At least, August hoped so. But he really had no idea how long a dog could remember.

Only two of the massive duffles fit in August's trunk. So Henry had to wedge two in the back seat, one on top of the other, and then try to find a spot for himself beside them. Meanwhile Seth settled into the front passenger seat, and Woody retreated to the driver's seat and gave him a long-distance sniff. The dog cocked his head slightly. He leaned in and took a close-up sniff of Seth's bare arm. Suddenly a noise escaped the dog's throat, sounding like a cross between a bark and a whimper. He leaped into Seth's lap and began sniffing – then licking – all around Seth's neck as Seth dropped his head back and laughed.

'See?' August said, relieved.

He began the difficult task of lowering himself into the driver's seat.

'Want help?' Henry asked immediately.

'Oh. No. Thanks, Henry, but no. The more I practice this, the better.'

Still Woody wiggled on Seth's lap, his paws up on the young man's chest, trying to direct his licks more toward Seth's face. Seth continued to hold his head back. And laugh. And the laughter filled a huge hole that had been gaping open in August's life, but he hadn't even known it. He hadn't consciously felt the gaping. But it struck him that he should have known.

He eased himself into the seat with a sigh, and placed his canes on the passenger side, near Seth's knees.

'Hey, Woody,' Henry said from the back, clearly tired of waiting. 'What about me?'

And Woody flew. It didn't even look like a jump. August never saw him push off. He appeared to just lift off like one of those military planes that go straight up on take-off. August looked over his shoulder in time to see him land in Henry's lap.

Henry didn't drop his head back. He allowed the dog to direct the torrent of kisses at his nose and mouth.

Henry opened his mouth to say something that sounded like, 'He remembers me.' But he shouldn't have. He should never have opened his mouth. August could hear him spitting and huffing, and see him wiping his face on his sleeve, trying to recover from dog kisses to his open mouth.

'You have to keep your mouth closed,' August said.

'Now you tell me,' Henry replied, holding the dog at arm's length long enough to say it.

'That is so cool,' Seth said.

He was watching August use a hand control to accelerate.

August was barely used to the new hand-operated throttle and brake, and he felt awkward using them, especially while being watched. But Seth didn't seem to notice his lack of ease.

'How long have you had them?'

'I only got the car back from installing them day before yesterday.'

'You're good at them.'

'Think so? Still feels awkward.'

'Seems like you're good with them.'

'You sure you can't stay a little longer?'

So there it was. He had said it.

August listened to the silent echo of his words. He'd had no idea he was about to say them. Part of him wished he hadn't. Another part of him knew he'd had to, sooner or later, and was glad he'd finally gotten it over with.

He watched the boys exchange another glance, until Henry caught August watching in the rear-view mirror and carefully looked away, out the window.

'It's just that . . . we haven't seen each other in so long.'

'You can say that again,' Seth said.

'Really,' Henry added.

'So why run off in the morning?'

'Don't worry,' Seth said. 'We'll have a great visit. Promise.'

'So you're staying another day or two?'

'We'll have a great visit. Take my word for it.'

'I can't stay up and talk all night the way I might have when I was younger. I get tired early.'

Another glance between the boys.

'August. Trust me. I'm promising you. We'll have a great visit.'

August didn't know how to get more specifics out of them, and he wasn't liking himself very well for trying.

So he abandoned the subject for the rest of the ride home.

The minute they'd finished eating Henry stood up at the dinner table, seeming slightly nervous. He banged his thighs on the edge of the table, then looked nervous and embarrassed at the same time.

'I'll start loading our stuff in the motorhome. Seth, you do the thing with August, OK?'

Then he disappeared without waiting to see if it was OK or not.

August looked over at Seth, who averted his gaze.

'What thing with August?' August asked.

'Oh. Well. I'll tell you. No, I'll show you. Which one is your room? Come on into your room, and I'll show you what the thing is.'

August tried to rise, but plunked back into his chair again. It was harder at the end of the day. Everything made him tired.

Seth ran around the table and helped him up.

'Thanks,' August said, and reached for his canes.

'Forget the canes,' Seth said. 'You have me. Come on. Let's do this thing.'

'This thing being . . .'

'You have to come with me into your room and then I'll show you.'

August sighed. He was curious. And accepting help seemed the fastest way to get where he wanted to go.

He threw an arm over Seth's shoulder, and Seth wrapped an arm firmly around his waist, and they walked slowly into August's bedroom. It was messy, because he'd been too tired to clean it. And he'd been hoping no one would see.

It was easy walking, because Seth supported a lot of his weight.

He eased himself down on the end of the bed with Seth's help.

'OK,' August said. 'We're here now. What's this all about?'

'I want you to point to everything you used to pack when you went away for the summer.'

August sighed again. He had been hoping there was more to the 'thing' than just that.

'It won't work,' he said. 'You needed to know all that before you left home. It's too late.'

'What?'

'Why didn't you ask me for a list of what to bring before you left? I have a special packing list for RV trips. I could have sent you a copy.'

'Oh. That's good. Where's that?'

'On the computer.'

'Can I print out a copy?'

'Seth, it's too late. Whatever you forgot to bring, it's too late. You'll have to buy it on the road or do without it. You missed your chance to organize your stuff.'

'*Our* stuff?' Seth burst into a grin. 'You still don't know, do you? You don't get it. All the mistakes Henry made. All the hints we dropped. And you still don't know. August. We don't want a list of what to pack for *us*. We want a list of what to pack for *you*.'

The words spun in August's head and added up to nothing. They never found their purpose.

'Still not getting it.'

'August. Geez. What does it take? Do I have to draw you a map? You're going.'

'I'm going?'

'You're going. We're taking you with us. Why do you think I kept saying we'd have a great visit? Even though we're leaving in the morning?'

August didn't answer. Instead he held perfectly still and tried to catch up. To let reality change for him. Adjust to what had been there all along, except in his brain. Or to begin to, anyway.

'I can't drive the motorhome.'

'I can.'

'I'm not good on those stairs.'

'We'll get you up and down them.'

'I can't—'

'August, stop. It doesn't matter what you can't. You don't have to. We'll do it all. Just like you did for us. We didn't have anything to contribute that summer. You just took us anyway. You just did it all.'

'Are you sure?'

'Never been surer of anything in my life.'

Again, August struggled in silence. He wanted to express some kind of gratitude, but he hadn't caught up yet. Everything was happening so fast.

Besides, Seth didn't give him time.

'Now what should I pack, August? Can I print out that list?'

'But we don't need a whole summer's worth of stuff just to go to Joshua Tree and Yosemite.'

'August. You're running on slow again. Did you see all that stuff we hauled up here on the bus? We're not just going to Joshua Tree and Yosemite. We're going both places, but they're just an appetizer. We're going out all summer.'

'Where?'

'You don't get to know that yet. Now come on. We have to leave first thing in the morning. Let's get you packed. You point to it, I pack it. Let's go.'

'I hate to even ask this,' August said, halfway through the socks and underwear. 'But I think I have to. I didn't budget for gas the way I usually do. I don't have enough money for a very long trip.'

'It's on us,' Seth said.

'You rob a bank?'

'Nope. Got a credit card. They push them hard on college students. Don't freak out, and don't lecture. I know it's not free money. I know it has to be paid back. But I don't care. I'll work all year to pay it back. We're doing this.'

'One more thing you have to bring,' Seth said.

He handed a stack of folded clothing to Henry at the bedroom doorway, and Henry disappeared with it.

'That's it for our list.'

'I know. But there's one more thing.'

'It's a very comprehensive list.'

'August . . .'

'OK, fine. What's the thing?'

'A little bit of Phillip's ashes. Doesn't have to be as much as last time. Just some. You didn't sprinkle all the rest or something, did you?'

'No, they're still in an urn over the fireplace. All but what we scattered in Yellowstone.'

'Do you trust me?'

'Of course I do.'

'I'll need a little plastic bag.'

'Top kitchen drawer next to the dishwasher.'

'Be right back.'

August remained sitting on the bed, still a bit stunned. Still not entirely adjusted to this sudden turn of events. Every time he tried to sort it out in his head, something outside his head distracted him.

'Seth,' he called, providing his own distraction this time. 'There's a plastic bag inside the urn. With a twist tie. You might want to undo it in the sink. It tends to get all over.'

'I know,' Seth called back. 'I've handled them. Remember?'

'Right,' August said. But too quietly for Seth to hear.

Seth appeared in the doorway three or four minutes later. August had actually had time to sort and think. He was closer to understanding that he was going away for the whole summer after all. With the boys.

Seth leaned a shoulder on the door frame as August looked up into his wide-open face.

'I still regret dropping that bottle,' Seth said.

'I thought you'd let that go.'

'Shoot, August, I don't let anything go. I say I do to get people off my back. In your case I said I did because I knew it hurt you that I didn't.'

'But it was a great place for those ashes to go.'

'But the bottle. You wanted to keep the bottle.'

'I hadn't really thought of what I would do with the bottle.'

'But you wouldn't have thrown it away.'

'I wouldn't have put it in the trash, no. Because it wasn't trash. I don't know if I would have kept it for ever.'

'Yes, you do. You know.'

'I do?'

'Absolutely you do. You would have kept it for ever. Come on, August. You told me the story. How the bottle made it so real. Made *him* so real. Like he might be just about to walk in and finish that tea.'

August nodded. Lost in thought. For a minute he couldn't find his way out again to answer.

When he did, he said, 'But he's not, though. I think the day you dropped that bottle it was high time for me to accept the fact that he's not.'

3
Rigorous Honesty

August woke slowly, like drifting up through a veil of translucent water. Even with his eyes open, he felt as though he were still asleep, and happy enough to stay that way. Or half that way.

He looked out through the bug-spattered windshield of the motorhome, vaguely still absorbing the difference in perspective. It was all different from the passenger's seat. He had never, until earlier that morning, ridden in the passenger's seat of his own rig. Maggie had been a less-than-confident driver, and had never been willing to take the wheel of a vehicle she considered an oversize beast.

It was dusk. Nearly dark. The landscape had the uninhabited blankness of flat California desert.

When he'd finally roused himself a bit more, he looked left, to Seth in the driver's seat, who glanced back and offered a little smile.

'Where are we?' August asked, his voice still a blur of
sleep.

It made him feel young, too young, like a child riding
in the back seat of a car. A child asking, 'Are we there
yet?' There was a strange, out-of-control sensation to
not being the adult. Like a child, ceding all the driving,
trip planning, and other details to the adult. He wasn't
used to it, to phrase it mildly. Yet he found he didn't
mind. He found almost a sense of comfort in handing
over the reins.

'Hopefully not too far from Joshua Tree,' Seth said.

August laughed out loud.

'What's funny?'

'I think we just set a new world record,' August said,
'for shortest amount of distance covered in the greatest amount of time. What would it be if you drove it
straight through? Like, two and a half hours?'

'Something like that, yeah. But why would you drive
it straight through when there are so many things to
stop and climb?'

August craned his neck around to check on Henry,
in his usual seat on the couch. If indeed one can still
have a 'usual' after an eight-year hiatus. Henry was fast
asleep, his chin resting on his narrow chest, one surprisingly large hand draped over Woody's back.

'So, I guess we'll have to find a place to stay outside
the park tonight,' August said.

'Nope.'

'How do you figure?'

'We have reservations.'

'Ah. Smart.'

'I may not know where we'll be each night for the rest of the trip, but I knew where we'd be tonight, and for the next few days. And it's gonna be so damned hot there, I may not get in any really good climbing except around dawn. I didn't want to waste a whole day.'

August allowed the dusky desert to flow by for a moment or two, in silence, nursing that responsibility-free sensation of being along for the ride.

Then he said, 'Still not going to tell me where we're going?'

'Nope. Not telling you where we're going in the long run. I *will* tell you where we're going next.'

August laughed again. 'I might guess Joshua Tree.'

'And you might be wrong. Next we're going to a meeting.'

'You found a meeting out here?'

'I did.'

'Did you work out a list of them for the whole trip?'

'Nope. Just called AA Area Service on my cell phone.'

'Are we going to a meeting for me? Or for you? Or both?'

'Yes,' Seth said.

August leaned back again and watched the desert vegetation streak by. For the first of what would be hundreds of times, he told himself, Memorize this. Enjoy it. Don't miss a moment. Not a sight, not a smell, not a sound. Make the most of this whole summer out on the road. Because it's going to be your last.

'Staying or coming?' Seth shot over his shoulder to his brother.

'What?'

Apparently Henry was slow to shake that veil of sleep as well.

'We're going to a meeting. Staying or going?'

'What kind of meeting?'

'AA meeting. Open. Anyone can go. Think fast, dude. Wake up.'

'Staying.'

'Fine.'

August opened the passenger-side door and used the handle over the door to help himself down. Seth jumped out and ran around the front of the cab to help him, but August waved him away.

'I'm fine. Just hand me my canes when I'm all ready to walk, OK?'

They set off in the direction of the meeting place together, a little storefront turned into a fellowship hall for a Unitarian Universalist congregation.

It was almost completely dark now, except for the expansive desert sky glowing with light at one edge. August saw dim stars and streaks of orange light through the clouds over a range of mountains. The natural features seemed out of place against the gas stations and strip malls spread out under that amazing sky.

Seth walked slowly to match August's pace.

Suddenly August heard, 'Hey, wait up!'

They stopped and turned to see Henry running after them.

'Changed my mind,' he said, catching up. 'I want to go to the meeting, too.'

They walked slowly together, the three of them. It seemed so few steps from the rig to the fellowship hall, yet it was a slow undertaking for August. Sooner or later, he told himself, he'd have to adjust to that new reality. Accept it through and through.

'Were you worried about staying alone?' August asked Henry as they walked.

'No. Not at all. Woody was there.'

'What changed your mind?'

At first Henry said nothing at all.

Then, standing at the open doorway, August smelling the coffee and watching group members bustle around placing literature and chairs, Henry spoke again.

'I just figured . . . you know. I've got to live with the guy and all.'

August spent the first three-quarters of the meeting watching Henry in his peripheral vision. Watching to see how the information he was hearing settled in. He never quite saw what he was looking for, though. Henry hadn't lost the knack of being present and saying absolutely nothing, betraying absolutely nothing, leaving August sure Henry was thinking hard, but not at all sure what he was thinking.

Suddenly Henry turned his head and met August's eyes. His gaze stuck there. There was something determined about the exchange, but August had no idea what it meant.

Henry leaned over and whispered in his ear.

'I need to talk to you outside,' he said.

August lumbered carefully to his feet. Henry handed him his canes, which he could just as easily have picked up on his own. But people liked to help, and there was no reason to say anything about it. They made their way out the door, one of Henry's hands lightly on August's upper arm.

Seth watched with mild curiosity but said nothing. He did not follow.

'What's up?' August asked, leaning against the facade of the building.

'I have to level with you about something.'

'OK.'

August's stomach tightened slightly, even as he told himself this was likely nothing at all. Or close enough to nothing.

'I was sitting in that meeting, listening. Listening to all those people talk about rigorous honesty. And at first all I could think about was my dad. I kept thinking, yeah, he must really belong in these meetings, because that's exactly what he's missing, all right. And then it hit me. I've got a little rigorous honesty of my own to get around to.'

'OK,' August said again, wishing they could get where they were going faster.

'I didn't get my dad's permission to come on this trip.'

August held still and silent for a moment, waiting for the information to settle in. But even after it did, he wasn't sure of the upshot of the news. What it really meant. How bad it would turn out to be.

'You just took off without telling him?'

'Yes and no. I left him a note.'

'But he doesn't know where you are?'

'I just told him I was going away for the summer with Seth.'

'But not with me.'

'No! Of course not with you. Then he never would have let me go.'

'Couldn't you have told him to his face you were going away with just Seth?'

'He would've asked questions. He would've gotten it out of me. Nothing was going to keep me from doing this, August. Nothing.'

August tipped his head back and looked at the stars. They were brilliant. He was shocked by their number and clarity. He'd briefly forgotten he was in the desert. The light cast by this tiny town didn't amount to much.

Before August could find words, Henry continued.

'OK, the truth is I'm a really bad liar. Probably because I don't do it much. I don't like to say stuff that isn't true, so I just don't say anything at all. I couldn't have lied to his face. He'd have known. And then he wouldn't have let me go.'

'What if he calls the police?'

'And tells them what? What did I do so wrong?'

'He could report you as a runaway.'

'I don't think he will if he thinks I'm just with Seth.'

On the mention of the name Seth, as if by magic, August saw Seth standing beside them in the barely cool evening.

'What's up, August? Are you OK?'

'I'm fine.'

'I'm the problem,' Henry said. 'I didn't tell Dad I was going. I mean, I left him a note.'

'And told him what?' Seth asked, sounding apprehensive.

'That I was going away with you for the summer.'

Seth dug his cell phone out of his pocket. Tapped a few times with his thumb. Peered at it in silence.

'Wonder why he hasn't called me.'

'Three guesses,' Henry said.

'Oh,' Seth said. 'Got it. He hasn't gotten home yet.'

August did a little thinking and figuring in his head. Tried to think when the boys had left home.

Apparently Wes had been gone for the better part of two days.

'I wish you wouldn't be mad at me,' Henry said as they drove down Indian Cove Road toward their campground.

The headlights of the rig illuminated jumbled piles of interconnected rocks on each side of the road – jumbles that added up to formations thirty or forty feet high. It was hard for August to take his eyes off them.

324   CATHERINE RYAN HYDE

'I'm not mad at you,' August said.

'He was talking to me,' Seth said.

'Yeah,' Henry said. 'I was talking to Seth.'

'I just don't want anything messing this up,' Seth said.

'And if I'd told him more . . . or asked his permission . . . that wouldn't have messed things up?'

'It's just not how I would have handled it.'

'Oh, get off my case, Seth. Would you, please? There's no way you put this whole thing off on me. Notice you never once asked me anything? Not how I got his permission. Not what I told him. You just didn't want to know. That's the truth and you know it.'

They pulled into Indian Cove Campground in silence. Seth eased the rig along the narrow dirt road, looking for the site number that matched the printed-out reservation confirmation on his lap. At one point he pulled over, turned on the overhead cab light. Checked the number again. Turned it off and drove on.

In time he turned in beside a fire ring and picnic table, the headlights illuminating a solid face of dusty reddish rock. Seth parked the rig with about a foot between the rocks and the front bumper.

His cell phone rang.

He turned off the engine. Cut the lights. Everything around them felt dark and motionless, and August wondered why all the other campers seemed silent and invisible.

Another ring.

Seth pulled it out of his shirt pocket, the LED light of its screen casting a soft glow on his face.

'Dad?' Henry asked. As if he simply couldn't hold the word in a moment longer.

'Dad,' Seth said solemnly.

Another ring.

'Are you going to get it?' Henry asked.

'I'm thinking. What do I tell him? Do I lie?'

'I think you'd better.'

'I don't like to do that. Then I feel like I'm no better than he is.'

A fourth ring.

'You can't tell him the truth or he'll sic the cops on me or something.'

'I have to think about this,' Seth said.

The phone stopped ringing. August figured it must have gone to voicemail.

'I guess for all he knows we're out of range,' Henry said.

'Yeah,' Seth said. 'I guess.'

August heard a tone from the phone that he could only guess was notification of a new voicemail message.

'I'm dead tired,' Seth said. 'I'll worry about this mess in the morning.'

He opened the glove compartment and threw his phone in. It landed on the plastic bag of Phillip's ashes.

4
Climbing

August opened his eyes, surprised to see the carpet-lined roof of the motorhome. As though, in his sleep, he had forgotten that such a thing could ever happen again. He looked out the window to see the dawn just breaking. The sun gleamed through a notch in a sand-colored rock wall, made up of a stacked jumble of smaller, rounded rocks, each strangely long and vertical. It shone into August's eyes in a way he found oddly pleasant, strobing into visible rays that radiated in all directions.

He reminded himself again: Take it in, imprint it. Enjoy it. Because this is your last summer out in the world.

He heard a noise, and looked up to see Henry dash into the kitchen and plug in the coffee pot, which was apparently all set up to brew. Two raw eggs sat out on the counter, and Henry quickly broke them into a small frying pan on the two-burner propane stove. He pushed the lever down on the toaster, and two pieces of nubby wheat bread disappeared into it.

'You look like you know your way around a kitchen,' August said.

'Yeah. Well. You know. If I hadn't learned to feed myself I'd've starved.'

August moved to sit up, but Henry stopped him with one raised hand.

'No. Don't get up. Not allowed. Unless you have to pee. Then you can get up. Otherwise I'm serving you breakfast in bed.'

August froze as Henry spoke, then settled again. Woody lay down with his back curled against August's hip.

'Why breakfast in bed?'

'I promised Seth I would. He wants you to have the best of everything this trip. We take care of everything for you. Just like you did for us last time.'

August absorbed that statement briefly. Then, a little embarrassed to address it directly, he asked, 'Where *is* Seth?'

'Three guesses.'

'Climbing?'

'Climbing.'

August watched the sun rise over the rock formations, his fingers in Woody's wiry white fur. He didn't speak again until Henry brought him a cup of coffee.

'Thanks,' August said. 'When did it get so bad again with your dad?'

Henry paused. Scratched his forehead distractedly with the heel of one hand.

'Um. I guess after Seth went off to college . . . my dad just kind of let his hair down. He always thought Seth was the one watching his every move, but I watch his every move, too; it's just that Seth watches his every move and says so. I don't say anything. So he figures he's getting off scot-free. I don't even think he cares what I see or what I think of what I see. I think he just doesn't want to hear anything about it. It's like he thinks if he doesn't have to hear about something then it isn't a problem.'

The phone rang again.

'Is that Seth's cell?' August asked.

'Must be. Unless you have one. I don't have one.'

'I have one along,' August said. 'But that's not it.'

Another ring.

'Crap,' Henry said. 'I'm going to do this myself. So Seth doesn't have to.'

He dug the phone out of the glove compartment.

'Hello . . . oh, yeah. Hi, Dad. Look, I'm sorry. I would have asked you, but it came up last minute. And you weren't home. I didn't want to miss the whole summer just because you weren't home.'

A pause. August would have given anything to hear the other side of the conversation.

'No, just the two of us,' Henry said.

But at that exact moment two other campers walked by their site, close behind the back door of the rig, and Woody barked sharply. August put a hand over his muzzle. But of course by then it was too late.

'No,' Henry said. 'Just the dog. We took his dog because he can't really much walk him any more.' A pause. 'No, I *am* telling you the truth. Look, I have to go. I have breakfast on the stove . . . Yes. I promise. Bye.'

Henry clicked off the phone and ran to the stove, turning off the burner under the eggs.

'Oh, good,' he said. 'They're perfect.'

'Think he believed you?'

'Not sure,' Henry said, with an exaggerated frown. 'I'm not even sure *he* knows if he believes me.'

August sat up on the couch, fully dressed, watching Henry. Henry was washing the breakfast dishes with almost obsessive concentration. August wasn't quite sure why he found the boy's simple but intense approach to dishes so fascinating. Maybe because it held clues to who he had become.

Henry looked up suddenly and caught August's eyes. His hands froze in place in the sudsy water.

'I'm sorry if I messed everything up,' he said.

August shrugged. 'I don't know what you should have done. What you *could* have done.'

'What would you have done?'

'I don't know. I really don't.' August paused to consider the situation for long enough that Henry returned his attention to the dishes. 'Maybe try to let him see how important it was to me. How much it meant to me to go. See if I could convince him.'

Henry shook his head hard. 'The more I tell him how

much it means to me to do it, the more he'll never let me go. That's exactly the problem. Don't you get that?'

'No,' August said. 'I guess I don't.'

'If you didn't mean so much to us, he wouldn't be so jealous of you.'

'Oh,' August said.

Then he felt himself weighted with self-consciousness, and didn't know if he could speak to Henry's statement any further. It seemed at odds with their track record of keeping in touch, but to say so might come out badly. So August just watched the boy dry the dishes and put them back in the cupboard.

Finally August said, 'I didn't know I meant that much to you guys.'

He regretted the words the moment they made their appearance.

Henry set down the cup and bowl he was holding and turned to face August, hands on his hips, mouth gaping open.

'Are you serious with that? You're our hero, August. You were like Superman. The guy who saved the day. We idolized you. How could you not know that? Why would you not know?'

August looked down at his hands, resting on Woody's fur. He felt his face redden. He didn't want to say what he had to say next, because he knew it would sound like a complaint. An ignoble complaint. But he was in too deep to back out.

'I guess because you didn't really keep in touch,' he said, eyes still cast down. 'You just seemed to kind of get on with your life. Not that there's anything wrong with that, really, but . . .'

Henry's mouth was still open.

'You trying to tell me you wanted us to keep bugging you?'

'You weren't bugging me. You were never bugging me. I loved hearing from you. I wanted to know how you were. I thought about you guys all the time.'

Henry stood in silence for a moment, then closed his mouth.

He plunked down on to the couch beside August, jostling his hip. Reaching over to scratch behind Woody's ear, he said, 'Damn it. Why do we ever believe him, anyway?'

Henry placed his face in his hands. August waited for him to speak again, but he didn't seem inclined to.

'Your dad?'

'Yeah,' Henry said through his hands.

'What did he tell you?'

'That we shouldn't make you sorry you ever agreed to take us. He said "How would you feel? You know. If you agreed to take some little strangers for the summer, and then at the end of the summer it turned out you were never getting rid of them for the whole rest of your life. Who would want that?"'

'I would,' August said. 'You weren't strangers by then.'

A long pause.

Then Henry said, 'It was actually one of the few things he told us that made sense.'

He sighed, rose to his feet, and resumed putting away the dishes.

'Do you know where Seth is?' August asked. 'I mean, where exactly he planned to climb?'

'I could probably find him. He said he was going to walk a mile back down the road. Back near the trail-head for the Boy Scout Trail. Why?'

'I just thought I'd like to watch him climb. I didn't get to see him yesterday.'

'No, you wouldn't like it,' Henry said.

'I wouldn't?'

'No.'

'Why wouldn't I?'

'It would scare you.'

'He's not careful? I can't picture Seth not being careful. He's so responsible and methodical about things.'

'Oh, he's all of that, all right. But it's still free solo.'

'Do I even want to know what that is?'

'Probably not. But we can go out and watch him if you really think that's what you want.'

'I don't know that I'm up for walking a mile up the road and back.'

'I can drive us. I have my learner's permit. I just need an adult with me. That's you.'

'You never drove the rig before, though.'

'So? My dad taught us both to drive on the big tow truck. You know, the one that towed this rig into the shop. He said if we could drive that monster we could drive anything.'

'Fine,' August said. 'Let's give it a try. A *careful* try.'

*

As he was struggling his way into the passenger's seat, self-conscious about his motor skills, August said, 'I guess I'm not like Superman now.'

Henry plunked into the driver's seat and fired up the engine.

Staring straight through the windshield at nothing but rock, as if he were embarrassed by his next words, Henry said, 'August. Don't say stuff like that. Your superpowers never had anything to do with your legs.'

'Ha!' Henry cried when he spotted his brother, and Woody jumped up on to his lap behind the wheel to see what the boy was so excited about.

'Oh, good,' August said. 'He's pretty close to the road.'

Henry eased the motorhome on to the narrow, sandy dirt shoulder. He had driven well, for as long as he had driven, which wasn't much. He had taken it slow, watched his clearance carefully, and hadn't made August wince once.

Henry cut the engine. They sat a moment in the silence. August wondered if everybody else in this section of the park was still asleep, or at least still in camp. He sure didn't see them out here.

'And there's some shade,' Henry said, pointing to a spot where a stand of rocks cast a long shadow.

August got out carefully while Henry ran two of the three camp chairs out to the shady seating area and set them up. Then he ran back and guided August by one elbow. August almost told him it wasn't necessary, but thought better of it. It might not have been necessary, but it was nice on this rocky, shrub-covered ground. It would be so easy to take a tumble.

When August was properly eased into a camp chair in the shade, Henry said, 'I'll go get Woody. And some bottled water.'

'Will you bring my camera, too, Henry? I want to take some pictures of him. It's in the map pocket on the passenger side.'

Henry set off at a trot.

August peered at Seth's back as he climbed. He was close enough to be clearly identified as Seth, but too far away for August's liking. He was wearing only shorts and a short-sleeved shirt, and some kind of minimal shoes. A helmet, August was happy to note. He looked forward to the zoom on the camera to help him make out more of what he was seeing.

Seth did not appear to know he was being watched.

Woody leapt into August's lap and kissed his face, and August's camera appeared at his left shoulder in Henry's hand.

'Thanks.'

'I'm putting a bottle of water right here.'

He indicated the mesh cup holder in the fabric arm of August's chair.

'Thanks.'

August powered up the camera and zoomed in close, looking to confirm a few details. He was sure his un-aided eyes were not seeing correctly.

He turned his head to look at Henry, who looked back.

'What?'

'Why am I not seeing ropes?' August asked.

'That would be the free solo thing we talked about. Well, Seth would say it's just bouldering, and that's different. But it's still solo. And free.'

'Well, I know what solo means. But . . . are you trying to tell me free means free of ropes? Carabiners? Pitons? Harnesses? All the stuff climbers use so they don't kill themselves? That's what it means to be free in climbing lingo?'

'He uses that stuff on the big walls. You know. When he goes high. Like when he's climbing Angels Landing at Zion, he'll rope up. Of course. And Yosemite. If he goes up The Nose on El Cap, he'll rope. He totally idolizes the climbers who do the big walls free, but he doesn't do it himself. But this is little stuff to him. Bouldering. Rock scrambling. This is barely a warm-up.'

'He's up about . . . what is that? By the time he gets to the top? Forty feet?'

'Thirty, maybe. Maybe thirty-five.'

'He could break his back falling from that height. He could fall on his head and kill himself.'

'Seth never falls, though.'

'That doesn't mean he never will.'

'August,' Henry said, a model of applied patience. 'Two things. First, notice I'm on the ground at all times. I'm not the one thirty feet up. Second, I told you this was something you didn't want to see. You really can't say I didn't warn you.'

August sighed and peered through the camera again. Snapped off a few shots.

'What exactly is he holding on to? It just looks like smooth rock.'

'Tiny cracks, if he can get them. Sometimes just big enough to wedge the tips of his fingers into. Or these little tiny nubs of rock that you can barely see, but it's just enough for him to grip.'

'This is terrifying.'

'Not for Seth, it's not. To repeat: don't say I didn't warn you.'

A moment later Seth topped out on the huge rock formation, stretching and turning around three hundred and sixty degrees. He spotted them, and waved in a big overhead arc. August waved back, a bit more reserved.

'Thank God he got up OK.'

'Seth always gets up OK,' Henry said.

August was anxious to see how Seth would get down. But watching him didn't answer many questions. He just disappeared over the top of the rocks. A few minutes later he came walking around the front of them, feet back on the ground.

August expected Seth to make a straight line for the shady spot where he and Henry were sitting, so he racked his brain for something positive to say about the climbing. Nothing emerged. It didn't really matter, though. Because Seth didn't come back. He just found another rock formation and started up its vertical face, seemingly hanging on to nothing.

'Oh,' August said, partly to Henry and partly to himself. He glanced down at the camera sitting in his lap. 'I guess I should take some more pictures of him.'

'Seth would like that. He doesn't have good pictures of himself climbing. Because the guys he climbs with don't want to bother with carrying a camera. Once he took me with him to Pinnacles, and I was supposed to work the camera from the ground. But I'm not a natural photographer like Seth is. The pictures were just OK. Not up to his standards.'

August zoomed in on Seth, nearly halfway up now. But it allowed him to see how little there was to hold, and it made August sweat. Yes, it was getting hotter, but this was a different kind of sweat. He forced himself to snap off a few good shots anyway. Then he put the camera down so he wouldn't have to see the climb in such horrifying detail.

'I still feel like I'm about to watch him break every bone in his body.'

'You get over that after a while,' Henry said, scratching Woody briskly behind both ears at once.

But August had a feeling that, even though Henry had gotten over it, maybe he never would.

By the time Seth arrived back at the camp chairs, holding his helmet under one arm and sweating profusely, it was nearly ten thirty. The shade patch had shrunk, forcing August and Henry to huddle close to the rocks, and August had taken to mopping his forehead obsessively with one sleeve.

'August is freaked out,' Henry said.

'About what?' Seth asked. As though August was not sitting right there, able to say for himself.

'Your climbing.'

'I thought I went pretty well today.'

'He thought you'd be roped up.'

'Oh,' Seth said. 'Well, this is small stuff, August. Bouldering.'

'But . . . no equipment at all—' August began.

'I have equipment!' He held up his helmet proudly. 'And . . .' He slid a belt around, bringing a small open bag to the front, where August could see it. 'I have chalk. For my fingers. That's enough for stuff like this where I don't even go high.'

Again Henry answered for August. 'He thinks it's high enough to break your back or something. Dad called. I talked to him. I lied to him so you wouldn't have to. But he heard Woody bark. So when you talk to him, remember. Woody is on the trip with us. August is not.'

'Well, I wasn't about to forget that last part,' Seth said. 'Think he believed you?'

'No idea.'

'Think he has any way to check?'

'No idea.'

Seth looked to August, and Henry followed suit.

'Think he's going to make trouble for us, August?'

'No idea,' August said.

*

The campfire snapped and crackled, its smoke and light reaching up toward the brilliant desert night sky. August could hear people in the neighboring camp-sites, but their presence seemed muted, as though a soft invisible wall hemmed their campsite in, making everything outside their own little world seem less relevant, less connected.

Memorize every detail, he told himself. Last summer of campfires.

August suddenly had a sharp memory of another campfire, the one he and the boys had built on their first night in Yellowstone. The fire into which they placed the first handful of Phillip's ashes. August wondered why they weren't sprinkling any of the ashes Seth had insisted on bringing. And, if not here, where?

'I'm tired of sitting,' Henry said. 'I'm taking Woody for a walk. Now that it's finally not hot.'

'How will you see where you're going?' August asked.

'I'll wear Seth's headlamp.'

Henry stood up and brushed sandy dirt off the seat of his shorts.

'Watch out for coyotes,' Seth said.

'Funny,' Henry shot back.

'It wasn't a joke.'

Henry shook his head and left the circle. Left Seth and August alone with all the words that had been sitting, so conspicuously unsaid, since earlier that morning.

'How long have you been doing this climbing?' August asked.

'Pretty much since you dropped me back home. You know. That September. When I was twelve. I built a climbing wall on the back of the shop. I was on it five hours a day. Then after I could drive I hit it for real. You know. Real walls.'

'You never mentioned it.'

'I was trying to avoid what we're doing right now.'

They stared at the fire in silence for a while. It was burning hotter now, and August could feel the heat on his cheeks. In his eyes.

'I feel responsible for this,' August said.

'Now why is that?'

'Because I took you to Zion. And put you on that shuttle bus and took you off again to see the climbers going up Angels Landing.'

'Geez, August. I thought I was the over-responsible one. You think sooner or later I wouldn't have seen something climbable? With somebody climbing it?'

August never answered that. The conversation stalled, and they stared into the fire in silence.

'It's my livelihood, August.'

'No, it isn't.'

'How can you say that? You think I don't know my own livelihood?'

'Obviously you don't. Your livelihood is your job.'

'I don't have a job right now.'

'You're not following me, Seth. You don't know what the word livelihood means. It doesn't mean the thing that keeps you lively. It means the way you earn your living. The thing that feeds you. Keeps you alive.'

'That doesn't sound like what it should mean.'

'English is a quirky language.'

'I guess.'

'It's your *raison d'être.*'

'Wow. English really is a quirky language.'

'That's French, actually.'

'I knew that. I was kidding.'

'Oh. Do you also know what it means?'

'I guessing it means like what I thought livelihood meant.'

'It means reason for existence. But I still don't think a physical activity should be the reason for your whole existence.'

More silence.

Then Seth said, 'All I know is, it's what makes me . . . you know . . . me. You know how when you're working, or going to school, and you just keep repeating the same days? Go to work, come home, eat. Do the laundry. Go to sleep. And then you notice the days are going by really fast. And they're all starting to look alike. And then you start to feel like, this can't be it. This can't be all. This can't be . . . you know . . . a whole life. There has to be more. That's what the climbing is to me. It's the more. That's the thing that makes me feel like life is enough. Come on. You know what I mean, August. What makes your life feel like enough?'

August sighed deeply, wishing he had a good, immediate answer.

'I've lived a pretty quiet life,' he said.

'But you traveled all summer. Every summer. That's your more. Right?'

'I guess it is, yeah.'

'So you know what I mean.'

August sighed again. 'I just can't imagine it's worth giving your life for.'

'You don't know I *will* give my life for it.'

'And you don't know you won't. Climbers die.'

'Drivers die, August. Do you have any idea how much risk you took? All those thousands of miles on the highways every summer? People die on highways. But drivers look at what I do and say, "Oh, my God. You could die." But then they get in their car and drive away, and never give it a thought. Some of them at eighty miles an hour. Some of them don't even buckle their seat belts. Not because it's really any safer. Because it *feels* safer. Because they're used to it. I bet if we could pull some good statistics we'd find out I'm a lot more likely to die driving on the highway to Joshua Tree than bouldering up some rocks to thirty or forty feet after I get there. But you still wouldn't say to me, "Seth, please. Don't get in that car. It's too dangerous. You could die."'

'No, I guess I wouldn't,' August said.

But it didn't really change the way he felt about the situation.

'So you understand?'

He almost said no. Just a flat no. But he caught it on the way out and changed it to something barely more supportive.

'I'm working on understanding,' he said.

Almost as though he was making some progress already.

But he wasn't.

5
Raison d'être

August opened his eyes. Looked out the motorhome window.

Zion was out there.

Not that he hadn't known, on some level, that it would be. Just that in his sleep he'd forgotten.

He looked up to see Henry in the kitchen, starting breakfast. And Seth was gone. Which is exactly what he'd seen for the last eight or nine days upon opening his eyes. Almost since they'd started their trip. Henry cooking. Seth gone.

'This is some intense déjà vu,' August said, indicating the view outside the windows.

'I'll say,' Henry answered, as if half there and half somewhere else.

'Even the way the cottonwood fluff is flying around. Just like it was eight years ago. Every detail.'

'Except I'm not scared.'

'You were still scared by the time we got to Zion?'

'Pretty much, yeah.' Woody sat up and begged for the toast Henry was buttering. Henry ignored him. 'I want to know what you really call that stuff. That cottonwood stuff. You're a scientist, August. I would think you would know stuff like that.'

'Science teacher.'

'There's a difference?'

'I'd say so. They probably just call them cottonwood seeds. Where's Seth?'

'Gone already.'

'He's always gone when I wake up. He's not on that big climb already, is he?'

'No. He's out looking for someone else climbing solo. Or a team that'll let him join. Because you gave him such a hard time about going solo.'

'Oh. Well. That's good, though. Right?'

Henry didn't answer.

'Sometimes you get really quiet,' August said, 'and it seems to mean something. It seems to fit in with a question you don't want to answer.'

Henry flipped two eggs in a frying pan on the burner, careful not to break the yolks. He maintained his silence.

'Confirm or deny,' August said.

'I don't like to tell people what to do.'

'What if they ask?'

'I still don't like it.'

'Isn't it better if he doesn't go alone?'

'I don't know. Maybe. But I do think it's why he's always gone before you get up. You've been awful hard on him about the climbing.'

'It's just because I care,' August said.

Henry didn't answer. August wondered if his silence meant the same thing as usual.

He stared out the window at the high rock faces, his view of them partially blocked by cottonwood trees. Smelled breakfast. Listened to the flow of the river.

'I hope he's careful who he picks,' August said, almost as if to himself. 'That could almost be more dangerous than going alone. Going with the wrong group. Someone who wants to go too fast, or isn't careful enough about belaying,' he said, repeating one of the few climbing terms he'd picked up from Seth. 'Or placing hardware. Or if their equipment is old and unreliable. I hope he knows how important that is.'

August looked at Henry, who was dishing up breakfast. The boy was literally biting his lip. It struck August as a sort of figurative way of biting his own tongue.

'You're doing it again,' August said.

'I don't like to tell people what to do, August.'

'Why don't you just tell me what you're thinking?'

August sat up, propped himself up with pillows behind his back, and Henry handed him breakfast. He watched the boy sit down on the couch with his own food. But Henry didn't eat. He just stared at it. As though the food had to make the first move.

Woody wiggled too close, but Henry didn't stop

him. August called Woody's name sharply and the dog jumped down in shame.

August was beginning to think Henry was never going to answer. Never going to say what he was thinking. But August was wrong. Hugely wrong.

'I'm just glad he left early, August. That's what I'm thinking. I'm glad he wasn't around to hear you say that. Do you have any idea how that would have made him feel? Seth's been climbing for eight years, August. Eight years. Since he was twelve. You have no idea how much he knows about it. You talk to him like you know the risks and he doesn't. He knows everything about climbing, including exactly what can go wrong. You have no idea how hard he works to keep the risks down. He's made a study of it. But you take all that away from him when you say things like that. Like you look at what he does, and it looks dangerous, and you start talking to him like he doesn't even know that. If it was somebody else he'd probably just shake his head and walk away. But he admires you so much. It's really hard for him. It hurts him, August.'

Then he stopped, just as suddenly. Turned his face away. Looked out the window. Nobody spoke. Or ate. August felt as though he'd suddenly lost his appetite.

'Sorry,' Henry said.

'I asked.'

'I don't like to talk to people that way. Well. I don't like to talk to people at all. Except you. I like to talk to you. But not like that.'

*

August and Henry took Woody for a short, slow walk later that morning, stopping for a time at the visitor's center. August sat on a bench with Woody while Henry went inside and looked around.

August watched men and women board shuttle buses dressed in hiking clothes, with day packs and trekking poles, and felt his mood sinking.

In time Henry rejoined him and they walked back to their campsite on a dirt trail beside the river, not talking at all.

Seth was back in camp. He had a friend with him, a young man a few years older, with wild black hair, dressed in only shorts and sneakers. His build was light and wiry, his chest narrow, but he was clearly in shape. His skin was bronze from many hours in the sun.

He and Seth were sorting through an amazing amount of climbing equipment, which was carefully laid out on the picnic table in front of them. Ropes and hardware, dozens of carabiners, loops of nylon strap, gear bags. A dozen other types of gear that August had never seen. August had no idea of the names for most of it, or the purpose. Neatly lined up, it covered every inch of the table.

Henry leaned in and whispered in August's ear. 'Bet you had no idea there was so much to it.'

'August!' Seth said, his head coming up suddenly. He sounded animated, almost artificially cheerful. 'This is Dwayne.'

August leaned carefully on his left cane, let the other

cane rest against his right leg, and shook hands with the young man.

'His climbing partner got the flu,' Seth continued.

'Maybe,' Dwayne said. 'Or maybe he got a good look at Moonlight Buttress.'

August noticed a slight wince on Seth's part.

Dwayne continued to sort and count gear while Seth pulled August aside.

'Please don't say anything bad about climbing in front of Dwayne,' he said.

August felt surprisingly stung. He wondered how long Henry had held his tongue before that morning, hesitating to speak on his brother's behalf, and if things were even worse than he'd made them out to be. He wondered if Seth's comment was the tip of an iceberg of August's own making.

'I wouldn't have,' he said.

'OK, good. Thanks.'

It may not have been entirely true, though, August thought. He might have. He wasn't sure any more.

'Moonlight Buttress?' he asked when they'd rejoined the others. 'I thought you were going up to Angels Landing.'

'Yeah. More or less,' Dwayne said. 'They're right next door.'

'We can still hike out down the Angels Landing Trail,' Seth added.

'So when do you leave?'

'Tonight. Last shuttle.'

'Not in the morning?'

'No, that's when everybody leaves – first shuttle in the morning. We'll go out tonight. Climb by moonlight and headlamps. It's safe in terms of holds, but if the routefinding is too hard, we may have to stop and bivvy. You have to cut me a lot of slack on this, August. Our plan is to do it non-stop in about twenty-four hours. But a lot of things can change the plan. We could get stuck behind other teams where we can't get by. We could lose the route in the dark. You have to accept that we could be gone for two or three days . . . maybe even longer . . . but that doesn't mean we're not OK.'

August swallowed hard, and self-consciously, his mouth feeling suddenly dry. He thought that sounded difficult and scary. To sit in the motorhome for two or three days, accepting. Trusting.

'OK,' he said, thinking it sounded weak. 'Maybe we'll take the shuttle out tomorrow and see if we can see you.'

Seth was threading hardware on to a nylon belt, and August wondered if that was the only reason he wouldn't meet August's eyes.

'Um . . .' he said after a time. 'We'll be too far away.'

'I've got my camera with the super zoom.'

Seth buckled the belt and threw it back on the picnic table with a huge, jangly clank. Then he took August by the arm and led him around to the rear door of the motorhome.

Speaking quietly, he said, 'Don't take this the wrong way, August. But . . . please don't watch. Please. It looks scarier than it is. Especially if you don't know much about climbing. I feel like . . . if I think you're watching . . . I'll be . . . I'll pick up that nervous energy from you. Well . . . not nervous exactly, but . . . negative. Like there's some kind of negative energy that I'll be able to feel. I mean, I know I won't really be able to feel it. I'm just worried that I'll be checking the feel of the air, because I'll be thinking about whether I can feel it. I'll be worried about whether you're worried. Every pitch, every hold, instead of just thinking about what I'm doing, I'll be thinking about how what I'm doing looks to you. And I worry it'll be a distraction. Please just let me do this with you not looking, OK?'

'Sure. Yeah. Sure, Seth. That's fine.'

Then August spent the next hour or two listening to the young climbers talk between themselves in what sounded like a foreign tongue. Joined here and there by bits of English, but full of a vernacular that might just as well have been Russian or Swahili for all he understood.

While he listened, August wondered if he had managed to cover over his hurt feelings as well as he hoped.

'I was just about to come looking for you,' Henry said as August made his way slowly back to the motorhome. 'I swear I was going to jump the shuttle and search every corner of the park.'

August wanted to argue, but he was too tired. It was too hard just to walk. He noticed the young man, Dwayne, was gone, and felt mildly relieved for reasons he couldn't quite pin down.

'Help me in, please,' he said.

Seth overheard, and came out, and they took their places to help August up the three back stairs. One on each side, arms reached up to brace firmly under August's upper arms, all the way up.

'Here, hold my bag,' he said, and handed it to Seth.

Seth set it down on the ground and they whisked him up the stairs. Almost too fast. It was cool inside the rig. The air conditioning was blowing hard. August sat on the couch with a sigh. Henry handed him a plastic cup of water immediately. As if the move had been rehearsed for maximum efficiency.

'I wasn't in the park,' he said to Henry, belatedly. 'I was in town. Springdale. I took the shuttle into Springdale.'

'Why alone, though?' Seth asked. 'That freaked me out a little.'

'I can go places alone.'

'I know. But why? Why wouldn't you want us to go?'

'I was looking for something. I just wanted to be alone to look. I bought you something.'

Seth looked around, as though August must be talking to Henry.

'Who? Me?'

'Yeah, you. Where's that bag?'

'Oops. Left it outside.'

Seth lunged out the door and came back with the bag in his hands. He brushed red dirt off it, then held it out to August.

'Don't give it to *me*,' August said. 'I told you it was for *you*.'

'Oh. Right.'

'But before you open it . . .' Everything seemed to hold still. And everyone. Even Woody didn't move. August wrestled with what to say. Truthfully, he was strangely self-conscious about the gift, and not sure of himself at all. It was either a wonderful present or a terrible one, the best or the worst thing he could have done. But given those choices, he wondered if he didn't just have to try. To find out. '. . . I still have the receipt. So I really want you to tell me if it doesn't feel like something you want. If you think it would be a distraction in any way. It won't hurt my feelings . . .'

Well, it will, August thought. *A little bit.* But he still wanted Seth to tell him the truth.

Seth peered into the bag.

'Oh, cool,' he said. 'A helmet cam!'

'You don't have to say you like it if you don't.'

'No, these are great, August. These are really cool. I've seen some of the footage climbers take with these. It's really intense. It's really close up, hands on. You know? Every time you look down to get something off your belt, you see down into all that exposure. You see these handholds that you mostly did by feel at the time. But, man, August. These are expensive! Why do you think I don't have one?'

'I have credit cards, too,' August said.

'Gosh, thanks, August.'

'I just thought . . . I really do want to see what you do, Seth. But you don't want me to watch, which I guess I understand, since I seem to be the nervous sort where this stuff is concerned. But I thought if you turned this on when you started climbing, I could see what you do later. When you're back. And I won't have to get nervous, because you're back. But if you think it would be heavy or awkward . . . well, it only weighs less than three ounces, but—'

'August,' Seth interrupted.

'What?'

'Please stop apologizing for it. It's a good present.'

'Really?'

'It's a good present.'

And he leaned over the couch where August sat and gave him an awkward but sincere hug. It felt like the reversal of some kind of magnetic polarity. Seth had been leaning away from him for days. But August hadn't realized how much so until Seth finally leaned back in.

'We should take the shuttle into Zion Canyon today,' August said.

It was morning. August was up and showered. Dressed. Henry was finishing up the breakfast dishes.

Seth had been gone since nine o'clock the previous night. Climbing. It was a fact that sat hard on August's mind, whatever else he tried to think or talk about.

When Henry didn't answer, August said, 'You know. Like the old days. Like we did eight years ago. Go up to Weeping Rock. Maybe even a tiny bit of the River Trail. We'll have to see how much I'm up for.'

Still no answer.

'Henry. Are you doing that thing again?'

'Which thing is that, August?' But he said it as though he knew which thing.

'You know. The one where you don't say anything because you don't like to tell people what to do. You don't like to talk to people like that.'

'I don't like to talk to people at all.'

'But this is me.'

'I was wondering if this is your way of breaking your promise not to watch Seth climb.'

'Well, we may see a trail of ants crawling up that big rock wall, but we won't be close enough to see which ones are Seth and Dwayne.'

'You told him you could use your super zoom.'

August sighed. Henry had been telling the truth when he said he watched everything, took in everything, but didn't say. But August was pressing him to say. And so he was saying.

'Tell you what,' August offered. 'Wide-angle shots only, and not of Moonlight Buttress. You can be my policeman.'

'Honest truth, August, why do you want to do this?'

'Because I'm a little nervous today, and I feel like I'm just waiting for Seth to get back, and it's going to be much too long a day if we just sit around camp all day and do nothing.'

'OK, fine,' Henry said. 'Good enough. Let's go.'

'You keep looking over there,' Henry said as they rode the shuttle along the narrow and twisting redrock road, drawing alongside Angels Landing and Moonlight Buttress.

'I guess I do. Is that cheating?'

'I don't know.'

'It's just such a huge wall, though. And so . . . vertical.'

'Actually, it's a little worse than vertical. It's slightly overhanging in places. Or . . . wait. Maybe not. Maybe I'm confusing it with The Nose route on El Capitan. But one of the walls he's doing this trip has some overhang.'

'Oh. Well. Thanks. I feel better now.'

'The thing you have to remember, August, is that Seth has climbed lots of big walls like that one. This is not some big special first time for him. This is just the first time you knew he was doing it while he was doing it.'

They rode in silence for a few moments, listening to the shuttle driver announce the sights, and the stops.

'Is that supposed to help?' August asked, at last.

'I figured it couldn't hurt,' Henry said.

Henry held one of August's canes on the short – but fairly steep – hike up to Weeping Rock, and August threw an arm over the boy's shoulder. He probably had a good half his weight on Henry, but Henry didn't seem to mind.

'This really does bring it back,' Henry said. 'Doesn't it?'

'Were you still afraid when we came up here?'

'Oh, yeah.'

'Of me?'

'Of you. Yeah. But also of everything else.'

'When did you stop being afraid of me?'

'When you carried me up the Angels Landing Trail on your back.'

They walked in silence for a while longer, then stood under the raining overhang and leaned on the rail, looking out. Like standing on your dry porch, looking off through the rain on a drizzly day. Henry did not lean his head out into the falling water.

'You going to college, too?' August asked.

'Not sure.'

'What would stop you?'

'I don't have Seth's grades. Nobody has Seth's grades. I probably couldn't get a full-ride scholarship like that.'

'Why not a community college?'

'We don't have one where I live. The closest one would be something like a ninety-mile round trip drive. Not sure where I'd get a good car and all that gas money. And besides, when I turn eighteen, I want to move. I want to get away.'

August leaned and stared through the weeping. Wondered briefly if Woody was sad back in camp alone. It was traditional to wonder that in this place.

The only other couple to stand under Weeping Rock with them started down, leaving August to feel as though he and Henry owned the park, and could enjoy it privately.

'So, go somewhere where there's a college.'

'Yeah, but . . . food. Rent. Car. Gas. Not sure I could afford to go to school if I'm working and paying my own way at the same time. Maybe I could. But it sounds scary. It sounds big.'

August nodded, and they reluctantly started down to the shuttle stop, slow and halting, and with much leaning on August's part.

'Am I putting too much weight on you?'

'No. Not at all. You're fine.'

'I weigh so much more than you do, though. Must be tiring.'

'Like carrying a kid on your back up to Scout Lookout on Angels Landing? That kind of tiring? You did your part, August. Now it's my turn to be tired.'

They paused and leaned their backs against the cool, damp rock face along the River Trail. Just watching the water flow. Letting people pass them.

August knew he was taking on too much exercise, but he had every intention of doing it anyway. He would be tired. But he wouldn't die. And maybe tired would do him good.

'There's a community college near where I live in San Diego,' he said after a time. 'Well, not very near. Fifteen miles, maybe. But we have public transportation. Buses. That's a cheap way to go.'

A long silence.

Then Henry said, 'Are you inviting me to come live with you while I go to college?'

'Yes, I guess I am. If you want to.'

'That's a pretty major offer, August. Sure you don't want to think about it?'

'Nothing to think about. I'd be happy to have you. Your dad wouldn't like it much, though.'

'Once I turn eighteen,' Henry said, 'it won't make a damn bit of difference what he likes and what he doesn't.'

6
Chalky White Hands

Henry and August sat in front of the campfire together in their comfortable camp chairs, in the dusk. Waiting. It was about eight o'clock that night, an hour or two before the soonest Seth might come back. August could pretend to be doing many things, such as relaxing and talking. And he couldn't speak for Henry. But inside, he was waiting. Waiting and preparing himself for several extra days. Resetting his internal clock by at least forty-eight hours. Because he preferred to expect the worst and be pleasantly surprised.

Well, not the worst. The worst time-wise. The actual worst he refused to consider.

August dropped one hand almost to the ground and scratched Woody between the shoulder blades.

Henry startled him by speaking.

'So, I'm going to ask you again at the end of the trip. In case you change your mind between now and then.'

'Ask me what?'

'If you really want me living in your house for four years.'

'I'm not going to change my mind.'

'I'm still going to ask again.'

Woody began to strain at the leash and whimper. August just assumed he'd smelled a critter. He didn't even bother to look.

'Hey!' Henry said. 'Seth's back a little early!'

August tried to spring to his feet, but failed. His happiness and relief had knocked all thoughts out of his head. Including the fact that he no longer sprang to his feet these days.

Seth wobbled toward camp looking like the twenty steps he still had to cover might or might not prove possible. He wore no shirt. His shirt was tied around his waist. His bare chest and legs looked painfully sunburned, and streaked with dirt and sweat. His hair had been plastered down to his head by a combination of the helmet and his own perspiration, and had dried that way. His hands were caked white with leftover chalk. What looked like ten or fifteen pounds of equipment hung in careful order around his waist, his climbing ropes neatly rolled into loops and hanging over one shoulder. Under his other arm he carried his helmet, the gift camera still attached with an elastic harness.

He looked like he might be about to drop into sleep on the spot, or hit the ground short of camp. But when he met August's eyes, he smiled in a way that looked genuinely happy.

In fact, he looked more genuinely happy than August could ever remember seeing him. Or being himself.

Henry jumped to his feet to offer his chair.

'Here. Flop here, Seth. I'll go get the other chair.'

Seth unceremoniously shed all of his equipment into the sandy dirt at his feet, and took Henry's instructions quite literally. He didn't lower himself. He flopped. August winced, waiting to see if the chair would take it.

It did.

'You're early.'

'Yup. We did good. We didn't get stuck behind anybody and we didn't lose the route. About nineteen or twenty hours up and a couple down. I don't know. I lost count coming down.'

'Is that some kind of new record?'

Seth brayed laughter, his defenses obviously down. 'Alex Honnold did it in eighty-three minutes.'

'How is that even possible?'

'He's Alex Honnold. Plus, he went free. He didn't rope up. Aid climbing takes time.'

August had no idea who Alex Honnold was, but he felt as though he should know, for some reason, and so didn't ask. In fact, there were many questions tumbling in his mind that he never asked.

What he did ask was, 'But I guess your time includes sleeping?'

'We did not sleep,' Seth said, slurring his words slightly with fatigue. 'We climbed.'

That raised even more questions in August's mind. Like what they would have done if they'd gotten stuck behind another team. So far as he could see, they had no portaledge, no sleeping bags, no extra food. Apparently they had wagered everything on speed. But August had no idea how to approach this issue, and had a strong sense that he should not.

Instead he asked, 'How'd the camera work out?'

'OK, I think. It was no trouble. I forgot it was even up there except when I saw the shadow of it on the rock. I guess we'll know when we see the video.'

'Did the memory card run out?'

'No idea. Too tired to check. But I took video the whole way up. Well, the part in sunlight, anyway. I didn't want to run out of memory in the dark and then find out the low-light video sucked. I think it held. I mean, sixty-four gigabytes.'

'It was the biggest card I could find,' August said.

Henry reappeared with the third camp chair and set it up.

Seth reached his helmet out to his brother and waited patiently for Henry to notice. 'Do me a favor, Henry, OK? Take the card out of this and start loading the video on to my computer?'

'Don't you want to sleep first?' August asked.

'Nope. Too wired. I don't want to move, but I'm not ready to sleep. I want to see what I got on that helmet cam.'

'Me, too,' August said. 'Now that I know you're safe.'

'So,' Seth said, the minute Henry was gone. 'Did *your* messages from my dad sound as bad as *my* messages from my dad?'

August's gut felt suddenly cold.

'I didn't get messages from your dad.'

'Hmm. That's funny. He said he called you every day.'

'I'm probably not even getting reception,' August said.

'Right. That's true. My phone probably only down-loaded messages when I took it up high.'

'So what did he say?'

'That he's called you every day. And every time you don't answer and don't call him back he gets more and more sure that you're along on the trip.'

'Oh,' August said. 'Wonder what we do about that?'

'No idea,' Seth said.

At nearly nine o'clock, Seth was still surprisingly awake. They hunched over the dinette table inside the motorhome, watching the video. Henry stood behind them, balancing with one hand on August's shoulder, and leaning to see over their heads.

It went fine at first.

It was a good twenty-five minutes of Dwayne going up the wall, seen from underneath. August found it a bit frightening how utterly vertical the wall really was, and how directly over Seth's head Dwayne was climbing. He couldn't help wondering what would happen if Dwayne fell. Wouldn't he take Seth off the wall on his way down?

Then again, he supposed that was why Dwayne was carefully placing hardware every few dozen feet and clipping his rope into it. To prevent just such an accident. August wondered if that climbing hardware always held in a fall. Or just usually.

He glanced over to see Seth sitting beside him, as if to remind himself that Seth was no longer on the wall. Seth shot back a weak, exhausted smile. Maybe a bit embarrassed, too.

'He doesn't lead every pitch, does he?' Henry asked, sounding bored.

'No. We're about to trade. In fact . . . somewhere around here I turned off the camera, so I'd be sure to get some of me leading. Right about . . .'

A few seconds passed, and then the film cut suddenly from one scene to another. Seth was looking down at his belt, reaching for a piece of equipment. August never saw which one. The camera looked down with him, and August found himself looking past Seth's bare chest, his legs and feet weirdly tiny from that perspective as they barely braced him on the rock, to a good five or six hundred feet down the perfectly vertical wall to the valley floor below.

'Holy crap!' he shouted, startling both boys. 'Oh. Sorry. I was not prepared for that. Made my stomach do that roller coaster thing.'

'Yeah, well, hold on, August,' Seth said. 'It gets hairier from here.'

August literally gripped the table and turned his eyes back to the screen.

The camera turned up. Looked up the wall. It did indeed look more than vertical. Slightly overhanging.

But that might have just been the perspective. The strange wide-angle perspective. Every time Seth reached up, it looked like he was reaching over the top of an outcrop of rock. Then, as he pulled himself up, it looked like that effect had been an illusion. But it was a scary illusion.

He watched Seth's hand come up into the picture again, dusted white with chalk. Watched Seth blow on the hand. Slap it against the rock to release the cloud of excess chalk. Then the hand reached up and found a crack in the rock as if by feel. The hold in the crack was already white with chalk, before Seth even touched it. From other climbers, August supposed.

Then, with nothing to hold him but his fingers wedged into that minuscule hold, Seth pulled himself up.

Somehow August hadn't been expecting that. He'd expected something more like Seth holding firmly to a rope and pulling himself up by it. But all the rope was underneath him. It was only there to shorten his fall if he fell. It did not hold him on to the wall. Nothing external held him on to the wall. Only those few chalky fingers supported Seth as he climbed hundreds of feet over the canyon floor.

August began to find it hard to breathe.

The camera looked down again, past Seth's bare chest and legs, and August squeezed his eyes closed. When he opened them again, Seth's hand was placing a piece of hardware into a crack in the rock. It had a loop of strap and a clip of some sort dangling from it, and Seth's chalky hand reached up and clipped the rope into it. But he had just set it loosely between the two faces of the crack. August expected Seth to screw or wedge it in tightly. Instead he just pulled hard on it and went on climbing.

August gasped when Seth put his weight on it.

'That doesn't look like it would hold you at all!'

'Relax, August. It expands.'

'Oh.'

'If it didn't, I wouldn't be here, right?'

'Oh. Right.'

August watched in silence for several minutes. Determined to keep his gasps and exclamations to himself.

He could hear Seth's winded breathing on the video, and it was making it harder and harder to breathe himself. Because Seth seemed so without options on that wall, and watching was making August feel panicky. He could hear the strain in Seth's breathing, the grunting of effort as he pulled himself up. He watched the white hand groping for holds in a way that felt exhausted and desperate. Or maybe that was something August was reading in.

It seemed so frighteningly exhausting, so hard, but what could Seth do? *You wouldn't want to downclimb a wall like that*, he thought, thinking in the jargon he'd begun to pick up during the summer. August wondered if Seth could give up and abseil down if he didn't want to go on. But of course Seth was doing no such thing.

Suddenly August felt as though no breath was coming into his lungs at all. Also as though he might vomit.

'I need air,' he gasped. 'I need to get outside. Help me get outside. Please.'

August could hear the strained puffing on the video-tape fade as both boys rushed him down the back stairs. All three of them nearly lost control of August in their haste. He pitched forward, expecting to land on his face in the dirt, but the boys caught him.

'Get him some water,' Seth told his brother.

Then he helped August over to one of the camp chairs to sit in front of the last of the dying fire. August still thought he might vomit, so he placed his head between his knees, waiting for the feeling to pass.

When he looked up again, Seth was watching him with a look of mild discontent.

'So I guess you really don't want to see what I do, then,' Seth said.

'I thought I did. But now I think I'm having a panic attack.'

'August. I'm right here. You know how it turned out.'

'But I also know you're going to keep doing it. Do you really have to keep doing it, Seth? It's like committing suicide. I feel like I'm watching you commit suicide.'

And Seth, who was, after all, sleep-deprived and exhausted, burst into a flare of anger.

'How can you even ask me that, August? Why would you ask a question like that? And say things like that to me! It's not suicide! I'm careful! I do it right and I'm good at it. You have no right to call it suicide! You know it means the world to me! You just don't want it to mean so much! You just don't want to believe that anything that requires fitness could be that important to anyone! Because *you* can't do fitness stuff any more!'

August watched helplessly as Henry flew across his chair, hitting Seth in the chest with his full weight. Up-ending Seth's chair. August watched his plastic water glass fall and tumble, the water soaking fast into the sandy dirt.

'Don't you *ever* talk to August that way!' Henry shouted. 'He's August! You never talk to him like that! Never!'

Henry delivered the words from a position on top of Seth and his camp chair, and it seemed Seth could not get up. Maybe he was too tired, or too surprised, or maybe Henry had knocked the wind out of him and he couldn't breathe.

God knows August still couldn't.

'You want to hold it down over there?' he heard a man shout from inside a tent at the next site over.

'Henry,' August said quietly. As calmly as possible. 'Stop. Leave your brother alone. Let him up.'

Henry did not let Seth up.

'You apologize to August,' Henry told his brother in a more controlled voice.

'No. Just let him up, Henry. He doesn't need to apologize. He's right.'

Henry stumbled to his feet and shot August a scorched look, as though August had thoroughly betrayed him.

'Well, he's partly right,' August corrected. 'It would be really hard for me right now to call climbing a good example of the most important pursuit in a life. When I can barely hike a half-mile uphill to Weeping Rock.'

Seth righted his chair and pulled himself up, leaning on it, gasping for breath. 'I'm sorry, August,' he said. 'Really I am. I'm so tired I don't know what I'm saying. I shouldn't even be talking.'

'No, don't apologize.' August said. 'You're right. I'm being an ass.'

Silence and lack of movement ruled for a long, awkward moment. Then Henry said, 'I'll go get you another glass of water, August.'

'No, it's OK,' August said. 'I think that knocked me out of it. I don't feel like I'm going to throw up any more.'

Henry scuffled inside without a word. And did not come out again.

'So, what's the other part?' Seth asked, poking at the dying embers with a rough stick.

August was amazed the young man was still awake and talking. August sighed.

'How can I explain this? It's like everybody lives every day knowing something terrible could happen. That this could be the day they get "the call". You know the one I mean. That dreadful call regretting to inform you that the worst has happened. I mean, we don't think about it every day. But if we thought about it, we'd know it could happen. But it seems like this weird quirk of human nature that we don't think it ever will. It never did before, so we figure it won't. Someone else will get the call. Someone who isn't us. But then you get the call. And it seems so real that you could again. Maybe even that you *will* again.'

'We studied that last semester in school,' Seth said. 'The way our subconscious tells us that if it never happened before, it never will. But if it happened, especially pretty recently, it tells us it's about to happen again. Like if somebody gets mugged on a certain corner in the city, every time they go through that intersection, their heart will beat faster. They'll break out in a sweat. Consciously they know it's not going to happen again just because of the location. But this reptilian part of our brain is giving off different signals.'

August sat in the dark for a time before answering.

Woody barked from inside the motorhome, and they looked up to see Dwayne standing at the edge of their campsite.

'Dwayne-o,' Seth said. 'What's up?'

'I was going through my equipment, and I have a couple things of yours. I have your belay plate. And this ascender.' He held it up in the dark.

'Can't believe you walked all the way over here tonight. I'd have thought you'd want to sleep first.'

'Yeah. Well. We're heading out first thing in the morning. And this is a nice ascender. These things aren't cheap.'

'Yeah, my dad gave me that,' Seth said.

Seth still wasn't getting up. August wondered if he even could.

It made August's stomach a little rocky and cool,

hearing that Seth's dad had given him a nice piece of expensive climbing equipment. So Seth's dad was supporting him in ways August couldn't manage. Wes was better at something.

'I haven't even sorted through my stuff to see if I accidentally got anything of yours.'

'Doesn't matter,' Dwayne said. 'Nothing missing that I care a damn about. We may have gotten some of each other's 'biners. But I have the right number, and the right number of locking ones. And all our 'biners are in good shape. So who cares?'

"Preciate your coming over, man. Not sure where you found the energy.'

'No worries. Have a good life. Climb high.'

And he set the belay plate and the ascender on the picnic table and walked back into the darkness from which he'd come.

August didn't know what to say to Seth. So he just said, 'You sound so awake. Alert, even.'

'I know. I was just marveling at that myself. So why do you not get these panic attacks over driving? Since that's how it happened.'

Oh, August thought. *We're still talking about this. Too bad.*

'I don't know. I guess because I blamed it on the alcohol. The combination of the alcohol and the driving. But I don't even know if I'm right.'

'Maybe we go exactly when it's our time to go, no sooner and no later, and the odds don't mean a thing.'

'I'm a science teacher, Seth.'

'Right. I think I better go to bed, August. I'm sorry. Again.'

'I wish you wouldn't be. I think it was mostly my fault.' As he watched Seth shuffle through the dirt like an exhausted old man, August asked, 'Any more big walls on this trip?'

'Yeah. One. At the very end of the summer. Yosemite. El Cap. Some climbing friends are going to meet me there. I won't be alone. Or with strangers.'

'At the end of the summer. Good. That gives me a little time. I'll try to do better by then.'

Seth smiled. But it was a sad smile. At least, it seemed sad to August.

'There it is,' Seth said, and pulled off the highway into a visitor's center parking lot.

'So that's Pikes Peak?' August asked.

'It is.'

'How can you tell?'

'I've seen a lot of pictures of it.'

They stepped out of the rig, and took a few more. Gave Woody a chance to stretch his legs and pee.

August was surprised there was still snow on Pikes Peak – and the surrounding mountains – in June. But maybe he shouldn't have been. Since it was over fourteen thousand feet.

'But that's not a climb, right?' August asked.

'No, there's a trail all the way up. It's a long hike.'

'How many feet of elevation do you gain?'

'Hmm. Don't remember exactly. It's something like twelve miles and over seven thousand feet.'

'That's a lot for one day. You're doing it in one day?'

'If nothing unexpected comes up.'

'That's a big hike. But, still . . . I can understand that. I can understand wanting to trudge up twelve miles and seven thousand feet in one grueling day.'

Silence. From both boys.

August wondered if it was *that* silence. The one that meant they were holding something back. And why he seemed intent on distinguishing one silence from another.

'In fact, I wish I could,' he added.

But he never got an answer.

Two days later, it still hadn't come up again.

Henry and August drove out of their RV park in Manitou Springs at ten in the morning, and Henry did an amazing job of navigating the steep, narrow, twisting streets up to the Pikes Peak Cog Railway Station. It was in essentially the same location as the trailhead for summit hikers, and alive with tourists on this June mid-morning. Cars sat jammed into tight parking places on both sides of the street, making the traffic lanes almost too narrow for the big motorhome, but Henry stayed calm. He went slow, occasionally asked August to check his clearance on the right, and when pairs or groups of people came walking through those narrow margins, Henry just stopped and let them by, not seeming to worry about the patience of any drivers behind him.

Nobody honked.

When they finally turned into a big parking lot,

where a train station employee pointed them up the hill to a second lot for larger vehicles, he heard Henry let out his breath. It was August's first indication that the stress of the difficult driving had gotten to him.

'You stay here, Woody,' Henry told the dog when he'd parked, and set the brake. 'Oh, no. Look at that, August. Look how his ears always go out and down when I say that. That's so sad.'

'No dogs on the cog railway. That's just the way it is.'

'I guess,' Henry said.

He didn't bother to add, "But I hate that it makes him sad." It was more or less memorized by then.

August tried to give Henry the window seat on the train, but he wouldn't hear of it.

A uniformed docent began a narration as the train pulled slowly up the grade. But August wasn't listening.

Henry leaned over August slightly to watch the view out the window. Even though it was only trees so far. It made August feel close to him, in more ways than just the literal one.

'I think we might be making a big mistake in how we're handling this thing with your dad,' August said.

'Making a mistake how?'

'Well. Every day he calls. And gets madder and madder.'

'How could we be making a mistake? We're not doing anything.'

'Exactly,' August said. 'I think that might be the mistake right there.'

A long silence. Very long. It lasted until they were well above the tree line.

Then Henry said, 'What do you think I should do?'

'Maybe call him.'

'And tell him what?'

'I'm thinking maybe the truth. Since he seems to know it already.'

'That's not going to be pretty.'

'Maybe not. But maybe neither is this.'

Henry sighed. Chewed on his lip a moment.

Then he said, 'First I want to get to—' he stopped himself abruptly. 'Um. Where we're going. If I don't get there with you guys, I swear . . . I just can't let him stop me until after that, August. It's too important to me.'

August nodded. Didn't speak.

'I mean, unless it was more like . . . you know . . . an order. That I call him. Not so much a suggestion.'

'It wasn't an order,' August said. 'More like a question. I really don't know what the right thing is. I just keep getting the feeling this isn't it.'

'Whoa,' August said as he waited in the line of passengers slowly shuffling off the train. 'You can really feel how thin the air is.'

'You OK, August?'

'I think so. It just makes every move harder.'

'Here, put your arm around my shoulder.'

August started to object, almost out of force of habit. Then he shut his mouth again and leaned on Henry's narrow but solid shoulders.

They stepped off into patchy snow on the summit. And cold.

'I haven't been cold for a long time,' Henry said. 'So where does the trail come up? Where's the top of it?'

'No idea,' August said. 'We'll have to go inside and ask.'

'You stay right here and look at the view. I'll go.'

August planted his canes carefully and looked around. The long red train comprised nearly half of his view. The summit looked as rocky and desolate as the surface of the moon. A place where nobody lives and nothing grows. And yet if he turned around he'd see a restaurant and gift shop behind him. So he didn't turn around.

He looked up to the sky. It was the most amazing color of blue. Brilliant and uniform, but a light blue. The few filmy clouds looked like cotton candy that someone had dragged a sleeve through.

He looked out into the distance and saw mountains and green valleys and lakes, and maybe even states beyond Colorado. He'd heard that on a clear day you could see several states from the summit of Pikes Peak. Off in the distance the clouds looked much darker and more serious, maybe the start of a classic mountain afternoon thunderstorm. But a good long way off.

Seth was a strong hiker. He'd beat it.

He closed his eyes and thought, *It's a good summer. A full one. With lots of good firsts. Which is good. Since it's the last.*

*

They sat on some rocks that were a bit too low for sitting, as near to the edge of the sudden grade as they dared, and let the train they'd taken up go down without them.

And waited for Seth.

'You really can't see the trail from here,' August said.

'No, but we should see him when he gets up here. They said it gets sketchier as it gets up to the summit. Less like a trail and more like just finding a good spot to scramble up. But they said most hikers come up right around here. We'll see him.'

'I'm getting hungry,' August said. 'But I don't want to eat without Seth.'

'Me neither.'

August closed his eyes and pulled his jacket more tightly around himself. It was barely forty degrees and the wind kept trying to cut right through his clothes.

'Hope he beats that storm,' August said.

Henry shielded his eyes from the sun with one hand. 'Oh, that's a good long way off,' he said. 'Seth knows all about getting up here by noon. He knows enough to be scared of lightning. Why do you think he hit the trail at three in the morning?'

They waited in silence for a few more minutes, August hugging himself against the cold.

'I'm jealous of Seth today,' he said.

That just sat there on the summit edge with them for a moment. Henry didn't answer.

'I look down there and I think, My God. What a huge job. What a huge undertaking to have ahead of you. To accomplish all in one day. So many hours of exertion. And yet I envy him. Because I know how he's going to feel when he comes trudging up over that last rise. I totally understand a challenge like this one. I wish he'd do more of this and less of the hanging on sheer walls. I keep wondering why this much adventure and challenge isn't enough.'

Henry stayed dead quiet.

'Penny for your thoughts,' August said.

'It shouldn't matter whether you understand it or not, August. Or whether it would be enough of a challenge for you or not. It's Seth's dream. Not yours. And I really hope that when he gets up here you won't say anything like that to him.'

'Oh,' August said. 'Right. I just did it again, didn't I? I don't even see them go by sometimes. They're just there. And they seem so natural and so right until you point out otherwise.'

'I'm really sorry Phillip died, August. You know I am. But that doesn't mean Seth will.'

Before August could even open his mouth to answer, he was startled by a voice from behind.

'What're you guys doing out here?'

The surprise almost knocked him right off his rock.

He turned to see Seth standing on the summit behind them, his pack slung over one shoulder. He looked relaxed. Not out of breath at all.

'Where did you come up?' August asked, struggling to his feet. Both Henry and Seth rushed to help him up. 'We were told you'd come up somewhere right around here.'

'I came up right around here,' Seth said. 'But over two hours ago. I've been sitting in the restaurant waiting for you guys. I'm starved. Come on. Let's go have something to eat.'

Before they boarded a train together to ride back down to Manitou Springs, Seth asked another tourist to take a picture of them in front of the sign. The Pikes Peak Summit sign that announced they stood 14,110 feet above sea level.

While he was posing for the photo, without canes, under the dark and gathering clouds, one arm around each boy's shoulder, August wondered two things about the finished photo.

He wondered how much different it would feel to look at it the way Seth would, after climbing to 14,110 feet above sea level. Not sitting on a plastic train seat and being hauled up the incline.

And he wondered, in years to come, when he was stuck home for the summer, if looking at the photo memory of this moment would make him feel better or worse.

8
The Truth

August woke with a start to find himself in the passenger seat of the rig. It was dark, and Seth was driving. He'd been driving all day, making time. But making time to where? August still wasn't sure.

He looked through the windshield as the landscape slid by. Wherever they were, it was flat here. There didn't seem to be much around in the way of habitation.

'Where are we?' August asked.

'Kansas,' Seth said.

'Really. Kansas.'

'Does that seem surprising?'

'It does, actually. In all the time I've had this motor-home – I mean, in all the time *I had* it – I never took it this far out into the world. I never left the Southwest, I think, except for Yellowstone. No, that's not true. I took it up to the Pacific Northwest once.'

'Yeah, well, you're with *us* now.' Seth smiled a little, as if to and for himself. Then he said, 'Here's what I want to know. It's still June. How in God's name did you make a trip like this last all summer? I swear I don't remember.'

It was August's turn to smile.

'You're rushing,' he said. 'You've got a few activities, a few destinations lined up. And you're rushing from one to the other. My pace was different. It's just a whole different mindset. It's more about being than doing. When you find a place you like, you just be there. You don't have to have something special to do every day. You don't have to move on to the next place just because you don't have plans. You camp for the sake of camping. You sit by your campfire in a park and just glory in the fact that you're there.'

'Wow,' Seth said. 'Sounds so unlike me. Did I do that eight years ago?'

'If you didn't, you kept it to yourself.'

'Well, anyway. I promise we'll try that. Later in the trip. Right now we're rushing on purpose.'

'Why is that?'

Henry's voice from the dinette area. 'Because he promised me he would.'

August wasn't sure why he had assumed Henry was sleeping.

Seth said, 'Henry's afraid Dad's going to freak out and come looking, or report him missing or something. Before we get to . . . this place. That it's important for us to get to. If he's going to get yanked off this trip, he wants to get to this special place first. So bear with us while we make some miles.'

August settled back, more than happy to bear with them, and let his eyes drift closed.

When he opened them, dawn was just about to break.

They were not moving. Not making miles.

The highway stretched out into nowhere, seeming to go on for ever before narrowing to a point at the horizon. This world was flat. They were out on some kind of plain. No homes as far as the eye could see, but now and then another car passed with a whoosh of air, slightly rocking the rig.

August craned around and looked into the back. Henry was lying on his back on the couch, awake, petting Woody, who sat on his chest. Seth was either in the bathroom or nowhere nearby.

'Where are we?' August asked.

'Haven't the slightest,' Henry said.

'Still in Kansas?'

'Don't even know that. Could be Missouri by now. No idea. We're broken down.'

'Oh,' August said. Then, after a time, 'Where's Seth?'

'He hitchhiked out for help.'

'Oh. No cell reception out here? It's so flat. I would think reception would be good.'

'The cell reception is fine. He didn't want to call for a tow because it's so expensive. He wants to try to fix it some cheaper way. Are you up? You want coffee? Breakfast?'

'Coffee would be nice. I have that service club, though. For RV-ers.'

'Still costs money when you have to tow it lots and lots of miles. And then he's afraid of getting towed into a shop that'll take us to the cleaners. He wants to find somebody who'll lend him tools. Or rent him tools. So he can fix it here. It's nothing complicated. Just the water pump. Seth could do one of those in his sleep. Otherwise he's worried the repair will eat up too much of our gas money. Well, gas credit. And we won't be able to make the big goal.'

He scooted Woody down and stood in the kitchen to start coffee.

August laughed.

'What's funny?' Henry asked.

'Nothing, really. I mean, funny is not the right word. I just remember that bind so well. How do you think I met you guys?'

'Oh,' Henry said. 'Right.'

They sat out on camp chairs in the dirt, fifty or so feet off the highway and their rig, watching the sun rise in the distance and drinking coffee. The sun was on such an angle, flat against the horizon, that August could almost look straight at it with his sunglasses on. But he didn't, anyway, on general principles.

The sky was a color like blue-tinged steel, with a flat pattern of thin clouds that seemed to sail over their heads. It seemed strange to August, because the morning was perfectly windless at camp-chair level. But up above, the clouds rolled over as if on a conveyor belt as wide as the Earth.

'It's almost like looking at time-lapse photography,' August said.

'I was just thinking that! I was just sitting here wondering if time was going by faster than I thought. Because it's like we're sitting here for a minute watching what clouds usually do in an hour. This must've been what you meant about "just being".'

'Yes,' August said. 'This is what I meant.'

'Except this is someplace we never meant to be.'

'Doesn't really matter,' August said. 'Here we are.'

They watched the sky in silence for a few minutes more.

Then Henry said, 'I've decided you're right about my dad. I should at least try telling him the truth. Otherwise, I think he'll do something mean and jealous, but if I say it was mean and jealous he'll say no, it was because I lied to him. He'll use that to put it back on me. On my mistakes.'

August wondered how much of Henry's new decision hinged on the fact that rushing to their destination was no longer an option. He waited, in case Henry wanted to say more.

'You're not saying anything, August.'

'I never really know how to comment about that, because I feel like I don't know the best thing, either. But if you're having trouble deciding, it's hard to imagine you could go far wrong with the truth. And even if it seems like you do . . . it's still hard to imagine that whatever happens is far wrong.'

Henry rose to his feet without a word and walked

back to the rig. Vaulted up the back stairs and disappeared inside. A moment later he stuck his head back out, Woody wagging by his feet.

'Seth has his cell phone with him.'

'Mine is in the glove compartment.'

Henry disappeared back inside again.

August regretted not being able to hear at least one end of the conversation, but he could understand why Henry would want privacy.

What seemed like only a minute or two later, Henry came back out and sat, this time carrying Woody, who he plunked on to his lap.

'Didn't get him?'

'Oh, I got him, all right.'

'How was it?'

'Not good.'

'Think it made things better, or worse?'

'No idea,' Henry said. 'He hung up on me before I could really figure that out. I just hope you're right about that "not going too far wrong with the truth" thing.'

'Yeah,' August said, 'I hope I am, too.'

Seth arrived back what might have been an hour later, only August wasn't wearing his watch, or feeling any need to.

Seth jumped out of the passenger seat of an ancient army-green pickup truck, looking miffed. He hauled a battered metal tool chest out of the bed of the truck. It was heavy enough that he had to carry it with both hands. August watched him wrestle it across the highway, over to the front bumper of the rig, and set it heavily in the dirt with a clanging noise. Then he trotted back to the truck and grabbed a cube-shaped cardboard carton, which he tucked under his arm. He nodded to the driver, who swung a U-turn on the highway, his truck shrinking into nothingness as he disappeared into the distance.

August expected Seth to come say good morning, or offer some progress report. Instead he just dropped the carton in the dirt and popped the hood from the inside.

August heard Henry sigh. 'Think we should go over there and find out why he's not a happy camper? Or should we just sit here and continue to "be"?'

'Hmm,' August said.

Truthfully, he was enjoying the feeling of being Not In Charge. He had never been Not In Charge before. In the past it would always have been August, hitchhiking out for help. Throwing stuff around. Muttering under his breath. But it struck him as an immature, unhelpful truth.

'We should at least see if we can do anything to help him,' he said.

'He's probably hot and thirsty. I'll get him some of that iced tea I made.'

'Do me a favor. Move my chair over there while I'm walking over.'

Seth didn't seem to notice as August settled in his chair by the front bumper. He was on his back in the dirt, almost half under the engine. Doing what, August wasn't sure. He had no tools out of the chest yet. Hadn't taken the new water pump out of its box. Maybe just making a plan. Checking his access from underneath.

Seth pulled out and sat up, still looking frowny and intense.

'Oh. Hi, August.'

'Everything OK now?'

'Ah, I'm pissed at that guy. He gouged me, August. A hundred bucks to use this toolbox for the day. A hundred bucks. For what? Every single thing in here is something he tossed off his A-list for one reason or another. I mean, I can use the stuff, but . . . a hundred bucks? But he knew he had me over a barrel. And then as if that's not bad enough, he holds my driver's license and my credit card, like I'm about to run off with these, like they're so desirable, you know? So incredibly valuable. But first he checks my card to make sure he can authorize a thousand dollars in case I skip with them. I almost laughed in his face. A thousand dollars! But it was fifty miles farther into anything like a real city. Anyplace I might've had a couple of choices on who to ask. So he took me to the cleaners. I don't like that. That bugs me.'

'I can afford the hundred.'

'So can I, August. We're not that tight on gas money that I can't absorb a hundred. It's the principle of the thing.'

He squatted in the dirt and opened the metal chest,

picking through and finding a few wrenches in basic sizes, then laying them out in size order in the dirt.

Henry showed up with a plastic glass of iced tea, and the intense look on Seth's face broke for the first time.

'Thanks,' he said. 'I could use that right about now.'

He accepted the drink and drained it all in one giant tip of the glass, his Adam's apple bobbing as he swallowed. Then he handed the glass back to Henry. It was stained with greasy fingerprints from handling the dirty tools.

'I'm taking Woody for a walk,' Henry said, and disappeared.

August sat quietly for a long time, though he and Seth didn't talk. He was hoping just sitting close by would provide Seth with a sense of companionship. Nobody likes to feel alone when they're broken down far from home. Everybody likes a little moral support at a time like that.

After a while August got into a rhythm of just being there, and it wasn't much different from sitting under the scudding clouds. Not at the heart of the thing.

He watched Seth reach into the open hood from above, a wrench in his hand. Saw the strain on his face and in his arm muscles as he coaxed a bolt to move. After five or six bolts, he pulled out the fan belt and set it in the dirt.

Then he dropped down on to his back and slid under again. A split second later he slid back out and chose a different wrench. He pulled his cell phone out of his back jeans pocket, where it clearly bothered him, and set it on top of the open tool chest. Then his upper body was gone again.

It startled August when he spoke, his voice drifting up from under the engine of the rig. Nobody had spoken for quite some time.

'Say what you want about my dad. He never gouged anybody who got stuck in our shop.'

'No, that's true. He didn't. I was over a barrel when I got there, and his prices were fair.'

'He was honest that way.' A long silence. Then Seth's detached voice said, 'I guess that sounds strange.'

'No. Why would it?'

'Well, because he lies. How can you be honest and dishonest at the same time?'

'I think people are mostly some combination of the two. Your dad doesn't lie for profit. He doesn't purposely lie to hurt people. He has a problem, and he lies to cover over the problem and protect it, because he can't figure his way out of it. That doesn't mean he wants to go out of his way to take advantage of anybody. It doesn't mean he ever really meant to hurt anybody. I hope you don't think I look at your dad like he's all bad.'

'No. You never said that. I'm more critical of him than you are.'

'I never had to live with him.'

'He docs hurt people, though.'

'I know.'

'So you can not mean to hurt anybody and still hurt people as much as he does?'

'Oh, yeah.'

'It's sort of like he's a good person and a bad person at the same time. Which I think is . . . not possible.'

'Seth. It's not only possible, it pretty much describes every human being on the planet. Everybody is a good person and a bad person at the same time. The only real variation is in the balance. How much good to how much bad. When a person has a bigger good side, we call him a good person. But it's never absolute.'

Seth grabbed the bumper and slid out. Pulled to his feet and reached into the engine compartment from above. Drew out the fan. Set it carefully in the dirt, blades up.

'I don't know,' he said. 'Feels so much easier to be just plain mad at him. Like it's absolute. When I think of things that are good about him, like not gouging people when it would be so easy to, it's harder. It's confusing. It would be easier if people were just good or bad and that was that.'

He switched wrenches again, and his arm disappeared up to the armpit in the engine compartment.

'I know,' August said. 'I guess that's why so many people try to treat the world like it *is* black and white. It's easier. While you were gone, Henry called him and told him the truth.'

'Oh. How'd that go?'

'Apparently not too well.'

'Is he going to try to pull him off the trip? Can he, even?'

'We're not really sure.'

'Did he say he would try?'

'He hung up before going into that kind of detail.'

'Yeah.' Seth shook his head. 'That sounds about right.'

August watched Seth work in silence for several minutes. Seth carefully laid bolts on the metal edge of the engine compartment as he extracted them. Then August heard a big splash, and watched a pool of greenish coolant form under the rig. Trickle out under Seth's feet. Seth stood upright and pulled the old water pump out, holding it up over his head like some kind of trophy.

'Well done,' August said.

'Looks like we really will get back on the road today. Maybe have half a chance to outrun him.' He pulled the new water pump out of the box and leaned into the engine compartment with it. 'Sometimes I think about the fact that you were an alcoholic, too.'

'I *am* an alcoholic.'

'That you were a practicing alcoholic, too. And now you're this.'

'I was always this. Under that.'

'Right. That's what I think about. I wonder about the dad under that. Who he could be. If I'll ever get to find out. Oh, shit. Oh, no. Do not even tell me. No. No, I have to be wrong. Please. Please tell me I'm wrong.'

'What?'

'I think the guy sold me the wrong water pump.'

'Oh, no. Are you sure?'

Seth pulled the new pump out again, and set it in the dirt next to the old one. August looked at them side by side.

'They look the same.'

'They're close. But the bolt holes don't line up.'

He put the two pumps together, their flat mating surfaces against each other, and held them up for August to see. The bolt holes didn't line up.

'Shit,' Seth said, and dropped them both on to the dirt.

He flopped over on to his back, one arm splayed across his face, and lay still for a long time. August didn't speak, because he wasn't sure if he should. If anything he could say would help.

In time, Seth said, 'Sorry I cussed, August.'

'I never really cared about cuss words. Never saw what the fuss was about. That was more a rule you made for yourself. It never mattered to me.'

Seth lay still for quite a while longer. Three or four minutes, August guessed. Then he sighed, and sat up. Wiped off the new water pump with a shop rag from the tool chest and packed it back in its box.

'Well, off I go,' he said.

'I'm sorry.'

'It's not like you didn't warn me there would be some maintenance involved.'

'Still sorry.'

'I'm not sorry this good old rig needs a repair now and then. I'm just sorry that idiot charged me a hundred bucks to use his crappy tools *and* sold me the wrong part. But no matter how long I sit here and stew about it, I still have to hitch a ride back to his shop.'

Henry got back nearly an hour later. Woody's tongue lolled happily from one side of his widely grinning mouth.

'Where's Seth?'

'He had to go back to exchange a part.'

'Oh. That's a pain. Shit. Just when you really want to hurry. Oh. Sorry about the language, August.'

'I never really cared about language,' August said.

August and Henry sat outside with Woody all day, and practiced just being.

Henry said, 'If we can just sit here and be at a time like this, imagine how easy it will be when we're in some really cool national park and everything is going fine.'

August said, 'Is that where we're going? A national park?'

Henry just smiled and said, 'You know I can't tell you that, August. It's a surprise.'

The sun went down, and still Seth was not back.

Henry said, 'Maybe nobody would give him a ride.'

August said, 'Maybe the guy didn't have the right one in stock.'

Then they firmly decided not to worry about it, and moved inside because it was cold.

*

At ten o'clock, with Seth still not back, they decided they'd have to go to bed and not worry about it.

After an hour of lying awake worrying, August said, 'Henry. You awake?'

'Yeah. Why?'

'I was just thinking . . . can you haul those tools inside? If someone comes by and steals them in the night, the guy'll charge Seth a thousand bucks.'

'A thousand bucks? Holy crap! They're worth that much?'

'No. They're not. But that's what it'll cost him to lose them, and that's the problem.'

Henry sat up and put on his shoes and slid out the driver's door. A minute later he pushed the big, heavy toolbox on to the driver's side floor. He peered at it for a moment in the dome light.

'I think I just figured out why he didn't call.'

'Why?'

'I'm looking at his cell phone right here.'

'Oh,' August said. 'That would explain it all right.'

9
Flashing Red

August blasted awake, after what might have amounted to a forty-five-minute night's sleep, to the sound of staticky two-way radio transmission. He opened his eyes to see the clear red of strobing emergency lights swirling around the inside of the cabin.

Woody raced out from under the covers and barked in no particular direction.

August sat up and looked over at Henry, who was also sitting up. Also looking freshly awakened.

'Tow truck?' Henry asked.

'Why would he bring back a tow truck if we just need another water pump?'

Henry shrugged.

But another thought flooded August's mind. If Seth had come back with a tow truck, curious a move as that may have been, it meant Seth was back, and OK.

A sharp knock on the back door sent Woody into a massive, howling attack of barking.

'I'll go,' Henry said. 'I can move faster.'

He ran the four steps to the back door in just his boxer shorts and tee-shirt, and swung the door wide. August blinked into the flashing red lights of what looked like some kind of state-police patrol car. Two uniformed officers stood in the dirt a few feet from the base of their back stairs, each with one hand rather alarmingly poised on his holstered weapon.

August struggled to his feet. His canes leaned against the bathroom door, but he didn't really need them inside the rig, because the middle aisle was so narrow, and there was always something to lean on. He teetered to the back door to help Henry, who appeared frozen, like a little bird suddenly caught in a child's hand.

'Officers,' he said. 'I know this looks like illegal camping, but we're broken down. A third member of our party is off getting parts to get us back on the road.'

'Sir, please step out of the vehicle,' the older of the two officers said.

He was maybe forty, beefy, with short blond hair, and his partner was a frightened-looking rookie who barely looked as old as Seth.

'I know it's probably illegal to park here, but this is emergency parking.'

'Sir, I don't want to have to ask you again. Step out of the vehicle.'

His tone settled hard into August's stomach like a sour and undigested meal.

Henry stepped down into the dirt, silent, still in just

his underwear and bare feet, his hands in the air as though he'd been caught robbing a bank.

'OK. Officer. I hear that request. And I want to comply. My goal is to comply. But I'm disabled, and it's very hard for me to come down the back stairs without assistance. I could go through the front and come out the passenger door. There's a handle there for me to hold.'

'No,' the officer said, still with one hand alarmingly perched on his sidearm. 'Where I can see you at all times.'

'I can't. I'll fall.'

The officer's eyes left him for a split second. Fastened on Henry. 'Can you get him down?'

'I think so,' he said, his voice sounding squeaky. It reminded August of the little cartoon mouse of his seven-year-old voice, so long ago.

'No fast moves. And always so I can see your hands.'

Still frightened, but thinking this was crossing the line into foolish overkill, August said, 'Officer, with all due respect, we're in our underwear and pajamas. The idea of a concealed weapon doesn't really fit the moment.'

'Sir,' the officer said, 'step out of the vehicle.'

'Woody, stay,' August said, and the dog sank into an uncomfortable-looking down position and turned his head away.

August held the metal ladder on the outside of the rig with one hand, though it became harder to hold as he stepped down, and Henry braced him with his whole body, under his other arm, tightly wrapping August's chest.

Then Henry tried to bolt up the stairs to get August's canes.

'Right where you are,' the officer said.

'He can't stand without his canes.'

'He's standing,' the officer said.

With a flip of his head he indicated August, who was standing with his back pressed against the rear of the motorhome, holding on to the ladder with both hands to steady himself.

'Just stand right there and keep your hands where I can see them.'

It struck August as unnecessary repetition, especially since he couldn't move his hands without risking falling on his ass in the dirt.

'I just have to close the screen door,' Henry said. 'So the dog won't come out.'

No reply. So he did. Slowly.

Dawn was just barely breaking, the steely sky perfectly cloudless. No cars came whooshing by to rock the rig. They might as well have been on the surface of a distant and uninhabited planet.

'What's this all about?' August asked. 'Is this really all because we're parked on the side of the highway?'

The officer ignored him completely and addressed Henry. 'Henry Reedy?'

August could see Henry's Adam's apple bob as he swallowed hard. Henry nodded so slightly that the movement was barely perceptible in the thin light.

'We're going to have to take you into custody, son.'

'What did I do?' the little cartoon mouse asked.

'You've been reported as a runaway minor. So we're taking you in. We'll release you when your father comes to take you back to California.'

Henry closed his eyes. Left them closed for a long time. August watched him in the strobing red. Wondering what Henry was feeling. Wondering what he himself was feeling. Waited for Henry to open them again. Or something. Or anything. He waited for anything to happen. While he waited, he not only wondered what would happen next, he wondered why he hadn't known, the minute he saw the flashing lights. Why hadn't he known?

Then, as a thought out of place, he remembered Seth was missing. It filled him with a complete and utter sense that all was lost. What would he do when they took Henry away and he was left here, broken down and alone?

'He's just being jealous and mean.' Henry's voice sounded a little deeper. 'He knew I was going away for the summer. He didn't care if I went away with Seth. He just doesn't like August, because he's jealous of August.'

'Son,' the officer said, 'I have a report of a runaway. You've been reported. We don't sort these things out in the field. I don't stand out here like some kind of family court. Your father reported you missing. He wants you back. We give you back. End of story.'

The officer stepped forward and took Henry by one elbow.

Henry reflexively jerked his arm away.

'Be very careful what you do from this moment on, son,' the officer told him, his voice a brick wall of warning. 'You're being asked to comply with the reasonable requests of an officer. You don't want to play games with that.'

August saw Henry deflate. Saw the air billow out of him, leaving him shorter, softer. Defeated. The officer took his arm again, and he allowed himself to be led. August watched him step away, and felt he was surely losing him. The promise of their summer together slipped away one step at a time.

'Aren't you even going to let him go in and get some clothes?' August asked.

The officer leading Henry stopped. Looked at the boy as if for the first time. Then he looked to his young partner.

'Take him inside and let him get dressed. You stay right here,' he added in August's direction.

'I hate him,' Henry said under his breath as he passed where August stood, still clutching the rig's ladder.

'Don't,' August said. 'Don't let him make you hate. Don't let anybody make you hate.'

He wondered how long it would be before he got to say anything to Henry again.

A few moments later the boy emerged on to the back steps in jeans and a tee-shirt, and flip-flop sandals. Standing tall on the top step, he said in a loud, deep voice, 'At least let me call him.'

'I'm not sure what good you think that'll do,' the officer said.

'Maybe I can get him to change his mind.'

'He'd actually have to withdraw the report.'

'Maybe I can get him to.'

The two cops, the younger of whom was still standing in the rig behind Henry, exchanged a glance.

'I guess it wouldn't hurt anything.'

Henry turned to bound back inside, but the young officer stopped him with one hand on his chest.

'We'll call him from the patrol car,' the older officer said. 'We'll have dispatch call him and then they'll patch you in.'

The young cop walked to the patrol car with Henry, and placed him in the back just the way you see on TV. One hand bending the top of his head down, so he couldn't hit it on the metal roof. Then he slammed the door, closing the boy in. He walked around to the driver's-side door, and sat inside with his long legs out, talking on the radio. August couldn't hear what he said.

He looked up at the older cop, still standing in the same spot in the dirt.

'May I sit down on the steps? It's hard on my arms, what I'm doing here.'

'Sure,' the cop said, and it was the first time he had sounded entirely human since August met him. He walked over and leaned his back against the rig. 'Sorry about the indignity of standing out here in your pajamas without your canes. Sorry about the thing with the hands on the guns. These stops can be dicey. You just don't know what you're walking into. Ninety-nine times it's gonna be fine, but the hundredth time stuff happens. And if it's gonna happen, it's gonna happen fast, and if you're not prepared it's gonna be too late.'

'I understand,' August said. And, to his surprise, he really did.

'I know family stuff is hard. We don't like this any better than you do. But once that report gets filed, there's nothing we can do but our jobs.'

August nodded slowly.

A moment passed in silence.

'His father is an alcoholic,' August said. Quietly. 'I really don't think he's a bad guy. But he's a difficult guy. He makes a lot of bad choices. He doesn't like me because I'm a recovering alcoholic. It's just one of those mirrors he doesn't like looking into. It was the boys' idea to do this for me. It's really important to them to take me on this trip. And the fact that it's so important to them sets him off. Because it shows I mean something to them.'

'Yeah, well. Like I say. Family stuff is hard. I know. I've got a family.'

They sat and leaned in silence for a moment, and then Henry's voice split the early morning chill. It was strong and deep. It was so loud August could hear it. All the way from the back seat of the patrol car.

Henry was yelling at his dad.

'This is the worst thing you ever did to me! How

could you do this? You do this because you hate August, because you think he's a better man than you are. Well, I've got news for you, Dad. He *is* a better man than you are. Because he would never do a thing like this. You do these mean, jealous things, and then you expect me to respect you. How can I respect you when you do things like this? If you think I look up to August more than I look up to you, maybe this is why. Maybe try acting like a good person and I could look up to you, too. Why don't you try that, Dad? Why don't you try showing me something I can respect, and then maybe I can respect you!'

Then silence. Maybe his dad was saying something. Maybe Henry'd just lowered his voice. August couldn't see enough from where he was sitting to tell.

'Wow,' the officer said. 'I never talked to my dad like that.' He didn't sound critical, though. He sounded almost admiring.

'Neither did Henry.'

They sat in silence for another long interval. Two minutes. Maybe three.

'This is a little mouse of a kid,' August said, 'who barely talks to anybody at all. For years he didn't talk to anybody but his brother. Now he talks to his brother and me. When I ask him for his opinion he goes silent on me. Says he doesn't like to tell people what to do.'

'Well, something woke up the lion in that mouse.'

They looked up to see the young officer approach them.

'He says he'll withdraw the report.' It was the first

time August had heard the young man's voice. He sounded even younger than he looked. 'But I think we have to sit here until he actually does.'

'Correct,' the older cop said.

His young partner went back to the car to wait by the radio.

'See, now I hate that. That just pisses me off,' the cop said to August.

It surprised him. The conversation he'd been having with the man had seemed so human.

'That he's pulling the report?'

'More that he filed it in the first place. That's just playing with the law. If he really thought his son was in any danger out here with you, he wouldn't pull the report. So he never should have filed it. We take our jobs seriously. I don't like it when people get us involved in their games.'

'Yeah,' August said. 'Unfortunately, that's just the kind of guy he is.'

They sat in silence, August watching the sun break over the horizon, shining into his eyes in a way that felt strangely comfortable.

Then he said, 'We actually have another big problem, but I'm thinking you can understand how the events of the last few minutes temporarily knocked it out of my head. His older brother, Seth, went off in search of a water pump yesterday morning. And he still isn't back. I'm getting worried.'

'Which way'd he go?'

'East. There was a guy in a shop east of here who

rented him some tools. But he sold him the wrong water pump. So he had to go back out to exchange it. Maybe he just couldn't find the right one in stock or something. But I'm sure you understand why I'd be worried about him. Hitchhiking all alone out in the middle of nowhere, and then gone all night.'

The cop sighed. 'I wish people would just call the state police when they break down. It's our job to help.'

'Oh. We didn't know you could do that.'

'Apparently nobody does. When we get this situation cleared up, we'll go down there and see if we can't find where he got off to. Was it Red's Automotive? That's the closest place east of here.'

'I don't know. He didn't say. I saw the guy drop him off, but I didn't get a real good look at him. He was driving a big old army-green pickup.'

'Yeah, that sounds like Red. We'll see what we can do.'

They looked up to see the kid officer step out of the driver's seat and shoot them a thumbs up. He opened the back door of the car and invited Henry to step out. Henry stood a moment in the dawn chill, as though he could barely accept his freedom. As though he'd been imprisoned for years, and had never seen the sun in all that time.

Then he shook the look away and walked back to August.

The older officer gave him a pat on the arm, and then both men packed it up and drove away, turning off those flashing red lights that August, amazingly, had forgotten were turning. They'd gotten to seem almost normal by that time.

Henry stood beside him for a long, silent time, clearly in shock.

Then August said, 'You were amazing. You were so good.'

A silence, then Henry broke into a sudden smile.

'I was, wasn't I?' he said.

Half an hour later, just as they were finishing their first cup of coffee – still too jangled to eat – the patrol car came back. It pulled into the dirt on the other side of the highway, and Seth stepped out with a familiar box under his arm.

He waved to the cops, who drove away.

August pulled a huge breath and realized that every breath he'd taken since Seth disappeared had been a shallow and frightened one.

Seth opened the driver's-side door and stuck his head in.

'Sorry, August. I know you must've been freaked out. I'll tell you later why I couldn't call. It's kind of a long story. I just want to get this pump on and get back on the road. Oh,' he said, looking down. 'You brought the tools inside. That was smart. Thanks.'

He looked in at Henry, who was sitting on the couch, smiling in a swallowed-a-secret sort of way.

'What's with you?' Seth asked him. 'What's so damn funny?'

'Sorry. I was just thinking it's nice not to be the one

who gets hauled back to the rig by the police this time.'

Seth shook his head in mock disgust. He hoisted up the heavy chest and disappeared, slamming the door behind him.

August eased himself into the passenger seat, then out the door, then reached in for one cane. He stood at the front of the engine compartment, leaning on it with one hand, bracing on his cane with the other. He watched Seth study the mating surfaces of the two pumps. Seth looked up and saw August watching, and held up the pumps for him to see.

'The bolt holes line up,' August said.

'Finally. Something went right.' Seth began to lay out tools again. 'I had the worst night, August. God. Whatever you were going through back here worrying about me, it couldn't have been worse than this. I get back there, and they don't have the pump I need in stock. They have to order it. So I knew right away I was stuck there till morning. The owner, that lousy thief, was gone. And he had my credit card. And the guy who was there, this other mechanic, he was either just a complete jerk, or maybe all he knew was that his boss was a hardass and he'd have to answer to him later. I forgot my cell phone. And he wouldn't let me use his phone. It's an expensive call, because your cell number is California. And I didn't have enough cash to use the payphone. And I couldn't get a room, because I didn't have my credit card. The jerk wouldn't even let me sleep in the shop. I guess he thought I might steal something. I had to sleep in an old car parked on their yard that wasn't locked. I'd like to choke that jackass who took my driver's license and credit card and then just went home. What if I'd come by to bring the tools back? You know. All ready to get on the road? He just wouldn't have bothered to be there. And he's charging me a hundred dollars for that. God. Why is everything going so wrong all of a sudden?'

'Not everything. You made it back OK. And you got the right part.'

'Yeah, and those cops were nice. They picked me up hitchhiking. Nobody would give me a ride. It's actually a misdemeanor to hitch a ride on this highway, but they let me off with a warning if I just promised to call the state police next time I break down. I didn't know you could do that. Did you?'

'Apparently nobody knows that. They didn't tell you why they came by here? How they knew you were stranded out there?'

'No. I thought they just happened to go by and see me.'

'They came by to get Henry and take him into custody, because your dad reported him as a runaway.'

Seth leapt to his feet, dropping one tool and accidentally kicking several others away.

'They took Henry? Why didn't you tell me? Where did they take him?'

'Duh,' Henry called from inside the rig. 'I'm right here. You were just shaking your head at me. Remember?'

'Oh, that's right,' Seth said, slumping against the

bumper. 'Geez, I'm tired. I didn't sleep much. I'm not thinking straight. What happened?'

'He yelled at your dad and backed him right down.'

'Aw, nice. See, I told you they were nice guys.'

'No. Not the cops, Seth. Henry.'

'*Henry* yelled at our dad?'

'Backed him right down.'

'That Henry? In there?'

'Hey!' Henry yelled out.

'Geez. And I missed it.' He gathered up the tools he had kicked and put them back in order.

'Don't you want to eat something first, Seth? Aren't you starving?'

Seth stopped moving, as if to consider that at length. 'I'm kind of starving. Even though I had a little cash to eat from the vending machine. But right now nothing's more important to me than getting this rig back in one piece and getting back on the road.'

A little past noon they drove into Red's Automotive, and parked out front.

Seth said, 'If he's still gone with my license and my credit card I'm going to want to hurt someone.'

Then he walked around to the back of the rig and pulled the tool chest out from behind the door. Lugged it into the shop.

August took his canes, lowered himself, and followed.

'You're going in, August?' Seth asked. 'You don't have to go in.'

'I want to have a talk with this guy,' August said.

Red was a gray-haired man with fair, damaged skin, who August figured must have been red-haired in his youth. He held an unlit cigarette with pursed lips. He looked up at Seth as if with some kind of preset contempt.

'You sold me the wrong pump,' Seth said. 'It cost me a day.'

The man did not answer. Instead he walked around the counter, squatted by the old tool chest, opened it, and began plowing through it.

'It's all there,' Seth said.

'Including a thing or two that never belonged to me,' Red said, and handed Seth his cell phone.

Then he walked back behind the counter and hit a button on the cash register. It opened with a 'bing' sound. He reached in and pulled out Seth's driver's license and credit card. Slid them across the counter.

Seth stuffed them into his pocket, seething but silent. He started for the door. August did not.

Red looked up at August and August held his gaze steadily.

'Something else I can do for you?'

'I have a bone to pick with you. You charged my friend a hundred bucks to use some dirty, rusty old tools. Then you sold him the wrong part. So he had to hitchhike all the way back to your shop for the right one. Which you didn't have in stock. So he was stuck overnight. But you had his credit card. He couldn't buy decent food, or get a room. Your employee didn't even have the courtesy to let him sleep indoors. He couldn't even make a phone call to tell me he was OK.'

Red's face was dispassionate. Unmoved.

'Card was in the register.'

'Which the only employee on the premises didn't know. So we've all had a nightmare of a day and a half thanks to your carelessness. And in return for that nightmare, which you could've prevented, you want to charge him a hundred dollars for nothing.'

Red stared into his face for a long moment, hands on his hips, cigarette bouncing from his tight lips.

'That's what we agreed on.'

'Don't you think an unstated part of the agreement is that you'd sell him the correct part, and that his card would be available to him when he showed up needing it?'

'I got work to do, mister. Your boy ought to be able to talk for himself.'

'I think he's afraid to, because he's so mad. I think he's afraid he couldn't be civil. I think we'll just stay while you consider your responsibility to this situation.'

Red sighed. Pointed to a sign on the wall behind the counter. It reserved his right to refuse service to anyone.

'I can ask you to leave.'

'Fine. We'll leave. Good idea. We'll just park on the street out front for a while. With a big sign on the side of the rig, telling passersby what we think of Red's Automotive.'

Red rubbed his face for a long moment. Then he leveled Seth with his flat stare. 'I knew the minute I laid eyes on you you'd be nothing but a pain in my ass.'

He opened the cash register drawer again with another 'bing', counted out five twenties, and threw them over the counter, where they fluttered apart on to the linoleum floor.

Then he headed toward the door into the shop. Stopped. Said, 'I drove him all the way back to where you were broke down.'

'That's true,' August said.

He picked up one of the twenties and set it back on the counter.

Red shook his head and disappeared into the shop.

Seth looked at August, his tight face softening and changing, one corner of his mouth twitching up. Then he bent down and picked up the rest of the cash.

They walked back to the motorhome, and August climbed in, ready to get back on the road again. All three of them.

Seth climbed into the driver's seat and smiled broadly for the first time in days. 'That was pretty cool, August.'

'What'd he do?' Henry asked.

'Got me most of my money back. It wasn't easy, either. He really told that guy off, but good.'

'I learned that from Henry,' August said.

Seth started the rig and pulled back out on to the highway. Back on the road. At last. 'Still can't believe Henry told off our dad,' he said.

'Hey!' Henry said. 'Don't talk about me like I never do anything good.'

'No, I didn't mean it like that. At all. You do lots of good things. Just . . . not usually . . . you know. Out loud.'

10
Falling

August woke from a nap on the couch to find the rig stopped. Which it hadn't been for quite some time. He'd gone ahead and taken a horizontal nap without his seat belt, because the boys seemed disinclined to even pause.

He sat up and blinked, noticing that the privacy curtain was up between him and the boys in the cab. And the blinds were pulled down. August figured they'd done that so he could sleep.

Henry ducked under the curtain just as August began to raise the blinds to see where they were.

'Oh, no you don't,' Henry said, and reached over and lowered the blinds again.

'I'm not allowed to look out?'

'Not for another twelve hours or so. Think of it like we're taking you there blindfolded. Only we thought this would be more comfortable for you.'

Seth ducked under the curtain and sat at the dinette table.

Henry began to root around in the fridge and set food out on the counter.

August rubbed his eyes.

'Where are we?' he asked.

Seth laughed. 'Geez, August. If we wanted you to know that we'd let you look out the window.'

'That wasn't exactly what I meant. I mean, is this a campsite? Are we here for the night?'

'Nope. We're making time. We're driving straight through. We want to get there before anything else can go wrong. This is just a highway rest stop. We're just stopping for something to eat and then we're back on the road.'

When August next woke up, he was in his fully made bed. Henry had made it up for him, so he could sleep normally while the boys took turns driving through the night.

He sat up just as the rig came to a full stop. He looked at his watch. It was not yet 5 a.m.

He could hear a sound, but it was a sound he could not identify. A heavy roar, like big machinery, but not quite like that. Like a plane landing close by, but not exactly. He sat listening, but it never changed, never shifted. Never got closer, or farther away.

The boys ducked under the privacy curtain one after the other.

'Get dressed,' Henry said, his voice barely containing tightly reined excitement. 'We're here.'

'What's the sound?'

'Get dressed and you'll see.'

August levered to his feet and rummaged through the overhead cupboards. He pulled on a pair of jeans, then a fleece jacket right over his pajama top. Henry handed him his sheepskin boots and he sat to put them on.

'You have to close your eyes,' Seth said.

'Seriously?'

'Work with us here, August.'

So August closed his eyes. The back door opened, letting in a more direct version of the roaring sound. There was so much power in that sound. It almost frightened August to approach it with his eyes closed. But he had the boys along. He trusted the boys.

He walked to the open door, leaning on walls and counters, and felt the pre-dawn morning sharp and cool. Surprisingly damp.

They helped him down the back steps. Then August felt a cane placed under each of his hands.

'No peeking,' Seth said. Then, to Henry, 'Go get the—'

'I know,' Henry said. 'Just go.'

Seth guided August with both his hands on August's left arm. They walked together toward the sound.

'I'm feeling mist hitting my face,' August said. 'So now I'm thinking water. Somehow that sound is water. I'm guessing waterfall, but I never heard a waterfall sound like that.'

'Maybe we're at Victoria Falls in Africa. Or Iguazu Falls in South America.'

'Or Niagara Falls,' August said, feeling an almost painful crush of reaction in his chest. *Of course*, he thought. *Why hadn't I guessed it*? But how could he possibly have imagined that these two crazy young guys would cross the entire United States diagonally just for him? And his late son? How could he have thought that?

'Now why would you think Niagara and not Victoria or Iguazu?'

'Because I think I would have noticed if we crossed the Panama Canal. Even with the curtains drawn. Same with the Atlantic Ocean.'

Henry caught up and placed one protective hand on August's other arm. And they walked, shivering slightly in the cool mist.

'OK,' Henry said. 'Open your eyes.'

August opened his eyes.

In front of him was a four-rung metal railing, forming a curved point at the edge of what August could only assume were the American falls. Since no one had brought a passport. Just beyond the railing, the Niagara River spilled over the edge, with a roar and a roiling mist, in the half-darkness before dawn. There seemed to be some light on the water, but August couldn't tell if it was purposely trained there, or if the light came from the shops and towers and hotels he could see in the distance, across the river. These weren't colored lights, like the ones he'd heard about, trained on the falls at night, and he was glad of that. The falls just seemed to glow. He looked to the sky to see they had moved into civil twilight, the sky barely shining with morning, but he wasn't sure if that could be enough.

He was surprised there wasn't a bigger crowd around, even at this hour. Especially in this one perfect spot where you could stand at the railing at the very lip of one part of the falls. Watch the river crest the falls just below you.

He saw several couples, and a small group, but only as spots in the distance. He saw many cars parked, and one making its way into a parking lot, but not very close by. Surprising though it seemed to August, especially in the summer, they were effectively alone.

'You guys are crazy, you know that? I hope you know I mean it in a good way, but . . . this is the entire opposite end of the country from where we started.'

'So?' Henry said. 'If you like it, it's worth it.'

'I like it. I like it a lot.'

'Here. You do the honors, August.'

August looked down to see Henry holding something that, in the partly dark morning, looked like a miniature barrel. A wooden barrel, but less than a foot tall. But banded with metal, like a real barrel.

'Where on earth did you get a little barrel like that?'

'Seth bought it online. We've had it with us the whole time. It was in a hiding place, though. Here.'

Henry grasped a metal handle and pulled hard, and the lid came off the barrel. Then Seth pulled the plastic bag of Phillip's ashes out of his pocket and handed them to August.

August noticed his hands were shaking slightly,

but couldn't quite put his finger on which among his current tangle of thoughts and emotions might have caused that.

Still, he managed to open the zipper lock on the bag and pour the ashes into the barrel. Henry took it back and wedged the lid carefully in place.

'You want to do this all three of us together?' Seth asked. 'You want us to all sort of hold it at once and . . . you know . . . one, two, three . . . let go?'

'I think we should walk farther up the river,' Henry said. 'That way he gets a longer ride. I mean, it's not just about going over the falls. Right? It's about racing along the river knowing you're *about* to go over the falls. That's the adventurous part.'

'I'd love to see it actually go over the edge, though,' August said.

Though he knew he might not. It might be too dark. The barrel might disappear under the water, held down by the strong current, and that might be the end of that. Once they let go of the barrel, they might never see it again. They might have to take it purely on faith that it had gone over.

Which shouldn't be hard, August thought. *Once something is in that raging river, where on earth could it go but over? Including objects – and even ships and people – much larger than this wooden toy.*

'Tell you what,' he said. 'If you're willing to split up, you guys go a few yards up the river and drop it in. And I'll stand right here and see if I can watch it go over.'

'Maybe we should wait till it's lighter,' Seth said.

'I don't know. It's awfully nice with nobody out here but us. I don't know how we got so lucky, and I don't imagine our luck'll hold long.'

The boys looked at each other and nodded.

August watched them as they set up, maybe fifty yards away. It wasn't completely dark, he realized. The sky was getting light. It was hard to know how much was the coming dawn, how much was the ambient light of so much civilization. Or lights trained on the water. If indeed lights were trained on the water. But it was light enough for August to see as much as he needed to see.

He watched them lean their upper bodies over the rail, and they both had the barrel. They each had one hand on it. They were working together.

Then August saw just a speck of it as it flew. Just saw it as a spot in the air. It rose up in an arc and seemed to slow. Or even to hang there. Just for a split second. Then it was gone.

The boys took off. August watched them running in his direction, stretching out. Sprinting. Peering over the rail as they ran.

'I can't see it!' Henry screamed. 'It's too dark to see it!'

'There it is!' Seth shouted. 'I think.'

But a second or two later, the barrel outpaced them. August could tell by the direction of their gaze. Ahead. The barrel was getting farther ahead.

A second after that, August spotted it. The current

hadn't pulled it under. Apparently it didn't have enough mass for that. It was too light. Too buoyant.

August saw it shoot by.

It shot off the edge, projected farther out than the water, and seemed to hang there by itself for just a split second. Like the cartoon coyote who hangs in the air, then perceives his situation, then accepts the inevitability of gravity, then falls. Or maybe August's mind played a trick on him, or time played a trick on August's mind. Maybe in that split second time was something just the slightest bit different than it had been before, or would be again.

See? he thought to Phillip in the silence of his brain. *We didn't forget about you.*

The barrel fell, quickly disappearing into the dimness and the mist.

As it did, the boys arrived, puffing.

August dropped his canes, which clattered on the concrete walkway. He fell forward on to the boys, and they caught him. He held them a moment, and they held him, without any of the three of them seeming to know exactly how the moment had come to be, or what it meant.

'You OK, August?' Seth asked.

August wanted to answer, but the words felt stuck in his chest. Then in his throat. He worked at knocking them loose, even though he didn't know exactly what words they would turn out to be.

'You guys just mean so damn much to me,' he said.

And they stood tangled up a moment longer.

Then August felt embarrassed, and straightened himself, and reached for his canes, which Henry dove for, and handed to him.

'That's enough of that,' August said. 'Sorry to get all mooshy on you.'

'It's OK, August,' Seth said.

'We don't mind,' Henry said. 'We like it when you get mooshy.'

They stood leaning on the rail for a long time, listening to the falls roar, watching the scene get lighter, watching millions of gallons of water careen over the edge.

'We didn't see it go over,' Henry said.

'I saw it go over,' August said.

'Well, that's good,' Seth said. 'That's what's most important.'

'What did it look like?' Henry asked.

'It's hard to describe. But it was really something. It was worth the price of admission.'

'Worth driving diagonally across the whole country for?'

'If you guys were willing to do it, then . . . hell, yeah.'

They stared in silence for a while longer. August heard a few more cars going by behind them. Knew this very busy tourist destination was waking up. Getting going for the morning. He wondered if the boys had timed their arrival for the maximum chance of having the rail to themselves. Or if that had been a happy accident.

'I'm sorry I got so emotional with you guys,' he said again.

'August, geez,' Seth said, 'will you stop?'

'Yeah,' Henry said. 'Way to apologize for caring.'

'Yeah, OK. I see your point.'

Another moment of silence, broken by the arrival of the first tour bus of the morning, parking and unloading its passengers in a lot somewhere behind them. August never looked around. Never took his eyes off all that mesmerizing water.

'So, now we made the big destination. Now what?'

Seth said, 'Now we practice that "be" mode. Because we've got a lot of summer left. Now we go back a lot more slowly than we got here.'

'But we're going to stay at the falls a while, though. Right? Now that we came all this way?'

'Long as you want, August. When you get enough Niagara Falls, you just say the word.'

'Hard to imagine getting enough of this.'

'Well,' Seth said. 'I think it's like what you told me about the hoodoos at Bryce Canyon. "Until you know them so well you can see them in your head when you close your eyes."'

'Good memory.'

'When you have that much Niagara Falls in your head, August, you say the word. And we'll make our way back to Yosemite. And then home.'

Part Four

August In Late August

Yosemite

August opened his eyes, then the blinds over his bed. He sat up and stared out the window at Yosemite's big granite walls through the trees.

It was the first full day Seth was gone, climbing. Climbing with his friends, August started to think, then corrected himself. Three of his friends from home had shown up. Two of them had looked up at The Nose route on El Capitan and decided to take a nice drive up through Tuolumne Meadows instead.

For several days August had been purposely post-poning walking, or taking the shuttle, or asking Henry to drive, so he could look up at the climbing route on El Capitan.

This was the second in what could be as long as five days of climbing for Seth. Or it could be longer.

He watched Henry putter in the kitchen, making breakfast. It was such a familiar routine. Now that the summer was nearly over, August dreaded the moment he would have to let it go.

'I think today's the day,' August said.

'What day would that be, August?' Henry asked without looking up.

'The day we go as far as we can out into that meadow and sit in our camp chairs and look through our binoculars and my zoom lens and watch those little ants go up that big wall.'

'Hmm,' Henry said. 'Sure you're ready for that? This is not Moonlight Buttress. That's small compared to this. Moonlight Buttress is like a thousand feet. Or maybe more. I forget. But less than fifteen hundred. El Cap is over thirty-five hundred feet. You sure you can handle watching?'

'I think I need to see it. It's a big deal for him, and I can't just look away. I think I have to handle it whether I can handle it or not.'

Henry hiked out and set up two chairs in the field for them while August waited in the rig, parked in a space along the curb of the main drive. A space they'd had to wait a long time to get.

He also carried out water, and hats, and sunscreen, and took Woody along for the walk.

Then he came back and got August, and they picked their way carefully through the grassy meadow to-gether.

August stopped at the chairs, but did not sit.

'I think we should go closer. Don't you?'

'I didn't want you to have to walk too far.'

'I'll manage. I want to have half a chance of seeing which one he is.'

'I doubt we can get that close.'

'Well, let's get as close as we can, anyway.'

So the three of them walked quite a bit farther, Henry wrestling both camp chairs, which fortunately had slings for his shoulder, and the water, and the camera, and the binoculars, and Woody's leash. He didn't complain, or seem as though he wanted to.

In fact, it was August who wore down.

But he kept walking anyway.

Finally it seemed that if they walked much closer to the stand of trees that stood between them and the granite monolith, their treetops would begin to intrude upon the view. So they settled in the sun and got comfortable.

August could hear car doors slamming, parents calling to their children and vice versa. Few parks were as busy as Yosemite in the summer. But the noise sounded distant, unrelated to him. A couple walked through the meadow hand in hand, but all in all it felt like an uncrowded place.

One of the few uncrowded places.

August looked up at the route.

'I see why they call it The Nose,' he said.

It had a protruding vertical section which August could only assume was the route in question. He held the binoculars to his eyes, and adjusted them, and could just make out little spots of climbers. Ants on the wall.

'You were right,' he said. 'There's no way we can see which one is him.'

'Yeah,' Henry said. 'I know. But one of them is him. And we know it. Is it better or worse than you thought?'

'A little of both,' August said. 'It's a terrifying wall. But it's not as scary to watch it from here as it was to watch that helmet-cam footage. I guess the distance hides a lot of things I don't want to see.'

'I think you've gotten better about the whole thing.'

'Do you? I'm glad to hear that. I didn't really feel like I had.'

They watched in silence for a time, though there was really nothing to watch. August could barely see climbers at all without the binoculars, or without viewing through his camera on full zoom. With them, from this distance, the little ants barely appeared to be moving at all.

'It's really hard to imagine sleeping up there,' August said.

'I know. I feel the same way.'

'They'd need so much stuff for five days. How do they get all that stuff up there with them?'

'Haul bag,' Henry said.

But he didn't explain how a haul bag worked, and August didn't really feel he needed to know.

'I guess I should just be happy he isn't into mountaineering at over twenty-five thousand feet in the Himalayas,' August said.

'Oh, that'll come next. As soon as he can afford it.'

'Oh, dear God. Please tell me you're not serious. He

doesn't really want to climb Mt Everest.'

'No. He doesn't. He thinks it's too commercial. Too much of a trash heap, you know? After all these expeditions. With all these rich guys paying for Sherpas to practically drag them up. He wants to do Dhaulagiri or Cho Oyu.'

'I've never heard of either one of those.'

'That's exactly the point.'

'I've been traveling with him all summer, and I didn't know that about him.'

'He still leans away from talking about the climbing around you.'

'That's too bad. It shouldn't be that way. I'm going to have to figure out how to do something about that.'

'He doesn't like to upset you, August.'

'No, I didn't mean that. I need to do something about me. Somehow get the part of me that's proud of him to be almost as big as the part of me that's terrified for him. And maybe somehow accent the first part and deal with the rest on my own.'

'That would be a very nice thing to do for him if you could manage it.'

They watched in silence for a long time. Maybe close to an hour. Though really it was more a case of being than watching.

'I hate to admit it,' August said at last, 'but this is about as interesting as watching paint dry.'

'Well, that's what *I* thought. But you were determined to do it. We can go back now if you want.'

'In a little bit,' August said. 'It's nice out here.'

They spent a few more minutes just being.

Then Henry said, 'I told you I was going to ask again. Right? I warned you about that. So I'm asking. You've had all summer to think about it.'

'Think about what?'

'You know.'

'Oh. The college thing? I haven't thought a thing about it. I told you, there's nothing to think about. It's a standing offer. It's a done deal unless you change your mind for some reason. The day you graduate high school, hop on a bus or a train and I'll have your room ready. If you don't have money for a bus or a train, I'll send you the money.'

'Think I could get to San Diego by bus for fifty dollars?'

August estimated the miles in his head.

'I doubt it. Why? Why is fifty dollars a magic number?'

'Because I still have that mad money you gave us.'

'You're kidding.'

'I wouldn't kid about a thing like that. When Seth went off to college he gave it to me and said, "Here. Here's your mad money from August."'

'That same fifty-dollar bill.'

'Same one.'

A silence as August chewed that over. Eight years of stashing the same fifty-dollar bill. Keeping it a secret from their dad. Never succumbing to the temptation to spend it on anything else.

'That's a long time to have money and not spend it.'

'It was from August.' A brief silence. Henry broke it.

'That's why things went as well as they did after you dropped us off. You know that, right?'

'I don't think a fifty-dollar bill can do all that.'

'Not the money, August. You. You're the reason things were pretty OK after that. I know you think we just went on with our lives, and I'm sorry we didn't know you really wanted us to keep in touch. Now I wish we had. But still. It changed everything. It changed *us*. Whether we talked to you or not. Before we met you, we were always scared that our dad was just about to let us down. But after that summer, we knew if he dropped us you'd be there to catch us. You have no idea how much of a difference it made.'

August looked over at Henry's face, but the boy resisted looking back. Probably a little embarrassed.

'Sorry, August,' Henry said. 'Didn't mean to get all mooshy on you.'

'Way to apologize for caring,' August said.

They sat in silence for another minute or two. August was beginning to feel that enough of watching ants on a granite wall was enough. It was one of those things that was entirely different to watch than to do.

He thought again about the enormity of the challenges Seth bit off. How inseparable they were from his character. From him.

'I wonder . . .' he said, but he didn't finish the thought out loud.

'You wonder what, August?'

But he didn't want to say it to Henry. Or to anyone.

He wondered who he would be at the end of the

summer, when the one part of his life that was so uniquely 'him' drew to a close. Would something else come in and take its place? And even if it did, how could it ever be the same? Wasn't thinking anything could replace these summers a little like telling a friend who's just lost his wife that he'll find another wife and she'll be just as good?

Or a son.

Not everything is so easily replaced.

'Nothing,' he said. 'We should probably go back now.'

'No, really, August. What were you going to say?'

'Never mind,' he said. 'I'd rather think about happier things.'

It was three days later, after dark, when Seth stumbled back into camp. Henry and August were toasting marshmallows in the last of the campfire. They had the third chair out and ready, a vote of confidence that this would be the night Seth made it back OK.

August watched him pile ropes and hardware and a heavy-looking canvas haul bag on the picnic table in the dark. Woody whimpered and pulled to get to him, and Henry dropped the leash and let him say hello.

'Hey, boy,' Seth said. 'Yes, I missed you, too. Yes, I love you, too, I just love you from up here. You're all the way down there, and it's just too far to go. I don't even want to bend over.'

He shuffled over to the empty camp chair and gingerly settled in. Woody jumped in his lap.

'Ow! Woody. Damn! Leg muscles. Leg muscles.' He patted and scratched the dog a few times, then picked him up and handed him to Henry. 'Ow,' he said as his arms supported the dog's weight.

'Marshmallow?' August asked, and held out one he'd toasted for himself.

'Ooh,' Seth said. 'That one's perfect.' He took the stick from August. Blew on the golden-brown marshmallow to cool it. 'I am so tired of dehydrated food. And I've barely slept in days. I think I want to sleep for a year.'

'Fair enough,' August said. Then he thought of something more to say. Put it away again. Took it back out. Doubted it. Finally he just forced it out. 'You know I'm proud of you for being able to do a thing as big as that. Right?'

A silence radiated. August couldn't see Seth's face well in the dark. But he watched as Seth took a tentative bite of marshmallow and clearly found it too hot.

'I didn't know that. Actually.' More silence. 'What about the part of you that's scared to death over the whole thing?'

'Oh, that's still there. I'm just telling you about the good part.'

'Oh,' Seth said. 'That's nice. Thanks.'

They sat in silence for a time.

Then Henry said, 'I'm going to bed. For a guy who says he wants to sleep for a year, you sure are awake.'

'Yeah,' Seth said. 'I haven't come down yet. I'm down, but I'm not down. You know how it is.'

'Well, I'll see you both in the morning.'

'You won't see *me* in the morning,' Seth said. 'I'll be sleeping for a year. Well. You may see *me*. But I'll bet I won't see *you*.'

Henry shook his head, handed the dog to August, and disappeared.

'You probably want something more to eat,' August said to Seth.

'I'm thinking about it. But right now I can't get beyond thinking.'

'Where's your friend? Your climbing partner?'

'He wasn't about to go a step farther than his own tent and I don't blame him. Toast me another marshmallow, would you please, August? I can't bear to get up yet.' Then, while August was threading it on the stick, Seth said, 'It was nice of you to say what you said.'

'No. It was wrong of me to not say it sooner.'

'Don't say that. That's not true. That's just you. It's how you are. I had this big revelation while I was climbing. I thought about how your fear is just you, like climbing is just me. And I shouldn't try to talk you out of being afraid any more than you should try to talk me out of climbing.'

'Well, there's one big difference, though, Seth. Fear isn't something to aspire to. It's not something I really want.'

'Still doesn't mean I can't be patient. So, what do you want to do? We've got six days left. You want to spend them in the park? Or have you had enough summer?

Would you rather just go home and have more time to get ready for school?'

So there it is, August thought. *The end. The summer is over.* He questioned whether he could possibly have enjoyed it more while it lasted. But there's always room for improvement on that score.

'That's up to you,' he said.

'No, I want you to decide. This is your summer.'

'It's been a good one. I have to say that. I'm sorry it's over, but . . . We really covered a lot of ground.'

'Yeah. No kidding.'

'Do I even want to know what the gas came to?'

'No. You don't even want to know. That's one thing we're going to have to do differently next summer, August. When school starts, you're going to have to start budgeting for gas like you used to. Because by the time we're ready to head out again next summer, I can just about guarantee you I won't have paid off this summer's gas yet. Not to mention the payments on the rig.'

August sat still with those sentences in his head, trying to figure out if there was any way they could mean something different from what they appeared to mean. Before he restated it out loud, he needed to be sure he wasn't wrong. But the examination just left him confused.

'Next summer?'

'Yeah. Next summer we're back on your dime.'

'We're going out again next summer?'

'Of course we are. How did you not know that?'

440 CATHERINE RYAN HYDE

'You never said it.'

'I thought it went without saying. This is you, August. This is what you do. What makes you you. What's that thing the French call it? Your . . .'

'*Raison d'être.*'

'Right. The summer we don't come pick you up and take you out on the road is the next summer after we come to San Diego for your memorial. Sorry. Didn't mean to be morbid. No offense.'

'None taken. We all have to go sometime. I didn't know this was ongoing. I thought this was my last summer.'

'Oh, come on, August. We wouldn't do that to you.'

'It could get harder, you know. I could end up in a wheelchair.'

'So? We strap the thing to a bicycle rack on the back ladder and off we go. If we have to carry you up the back stairs, then that's just what we do. Climbing muscles,' he added, flexing for August in the dark.

They sat with that for a while, August readjusting his head to the news. Restructuring his entire future in his brain.

'You don't get to pay me for the rig, then.'

'I have to pay you for it.'

'You don't get to. I won't allow it. Get serious, Seth. It's as much use to me this way as it always was. I'm lucky I don't have to pay a fee for the chauffeuring.'

'Well, I guess I hadn't looked at it that way. I need to go to bed. I've had it. So when do you want to go home?'

August reached inside and found that the idea of home had gone completely neutral to him. It no longer stung to think of going home. Because it was only temporary. It didn't matter when they went home at all. Because it was only home from *this* summer.

'Doesn't matter to me,' he said. 'I'm done when you are. Sleep for a year, and when you're ready, I'm happy to go.'

Seth stayed stuck in his chair, though, and did not go off to bed as he'd said he must.

Instead they watched the fire together until the last of the embers winked out and died.

In the morning, when August woke up, Seth was wide awake, sitting up in his bed on the folded-out couch, looking worn down but happy. Watching Henry make breakfast.

'Hey there,' August said. 'Thought you were going to sleep for a year.'

'Yeah, I was slightly off on that. Turns out I'm going to eat for a year. Henry is making scrambled eggs and sausage and pancakes the way he always used to do when I'd been climbing.'

'That sounds good,' August said.

'How many eggs, August?' Henry asked over his shoulder.

'Two.'

'Seth? Three, I suppose?'

'Make it four.'

'Four?'

'Hey. Stand at the bottom of The Nose of El Cap and look up before you judge me.'

'Right,' Henry said. 'Whatever.'

August raised the window blinds to better see Yosemite. To wish it goodbye.

'Henry,' August said. 'Why didn't you tell me we were going out again next summer? And every summer after that?'

'Thought it went without saying, August. What did you think we'd do? Go off and leave you home and have fun without you?'

'Pretty much. Yeah. I thought this was going to be my last summer out in the world.'

That stayed in the air for a moment while Henry whisked eggs in a bowl. August could already smell the sausage cooking. Hear the links sizzle.

'How was it different?' Henry asked after a time. 'Thinking this was the last summer, I mean. How did it change the trip for you? Were you sad?'

August thought a moment. Resisted the temptation to answer off the top of his head.

'Sometimes. But mostly I just kept reminding myself to burn every moment into my memory. I just tried to be sure I was always there. That I didn't miss anything. I kept thinking, Enjoy this. Don't let a moment of it go by unenjoyed. Or unmemorized. Or unappreciated.'

'Then I'm glad you didn't know,' Henry said. 'Because that's the way to do a summer anyway.'

'You're right,' August said, completely releasing the idea that he wished he had known. Watching it lift away. Feeling lighter and cleaner without it. 'I think I'll do it that way every summer.'

'We should all do it that way every summer,' Henry said.

'I'm in for that,' Seth said.

It was promise enough to last August through the long year ahead, and he knew it.

THE END

Where We Belong
Catherine Ryan Hyde

*A remarkable, moving story about family and the
many forms this can take, which will be loved by
fans of Jodi Picoult and Susan Lewis.*

Fourteen-year-old Angie and her mum are on the brink
of homelessness . . . again. The problem is her little sister,
Sophie. Sophie has a form of autism, and a tendency to
shriek. Home never seems to last long.

Until they move in with Aunt Vi, across the fence from
a huge Great Dane. Sophie falls in love, and begins
to imitate the dog's calm nature. The shrieking stops.
Everyone relaxes. Until Paul, the dog's grumpy, socially
isolated owner, moves away.

Much to Angie's humiliation, her mum thinks they can
follow Paul and his dog. Once reunited, despite a huge
age gap, Angie and Paul form the closest friendship
either has known. But Angie risks everything to help
Paul's dream come true, even their friendship and
her one chance at a real home – the only thing she's
dreamed of since her father was killed. A place she won't
be thrown out of. A place she can feel she belongs.

The Hardest Part of Love
Catherine Ryan Hyde

*There's a split second between having it all,
and losing everything.*

Hayden briefly has it all: a wife and daughter he adores and a baby on the way. But when his son dies at birth, a deep anger emerges, robbing Hayden of everything.

Years on, Hayden is living in self-imposed exile. He's just lost his beloved dog and is now losing Laurel, the only woman he's loved since . . .

But just as Hayden's rage rises again, a young figure from the past emerges, forcing him to re-visit his long-buried childhood . . .

Walk Me Home
Catherine Ryan Hyde

Two sisters. One life-changing tragedy.

Carly and her little sister Jen are walking. Something terrible has happened. Something that has left Carly in charge, her faith in humanity shattered. She knows they need help. But she is terrified of her sister being taken away from her. All they have is each other.

Carly wants them to find their way back to the last person she knew she could trust – their stepfather. But Jen holds a secret about him which, if she's telling the truth, will put them both at far more risk than they could imagine.

And so begins a journey, across hundreds of miles, which neither girl could have anticipated. It isn't an easy one, and is often dangerous. But along the way they are also confronted with the unexpected kindness of strangers. And ultimately, should they choose to accept it, some new relationships that hold the potential to change everything . . .

When You Were Older
Catherine Ryan Hyde

I was doing my best to get out the door.
And then the phone rang. I almost let it go.

New York, September 11th 2001

Russell Ammiano is rushing to work when he gets a phone call that saves his life. As the city he loves is hit by unimaginable tragedy, Russell must turn his back and hurry home to Kansas.

Kansas, September 14th 2001

Ben Ammiano is mentally disabled, and a creature of habit. Any change to his routine sends him into a spin. But now his estranged brother has reappeared, and Ben's simple, ordered world has turned upside down.

**In a story as heartbreaking as it is uplifting,
two brothers must bury their pasts and learn
from each other, if they are to survive.**

Do you love talking about your favourite books?

From big tearjerkers to unforgettable love stories, to family dramas and feel-good chick lit, to something clever and thought-provoking, discover the very best **new fiction** around – and find your **next favourite read**.

See **new covers** before anyone else, and read **exclusive extracts** from the books everybody's talking about.

With plenty of **chat**, **gossip and news** about **the authors and stories you love**, you'll never be stuck for what to read next.

And with our **weekly giveaways**, you can **win** the latest laugh-out-loud romantic comedy or heart-breaking book club read before they hit the shops.

Curl up with another good book today.

Join the conversation at
www.facebook.com/ThePageTurners
And sign up to our free newsletter on
www.transworldbooks.co.uk